WITHDRAWN

Vampire
Stories

Vampire Stories

Introduction *by* PETER CUSHING

Edited by RICHARD DALBY

GRAMERCY BOOKS

NEW YORK

This 2006 edition is published by Gramercy Books, an imprint of Random House Value Publishing, a division of Random House, Inc., New York, by arrangement with Michael O'Mara Books Limited.

Gramercy is a registered trademark and the colophon is a trademark of Random House, Inc.

Random House
New York • Toronto • London • Sydney • Auckland
www.randomhouse.com

Printed and bound in the United States of America

Library of Congress Cataloging-in-Publication Data

Vampire stories / introduction by Peter Cushing ; edited by Richard Dalby.
    p. cm.
  ISBN-13: 978-0-517-22867-8
  ISBN-10: 0-517-22867-X
    1. Vampires—Fiction. 2. Horror tales, English. 3. Horror tales, American.
I. Dalby, Richard.
PR1309.H6V34 2006
823'.0873808375—dc22

                           2006041233

10 9 8 7 6 5 4 3 2 1

CONTENTS

FOREWORD

It was my pleasure to write the Foreword for Mr Richard Dalby's collection of crime stories, published in 1991 and entitled *Crime for Christmas*. I was delighted to be invited to do the same for his latest anthology which consists of vampire tales, told by a variety of distinguished authors, among them being Bram Stoker (of course), Ivan Turgenev, E. F. Benson and Edith Nesbit, the lady who achieved fame eventually in writing books for children! Her story, entitled *The Haunted House*, appeared in the *Strand* magazine in 1913 and has only recently been reprinted. In fact, many of those selected for this volume have been neglected over the years.

Conan Doyle's Sherlock Holmes has so gripped the imagination of the public worldwide, that many still write to him at his Baker Street address, seeking help over some problem or other.

Bram Stoker succeeded in a similar fashion, but with a very different fictitious character – Dracula.

What is it that attracts so many people to this quite repellent creature, I wonder. It could be a throw-back to childhood, when the fear of a lurking bogey-man was never far away when alone and in the dark. Perhaps that fear was overcome to a certain extent by the seaside holiday treat of watching 'Punch and Judy', tending to make them immune to such bizarre goings-on. (After all, that version of Grand Guignol is pretty grisly fare for the young, don't you think?)

In later years, they become more sophisticated in their taste for excitement, visiting 'The Chamber of Horrors' at Madame Tussaud's and elsewhere.

Come adulthood, those youthful amusements are replaced by a fascination for the loathsome Lord of the Undead, Dracula, who has an hypnotic power, like the stoat which can mesmerize its prey. (An apt simile, since that carnivore's custom of licking blood from its victim's fur has given rise to the legend that it sucks blood.)

The character originates from a 15th century prince of Wallachia in Rumania, Vlad V, whose nickname was 'The Impaler', owing to his beastly little habit of slowly impaling the Turkish invaders of his country, and drinking their blood with his dinner.

The name 'Dracula' derives from his father, who was known as Vlad Drakul (the Devil), and Castle Dracula in the Carpathian Mountains, north of Bucharest.

A number of quite learned people believe in the existence of the Yeti and Loch Ness Monster, and there are those who are convinced that Dracula, or his equivalent, is out there somewhere.

I had the good fortune to appear in several Dracula pictures made by Hammer, in which my very dear friend Christopher Lee was quite magnificent as the Count. They became known as Hammer Horror Films, but we both prefer the title Fantasy Films, because that is what they are. I am told that at least one of those movies, most of which were made during the Fifties and Sixties, is shown on television every day of every week somewhere in the world.

In my second book of autobiography, *Past Forgetting*, I wrote about that period of our careers: '. . . "Dracula". Now that was a part my old chum Christopher Lee could really get his teeth into, and, by gum, he *did*! – several times. I think he showed great courage when he weighed anchor, and sought different characters to play in Hollywood, where he spent about ten years before returning home to Britain. He intuited that when the demand for so-called 'horror' films waned, he might wane with them, and he wanted to cast off the mantle of the Count that shackled him. When asked by the Press why he didn't want to play Dracula anymore, he replied, with typical humour, "Because I'm getting too long in the tooth" . . .'

As a party piece he invariably recited 'Welsh Vampire' by Dylan Thomas with blood-curdling relish, which always went down extremely well:

> 'Councillors' jugulars suck I with glee
> Oh! Oh! For the taste of a scrumptious JP
> Tremble ye alderman!
> Town clerk beware!
> As I hoover the veins
> Of your succulent mayor.'

Mr Dalby's selection is well chosen, and it is interesting to note how a very diverse group of authors set about tackling the problem of variations upon the theme.

For those who like such stories, his anthology is an ideal bedside companion, even though it might induce a few nightmares! But how nice to wake up, with relief, knowing that the experience was nothing worse!

I loved making those films with Christopher, films which give lasting pleasure to so many; and to give readers some idea of the impact Dalby's choice had upon me, if I found myself on the horns of a dilemma by having to choose his book or one other when marooned on a desert island, I'd plump for a Billy Bunter! I'd rather risk dreaming of being eaten alive by that perpetually ravenous schoolboy than being sucked dry by a vampire, Welsh or otherwise!

You have been warned . . .

Peter Cushing OBE

ACKNOWLEDGMENTS

The Publisher has made every effort to contact the copyright holders of material reproduced in this book, and wishes to apologize to those he has been unable to trace. Grateful acknowledgment is made for permission to reprint the following.

'Close Behind Him' by John Wyndham, reprinted by permission of the estate of John Wyndham and 'Fantastic Magazine'.
'Vampires Ltd' by Josef Nesvadba, reprinted by permission of Aura-Pont, Prague and Mrs Iris Lewit-Unwin.
'Chastel' by Manly Wade Wellman, reprinted by permission of Karl Edward Wagner, Literary Executor for the Estate of Manly Wade Wellman.
'The Master of Rampling Gate' copyright © 1984 by Anne O'Brien Rice. Originally published in Redbook. Reprinted by permission of Anne Rice.
'The Undead' by Robert Bloch. Copyright © 1984 by Robert Bloch. Reproduced by kind permission of Ralph M. Vicinanza, Ltd.
'The Author's Tale' © 1934 by L.A. Lewis. Reprinted by permission of Richard Dalby.

The following stories are reproduced by permission of the authors:
'The Apples of Sodom' © 1980 by David G. Rowlands.
'China Rose' © 1992 by Ron Weighell.
'Saint Sebastian and the Mona Lisa' © 1992 by A.F. Kidd.
'Quiet is the Night' © 1992 by Jessica Palmer.
'The Last Sin' © 1992 by Ken Cowley.

[x]

PHANTOMS

Ivan Turgenev

Ivan Turgenev (1818–1883) was one of the
most important of all Russian novelists, and an
outstanding stylist. His works were the first of
any Russian to be read widely outside his own
country. Among his most notable works are *A
Sportsman's Sketches* (1852) which with its vivid
descriptions of the suffering of Russian farmers
helped to hasten the emancipation of the serfs in
Russia; and *Fathers and Sons* in which he coined
the word 'nihilist'.
'Phantoms' (1864) is Turgenev's brilliant
literary masterpiece of the supernatural.

For a long time I could not get to sleep, and kept turning from side
to side. 'Confound this foolishness about table-turning!' I
thought. 'It simply upsets one's nerves.'.. Drowsiness began to
overtake me at last . . .

Suddenly it seemed to me as though there were the faint and plaintive
sound of a harp-string in the room.

I raised my head. The moon was low in the sky, and looked me straight
in the face. White as chalk lay its light upon the floor . . . The strange
sound was distinctly repeated.

I leaned on my elbow. A faint feeling of awe plucked at my heart. A
minute passed, another . . . Somewhere, far away, a cock crowed;
another answered still more remote.

I let my head sink back on the pillow. 'See what one can work oneself
up to,' I thought again, . . . 'there's a singing in my ears.'

After a little while I fell asleep – or I thought I fell asleep. I had an extraordinary dream. I fancied I was lying in my room, in my bed – and was not asleep, could not even close my eyes. And again I heard the sound . . . I turned over . . . The moonlight on the floor began softly to lift, to rise up, to round off slightly above . . . Before me, impalpable as mist, a white woman was standing motionless.

'Who are you?' I asked with an effort.

A voice made answer, like the rustle of leaves: 'It is I . . . I . . . I . . . I have come for you.'

'For me? But who are you?'

'Come by night to the edge of the wood where there stands an old oak-tree. I will be there.'

I tried to look closely into the face of the mysterious woman – and suddenly I gave an involuntary shudder: there was a chilly breath upon me. And then I was not lying down, but sitting up in my bed; and where, as I fancied, the phantom had stood, the moonlight lay in a long streak of white upon the floor.

The day passed somehow. I tried, I remember, to read, to work . . . everything was a failure. The night came. My heart was throbbing within me, as though it expected something. I lay down, and turned with my face to the wall.

'Why did you not come?' sounded a distinct whisper in the room.

I looked around quickly.

Again she . . . again the mysterious phantom. Motionless eyes in a motionless face, and a gaze full of sadness.

'Come!' I heard the whisper again.

'I will come,' I replied with instinctive horror. The phantom bent slowly forward, and undulating faintly like smoke, melted away altogether. And again the moon shone white and untroubled on the smooth floor.

I passed the day in unrest. At supper I drank almost a whole bottle of wine, and all but went out on to the steps; but I turned back and flung myself into my bed. My blood was pulsing painfully.

Again the sound was heard . . . I started, but did not look round. All at once I felt that someone had tight hold of me from behind, and was whispering in my very ear: 'Come, come, come.' . . . Trembling with terror, I moaned out: 'I will come!' and sat up.

A woman stood stooping close to my very pillow. She smiled dimly

[2]

and vanished. I had time, though, to make out her face. It seemed to me I had seen her before – but where, when? I got up late, and spent the whole day wandering about the country. I went to the old oak at the edge of the forest, and looked carefully all around.

Towards evening I sat at the open window in my study. My old housekeeper set a cup of tea before me, but I did not touch it . . . I kept asking myself in bewilderment: 'Am not I going out of my mind?' The sun had just set: and not the sky alone was flushed with red; the whole atmosphere was suddenly filled with an almost unnatural purple. The leaves and grass never stirred, stiff as though freshly coated with varnish. In their stony rigidity, in the vivid sharpness of their outlines, in this combination of intense brightness and death-like stillness, there was something weird and mysterious. A rather large grey bird suddenly flew up without a sound and settled on the very window sill . . . I looked at it, and it looked at me sideways with its round, dark eye. 'Were you sent to remind me, then?' I wondered.

At once the bird fluttered its soft wings, and without a sound – as before – flew away. I sat a long time still at the window, but I was no longer a prey to uncertainty. I had, as it were, come within the enchanted circle, and I was borne along by an irresistible though gentle force, as a boat is borne along by the current long before it reaches the waterfall. I started up at last. The purple had long vanished from the air, the colours were darkened, and the enchanted silence was broken. There was the flutter of a gust of wind, the moon came out brighter and brighter in the sky that was growing bluer, and soon the leaves of the trees were weaving patterns of black and silver in her cold beams. My old housekeeper came into the study with a lighted candle, but there was a draught from the window and the flame went out. I could restrain myself no longer. I jumped up, clapped on my cap, and set off to the corner of the forest, to the old oak-tree.

This oak had, many years before, been struck by lightening; the top of the tree had been shattered, and was withered up, but there was still life left in it for centuries to come. As I was coming up to it, a cloud passed over the moon: it was very dark under its thick branches. At first I noticed nothing special; but I glanced on one side, and my heart fairly failed me – a white figure was standing motionless beside a tall bush between the oak and the forest. My hair stood upright on my head, but I plucked up my courage and went towards the forest.

Yes, it was she, my visitor of the night. As I approached her, the moon

[3]

shone out again. She seemed all, as it were, spun out of half-transparent, milky mist, – through her face I could see a branch faintly stirring in the wind; only the hair and eyes were a little dark, and on one of the fingers of her clasped hands a slender ring shone with a gleam of pale gold. I stood still before her, and tried to speak; but the voice died away in my throat, though it was no longer fear exactly I felt. Her eyes were turned upon me; their gaze expressed neither distress nor delight, but a sort of lifeless attention. I waited to see whether she would utter a word, but she remained motionless and speechless, and still gazed at me with her deathly intent eyes. Dread came over me again.

'I have come!' I cried at last with an effort. My voice sounded muffled and strange to me.

'I love you,' I heard her whisper.

'You love me!' I repeated in amazement.

'Give yourself up to me,' was whispered me again in reply.

'Give myself up to you! But you are a phantom; you have no body even.' A strange animation came upon me. 'What are you – smoke, air, vapour? Give myself up to you! Answer me first, Who are you? Have you lived upon the earth? Whence have you come?'

'Give yourself up to me. I will do you no harm. Only say two words: "Take me."'

I looked at her. 'What is she saying?' I thought. 'What does it all mean? And how can she take me? Shall I try?'

'Very well,' I said, and unexpectedly loudly, as though someone had given me a push from behind; 'take me!'

I had hardly uttered these words when the mysterious figure, with a sort of inward laugh, which set her face quivering for an instant, bent forward, and stretched out her arms wide apart . . . I tried to dart away, but I was already in her power. She seized me, my body rose a foot from the ground, and we both floated smoothly and not too swiftly over the wet, still grass.

At first I felt giddy, and instinctively I closed my eyes . . . A minute later I opened them again. We were floating as before; but the forest was now nowhere to be seen. Under us stretched a plain, spotted here and there with dark patches. With horror I felt that we had risen to a fearful height.

'I am lost; I am in the power of Satan,' flashed through me like lightning. Till that instant the idea of a temptation of the evil one, of the possibility of perdition, had never entered my head. We still whirled on, and seemed to be mounting higher and higher.

[4]

'Where will you take me?' I moaned at last.

'Where you like,' my companion answered. She clung close to me; her face was almost resting upon my face. But I was scarcely conscious of her touch.

'Let me sink down to the earth, I am giddy at this height.'

'Very well; only shut your eyes and hold your breath.'

I obeyed, and at once felt that I was falling like a stone flung from the hand . . . the air whistled in my ears. When I could think again, we were floating smoothly once more just above the earth, so that we caught our feet in the tops of the tall grass.

'Put me on my feet,' I began. 'What pleasure is there in flying? I'm not a bird.'

'I thought you would like it. We have no other pastime.'

'You? Then what are you?'

There was no answer.

'You don't dare to tell me that?'

The plaintive sound which had awakened me the first night quivered in my ears. Meanwhile we were still, scarcely perceptibly, moving in the damp night air.

'Let me go!' I said. My companion moved slowly away, and I found myself on my feet. She stopped before me and again folded her hands. I grew more composed and looked into her face; as before it expressed submissive sadness.

'Where are we?' I asked. I did not recognize the country about me.

'Far from your home, but you can be there in an instant.'

'How can that be done? By trusting myself to you again?'

'I have done you no harm and will do you none. Let us fly till dawn, that is all. I can bear you away wherever you fancy – to the ends of the earth. Give yourself up to me! Say only: "Take me!"'

'Well . . . take me!'

She again pressed close to me, again my feet left the earth – and we were flying.

'Which way?' she asked me.

'Straight on, keep straight on.'

'But here is a forest.'

'Lift us over the forest, only slower.'

We darted upwards like a wild snipe flying up into a birch-tree, and again flew on in a straight line. Instead of grass, we caught glimpses of tree-tops just under our feet. It was strange to see the forest from above,

[5]

its bristling back lighted up by the moon. It looked like some huge slumbering wild beast, and accompanied us with a vast unceasing murmur, like some inarticulate roar. In one place we crossed a small glade; intensely black was the jagged streak of shadow along one side of it. Now and then there was the plaintive cry of a hare below us; above us the owl hooted, plaintively too; there was a scent in the air of mushrooms, buds, and dawn-flowers; the moon fairly flooded everything on all sides with its cold, hard light; the Pleiades gleamed just over our heads. And now the forest was left behind; a streak of fog stretched out across the open country; it was the river. We flew along one of its banks, above the bushes, still and weighed down with moisture. The river's waters at one moment glimmered with a flash of blue, at another flowed on in darkness, as it were, in wrath. Here and there a delicate mist moved strangely over the water, and the water-lilies' cups shone white in maiden pomp with every petal open to its full, as though they knew their safety out of reach. I longed to pick one of them, and behold, I found myself at once on the river's surface . . . The damp air struck me an angry blow in the face, just as I broke the thick stalk of a great flower. We began to fly across from bank to bank, like the water-fowl we were continually waking up and chasing before us. More than once we chanced to swoop down on a family of wild ducks, settled in a circle on an open spot among the reeds, but they did not stir; at most one of them would thrust out its neck from unders its wing, stare at us, and anxiously poke its beak away again in its fluffy feathers, and another faintly quacked, while its body twitched a little all over. We startled one heron; it flew up out of a willow bush, brandishing its legs and fluttering its wings with clumsy eagerness: it struck me as remarkably like a German. There was not the splash of a fish to be heard, they too were asleep. I began to get used to the sensation of flying, and even to find a pleasure in it; any one will understand me, who has experienced flying in dreams. I proceeded to scrutinize with close attention the strange being, by whose good offices such unlikely adventures had befallen me.

She was a woman with a small un-Russian face. Greyish-white, half-transparent, with scarcely marked shades, she reminded one of the alabaster figures on a vase lighted up within, and again her face seemed familiar to me.

'Can I speak with you?' I asked.

'Speak.'

'I see a ring on your finger; you have lived then on the earth, you have been married?'

I waited ... There was no answer.

'What is your name, or, at least, what was it?'

'Call me Alice.'

'Alice! That's an English name! Are you an Englishwoman? Did you know me in former days?'

'No'.

'Why is it then you have come to me?'

'I love you.'

'And are you content?'

'Yes; we float, we whirl together in the fresh air.'

'Alice!' I said all at once, 'you are perhaps a sinful, condemned soul?'

My companion's head bent towards me. 'I don't understand you,' she murmured.

'I adjure you in God's name ...' I was beginning.

'What are you saying?' she put in in perplexity. 'I don't understand.'

I fancied that the arm that lay like a chilly girdle about my waist softly trembled ...

'Don't be afraid,' said Alice, 'don't be afraid, my dear one!' Her face turned and moved towards my face ... I felt on my lips a strange sensation, like the faintest prick of a soft and delicate sting ... Leeches might prick so in mild and drowsy mood.

I glanced downwards. We had now risen again to a considerable height. We were flying over some provincial town I did not know, situated on the side of a wide slope. Churches rose up high among the dark mass of wooden roofs and orchards; a long bridge stood out black at the bend of a river; everything was hushed, buried in slumber. The very crosses and cupolas seemed to gleam with a silent brilliance; silently stood the tall posts of the wells beside the round tops of the willows; silently the straight whitish road darted arrow-like into one end of the town, and silently it ran out again at the opposite end on to the dark waste of monotonous fields.

'What town is this?' I asked.

'X ...'

'X ... in Y ... province?'

'Yes.'

'I'm a long distance indeed from home!'

'Distance is not for us.'

[7]

'Really?' I was fired by a sudden recklessness. 'Then take me to South America!'

'To America I cannot. It's daylight there by now.'

'And we are night-birds. Well, anywhere, where you can, only far, far away.'

'Shut your eyes and hold your breath,' answered Alice, and we flew along with the speed of a whirlwind. With a deafening noise the air rushed into my ears. We stopped, but the noise did not cease. On the contrary, it changed to a sort of menacing roar, the roll of thunder . . .

'Now you can open your eyes,' said Alice.

I obeyed . . . Good God, where was I?

Overhead, ponderous, smoke-like storm-clouds; they huddled, they moved on like a herd of furious monsters . . . and there below, another monster; a raging, yes, raging, sea . . . The white foam gleamed with spasmodic fury, and surged up in hillocks upon it, and hurling up shaggy billows, it beat with a sullen roar against a huge cliff, black as pitch. The howling of the tempest, the chilling gasp of the storm-rocked abyss, the weighty splash of the breakers, in which from time to time one fancied something like a wail, like distant cannon-shots, like a bell ringing – the tearing crunch and grind of the shingle on the beach, the sudden shriek of an unseen gull, on the murky horizon the disabled hulk of a ship – on every side death, death and horror . . . Giddiness overcame me, and I shut my eyes again with a sinking heart . . .

'What is this? Where are we?'

'On the south coast of the Isle of Wight opposite the Blackgang cliff where ships are so often wrecked,' said Alice, speaking this time with peculiar distinctness, and as it seemed to me with a certain malignant pleasure . . .

'Take me away, away from here . . . home! home!' I shrank up, hid my face in my hands . . . I felt that we were moving faster than before, the wind now was not roaring or moaning, it whistled in my hair, in my clothes . . . I caught my breath . . .

'Stand on your feet now,' I heard Alice's voice saying. I tried to master myself, to regain consciousness . . . I felt the earth under the soles of my feet and I heard nothing, as though everything had swooned away about me . . . only in my temples the blood throbbed irregularly, and my head was still giddy with a faint ringing in my ears. I drew myself up and opened my eyes.

We were on the bank of my pond. Straight before me there were glimpses through the pointed leaves of the willows of its broad surface with threads of fluffy mist clinging here and there upon it. To the right a field of rye shone dimly; on the left stood up my orchard trees, tall, rigid, drenched it seemed in dew . . . The breath of the morning was already upon them. Across the pure grey sky stretched like streaks of smoke, two or three slanting clouds; they had a yellowish tinge, the first faint glow of dawn fell on them; one could not say whence it came; the eye could not detect on the horizon, which was gradually growing lighter, the spot where the sun was to rise. The stars had disappeared; nothing was astir yet, though everything was already on the point of awakening in the enchanted stillness of the morning twilight.

'Morning! see, it is morning!' cried Alice in my ear. 'Farewell till to-morrow.'

I turned round . . . Lightly rising from the earth, she floated by, and suddenly she raised both hands above her head. The head and hands and shoulders glowed for an instant with warm corporeal light; living sparks gleamed in the dark eyes; a smile of mysterious tenderness stirred the reddening lips . . . A lovely woman had suddenly arisen before me . . . But as though dropping into a swoon, she fell back instantly and melted away like vapour.

I remained passive.

When I recovered myself and looked round me, it seemed to me that the corporeal, pale-rosy colour that had flitted over the figure of my phantom had not yet vanished, and was enfolding me, diffused in the air . . . It was the flush of dawn. All at once I was conscious of extreme fatigue and turned homewards. As I passed the poultry-yard, I heard the first morning cackling of the geese (no birds wake earlier than they do); along the roof at the end of each beam sat a rook, and they were all busily and silently pluming themselves, standing out in sharp outline against the milky sky. From time to time they all rose at once, and after a short flight, settled again in a row, without uttering a caw . . . From the wood close by came twice repeated the drowsy, fresh chuck-chuck of the black-cock, beginning to fly into the dewy grass, overgrown by brambles . . . With a faint tremor all over me I made my way to my bed, and soon fell into a sound sleep.

The next night, as I was approaching the old oak, Alice moved to meet me, as if I were an old friend. I was not afraid of her as I had been the day before, I was almost rejoiced at seeing her; I did not even attempt to comprehend what was happening to me; I was simply longing to fly farther to interesting places.

Alice's arm again twined about me, and we took flight again.

'Let us go to Italy,' I whispered in her ear.

'Wherever you wish, my dear one,' she answered solemnly and slowly, and slowly and solemnly she turned her face towards me. It struck me as less transparent than on the eve; more womanlike and more imposing; it recalled to me the being I had had a glimpse of in the early dawn at parting.

'This night is a great night,' Alice went on. 'It comes rarely – when seven times thirteen . . .'

At this point I could not catch a few words.

'Tonight we can see what is hidden at other times.'

'Alice!' I implored, 'but who are you, tell me at last?'

Silently she lifted her long white hand. In the dark sky, where her finger was pointing, a comet flashed, a reddish streak among the tiny stars.

'How am I to understand you?' I began, 'Or, as that comet floats between the planets and the sun, do you float among men . . . or what?'

But Alice's hand was suddenly passed before my eyes . . . It was as though a white mist from the damp valley had fallen on me . . .

'To Italy! to Italy!' I heard her whisper. 'This night is a great night!'

The mist cleared away from before my eyes, and I saw below me an immense plain. But already, by the mere breath of the warm soft air upon my cheeks, I could tell I was not in Russia; and the plain, too, was not like our Russian plains. It was a vast dark expanse, apparently desert and not overgrown with grass; here and there over its whole extent gleamed pools of water, like broken pieces of looking-glass; in the distance could be dimly descried a noiseless motionless sea. Great stars shone bright in the spaces between the big beautiful clouds; the murmur of thousands, subdued but never-ceasing, rose on all sides, and very strange was this shrill but drowsy chorus, this voice of the darkness and the desert . . .

'The Pontine marshes,' said Alice. 'Do you hear the frogs? do you smell the sulphur?'

'The Pontine marshes . . .' I repeated, and a sense of grandeur and of desolation came upon me. 'But why have you brought me here, to this gloomy forsaken place? Let us fly to Rome instead.'

'Rome is near,' answered Alice . . . 'Prepare yourself!'

We sank lower, and flew along an ancient Roman road. A bullock slowly lifted from the slimy mud its shaggy monstrous head, with short tufts of bristles between its crooked backward-bent horns. It turned the whites of its dull malignant eyes askance, and sniffed a heavy snorting breath into its wet nostrils, as though scenting us.

'Rome, Rome is near . . .' whispered Alice. 'Look, look in front . . .'

I raised my eyes.

What was the blur of black on the edge of the night sky? Were these the lofty arches of an immense bridge? What river did it span? Why was it broken down in parts? No, it was not a bridge, it was an ancient aqueduct. All around was the holy ground of the Campagna, and there, in the distance, the Albanian hills, and their peaks and the grey ridge of the old aqueduct gleamed dimly in the beams of the rising moon . . .

We suddenly darted upwards, and floated in the air before a deserted ruin. No one could have said what it had been: sepulchre, palace, or castle . . . Dark ivy encircled it all over in its deadly clasp, and below gaped yawning a half-ruined vault. A heavy underground smell rose in my face from this heap of tiny closely-fitted stones, whence the granite facing of the wall had long crumbled away.

'Here,' Alice pronounced, and she raised her hand: 'Here! call aloud three times running the name of the mighty Roman!'

'What will happen?'

'You will see.'

I wondered. 'Divus Caius Julius Caesar!' I cried suddenly; 'divus Caius Julius Caesar!' I repeated deliberately; 'Caesar!'

The last echoes of my voice had hardly died away, when I heard . . .

It is difficult to say what I did hear. At first there reached me a confused din the ear could scarcely catch, the endlessly-repeated clamour of the blare of trumpets, and the clapping of hands. It seemed that somewhere, immensely far away, at some fathomless depth, a multitude innumerable was suddenly astir, and was rising up, rising up in agitation, calling to one another, faintly, as if muffled in sleep, the suffocating sleep of ages. Then the air began moving in dark currents over the ruin . . . Shades began flitting before me, myriads of shades, millions of outlines, the rounded curves of helmets, the long straight lines of lances; the moonbeams were broken into momentary gleams of blue upon these helmets and lances, and all this army, this multitude, came closer and closer, and grew, in more and more rapid movement . . . An indescribable force, a force fit to set the whole world moving, could be felt in it; but not one figure stood out clearly . . . And suddenly I

[11]

fancied a sort of tremor ran all round, as if it were the rush and rolling apart of some huge waves . . . '*Caesar, Caesar venit!*' sounded voices, like the leaves of a forest when a storm has suddenly broken upon it . . . a muffled shout thundered through the multitude, and a pale stern head, in a wreath of laurel, with downcast eyelids, the head of the emperor, began slowly to rise out of the ruin . . .

There is no word in the tongue of man to express the horror which clutched at my heart . . . I felt that were that head to raise its eyes, to part its lips, I must perish on the spot! 'Alice!' I moaned, 'I won't, I can't, I don't want Rome, coarse, terrible Rome . . . Away, away from here!'

'Coward!' she whispered, and away we flew. I just had time to hear behind me the iron voice of the legions, like a peal of thunder . . . then all was darkness.

'Look round,' Alice said to me, 'and don't fear.'

I obeyed – and, I remember, my first impression was so sweet that I could only sigh. A sort of smoky-grey, silvery-soft, half-light, half-mist, enveloped me on all sides. At first I made out nothing: I was dazzled by this azure brilliance; but little by little began to emerge the outlines of beautiful mountains and forests; a lake lay at my feet, with stars quivering in its depths, and the musical splash of waves. The fragrance of orange flowers met me with a rush, and with it – and also as it were with a rush – came floating the pure powerful notes of a woman's young voice. This fragrance, this music, fairly drew me downwards, and I began to sink . . . to sink down towards a magnificent marble palace, which stood, invitingly white, in the midst of a wood of cypress. The music flowed out from its wide open windows, the waves of the lake, flecked with the pollen of flowers, splashed upon its walls, and just opposite, all clothed in the dark green of orange flowers and laurels, enveloped in shining mist, and studded with statues, slender columns, and the porticoes of temples, a lofty round island rose out of the water . . .

'Isola Bella!' said Alice. . . . 'Lago Maggiore . . .'

I murmured only 'Ah!' and continued to drop. The woman's voice sounded louder and clearer in the palace; I was irresistibly drawn towards it . . . I wanted to look at the face of the singer, who, in such music, gave voice to such a night. We stood still before the window.

In the centre of a room, furnished in the style of Pompeii, and more like an ancient temple than a modern drawing-room, surrounded by Greek statues, Etruscan vases, rare plants, and precious stuffs, lighted up by the soft radiance of two lamps enclosed in crystal globes, a young woman was sitting at the piano. Her head slightly bowed and her eyes half-closed, she sang an Italian melody; she sang and smiled, and at the same time her face wore an expression of gravity, almost of sternness . . . a token of perfect rapture! She smiled . . . and Praxiteles' Faun, indolent, youthful as she, effeminate, and voluptuous, seemed to smile back at her from a corner, under the branches of an oleander, across the delicate smoke that curled upwards from a bronze censer on an antique tripod. The beautiful singer was alone. Spell-bound by the music, her beauty, the splendour and sweet fragrance of the night, moved to the heart by the picture of this youthful, serene, and untroubled happiness, I utterly forgot my companion, I forgot the strange way in which I had become a witness of this life, so remote, so completely apart from me, and I was on the point of tapping at the window, of speaking . . .

I was set trembling all over by a violent shock – just as though I had touched a galvanic battery. I looked round . . . The face of Alice was – for all its transparency – dark and menacing; there was a dull glow of anger in her eyes, which were suddenly wide and round . . .

'Away!' she murmured wrathfully, and again whirling and darkness and giddiness . . . Only this time not the shout of legions, but the voice of the singer, breaking on a high note, lingered in my ears . . .

We stopped. The high note, the same note was still ringing and did not cease to ring in my ears, though I was breathing quite a different air, a different scent . . . a breeze was blowing upon me, fresh and invigorating, as though from a great river, and there was a smell of hay, smoke and hemp. The long-drawn-out note was followed by a second, and a third, but with an expression so unmistakable, a trill so familiar, so peculiarly our own, that I said to myself at once: 'That's a Russian singing a Russian song!' and at that very instant everything grew clear about me.

We found ourselves on a flat riverside plain. To the left, newly-mown meadows, with rows of huge haystacks, stretched endlessly till they were lost in the distance; to the right extended the smooth surface of a vast mighty river, till it too was lost in the distance. Not far from the bank, big dark barges slowly rocked at anchor, slightly tilting their slender masts, like pointing fingers. From one of these barges came floating up to me the sounds of a liquid voice, and a fire was burning in it, throwing a long red light that danced and quivered on the water. Here and there, both on the river and in the fields other lights were glimmering, whether close at hand or far away, the eye could not distinguish; they shrank together, then suddenly lengthened out into great blurs of light; grasshoppers innumer-

[13]

able kept up an unceasing churr, persistent as the frogs of the Pontine marshes; and across the cloudless, but dark lowering sky floated from time to time the cries of unseen birds.

'Are we in Russia?' I asked of Alice.

'It is the Volga,' she answered.

We flew along the river-bank. 'Why did you tear me away from there, from that lovely country?' I began. 'Were you envious, or was it jealousy in you?'

The lips of Alice faintly stirred, and again there was a menacing light in her eyes . . . But her whole face grew stony again at once.

'I want to go home,' I said.

'Wait a little, wait a little,' answered Alice. 'Tonight is a great night. It will not soon return. You may be a spectator . . . Wait a little.'

And we suddenly flew across the Volga in a slanting direction, keeping close to the water's surface, with the low impetuous flight of swallows before a storm. The broad waves murmured heavily below us, the sharp river breeze beat upon us with its strong cold wing . . . the high right bank began soon to rise up before us in the half-darkness. Steep mountains appeared with great ravines between. We came near to them.

'Shout: "Lads, to the barges!"' Alice whispered to me. I remembered the terror I had suffered at the apparition of the Roman phantoms. I felt weary and strangely heavy, as though my heart were ebbing away within me. I wished not to utter the fatal words; I knew beforehand that in response to them there would appear, as in the wolves' valley of the Freischütz, some monstrous thing; but my lips parted against my will, and in a weak forced voice I shouted, also against my will: 'Lads, to the barges!'

At first all was silence, even as it was at the Roman ruins, but suddenly I heard close to my very ear a coarse bargeman's laugh, and with a moan something dropped into the water and a gurgling sound followed . . . I looked round: no one was anywhere to be seen, but from the bank the echo came bounding back, and at once from all sides rose a deafening din. There was a medley of everything in this chaos of sound: shouting and whining, furious abuse and laughter, laughter above everything; the plash of oars and the cleaving of hatchets, a crash as of the smashing of doors and chests, the grating of rigging and wheels, and the neighing of horses, and the clang of the alarm bell and the clink of chains, the roar and crackle of fire, drunken songs and quick, gnashing chatter, weeping inconsolable, plaintive despairing prayers, and shouts of command, the dying gasp and the reckless whistle, the guffaw and the thud of the dance . . . 'Kill them! Hang them! Drown them! rip them up! bravo! bravo! don't spare them!' could be heard distinctly; I could even hear the hurried breathing of men panting. And meanwhile all around, as far as the eye could reach, nothing could be seen, nothing was changed; the river rolled by mysteriously, almost sullenly, the very bank seemed more deserted and desolate – that was all.

I turned to Alice, but she put her finger to her lips . . .

'Stepan Timofeitch! Stepan Timofeitch is coming!' was shouted noisily all round; 'he is coming, our father, our ataman, our breadgiver!' As before I saw nothing but it seemed to me as though a huge body were moving straight at me . . . 'Frolka! where art thou, dog?' thundered an awful voice. 'Set fire to every corner at once – and to the hatchet with them, the white-handed scoundrels!'

I felt the hot breath of the flame close by, and tasted the bitter savour of the smoke; and at the same instant something warm like blood spurted over my face and hands . . . A savage roar of laughter broke out all round . . .

I lost consciousness, and when I came to myself, Alice and I were gliding along beside the familiar bushes that bordered my wood, straight towards the old oak . . .

'Do you see the little path?' Alice said to me, 'where the moon shines dimly and where are two birch-trees overhanging? Will you go there?'

But I felt so shattered and exhausted that I could only say in reply: 'Home! home!'

'You are at home,' replied Alice.

I was in fact standing at the very door of my house – alone. Alice had vanished. The yard-dog was about to approach, he scanned me suspiciously – and with a bark ran away.

With difficulty I dragged myself up to my bed and fell asleep without undressing.

All the following morning my head ached, and I could scarcely move my legs; but I cared little for my bodily discomfort; I was devoured by regret, overwhelmed with vexation.

I was excessively annoyed with myself. 'Coward!' I repeated incessantly; 'yes – Alice was right. What was I frightened of? how could I miss such an opportunity? . . . I might have seen Caesar himself – and I was senseless with terror, I whimpered and turned away, like a child at the sight of the rod. Razin, now – that's another matter. As a nobleman and landowner ... though, indeed, even then what had I really to fear? Coward! coward!' ...

'But wasn't it all a dream?' I asked myself at last. I called my housekeeper.

'Marfa, what o'clock did I go to bed yesterday – do you remember?'

'Why, who can tell, master? ... Late enough, surely. Before it was quite dark you went out of the house; and you were tramping about in your bedroom when the night was more than half over. Just on morning – yes. And this is the third day it's been the same. You've something on your mind, it's easy to see.'

'Aha-ha!' I thought. 'Then there's no doubt about the flying. Well, and how do I look today?' I added aloud.

'How do you look? Let me have a look at you. You've got thinner a bit. Yes, and you're pale, master; to be sure, there's not a drop of blood in your face.'

I felt a slight twinge of uneasiness ... I dismissed Marfa.

'Why, going on like this, you'll die, or go out of your mind, perhaps,' I reasoned with myself, as I sat deep in thought at the window. 'I must give it all up. It's dangerous. And now my heart beats so strangely. And when I fly, I keep feeling as though someone were sucking at it, or as it were drawing something out of it – as the spring sap is drawn out of the birch-tree, if you stick an axe into it. I'm sorry, though. And Alice too ... She is playing cat and mouse with me ... still she can hardly wish me harm. I will give myself up to her for the last time – and then ... But if she is drinking my blood? That's awful. Besides, such rapid locomotion cannot fail to be injurious; even in England, I'm told, on the railways, it's against the law to go more than one hundred miles an hour ...'

So I reasoned with myself – but at ten o'clock in the evening, I was already at my post before the old oak tree.

The night was cold, dull, grey; there was a feeling of rain in the air. To my amazement, I found no one under the oak; I walked several times round it, went up to the edge of the wood, turned back again, peered anxiously into the darkness ... All was emptiness. I waited a little, then several times I uttered the name, Alice, each time a little louder, ... but she did not appear. I felt sad, almost sick at heart; my previous apprehensions vanished; I could not resign myself to the idea that my companion would not come back to me again.

'Alice! Alice! come! Can it be you will not come?' I shouted, for the last time.

A crow, who had been waked by my voice, suddenly darted upwards into a tree-top close by, and catching in the twigs, fluttered his wings . . . But Alice did not appear.

With downcast head, I turned homewards. Already I could discern the black outlines of the willows on the pond's edge, and the light in my window peeped out at me through the apple-trees in the orchard – peeped at me, and hid again, like the eye of some man keeping watch on me – when suddenly I heard behind me the faint swish of the rapidly parted air, and something at once embraced and snatched me upward, as a buzzard pounces on and snatches up a quail . . . It was Alice sweeping down upon me. I felt her cheek against my cheek, her enfolding arm about my body, and like a cutting cold her whisper pierced to my ear, 'Here I am.' I was frightened and delighted both at once . . . We flew at no great height above the ground.

'You did not mean to come today?' I said.

'And you were dull without me? You love me? Oh, you are mine!'

The last words of Alice confused me . . . I did not know what to say.

'I was kept,' she went on; 'I watched.'

'Who could keep you?'

'Where would you like to go?' inquired Alice, as usual not answering my question.

'Take me to Italy – to that lake, you remember.'

Alice turned a little away, and shook her head in refusal. At that point I noticed for the first time that she had ceased to be transparent. And her face seemed tinged with colour; there was a faint glow of red over its misty whiteness. I glanced at her eyes . . . and felt a pang of dread; in those eyes something was astir – with the slow, continuous, malignant movement of the benumbed snake, twisting and turning as the sun begins to thaw it.

'Alice,' I cried, 'who are you? Tell me who you are.'

Alice simply shrugged her shoulders.

I felt angry . . . I longed to punish her; and suddenly the idea occurred to me to tell her to fly with me to Paris. 'That's the place for you to be jealous,' I thought. 'Alice,' I said aloud, 'you are not afraid of big towns – Paris, for instance?'

'No.'

'Not even those parts where it is as light as in the boulevards?'

'It is not the light of day.'

'Good; then take me at once to the Boulevard des Italiens.'

Alice wrapped the end of her long hanging sleeve about my head. I was at once enfolded in a sort of white vapour full of the drowsy fragrance of the poppy. Everything disappeared at once; every light, every sound, and almost consciousness itself. Only the sense of being alive remained, and that was not unpleasant.

Suddenly the vapour vanished; Alice took her sleeve from my head, and I saw at my feet a huge mass of closely packed buildings, brilliant light, movement, noisy traffic . . . I saw Paris.

I had been in Paris before, and so I recognised at once the place to which Alice had directed her course. It was the Garden of the Tuileries with its old chestnut-trees, its iron railings, its fortress moat, and its brutal-looking Zouave sentinels. Passing the palace, passing the Church of St Roche, on the steps of which the first Napoleon for the first time shed French blood, we came to a halt high over the Boulevard des Italiens, where the third Napoleon did the same thing and with the same success. Crowds of people, dandies young and old, workmen in blouses, women in gaudy dresses, were thronging on the pavements; the gilded restaurants and cafés were flaring with lights; omnibuses, carriages of all sorts and shapes, moved to and fro along the boulevard; everything was bustle, everything was brightness, wherever one chanced to look . . . But, strange to say, I had no inclination to forsake my pure dark airy height. I had no inclination to get nearer to this human ant-hill. It seemed as though a hot, heavy, reddish vapour rose from it, half-fragrance, half-stench; so many lives were flung struggling in one heap together there. I was hesitating . . . But suddenly, sharp as the clang of iron bars, the voice of a harlot of the streets floated up to me; like an insolent tongue, it was thrust out, this voice; it stung me like the sting of a viper. At once I saw in imagination the strong, heavy-jawed, greedy, flat Parisian face, the mercenary eyes, the paint and powder, the frizzed hair, and the nosegay of gaudy artificial flowers under the high-pointed hat, the polished nails like talons, the hideous crinoline . . . I could fancy too one of our sons of the steppes running with pitiful eagerness after the doll put up for sale . . . I could fancy him with clumsy coarseness and violent stammering, trying to imitate the manners of the waiters at Véfour's, mincing, flattering, wheedling . . . and a feeling of loathing gained possession of me . . . 'No,' I thought, 'here Alice has no need to be jealous . . .'

Meanwhile I perceived that we had gradually begun to descend . . . Paris was rising to meet us with all its din and odour . . .

'Stop,' I said to Alice. 'Are you not stifled and oppressed here?'

'You asked me to bring you here yourself.'

'I am to blame, I take back my word. Take me away, Alice, I beseech you. To be sure, here is Prince Kulmametov hobbling along the boulevard; and his friend, Serge Varaksin, waves to him, shouting: "Ivan Stepanitch, *allons souper*, make haste, zhay angazha Rigol-bouche itself!" Take me away from these furnished apartments and *maisons dorées*, from the Jockey Club and the Figaro, from close-shaven military heads and varnished barracks, from sergents-de-ville with Napoleonic beards, and from glasses of muddy absinthe, from gamblers playing dominoes at the cafés, and gamblers on the Bourse, from red ribbons in button-holes, from M. de Four, inventor of 'matrimonial specialities', and the gratuitous consultations of Dr Charles Albert, from liberal lectures and government pamphlets, from Parisian comedies and Parisian operas, from Parisian wit and Parisian ignorance . . . Away! away! away!'

'Look down,' Alice answered; 'you are not now in Paris.'

I lowered my eyes . . . It was true. A dark plain, intersected here and there by the whitish lines of roads, was rushing rapidly by below us, and only behind us on the horizon, like the reflection of an immense conflagration, rose the great glow of the innumerable lights of the capital of the world.

Again a veil fell over my eyes . . . Again I lost consciousness. The veil was withdrawn at last. What was it down there below? What was this part, with avenues of lopped lime-trees, with isolated fir-trees of the shape of parasols, with porticoes and temples in the Pompadour style, with statues of satyrs and nymphs of the Bernini school, with rococo tritons in the midst of meandering lakes, closed in by low parapets of blackened marble? Wasn't it Versailles? No, it was not Versailles. A small palace, also rococo, peeped out behind a clump of bushy oaks. The moon shone dimly, shrouded in mist, and over the earth there was, as it were spread out, a delicate smoke. The eye could not decide what it was, whether moonlight or fog. On one of the lakes a swan was asleep; its long back was white as the snow of the frost-bound steppes, while glow-worms gleamed like diamonds in the bluish shadow at the base of a statue.

'We are near Mannheim,' said Alice; 'this is the Schwetzingen garden.'

'We are in Germany,' I thought, and I fell to listening. All was silence, except somewhere, secluded and unseen, the splash and babble of falling water. It seemed continually to repeat the same words: 'Aye, aye, aye, for aye, aye.' And all at once I fancied that in the very centre of one of the avenues, between clipped walls of green, a cavalier came tripping along in red-heeled boots, a gold-braided coat, with lace ruffs at his wrists, a light

[19]

steel rapier at his thigh, smilingly offering his arm to a lady in a powdered wig and a gay chintz . . . Strange, pale faces . . . I tried to look into them . . . But already everything had vanished, and as before there was nothing but the babbling water.

'Those are dreams wandering,' whispered Alice; 'yesterday there was much – oh, much – to see; today, even the dreams avoid man's eyes. Forward! forward!'

We soared higher and flew farther on. So smooth and easy was our flight that it seemed that we moved not, but everything moved to meet us. Mountains came into view, dark, undulating, covered with forest; they rose up and swam towards us . . . And now they were slipping by beneath us, with all their windings, hollows, and narrow glades, with gleams of light from rapid brooks among the slumbering trees at the bottom of the dales; and in front of us more mountains sprung up again and floated towards us . . . We were in the heart of the Black Forest.

Mountains, still mountains . . . and forest, magnificent, ancient, stately forest. The night sky was clear; I could recognize some kinds of trees, espcially the splendid firs, with their straight white trunks. Here and there on the edge of the forest, wild goats could be seen; graceful and alert, they stood on their slender legs and listened, turning their heads prettily and pricking up their great funnel-shaped ears. A ruined tower, sightless and gloomy, on the crest of a bare cliff, laid bare its crumbling turrets; above the old forgotten stones, a little golden star was shining peacefully. From a small almost black lake rose, like a mysterious wail, the plaintive croak of tiny frogs. I fancied other notes, long-drawn-out, languid like the strains of an Æolian harp . . . Here we were in the home of legend! The same delicate moonlight mist, which had struck me in Schwetzingen, was shed here on every side, and the farther away the mountains, the thicker was this mist. I counted up five, six, ten different tones of shadow at different heights on the mountain slopes, and over all this realm of varied silence the moon queened it pensively. The air blew in soft, light currents. I felt myself a lightness at heart, and, as it were, a lofty calm and melancholy . . .

'Alice, you must love this country!'

'I love nothing.'

'How so? Not me?'

'Yes . . . you!' she answered indifferently.

It seemed to me that her arm clasped my waist more tightly than before.

'Forward! forward!' said Alice, with a sort of cold fervour.

'Forward!' I repeated.

A loud, thrilling cry rang out suddenly over our heads, and was at once repeated a little in front.

'Those are belated cranes flying to you, to the north,' said Alice; 'would you like to join them?'

'Yes, yes! raise me up to them.'

We darted upwards and in one instant found ourselves beside the flying flock.

The big handsome birds (there were thirteen of them) were flying in a triangle, with slow sharp flaps of their hollow wings; with their heads and legs stretched rigidly out, and their breasts stiffly pressed forward, they pushed on persistently and so swiftly that the air whistled about them. It was marvellous at such a height, so remote from all things living, to see such passionate, strenuous life, such unflinching will, untiringly cleaving their triumphant way through space. The cranes now and then called to one another, the foremost to the hindmost; and there was a certain pride, dignity, and invincible faith in these loud cries, this converse in the clouds. 'We shall get there, be sure, hard though it be,' they seemed to say, cheering one another on. And then the thought came to me that men, such as these birds – in Russia – nay, in the whole world, are few.

'We are flying towards Russia now,' observed Alice. I noticed now, not for the first time, that she almost always knew what I was thinking of. 'Would you like to go back?'

'Let us go back . . . or no! I have been in Paris; take me to Petersburg.'

'Now?'

'At once . . . Only wrap my head in your veil, or it will go ill with me.'

Alice raised her hand . . . but before the mist enfolded me, I had time to feel on my lips the contact of that soft, dull sting . . .

'Li-i-isten!' sounded in my ears a long-drawn-out cry. 'Li-i-isten!' was echoed back with a sort of desperation in the distance. 'Li-i-isten!' died away somewhere far, far away. I started. A tall golden spire flashed on my eyes; I recognized the fortress of St Peter and St Paul.

A northern, pale night! But was it night at all? Was it not rather a pallid, sickly daylight? I never liked Petersburg nights; but this time the night seemed even fearful to me; the face of Alice had vanished completely, melted away like the mist of morning in the July sun, and I saw her whole body clearly, as it hung, heavy and solitary on a level with the Alexander column. So here was Petersburg! Yes, it was Petersburg, no doubt. The wide empty grey streets; the greyish-white, and yellowish-grey and greyish-lilac houses, covered with stucco, which was peeling off, with their sunken windows, gaudy sign-boards, iron canopies over steps, and wretched little greengrocer's shops; the façades, inscriptions, sentry-boxes, troughs; the golden cap of St Isaac's; the senseless motley Bourse; the granite walls of the fortress, and the broken wooden pavement; the barges loaded with hay and timber; the smell of dust, cabbage, matting, and hemp; the stony-faced dvorniks in sheepskin coats, with high collars; the cab-drivers, huddled up dead asleep on their decrepit cabs – yes, this was Petersburg, our northern Palmyra. Everything was visible; everything was clear – cruelly clear and distinct – and everything was mournfully sleeping, standing out in strange huddled masses in the dull clear air. The flush of sunset – a hectic flush – had not yet gone, and would not be gone till morning from the white starless sky; it was reflected on the silken surface of the Neva, while faintly gurgling and faintly moving, the cold blue waves hurried on ...

'Let us fly away,' Alice implored.

And without waiting for my reply, she bore me away across the Neva, over the palace square to Liteiny Street. Steps and voices were audible beneath us; a group of young men, with worn faces, came along the street talking about dancing-classes. 'Sub-lieutenant Stolpakov's seventh!' shouted suddenly a soldier standing half-asleep on guard at a pyramid of rusty bullets; and a little farther on, at an open window in a tall house, I saw a girl in a creased silk dress, without cuffs, with a pearl net on her hair, and a cigarette in her mouth. She was reading a book with reverent attention; it was a volume of the works of one of our modern Juvenals.

'Let us fly away!' I said to Alice.

One instant more, and there were glimpses below us of the rotting pine copses and mossy bogs surrounding Petersburg. We bent our course straight to the south; sky, earth, all grew gradually darker and darker. The sick night; the sick daylight; the sick town – all were left behind us.

We flew more slowly than usual, and I was able to follow with my eyes the immense expanse of my native land gradually unfolding before me, like the unrolling of an endless panorama. Forests, copses, fields, ravines, rivers – here and there villages and churches – and again fields and forests and copses and ravines ... Sadness came over me, and a kind of indifferent dreariness. And I was not sad and dreary simply because it was Russia I was flying over. No. The earth itself, this flat surface which lay spread out beneath me; the whole earthly globe, with its populations, multitudinous, feeble, crushed by want, grief and diseases, bound to a clod of pitiful dust; this brittle, rough crust, this shell over the fiery sands of our planet, overspread with the mildew we call the organic, vegetable kingdom; these human flies, a thousand times paltrier than flies; their dwellings glued together with filth, the pitiful traces of their tiny, monotonous bustle, of their comic struggle with the unchanging and inevitable, how revolting it all suddenly was to me. My heart turned slowly sick, and I could not bear to gaze longer on these trivial pictures, on this vulgar show . . . Yes, I felt dreary, worse than dreary. Even pity I felt nothing of for my brother men: all feelings in me were merged in one which I scarcely dare to name: a feeling of loathing, and stronger than all and more than all within me was the loathing – for myself.

'Cease,' whispered Alice, 'cease, or I cannot carry you. You have grown heavy.'

'Home,' I answered her in the very tone in which I used to say the word to my coachman, when I came out at four o'clock at night from some Moscow friends', where I had been talking since dinner-time of the future of Russia and the significance of the commune. 'Home,' I repeated, and closed my eyes.

But I soon opened them again. Alice seemed huddling strangely up to me; she was almost pushing against me. I looked at her and my blood froze at the sight. One who has chanced to behold on the face of another a sudden look of intense terror, the cause of which he does not suspect, will understand me. By terror, overmastering terror, the pale features of Alice were drawn and contorted, almost effaced. I had never seen anything like it even on a living human face. A lifeless, misty phantom, a shade, . . . and this deadly horror . . .

'Alice, what is it?' I said at last.

'She . . . she . . .' she answered with an effort. 'She.'

'She? Who is she?'

'Do not utter her name, not her name,' Alice faltered hurriedly. 'We must escape, or there will be an end to everything, and for ever . . . Look, over there!'

I turned my head in the direction in which her trembling hand was pointing, and discerned something . . . something horrible indeed.

This something was the more horrible that it had no definite shape. Something bulky, dark, yellowish-black, spotted like a lizard's belly, not a storm-cloud, and not smoke, was crawling with a snake-like motion over the earth. A wide rhythmic undulating movement from above

[23]

downwards, and from below upwards, an undulation recalling the malignant sweep of the wings of a vulture seeking its prey; at times an indescribably revolting grovelling on the earth, as of a spider stooping over its captured fly . . . Who are you, what are you, menacing mass? Under her influence, I saw it, I felt it – all sank into nothingness, all was dumb . . .

A putrefying, pestilential chill came from it. At this chill breath the heart turned sick, and the eyes grew dim, and the hair stood up on the head. It was a power moving; that power which there is no resisting, to which all is subject, which sightless, shapeless, senseless, sees all, knows all, and like a bird of prey picks out its victims, like a snake, stifles them and stabs them with its frozen sting . . .

'Alice! Alice!' I shrieked like one in frenzy. 'It is death! death itself!'

The wailing sound I had heard before broke from Alice's lips; this time it was more like a human wail of despair, and we flew. But our flight was strangely and alarmingly unsteady; Alice turned over in the air, fell, rushed from side to side like a partridge mortally wounded, or trying to attract a dog away from her young. And meanwhile in pursuit of us, parting from the indescribable mass of horror, rushed sort of long undulating tentacles, like outstretched arms, like talons . . . Suddenly a huge shape, a muffled figure on a pale horse, sprang up and flew upwards into the very heavens . . . Still more fearfully, still more desperately Alice struggled. 'She has seen! All is over! I am lost!' I heard her broken whisper. 'Oh, I am miserable! I might have profited, have won life, . . . and now . . . Nothingness, nothingness!' It was too unbearable . . . I lost consciousness.

When I came to myself, I was lying on my back in the grass, feeling a dull ache all over me, as from a bad bruise. The dawn was beginning in the sky: I could clearly distinguish things. Not far off, alongside a birch copse, ran a road planted with willows: the country seemed familiar to me. I began to recollect what had happened to me, and shuddered all over directly my mind recalled the last, hideous apparition . . .

'But what was Alice afraid of?' I thought. 'Can she too be subject to that power? Is she not immortal? Can she too be in danger of annihilation, dissolution? How is it possible?'

A soft moan sounded close by me. I turned my head. Two paces from me lay stretched out motionless a young woman in a white gown, with thick disordered tresses, with bare shoulders. One arm was thrown behind her head, the other had fallen on her bosom. Her eyes were closed, and on her tightly shut lips stood a fleck of crimson stain. Could it be Alice? But Alice was a phantom, and I was looking upon a living woman. I crept up to her, bent down . . .

'Alice, it is you?' I cried. Suddenly, slowly quivering, the wide eyelids rose; dark piercing eyes were fastened upon me, and at the same instant lips too fastened upon me, warm, moist, smelling of blood . . . soft arms twined tightly round my neck, a burning, full heart pressed convulsively to mine. 'Farewell, farewell for ever!' the dying voice uttered distinctly, and everything vanished.

I got up, staggering like a drunken man, and passing my hands several times over my face, looked carefully about me. I found myself near the high road, a mile and a half from my own place. The sun had just risen when I got home.

All the following nights I awaited – and I confess not without alarm – the appearance of my phantom; but it did not visit me again. I even set off one day, in the dusk, to the old oak, but nothing took place there out of the common. I did not, however, overmuch regret the discontinuance of this strange acquaintance. I reflected much and long over this inexplicable, almost unintelligible phenomenon; and I am convinced that not only science cannot explain it, but that even in fairy tales and legends nothing like it is to be met with. What was Alice, after all? An apparition, a restless soul, an evil spirit, a sylphide, a vampire, or what? Sometimes it struck me again that Alice was a woman I had known at some time or other, and I made tremendous efforts to recall where I had seen her . . . Yes, yes, I thought sometimes, directly, this minute, I shall remember . . . In a flash everything had melted away again like a dream. Yes, I thought a great deal, and, as is always the way, came to no conclusion. The advice or opinion of others I could not bring myself to invite; fearing to be taken for a madman. I gave up all reflection upon it at last; to tell the truth, I had no time for it. For one thing, the emancipation had come along with the redistribution of property, etc.; and for another, my own health failed; I suffered with my chest, with sleeplessness, and a cough. I got thin all over. My face was yellow as a dead man's. The doctor declares I have too little blood, calls my illness by the Greek name, 'anaemia', and is sending me to Gastein. The arbitrator swears that without me there's no coming to an understanding with the peasants. Well, what's one to do?

But what is the meaning of the piercingly-pure, shrill notes, the notes of an harmonica, which I hear directly any one's death is spoken of before me? They keep growing louder, more penetrating . . . And why do I shudder in such anguish at the mere thought of annihilation?

[25]

DRACULA'S GUEST

Bram Stoker

Bram Stoker (1847–1912), was the creator of
the world's most celebrated vampire, Dracula.
This independent tale did not fit comfortably
into the novel *Dracula* itself, and was remoulded
as a fine short story in its own right forming the
title story in a posthumous collection of his
horror tales published in 1914.

W hen we started for our drive the sun was shining brightly on
Munich, and the air was full of the joyousness of early
summer. Just as we were about to depart, Herr Delbrück
(the maitre d'hôtel of the Quatre Saisons, where I was staying) came
down, bareheaded, to the carriage and, after wishing me a pleasant drive,
said to the coachman, still holding his hand on the handle of the carriage
door:

'Remember you are back by nightfall. The sky looks bright but there
is a shiver in the north wind that says there may be a sudden storm. But
I am sure you will not be late.' Here he smiled, and added, 'for you know
what night it is.'

Johann answered with an emphatic, 'Ja, mein Herr,' and, touching his
hat, drove off quickly. When we had cleared the town, I said, after
signalling to him to stop:

'Tell me, Johann, what is tonight?'

He crossed himself, as he answered laconically: 'Walpurgis nacht.'

Then he took out his watch, a great, old-fashioned German silver thing as big as a turnip, and looked at it, with his eyebrows gathered together and a little impatient shrug of his shoulders. I realized that this was his way of respectfully protesting against the unnecessary delay, and sank back in the carriage, merely motioning him to proceed. He started off rapidly, as if to make up for lost time. Every now and then the horses seemed to throw up their heads and sniffed the air suspiciously. On such occasions I often looked round in alarm. The road was pretty bleak, for we were traversing a sort of high, wind-swept plateau. As we drove, I saw a road that looked but little used, and which seemed to dip through a little, winding valley. It looked so inviting that, even at the risk of offending him, I called Johann to stop – and when he had pulled up, I told him I would like to drive down that road. He made all sorts of excuses, and frequently crossed himself as he spoke. This somewhat piqued my curiosity, so I asked him various questions. He answered fencingly, and repeatedly looked at his watch in protest. Finally I said:

'Well, Johann, I want to go down this road. I shall not ask you to come unless you like; but tell me why you do not like to go, that is all I ask.' For answer he seemed to throw himself off the box, so quickly did he reach the ground. Then he stretched out his hands appealingly to me, and implored me not to go. There was just enough of English mixed with the German for me to understand the drift of his talk. He seemed always just about to tell me something – the very idea of which evidently frightened him; but each time he pulled himself up, saying, as he crossed himself: 'Walpurgis nacht!'

I tried to argue with him, but it was difficult to argue with a man when I did not know his language. The advantage certainly rested with him, for although he began to speak in English, of a very crude and broken kind, he always got excited and broke into his native tongue – and every time he did so, he looked at his watch. Then the horses became restless and sniffed the air. At this he grew very pale, and, looking around in a frightened way, he suddenly jumped forward, took them by the bridles and led them on some twenty feet. I followed, and asked why he had done this. For answer he crossed himself, pointed to the spot we had left and drew his carriage in the direction of the other road, indicating a cross, and said, first in German, then in English: 'Buried him – him what killed themselves.'

I remembered the old custom of burying suicides at cross-roads: 'Ah! I see, a suicide. How interesting!' But for the life of me I could not make out why the horses were frightened.

Whilst we were talking, we heard a sort of sound between a yelp and a bark. It was far away; but the horses got very restless, and it took Johann all his time to quiet them. He was pale, and said: 'It sounds like a wolf – but yet there are no wolves here now.'

'No?' I said, questioning him; 'isn't it long since the wolves were so near the city?'

'Long, long,' he answered, 'in the spring and summer; but with the snow the wolves have been here not so long.'

Whilst he was petting the horses and trying to quiet them, dark clouds drifted rapidly across the sky. The sunshine passed away, and a breath of cold wind seemed to drift past us. It was only a breath, however, and more in the nature of a warning than a fact, for the sun came out brightly again. Johann looked under his lifted hand at the horizon and said:

'The storm of snow, he comes before long time.' Then he looked at his watch again, and, straightway holding his reins firmly – for the horses were still pawing the ground restlessly and shaking their heads – he climbed to his box as though the time had come for proceeding on our journey.

I felt a little obstinate and did not at once get into the carriage.

'Tell me,' I said, 'about this place where the road leads,' and I pointed down.

Again he crossed himself and mumbled a prayer, before he answered: 'It is unholy.'

'What is unholy?' I enquired.

'The village.'

'Then there is a village?'

'No, no. No one lives there hundreds of years.' My curiosity was piqued: 'But you said there was a village.'

'There was.'

'Where is it now?'

Whereupon he burst out into a long story in German and English, so mixed up that I could not quite understand exactly what he said, but roughly I gathered that long ago, hundreds of years, men had died there and been buried in their graves; and sounds were heard under the clay, and when the graves were opened, men and women were found rosy with life and their mouths red with blood. And so, in haste to save their lives (aye, and their souls! – and here he crossed himself) those who were left fled away to other places, where the living lived, and the dead were dead and not – not something. He was evidently afraid to speak the last words. As he proceeded with his narration, he grew more and more excited. It

[28]

seemed as if his imagination had got hold of him, and he ended in a perfect paroxysm of fear – white-faced, perspiring, trembling and looking round him, as if expecting that some dreadful presence would manifest itself there in the bright sunshine on the open plain. Finally, in an agony of desperation, he cried:

'Walpurgis nacht!' and pointed to the carriage for me to get in. All my English blood rose at this, and, standing back, I said:

'You are afraid, Johann – you are afraid. Go home; I shall return alone; the walk will do me good.' The carriage door was open. I took from the seat my oak walking-stick – which I always carry on my holiday excursions – and closed the door, pointing back to Munich, and said, 'Go home, Johann – Walpurgis nacht doesn't concern Englishmen.'

The horses were now more restive than ever, and Johann was trying to hold them in, while excitedly imploring me not to do anything so foolish. I pitied the poor fellow, he was so deeply in earnest; but all the same I could not help laughing. His English was quite gone now. In his anxiety he had forgotten that his only means of making me understand was to talk my language, so he jabbered away in his native German. It began to be a little tedious. After giving the direction, 'Home!' I turned to go down the cross-road into the valley.

With a despairing gesture, Johann turned his horses towards Munich. I leaned on my stick and looked after him. He went slowly along the road for a while: then there came over the crest of the hill a man tall and thin. I could see so much in the distance. When he drew near the horses, they began to jump and kick about, then to scream with terror. Johann could not hold them in; they bolted down the road, running away madly. I watched them out of sight, then looked for the stranger, but I found that he, too, was gone.

With a light heart I turned down the side road through the deepening valley to which Johann had objected. There was not the slightest reason, that I could see, for his objection; and I daresay I tramped for a couple of hours without thinking of time or distance, and certainly without seeing a person or a house. So far as the place was concerned, it was desolation itself. But I did not notice this particularly till, on turning a bend in the road, I came upon a scattered fringe of wood; then I recognized that I had been impressed unconsciously by the desolation of the region through which I had passed.

I sat down to rest myself, and began to look around. It struck me that it was considerably colder than it had been at the commencement of my walk – a sort of sighing sound seemed to be around me, with, now and then, high overhead, a sort of muffled roar. Looking upwards I noticed that great thick clouds were drifting rapidly across the sky from North to South at a great height. There were signs of coming storm in some lofty stratum of the air. I was a little chilly, and, thinking that it was the sitting still after the exercise of walking, I resumed my journey.

The ground I passed over was now much more picturesque. There were no striking objects that the eye might single out; but in all there was a charm of beauty. I took little heed of time and it was only when the deepening twilight forced itself upon me that I began to think of how I should find my way home. The brightness of the day had gone. The air was cold, and the drifting of clouds high overhead was more marked. They were accompanied by a sort of far-away rushing sound, through which seemed to come at intervals that mysterious cry which the driver had said came from a wolf. For a while I hesitated. I had said I would see the deserted village, so on I went, and presently came on a wide stretch of open country, shut in by hills all around. Their sides were covered with trees which spread down to the plain, dotting, in clumps, the gentler slopes and hollows which showed here and there. I followed with my eye the winding of the road, and saw that it curved close to one of the densest of these clumps and was lost behind it.

As I looked there came a cold shiver in the air, and the snow began to fall. I thought of the miles and miles of bleak country I had passed, and then hurried on to seek the shelter of the wood in front. Darker and darker grew the sky, and faster and heavier fell the snow, till the earth before and around me was a glistening white carpet the further edge of which was lost in misty vagueness. The road was here but crude, and when on the level its boundaries were not so marked, as when it passed through the cuttings; and in a little while I found that I must have strayed from it, for I missed underfoot the hard surface, and my feet sank deeper in the grass and moss. Then the wind grew stronger and blew with ever increasing force, till I was fain to run before it. The air became icy-cold, and in spite of my exercise I began to suffer. The snow was now falling so thickly and whirling around me in such rapid eddies that I could hardly keep my eyes open. Every now and then the heavens were torn asunder by vivid lightning, and in the flashes I could see ahead of me a great mass of trees, chiefly yew and cypress all heavily coated with snow.

I was soon amongst the shelter of the trees, and there, in comparative silence, I could hear the rush of the wind high overhead. Presently the blackness of the storm had become merged in the darkness of the night. By-and-by the storm seemed to be passing away: it now only came in fierce puffs or blasts. At such moments the weird sound of the wolf appeared to be echoed by many similar sounds around me.

Now and again, through the black mass of drifting cloud, came a straggling ray of moonlight, which lit up the expanse, and showed me that I was at the edge of a dense mass of cypress and yew trees. As the snow had ceased to fall, I walked out from the shelter and began to investigate more closely. It appeared to me that, amongst so many old foundations as I had passed, there might be still standing a house in which, though in ruins, I could find some sort of shelter for a while. As I skirted the edge of the copse, I found that a low wall encircled it, and following this I presently found an opening. Here the cypresses formed an alley leading up to a square mass of some kind of building. Just as I caught sight of this, however, the drifting clouds obscured the moon, and I passed up the path in darkness. The wind must have grown colder, for I felt myself shiver as I walked; but there was hope of shelter, and I groped my way blindly on.

I stopped, for there was a sudden stillness. The storm had passed; and, perhaps in sympathy with nature's silence, my heart seemed to cease to beat. But this was only momentarily; for suddenly the moonlight broke through the clouds, showing me that I was in a graveyard, and that the square object before me was a great massive tomb of marble, as white as the snow that lay on and all around it. With the moonlight there came a fierce sigh of the storm, which appeared to resume its course with a long, low howl, as of many dogs or wolves. I was awed and shocked, and felt the cold perceptibly grow upon me till it seemed to grip me by the heart. Then while the flood of moonlight still fell on the marble tomb the storm gave further evidence of renewing, as though it was returning on its track. Impelled by some sort of fascination, I approached the sepulchre to see what it was, and why such a thing stood alone in such a place. I walked around it, and read, over the Doric door, in German—

COUNTESS DOLINGEN OF GRATZ

IN STYRIA

SOUGHT AND FOUND DEATH

1801.

On the top of the tomb, seemingly driven through the solid marble – for the structure was composed of a few vast blocks of stone – was a great iron spike or stake. On going to the back I saw, graven in great Russian letters:

The dead travel fast.

There was something so weird and uncanny about the whole thing that it gave me a turn and made me feel quite faint. I began to wish, for the first time, that I had taken Johann's advice. Here a thought struck me, which came under almost mysterious circumstances and with a terrible shock. This was Walpurgis Night!

Walpurgis Night, when, according to the belief of millions of people, the devil was abroad – when the graves were opened and the dead came forth and walked. When all evil things of earth and air and water held revel. This very place the driver had specially shunned, This was the depopulated village of centuries ago. This was where the suicide lay; and this was the place where I was alone – unmanned, shivering with cold in a shroud of snow with a wild storm gathering again upon me! It took all my philosophy, all the religion I had been taught, all my courage, not to collapse in a paroxysm of fright.

And now a perfect tornado burst upon me. The ground shook as though thousands of horses thundered across it; and this time the storm bore on its icy wings, not snow, but great hailstones which drove with such violence that they might have come from the thongs of Balearic slingers – hailstones that beat down leaf and branch and made the shelter of the cypresses of no more avail than though their stems were standing-corn. At the first I rushed to the nearest tree; but I was soon fain to leave it and seek the only spot that seemed to afford refuge, the deep Doric doorway of the marble tomb. There, crouching against the massive bronze-door, I gained a certain amount of protection from the beating of the hailstones, for now they only drove against me as they ricochetted from the ground and the side of the marble.

As I leaned against the door, it moved slightly and opened inwards. The shelter of even a tomb was welcome in that pitiless tempest, and I was about to enter it when there came a flash of forked lightning that lit up the whole expanse of the heavens. In the instant, as I am a living man, I saw, as my eyes were turned into the darkness of the tomb, a beautiful woman, with rounded cheeks and red lips, seemingly sleeping on a bier. As the thunder broke overhead, I was grasped as by the hand of a giant and hurled out into the storm. The whole thing was so sudden that, before I could realize the shock, moral as well as physical, I found the hailstones beating me down. At the same time I had a strange, dominating feeling that I was not alone. I looked towards the tomb. Just then there came another blinding flash, which seemed to strike the iron stake that surmounted the tomb and to pour through to the earth, blasting and crumbling the marble, as in a burst of flame. The dead woman rose for a moment of agony, while she was lapped in the flame, and her bitter scream of pain was drowned in the thundercrash. The last thing I heard was this mingling of dreadful sound, as again I was seized in the giant-grasp and dragged away, while the hailstones beat on me, and the air around seemed reverberant with the howling of wolves. The last sight that I remembered was a vague, white, moving mass, as if all the graves around me had sent out the phantoms of their sheeted-dead, and that they were closing in on me through the white cloudiness of the driving hail.

Gradually there came a sort of vague beginning of consciousness; then a sense of weariness that was dreadful. For a time I remembered nothing; but slowly my senses returned. My feet seemed positively racked with pain, yet I could not move them. They seemed to be numbed. There was an icy feeling at the back of my neck and all down my spine, and my ears, like my feet, were dead, yet in torment; but there was in my breast a sense of warmth which was, by comparison, delicious. It was as a nightmare – a physical nightmare, if one may use such an expression; for some heavy weight on my chest made it difficult for me to breathe.

This period of semi-lethargy seemed to remain a long time, and as it faded away I must have slept or swooned. Then came a sort of loathing, like the first stage of sea-sickness, and a wild desire to be free from something – I knew not what. A vast stillness enveloped me as though all the world were asleep or dead – only broken by the low panting as of some animal close to me. I felt a warm rasping at my throat, then came a consciousness of the awful truth, which chilled me to the heart and sent the blood surging up through my brain. Some great animal was lying on me and now licking my throat. I feared to stir, for some instinct of prudence bade me lie still; but the brute seemed to realize that there was now some change in me, for it raised its head. Through my eyelashes I saw above me the two great flaming eyes of a gigantic wolf. Its sharp white teeth gleamed in the gaping red mouth, and I could feel its hot breath fierce and acrid upon me.

For another spell of time I remembered no more. Then I became conscious of a low growl, followed by a yelp, renewed again and again. Then, seemingly very far away, I heard a 'Holloa! holloa!' as of many voices calling in unison. Cautiously I raised my head and looked in the direction whence the sound came; but the cemetery blocked my view. The wolf still continued to yelp in a strange way, and a red glare began to move round the grove of cypresses, as though following the sound. As the voices drew closer, the wolf yelped faster and louder. I feared to make either sound or motion. Nearer came the red glow, over the white pall which stretched into the darkness around me. Then all at once from beyond the trees there came at a trot a troop of horsemen bearing torches. The wolf rose from my breast and made for the cemetery. I saw one of the horsemen (soldiers by their caps and their long military cloaks) raise his carbine and take aim. A companion knocked up his arm, and I heard the ball whizz over my head. He had evidently taken my body for that of the wolf. Another sighted the animal as it slunk away, and a shot followed. Then, at a gallop, the troop rode forward – some towards me, others following the wolf as it disappeared amongst the snow-clad cypresses.

As they drew nearer I tried to move, but was powerless, although I could see and hear all that went on around me. Two or three of the soldiers jumped from their horses and knelt beside me. One of them raised my head, and placed his hand over my heart.

'Good news, comrades!' he cried. 'His heart still beats!'

Then some brandy was poured down my throat; it put vigour into me, and I was able to open my eyes fully and look around. Lights and shadows were moving among the trees, and I heard men call to one another. They drew together, uttering frightened exclamations; and the lights flashed as the others came pouring out of the cemetery pell-mell, like men possessed. When the further ones came close to us, those who were around me asked them eagerly:

'Well, have you found him?'

The reply rang out hurriedly:

'No! no! Come away quick – quick! This is no place to stay, and on this of all nights!'

'What was it?' was the question, asked in all manner of keys. The answer came variously and all indefinitely as though the men were moved by some common impulse to speak, yet were restrained by some common fear from giving their thoughts.

'It – it – indeed!' gibbered one, whose wits had plainly given out for the moment.

'A wolf – and yet not a wolf!' another put in shudderingly.

'No use trying for him without the sacred bullet,' a third remarked in a more ordinary manner.

'Serve us right for coming out on this night! Truly we have earned our thousand marks!' were the ejaculations of a fourth.

'There was blood on the broken marble,' another said after a pause – 'the lightning never brought that there. And for him – is he safe? Look at his throat! See, comrades, the wolf has been lying on him and keeping his blood warm.'

The officer looked at my throat and replied:

'He is all right; the skin is not pierced. What does it all mean? We should never have found him but for the yelping of the wolf.'

'What became of it?' asked the man who was holding up my head, and who seemed the least panic-stricken of the party, for his hands were steady and without tremor. On his sleeve was the chevron of a petty officer.

'It went to its home,' answered the man, whose long face was pallid, and who actually shook with terror as he glanced around him fearfully. 'There are graves enough there in which it may lie. Come, comrades – come quickly! Let us leave this cursed spot.'

The officer raised me to a sitting posture, as he uttered a word of command; then several men placed me upon a horse. He sprang to the saddle behind me, took me in his arms, gave the word to advance; and, turning our faces away from the cypresses, we rode away in swift, military order.

As yet my tongue refused its office, and I was perforce silent. I must have fallen asleep; for the next thing I remembered was finding myself standing up, supported by a soldier on each side of me. It was almost broad daylight, and to the north a red streak of sunlight was reflected, like a path of blood, over the waste of snow. The officer was telling the men to say nothing of what they had seen, except that they found an English stranger, guarded by a large dog.

'Dog! that was no dog,' cut in the man who had exhibited such fear. 'I think I know a wolf when I see one.'

The young officer answered calmly: 'I said a dog.'

'Dog!' reiterated the other ironically. It was evident that his courage was rising with the sun; and, pointing to me, he said, 'Look at his throat. Is that the work of a dog, master?'

Instinctively I raised my hand to my throat, and as I touched it I cried out in pain. The men crowded round to look, some stooping down from their saddles; and again there came the calm voice of the young officer:

'A dog, as I said. If aught else were said we should only be laughed at.'

I was then mounted behind a trooper, and we rode on into the suburbs of Munich. Here we came across a stray carriage, into which I was lifted, and it was driven off to the Quatre Saisons – the young officer accompanying me, whilst a trooper followed with his horse, and the others rode off to their barracks.

When we arrived, Herr Delbrück rushed so quickly down the steps to meet me, that it was apparent he had been watching within. Taking me by both hands he solicitously led me in. The officer saluted me and was turning to withdraw, when I recognized his purpose, and insisted that he should come to my rooms. Over a glass of wine I warmly thanked him and his brave comrades for saving me. He replied simply that he was more than glad, and that Herr Delbrück had at the first taken steps to make all the searching party pleased; at which ambiguous utterance the maître d'hôtel smiled, while the officer pleaded duty and withdrew.

'But Herr Delbrück,' I enquired, 'how and why was it that the soldiers searched for me?'

He shrugged his shoulders, as if in depreciation of his own deed, as he replied:

'I was so fortunate as to obtain leave from the commander of the regiment in which I served, to ask for volunteers.'

'But how did you know I was lost?' I asked.

'The driver came hither with the remains of his carriage, which had been upset when the horses ran away.'

'But surely you would not send a search-party of soldiers merely on this account?'

'Oh, no!' he answered; 'but even before the coachman arrived, I had this telegram from the Boyar whose guest you are,' and he took from his pocket a telegram which he handed to me, and I read:

BISTRITZ

BE CAREFUL OF MY GUEST – HIS SAFETY IS MOST PRECIOUS TO ME. SHOULD AUGHT HAPPEN TO HIM, OR IF HE BE MISSED, SPARE NOTHING TO FIND HIM AND ENSURE HIS SAFETY. HE IS ENGLISH AND THEREFORE ADVENTUROUS. THERE ARE OFTEN DANGERS FROM SNOW AND WOLVES AND NIGHT. LOSE NOT A MOMENT IF YOU SUSPECT HARM TO HIM. I ANSWER YOUR ZEAL WITH MY FORTUNE. – DRACULA

As I held the telegram in my hand, the room seemed to whirl around me; and, if the attentive maître d'hôtel had not caught me, I think I should have fallen. There was something so strange in all this, something so weird and impossible to imagine, that there grew on me a sense of my being in some way the sport of opposite forces – the mere vague idea of which seemed in a way to paralyse me. I was certainly under some form of mysterious protection. From a distant country had come, in the very nick of time, a message that took me out of the danger of the snow-sleep and the jaws of the wolf.

THE HAUNTED HOUSE

E. Nesbit

E. Nesbit (1858–1924) is best known today for
her classic novels for children, most notably *The
Railway Children* (1906). However, she also
wrote several dramatic horror stories, some of
which have not been reprinted since their
original appearance in magazines. One of the
best of these forgotten stories is 'The Haunted
House', first published in the *Strand* magazine, in
December 1913 under her married name of
E. Bland.

It was by the merest accident that Desmond ever went to the Haunted
House. He had been away from England for six years, and the nine
months' leave taught him how easily one drops out of one's place.

He had taken rooms at the Greyhound before he found that there was
no reason why he should stay in Elmstead rather than in any other of
London's dismal outposts. He wrote to all the friends whose addresses
he could remember, and settled himself to await their answers.

He wanted someone to talk to, and there was no one. Meantime he
lounged on the horsehair sofa with the advertisements, and his pleasant
grey eyes followed line after line with intolerable boredom. Then,
suddenly, 'Halloa!' he said, and sat up. This is what he read:

A HAUNTED HOUSE. – Advertiser is anxious to have phenomena

investigated. Any properly-accredited investigator will be given full facilities. Address, by letter only, Wildon Prior, 237, Museum Street, London.

'That's rum!' he said. Wildon Prior had been the best wicket-keeper in his club. It wasn't a common name. Anyway, it was worth trying, so he sent off a telegram.

WILDON PRIOR, 237, MUSEUM STREET, LONDON. MAY I COME TO YOU FOR A DAY OR TWO AND SEE THE GHOST? – WILLIAM DESMOND

On returning the next day from a stroll there was an orange envelope on the wide Pembroke table in his parlour.

DELIGHTED – EXPECT YOU TODAY. BOOK TO CRITTENDEN FROM CHARING CROSS. WIRE TRAIN – WILDON PRIOR, ORMEHURST RECTORY, KENT.

'So that's all right,' said Desmond, and went off to pack his bag and ask in the bar for a time-table. 'Good old Wildon; it will be ripping, seeing him again.'

A curious little omnibus, rather like a bathing-machine, was waiting outside Crittenden Station, and its driver, a swarthy, blunt-faced little man, with liquid eyes, said, 'You a friend of Mr Prior, sir?' shut him up in the bathing-machine, and banged the door on him. It was a very long drive, and less pleasant than it would have been in an open carriage.

The last part of the journey was through a wood; then came a churchyard and a church, and the bathing-machine turned in at a gate under heavy trees and drew up in front of a white house with bare, gaunt windows.

'Cheerful place, upon my soul!' Desmond told himself, as he tumbled out of the back of the bathing-machine.

The driver set his bag on the discoloured doorstep and drove off. Desmond pulled a rusty chain, and a big-throated bell jangled above his head.

Nobody came to the door, and he rang again. Still nobody came, but he heard a window thrown open above the porch. He stepped back on to the gravel and looked up.

A young man with rough hair and pale eyes was looking out. Not Wildon, nothing like Wildon. He did not speak, but he seemed to be making signs; and the signs seemed to mean, 'Go away!'

'I came to see Mr Prior,' said Desmond. Instantly and softly the window closed.

'Is it a lunatic asylum I've come to by chance?' Desmond asked himself, and pulled again at the rusty chain.

Steps sounded inside the house, the sound of boots on stone. Bolts were shot back, the door opened, and Desmond, rather hot and a little annoyed, found himself looking into a pair of very dark, friendly eyes, and a very pleasant voice said: 'Mr Desmond, I presume? Do come in and let me apologize.'

The speaker shook him warmly by the hand, and he found himself following down a flagged passage a man of more than mature age, well dressed, handsome, with an air of competence and alertness which we associate with what is called 'a man of the world'. He opened a door and led the way into a shabby, bookish, leathery room.

'Do sit down, Mr Desmond.'

'This must be the uncle, I suppose,' Desmond thought, as he fitted himself into the shabby, perfect curves of the arm-chair. 'How's Wildon?' he asked, aloud. 'All right, I hope?'

The other looked at him. 'I beg your pardon,' he said, doubtfully.

'I was asking how Wildon is?'

'I am quite well, I thank you,' said the other man, with some formality.

'I beg your pardon' – it was now Desmond's turn to say it – 'I did not realize that your name might be Wildon, too. I meant Wildon Prior.'

'I am Wildon Prior,' said the other, 'and you, I presume, are the expert from the Psychical Society?'

'Good Lord, no!' said Desmond. 'I'm Wildon Prior's friend, and, of course, there must be two Wildon Priors.'

'You sent the telegram? You are Mr Desmond? The Psychical Society were to send an expert, and I thought—'

'I see,' said Desmond; 'and I thought you were Wildon Prior, an old friend of mine – a young man,' he said, and half rose.

'Now, don't,' said Wildon Prior. 'No doubt it is my nephew who is your friend. Did he know you were coming? But of course he didn't. I am wandering. But I'm exceedingly glad to see you. You will stay, will you not? If you can endure to be the guest of an old man. And I will write to Will tonight and ask him to join us.'

'That's most awfully good of you,' Desmond assured him. 'I shall be glad to stay. I was awfully pleased when I saw Wildon's name in the paper, because—' And out came the tale of Elmstead, its loneliness and disappointment.

Mr Prior listened with the kindest interest. 'And you have not found your friends? How sad! But they will write to you. Of course, you left your address?'

'I didn't, by Jove!' said Desmond. 'But I can write. Can I catch the post?'

[39]

'Easily,' the elder man assured him. 'Write your letters now. My man shall take them to the post, and then we will have dinner, and I will tell you about the ghost.'

Desmond wrote his letters quickly, Mr Prior just then reappearing.

'Now I'll take you to your room,' he said, gathering the letters in long, white hands. 'You'll like a rest. Dinner at eight.'

The bed-chamber, like the parlour, had a pleasant air of worn luxury and accustomed comfort.

'I hope you will be comfortable,' the host said, with courteous solicitude. And Desmond was quite sure that he would.

Three covers were laid, the swarthy man who had driven Desmond from the station stood behind the host's chair, and a figure came towards Desmond and his host from the shadows beyond the yellow circles of the silver-sticked candles.

'My assistant, Mr Verney,' said the host, and Desmond surrendered his hand to the limp, damp touch of the man who had seemed to say to him, from the window of the porch, 'Go away!' Was Mr Prior perhaps a doctor who received 'paying guests', persons who were, in Desmond's phrase, 'a bit balmy'? But he had said 'assistant'.

'I thought,' said Desmond, hastily, 'you would be a clergyman. The Rectory, you know – I thought Wildon, my friend Wildon, was staying with an uncle who was a clergyman.'

'Oh no,' said Mr Prior. 'I rent the Rectory. The rector thinks it is damp. The church is disused, too. It is not considered safe, and they can't afford to restore it. Claret to Mr Desmond, Lopez.' And the swarthy, blunt-faced man filled his glass.

'I find this place very convenient for my experiments. I dabble a little in chemistry, Mr Desmond, and Verney here assists me.'

Verney murmured something that sounded like 'only too proud', and subsided.

'We all have our hobbies, and chemistry is mine,' Mr Prior went on. 'Fortunately, I have a little income which enables me to indulge it. Wildon, my nephew, you know, laughs at me, and calls it the science of smells. But it's absorbing, very absorbing.'

After dinner Verney faded away, and Desmond and his host stretched their feet to what Mr Prior called a 'handful of fire', for the evening had grown chill.

'And now,' Desmond said, 'won't you tell me the ghost story?'

The other glanced round the room.

'There isn't really a ghost story at all. It's only that – well, it's never happened to me personally, but it happened to Verney, poor lad, and he's never been quite his own self since.'

Desmond flattered himself on his insight.

'Is mine the haunted room?' he asked.

'It doesn't come to any particular room,' said the other, slowly, 'nor to any particular person.'

'Anyone may happen to see it?'

'No one sees it. It isn't the kind of ghost that's seen or heard.'

'I'm afraid I'm rather stupid, but I don't understand,' said Desmond, roundly. 'How can it be a ghost, if you neither hear it nor see it?'

'I did not say it was a ghost,' Mr Prior corrected. 'I only say that there is something about this house which is not ordinary. Several of my assistants have had to leave; the thing got on their nerves.'

'What became of the assistants?' asked Desmond.

'Oh, they left, you know; they left,' Prior answered, vaguely. 'One couldn't expect them to sacrifice their health. I sometimes think – village gossip is a deadly thing, Mr Desmond – that perhaps they were prepared to be frightened; that they fancy things. I hope that Psychical Society's expert won't be a neurotic. But even without being a neurotic one might – but you don't believe in ghosts, Mr Desmond. Your Anglo-Saxon common sense forbids it.'

'I'm afraid I'm not exactly Anglo-Saxon,' said Desmond. 'On my father's side I'm pure Celt; though I know I don't do credit to the race.'

'And on your mother's side?' Mr Prior asked, with extraordinary eagerness; an eagerness so sudden and disproportioned to the question that Desmond stared. A faint touch of resentment as suddenly stirred in him, the first spark of antagonism to his host.

'Oh,' he said lightly, 'I think I must have Chinese blood, I get on so well with the natives in Shanghai, and they tell me I owe my nose to a Red Indian great grandmother.'

'No negro blood, I suppose?' the host asked, with almost discourteous insistence.

'Oh, I wouldn't say that,' Desmond answered. He meant to say it laughing, but he didn't. 'My hair, you know – it's a very stiff curl it's got, and my mother's people were in the West Indies a few generations ago. You're interested in distinctions of race, I take it?'

'Not at all, not at all,' Mr Prior surprisingly assured him; 'but, of course, any details of your family are necessarily interesting to me. I feel,' he added, with another of his winning smiles, 'that you and I are already friends.'

Desmond could not have reasoningly defended the faint quality of dislike that had begun to tinge his first pleasant sense of being welcomed and wished for as a guest.

'You're very kind,' he said; 'it's jolly of you to take in a stranger like this.'

Mr Prior smiled, handed him the cigar-box, mixed whisky and soda, and began to talk about the history of the house.

'The foundations are almost certainly thirteenth century. It was a priory, you know. There's a curious tale, by the way, about the man Henry gave it to when he smashed up the monasteries. There was a curse; there seems always to have been a curse—'

The gentle, pleasant, high-bred voice went on. Desmond thought he was listening, but presently he roused himself and dragged his attention back to the words that were being spoken.

'– that made the fifth death . . . There is one every hundred years, and always in the same mysterious way.'

Then he found himself on his feet, incredibly sleepy, and heard himself say: 'These old stories are tremendously interesting. Thank you very much. I hope you won't think me very uncivil, but I think I'd rather like to turn in; I feel a bit tired, somehow.'

'But of course, my dear chap.'

Mr Prior saw Desmond to his room.

'Got everything you want? Right. Lock the door if you should feel nervous. Of course, a lock can't keep ghosts out, but I always feel as if it could,' and with another of those pleasant, friendly laughs he was gone.

William Desmond went to bed a strong young man, sleepy indeed beyond his experience of sleepiness, but well and comfortable. He awoke faint and trembling, lying deep in the billows of the feather bed; and lukewarm waves of exhaustion swept through him. Where was he? What had happened? His brain, dizzy and weak at first, refused him any answer. When he remembered, the abrupt spasm of repulsion which he had felt so suddenly and unreasonably the night before came back to him in a hot, breathless flush. He had been drugged, he had been poisoned!

'I must get out of this,' he told himself, and blundered out of bed towards the silken bell-pull that he had noticed the night before hanging near the door.

As he pulled it, the bed and the wardrobe and the room rose up round him and fell on him, and he fainted.

When he next knew anything someone was putting brandy to his lips. He saw Prior, the kindest concern in his face. The assistant, pale and watery-eyed. The swarthy manservant, stolid, silent, and expressionless. He heard Verney say to Prior: 'You see it was too much – I told you—' 'Hush,' said Prior, 'he's coming to.'

Four days later Desmond, lying on a wicker chair on the lawn, was a little disinclined for exertion, but no longer ill. Nourishing foods and drinks, beef-tea, stimulants, and constant care – these had brought him back to something like his normal state. He wondered at the vague suspicions, vaguely remembered, of that first night; they had all been proved absurd by the unwavering care and kindness of everyone in the Haunted House.

'But what caused it?' he asked his host, for the fiftieth time. 'What made me make such a fool of myself?' And this time Mr Prior did not put him off, as he had always done before by begging him to wait till he was stronger.

'I am afraid, you know,' he said, 'that the ghost really did come to you. I am inclined to revise my opinion of the ghost.'

'But why didn't it come again?'

'I have been with you every night, you know,' his host reminded him. And, indeed, the sufferer had never been left alone since the ringing of his bell on that terrible first morning.

'And now,' Mr Prior went on, 'if you will not think me inhospitable, I think you will be better away from here. You ought to go the seaside.'

'There haven't been any letters for me, I suppose?' Desmond said, a little wistfully.

'Not one. I suppose you gave the right address? Ormehurst Rectory, Crittenden, Kent?'

'I don't think I put Crittenden,' said Desmond. 'I copied the address from your telegram.' He pulled the pink paper from his pocket.

'Ah, that would account,' said the other.

'You've been most awfully kind all through,' said Desmond, abruptly.

'Nonsense, my boy,' said the elder man, benevolently. 'I only wish Willie had been able to come. He's never written, the rascal! Nothing but the telegram to say he could not come and was writing.'

'I suppose he's having a jolly time somewhere,' said Desmond, enviously; 'but look here – do tell me about the ghost, if there's anything to tell. I'm almost quite well now, and I *should* like to know what it was that made a fool of me like that.'

'Well' – Mr Prior looked round him at the gold and red of dahlias and sunflowers, gay in the September sunshine – 'here, and now, I don't know that it could do any harm. You remember that story of the man

[43]

who got this place from Henry VIII. and the curse? That man's wife is buried in a vault under the church. Well, there were legends, and I confess I was curious to see her tomb. There are iron gates to the vault. Locked, they were. I opened them with an old key – and I couldn't get them to shut again.'

'Yes?' Desmond said.

'You think I might have sent for a locksmith; but the fact is, there is a small crypt to the church, and I have used that crypt as a supplementary laboratory. If I had called anyone in to see to the lock they would have gossiped. I should have been turned out of my laboratory – perhaps out of my house.'

'I see.'

'Now the curious thing is,' Mr Prior went on, lowering his voice, 'that it is only since that grating was opened that this house has been what they call "haunted". It is since then that all the things have happened.'

'What things?'

'People staying here, suddenly ill – just as you were. And the attacks always seem to indicate loss of blood. And—' He hesitated a moment. 'That wound in your throat. I told you you had hurt yourself falling when you rang the bell. But that was not true. What is true is that you had on your throat just the same little white wound that all the others have had. I wish' – he frowned – 'that I could get that vault gate shut again. The key won't turn.'

'I wonder if I could do anything?' Desmond asked, secretly convinced that he *had* hurt his throat in falling, and that his host's story was, as he put it, 'all moonshine'. Still, to put a lock right was but a slight return for all the care and kindness. 'I'm an engineer, you know,' he added, awkwardly, and rose. 'Probably a little oil. Let's have a look at this same lock.'

He followed Mr Prior through the house to the church. A bright, smooth old key turned readily, and they passed into the building, musty and damp, where ivy crawled through the broken windows, and the blue sky seemed to be laid close against the holes in the roof. Another key clicked in the lock of a low door beside what had once been the Lady Chapel, a thick oak door grated back, and Mr Prior stopped a moment to light a candle that waited in its rough iron candlestick on a ledge of the stonework. Then down narrow stairs, chipped a little at the edges and soft with dust. The crypt was Norman, very simply beautiful. At the end of it was a recess, masked with a grating of rusty ironwork.

'They used to think,' said Mr Prior, 'that iron kept off witchcraft. This

[44]

is the lock,' he went on, holding the candle against the gate, which was ajar.

They went through the gate, because the lock was on the other side. Desmond worked a minute or two with the oil and feather that he had brought. Then with a little wrench the key turned and re-turned.

'I think that's all right,' he said, looking up, kneeling on one knee, with the key still in the lock and his hand on it.

'May I try it?'

Mr Prior took Desmond's place, turned the key, pulled it out, and stood up. Then the key and the candlestick fell rattling on the stone floor, and the old man sprang upon Desmond.

'Now I've got you,' he growled, in the darkness, and Desmond says that his spring and his clutch and his voice were like the spring and the clutch and the growl of a strong savage beast.

Desmond's little strength snapped like a twig at his first bracing of it to resistance. The old man held him as a vice holds. He had got a rope from somewhere. He was tying Desmond's arms.

Desmond hates to know that there in the dark he screamed like a caught hare. Then he remembered that he was a man, and shouted 'Help! Here! Help!'

But a hand was on his mouth, and now a handkerchief was being knotted at the back of his head. He was on the floor, leaning against something. Prior's hands had left him.

'Now,' said Prior's voice, a little breathless, and the match he struck showed Desmond the stone shelves with long things on them – coffins he supposed. 'Now, I'm sorry I had to do it, but science before friendship, my dear Desmond,' he went on, quite courteous and friendly. 'I will explain to you, and you will see that a man of honour could not act otherwise. Of course, you having no friends who know where you are is most convenient. I saw that from the first. Now I'll explain. I didn't expect you to understand by instinct. But no matter. I am, I say it without vanity, the greatest discoverer since Newton. I know how to modify men's natures. I can make men what I choose. It's all done by transfusion of blood. Lopez – you know, my man Lopez – I've pumped the blood of dogs into his veins, and he's my slave – like a dog. Verney, he's my slave, too – part dog's blood and partly the blood of people who've come from time to time to investigate the ghost, and partly my own, because I wanted him to be clever enough to help me. And there's a bigger thing behind all this. You'll understand me when I say' – here he became very

[45]

technical indeed, and used many words that meant nothing to Desmond, whose thoughts dwelt more and more on his small chance of escape.

To die like a rat in a hole, a rat in a hole! If he could only loosen the handkerchief and shout again!

'Attend, can't you?' said Prior, savagely, and kicked him. 'I beg your pardon, my dear chap,' he went on suavely, 'but this is important. So you see the elixir of life is really the blood. The blood is the life, you know, and my great discovery is that to make a man immortal, and restore his youth, one only needs blood from the veins of a man who unites in himself blood of the four great races – the four colours, black, white, red, and yellow. Your blood unites these four. I took as much as I dared from you that night. I was the vampire, you know.' He laughed pleasantly. 'But your blood didn't act. The drug I had to give you to induce sleep probably destroyed the vital germs. And, besides, there wasn't enough of it. Now there is going to be enough!'

Desmond had been working his head against the thing behind him, easing the knot of the handkerchief down till it slipped from head to neck. Now he got his mouth free, and said, quickly: 'That was not true what I said about the Chinamen and that. I was joking. My mother's people were all Devon.'

'I don't blame you in the least,' said Prior, quietly. 'I should lie myself in your place.'

And he put back the handkerchief. The candle was now burning clearly from the place where it stood – on a stone coffin. Desmond could see that the long things on the shelves *were* coffins, not all of stone. He wondered what this madman would do with his body when everything was over. The little wound in his throat had broken out again. He could feel the slow trickle of warmth on his neck. He wondered whether he would faint. It felt like it.

'I wish I'd brought you here the first day – it was Verney's doing, my tinkering about with pints and half-pints. Sheer waste – sheer wanton waste!'

Prior stopped and stood looking at him.

Desmond, despairingly conscious of growing physical weakness, caught himself in a real wonder as to whether this might not be a dream – a horrible, insane dream – and he could not wholly dismiss the wonder, because incredible things seemed to be adding themselves to the real horrors of the situation, just as they do in dreams. There seemed to be something stirring in the place – something that wasn't Prior. No – nor Prior's shadow, either. That was black and sprawled big across the arched roof. This was white, and very small and thin. But it stirred, it grew – now it was no longer just a line of white, but a long, narrow, white wedge – and it showed between the coffin on the shelf opposite him and that coffin's lid.

And still Prior stood very still looking down on his prey. All emotion but a dull wonder was now dead in Desmond's weakened senses. In dreams – if one called out, one awoke – but he could not call out. Perhaps if one moved – But before he could bring his enfeebled will to the decision of movement – something else moved. The black lid of the coffin opposite rose slowly – and then suddenly fell, clattering and echoing, and from the coffin rose a form, horribly white and shrouded, and fell on Prior and rolled with him on the floor of the vault in a silent, whirling struggle. The last thing Desmond heard before he fainted in good earnest was the scream Prior uttered as he turned at the crash and saw the white-shrouded body leaping towards him.

'It's all right,' he heard next. And Verney was bending over him with brandy. 'You're quite safe. He's tied up and locked in the laboratory. No. That's all right, too.' For Desmond's eyes had turned towards the lidless coffin. 'That was only me. It was the only way I could think of, to save you. Can you walk now? Let me help you, so. I've opened the grating. Come.'

Desmond blinked in the sunlight he had never thought to see again. Here he was, back in his wicker chair. He looked at the sundial on the house. The whole thing had taken less than fifty minutes.

'Tell me,' said he. And Verney told him in short sentences with pauses between.

'I tried to warn you,' he said, 'you remember, in the window. I really believed in his experiments at first – and – he'd found out something about me – and not told. It was when I was very young. God knows I've paid for it. And when you came I'd only just found out what really had happened to the other chaps. That beast Lopez let it out when he was drunk. Inhuman brute! And I had a row with Prior that first night, and he promised me he wouldn't touch you. And then he did.'

'You might have told me.'

'You were in a nice state to be told anything, weren't you? He promised me he'd send you off as soon as you were well enough. And he *had* been good to me. But when I heard him begin about the grating and the key I *knew* – so I just got a sheet and—'

[47]

'But why didn't you come out before?'

'I didn't dare. He could have tackled me easily if he had known what he was tackling. He kept moving about. It had to be done suddenly. I counted on just that moment of weakness when he really thought a dead body had come to life to defend you. Now I'm going to harness the horse and drive you to the police-station at Crittenden. And they'll send and lock him up. Everyone knew he was as mad as a hatter, but somebody had to be nearly killed before anyone would lock him up. The law's like that, you know.'

'But you – the police – won't they—'

'It's quite safe,' said Verney, dully. 'Nobody knows but the old man, and now nobody will believe anything he says. No, he never posted your letters, of course, and he never wrote to your friend, and he put off the Psychical man. No, I can't find Lopez; he must know that something's up. He's bolted.'

But he had not. They found him, stubbornly dumb, but moaning a little, crouched against the locked grating of the vault when they came, a prudent half-dozen of them, to take the old man away from the Haunted House. The master was dumb as the man. He would not speak. He has never spoken since.

AN EPISODE OF
CATHEDRAL
HISTORY

M. R. James

Montague Rhodes James (1862–1936), regarded
by many contemporaries as the greatest scholar
of his generation, succeeded more than any
other writer in reviving and restyling the fine art
of the ghost story. Several of his best stories,
including 'Count Magnus' and 'Wailing Well',
have undercurrents of vampirism. The story
reprinted here originally appeared in the
Cambridge Review, 10 June 1914. James later
wrote that Southminster incorporated 'blends of
Canterbury, Salisbury, and Hereford'.

There was once a learned gentleman who was deputed to examine
and report upon the archives of the Cathedral of Southminster.
The examination of these records demanded a very considerable
expenditure of time: hence it became advisable for him to engage
lodgings in the city: for though the Cathedral body were profuse in their
offers of hospitality, Mr Lake felt that he would prefer to be master of his
day. This was recognized as reasonable. The Dean eventually wrote
advising Mr Lake, if he were not already suited, to communicate with Mr
Worby, the principal Verger, who occupied a house convenient to the
church and was prepared to take in a quiet lodger for three or four weeks.
Such an arrangement was precisely what Mr Lake desired. Terms were
easily agreed upon, and early in December, like another Mr Datchery (as

he remarked to himself), the investigator found himself in the occupation of a very comfortable room in an ancient and 'cathedraly' house.

One so familiar with the customs of Cathedral churches, and treated with such obvious consideration by the Dean and Chapter of this Cathedral in particular, could not fail to command the respect of the Head Verger. Mr Worby even acquiesced in certain modifications of statements he had been accustomed to offer for years to parties of visitors. Mr Lake, on his part, found the Verger a very cheery companion, and took advantage of any occasion that presented itself for enjoying his conversation when the day's work was over.

One evening, about nine o'clock, Mr Worby knocked at his lodger's door. 'I've occasion,' he said, 'to go across to the Cathedral, Mr Lake, and I think I made you a promise when I did so next I would give you the opportunity to see what it looks like at night time. It's quite fine and dry outside, if you care to come.'

'To be sure I will; very much obliged to you, Mr Worby, for thinking of it, but let me get my coat.'

'Here it is, sir, and I've another lantern here that you'll find advisable for the steps, as there's no moon.'

'Anyone might think we were Jasper and Durdles, over again, mightn't they?' said Lake, as they crossed the close, for he had ascertained that the Verger had read *Edwin Drood*.

'Well, so they might,' said Mr Worby, with a short laugh, 'though I don't know whether we ought to take it as a compliment. Odd ways, I often think, they had at that Cathedral, don't it seem so to you, sir? Full choral matins at seven o'clock in the morning all the year round. Wouldn't suit our boys' voices nowadays, and I think there's one or two of the men would be applying for a rise if the Chapter was to bring it in – particular the altos.'

They were now at the south-west door. As Mr Worby was unlocking it Lake said, 'Did you ever find anybody locked in here by accident?'

'Twice I did. One was a drunk sailor; however he got in I don't know. I s'pose he went to sleep in the service, but by the time I got to him he was praying fit to bring the roof in. Lor'! what a noise that man did make! Said it was the first time he'd been inside a church for ten years, and blest if ever he'd try it again. The other was an old sheep: them boys it was, up to their games. That was the last time they tried it on though. There, sir, now you see what we look like; our late Dean used now and again to bring parties in, but he preferred a moonlight night, and there was a piece of

[50]

verse he'd quote to 'em, relating to a Scotch cathedral, I understand; but I don't know; I almost think the effect's better when it's all dark-like. Seems to add to the size and heighth. Now if you won't mind stopping somewhere in the nave while I go up into the choir where my business lays, you'll see what I mean.'

Accordingly Lake waited, leaning against a pillar, and watched the light wavering along the length of the church, and up the steps into the choir, until it was intercepted by some screen or other furniture, which only allowed the reflection to be seen on the piers and roof. Not many minutes had passed before Worby reappeared at the door of the choir and by waving his lantern signalled to Lake to rejoin him.

'I suppose it is Worby, and not a substitute,' thought Lake to himself, as he walked up the nave. There was, in fact, nothing untoward. Worby showed him the papers which he had come to fetch out of the Dean's stall, and asked him what he thought of the spectacle: Lake agreed that it was well worth seeing. 'I suppose,' he said, as they walked towards the altar-steps together, 'that you're too much used to going about here at night to feel nervous – but you must get a start every now and then, don't you, when a book falls down or a door swings to?'

'No, Mr Lake, I can't say I think much about noises, not nowadays: I'm much more afraid of finding an escape of gas or a burst in the stove pipes than anything else. Still there have been times, years ago. Did you notice that plain altar-tomb there – fifteenth century we say it is, I don't know if you agree to that? Well, if you didn't look at it, just come back and give it a glance, if you'd be so good.' It was on the north side of the choir, and rather awkwardly placed: only about three feet from the enclosing stone screen. Quite plain, as the Verger had said, but for some ordinary stone panelling. A metal cross of some size on the northern side (that next to the screen) was the solitary feature of any interest.

Lake agreed that it was not earlier than the Perpendicular period: 'but,' he said, 'unless it's the tomb of some remarkable person, you'll forgive me for saying that I don't think it's particularly noteworthy.'

'Well, I can't say as it is the tomb of anybody noted in history,' said Worby, who had a dry smile on his face, 'for we don't own any record whatsoever of who it was put up to. For all that, if you've half an hour to spare, sir, when we get back to the house, Mr Lake, I could tell you a tale about that tomb. I won't begin on it now; it strikes cold here, and we don't want to be dawdling about all night.'

'Of course I should like to hear it immensely.'

'Very well, sir, you shall. Now if I might put a question to you,' he

[51]

went on, as they passed down the choir aisle, 'in our little local guide – and not only there, but in the little book on our Cathedral in the series – you'll find it stated that this portion of the building was erected previous to the twelfth century. Now of course I should be glad enough to take that view, but – mind the step, sir – but, I put it to you – does the lay of the stone 'ere in this portion of the wall (which he tapped with his key), does it to your eye carry the flavour of what you might call Saxon masonry? No, I thought not; no more it does to me: now, if you'll believe me, I've said as much to those men – one's the librarian of our Free Library here, and the other came down from London on purpose – fifty times, if I have once, but I might just as well have talked to that bit of stonework. But there it is, I suppose everyone's got their opinions.'

The discussion of this peculiar trait of human nature occupied Mr Worby almost up to the moment when he and Lake re-entered the former's house. The condition of the fire in Lake's sitting-room led to a suggestion from Mr Worby that they should finish the evening in his own parlour. We find them accordingly settled there some short time afterwards.

Mr Worby made his story a long one, and I will not undertake to tell it wholly in his own words, or in his own order. Lake committed the substance of it to paper immediately after hearing it, together with some few passages of the narrative which had fixed themselves *verbatim* in his mind; I shall probably find it expedient to condense Lake's record to some extent.

Mr Worby was born, it appeared, about the year 1828. His father before him had been connected with the Cathedral, and likewise his grandfather. One or both had been choristers, and in later life both had done work as mason and carpenter respectively about the fabric. Worby himself, though possessed, as he frankly acknowledged, of an indifferent voice, had been drafted into the choir at about ten years of age.

It was in 1840 that the wave of the Gothic revival smote the Cathedral of Southminster. 'There was a lot of lovely stuff went then, sir,' said Worby, with a sigh. 'My father couldn't hardly believe it when he got his orders to clear out the choir. There was a new dean just come in – Dean Burscough it was – and my father had been 'prenticed to a good firm of joiners in the city, and knew what good work was when he saw it. Crool it was, he used to say: all that beautiful wainscot oak, as good as the day it was put up, and garlands-like of foliage and fruit, and lovely old gilding work on the coats of arms and the organ pipes. All went to the timber yard – every bit except some little pieces worked up in the Lady Chapel, and 'ere in this overmantel. Well – I may be mistook, but I say our choir never looked as well since. Still there was a lot found out about the history of the church, and no doubt but what it did stand in need of repair. There was very few winters passed but what we'd lose a pinnicle.' Mr Lake expressed his concurrence with Worby's views of restoration, but owns to a fear about this point lest the story proper should never be reached. Possibly this was perceptible in his manner.

Worby hastened to reassure him, 'Not but what I could carry on about that topic for hours at a time, and do do when I see my opportunity. But Dean Burscough he was very set on the Gothic period, and nothing would serve him but everything must be made agreeable to that. And one morning after service he appointed for my father to meet him in the choir, and he came back after he'd taken off his robes in the vestry, and he'd got a roll of paper with him, and the verger that was then brought in a table, and they begun spreading it out on the table with prayer books to keep it down, and my father helped 'em, and he saw it was a picture of the inside of a choir in a Cathedral; and the Dean – he was a quick-spoken gentleman – he says, "Well, Worby, what do you think of that?" "Why," says my father, "I don't think I 'ave the pleasure of knowing that view. Would that be Hereford Cathedral, Mr Dean?" "No, Worby," says the Dean, "that's Southminster Cathedral as we hope to see it before many years." "Indeed, sir," says my father, and that was all he did say – leastways to the Dean – but he used to tell me he felt reelly faint in himself when he looked round our choir as I can remember it, all comfortable and furnished-like, and then see this nasty little dry picter, as he called it, drawn out by some London architect. Well, there I am again. But you'll see what I mean if you look at this old view.'

Worby reached down a framed print from the wall. 'Well, the long and the short of it was that the Dean he handed over to my father a copy of an order of the Chapter that he was to clear out every bit of the choir – make a clean sweep – ready for the new that was being designed up in town, and he was to put it in hand as soon as ever he could get the breakers together. Now then, sir, if you look at that view, you'll see where the pulpit used to stand: that's what I want you to notice, if you please.' It was, indeed, easily seen; an unusually large structure of timber with a domed sounding-board, standing at the east end of the stalls on the north side of the choir, facing the bishop's throne. Worby proceeded to explain that during the alterations, services were held in the nave, the members of the choir being thereby disappointed of an anticipated holiday, and the organist in particular incurring the suspicion of having wilfully damaged the mechanism of the temporary organ that was hired at considerable expense from London.

The work of demolition began with the choir screen and organ loft, and proceeded gradually eastwards, disclosing, as Worby said, many interesting features of older work. While this was going on, the members of the Chapter were, naturally, in and about the choir a great deal, and it soon became apparent to the elder Worby - who could not help overhearing some of their talk - that, on the part of the senior Canons especially, there must have been a good deal of disagreement before the policy now being carried out had been adopted. Some were of the opinion that they should catch their deaths of cold in the return-stalls, unprotected by a screen from the draughts in the nave: others objected to being exposed to the view of persons in the choir aisles, especially, they said, during the sermons, when they found it helpful to listen in a posture which was liable to misconstruction. The strongest opposition, however, came from the oldest of the body, who up to the last moment objected to the removal of the pulpit. 'You ought not to touch it, Mr Dean,' he said with great emphasis one morning, when the two were standing before it: 'you don't know what mischief you may do.' 'Mischief? it's not a work of any particular merit, Canon.' 'Don't call me Canon,' said the old man with great asperity, 'that is, for thirty years I've been known as Dr Ayloff, and I shall be obliged, Mr Dean, if you would kindly humour me in that matter. And as to the pulpit (which I've preached from for thirty years, though I don't insist on that), all I'll say is, I *know* you're doing wrong in moving it.' 'But what sense could there be, my dear Doctor, in leaving it where it is, when we're fitting up the rest of the choir in a totally different *style*? What reason could be given - apart from the look of the thing?' 'Reason! reason!' said old Dr Ayloff; 'if you young men - if I may say so without any disrespect, Mr Dean - if you'd only listen to reason a little, and not be always asking for it, we should get on better. But there, I've said my say.' The old gentleman hobbled off, and as it proved, never entered the Cathedral again. The season - it was a hot summer - turned sickly on a sudden. Dr Ayloff was one of the first to go, with some affection of the muscles of the thorax, which took him painfully at night. And at many services the number of choirmen and boys was very thin.

Meanwhile the pulpit had been done away with. In fact, the sounding-board (part of which still exists as a table in a summer-house in the palace garden) was taken down within an hour or two of Dr Ayloff's protest. The removal of the base - not effected without considerable trouble -

disclosed to view, greatly to the exultation of the restoring party, an altar-tomb – the tomb, of course, to which Worby had attracted Lake's attention that same evening. Much fruitless research was expended in attempts to identify the occupant; from that day to this he has never had a name put to him. The structure had been most carefully boxed in under the pulpit-base, so that such slight ornament as it possessed was not defaced; only on the north side of it there was what looked like an injury; a gap between two of the slabs composing the side. It might be two or three inches across. Palmer, the mason, was directed to fill it up in a week's time, when he came to do some other small jobs near that part of the choir.

The season was undoubtedly a very trying one. Whether the church was built on a site that had once been a marsh, as was suggested, or for whatever reason, the residents in its immediate neighbourhood had, many of them, but little enjoyment of the exquisite sunny days and the calm nights of August and September. To several of the older people – Dr Ayloff, among others, as we have seen – the summer proved downright fatal, but even among the younger, few escaped either a sojourn in bed for a matter of weeks, or at the least, a brooding sense of oppression, accompanied by hateful nightmares. Gradually there formulated itself a suspicion – which grew into a conviction – that the alterations in the Cathedral had something to say in the matter. The widow of a former old verger, a pensioner of the Chapter of Southminster, was visited by dreams, which she retailed to her friends, of a shape that slipped out of the little door of the south transept as the dark fell in, and flitted – taking a fresh direction every night – about the Close, disappearing for a while in house after house, and finally emerging again when the night sky was paling. She could see nothing of it, she said, but that it was a moving form: only she had an impression that when it returned to the church, as it seemed to do in the end of the dream, it turned its head: and then, she could not tell why, but she thought it had red eyes. Worby remembered hearing the old lady tell this dream at a tea-party in the house of the chapter clerk. Its recurrence might, perhaps, he said, be taken as a symptom of approaching illness; at any rate before the end of September the old lady was in her grave.

The interest excited by the restoration of this great church was not confined to its own county. One day that summer an F.S.A., of some celebrity, visited the place. His business was to write an account of the discoveries that had been made, for the Society of Antiquaries, and his wife, who accompanied him, was to make a series of illustrative drawings for his report. In the morning she employed herself in making a general sketch of the choir; in the afternoon she devoted herself to details. She first drew the newly exposed altar-tomb, and when that was finished, she called her husband's attention to a beautiful piece of diaper-ornament on the screen just behind it, which had, like the tomb itself, been completely concealed by the pulpit. Of course, he said, an illustration of that must be made; so she seated herself on the tomb and began a careful drawing which occupied her till dusk.

Her husband had by this time finished his work of measuring and description, and they agreed that it was time to be getting back to their hotel. 'You may as well brush my skirt, Frank,' said the lady, 'it must be covered with dust, I'm sure.' He obeyed dutifully; but, after a moment, he said, 'I don't know whether you value this dress particularly, my dear, but I'm inclined to think it's seen its best days. There's a great bit of it gone.' 'Gone? Where?' said she. 'I don't know where it's gone, but it's off at the bottom edge behind here.' She pulled it hastily into sight, and was horrified to find a jagged tear extending some way into the substance of the stuff; very much, she said, as if a dog had rent it away. The dress was, in any case, hopelessly spoilt, to her great vexation, and though they looked everywhere, the missing piece could not be found. There were many ways, they concluded, in which the injury might have come about, for the choir was full of old bits of woodwork with nails sticking out of them. Finally, they could only suppose that one of these had caused the mischief, and that the workmen, who had been about all day, had carried off the particular piece with the fragment of dress still attached to it.

It was about this time, Worby thought, that his little dog began to wear an anxious expression when the hour for it to be put into the shed in the back yard approached. (For his mother had ordained that it must not sleep in the house.) One evening, he said, when he was just going to pick it up and carry it out, it looked at him 'like a Christian, and waved its 'and, I was going to say – well, you know 'ow they do carry on sometimes, and the end of it was I put it under my coat, and 'uddled it upstairs – and I'm afraid I as good as deceived my poor mother on the subject. After that the dog acted very artful with 'iding itself under the bed for half an hour or more before bed-time came, and we worked it so as my mother never found out what we'd done.' Of course Worby was glad of its company anyhow, but more particularly when the nuisance that is still remembered in Southminster as 'the crying' set in.

'Night after night,' said Worby, 'that dog seemed to know it was coming; he'd creep out, he would, and snuggle into the bed and cuddle right up to me shivering, and when the crying come he'd be like a wild thing, shoving his head under my arm, and I was fully near as bad. Six or seven times we'd hear it, not more, and when he'd dror out his 'ed again I'd know it was over for that night. What was it like, sir? Well, I never heard but one thing that seemed to hit it off. I happened to be playing about in the Close, and there was two of the Canons met and said "Good morning" one to another. "Sleep well last night?" says one – it was Mr Henslow that one, and Mr Lyall was the other. "Can't say I did," says Mr Lyall, "rather too much of Isaiah xxxiv. 14 for me." "xxxiv. 14," says Mr Henslow, "what's that?" "You call yourself a Bible reader!" says Mr Lyall. (Mr Henslow, you must know, he was one of what used to be termed Simeon's lot – pretty much what we should call the Evangelical party.) "You go and look it up." I wanted to know what he was getting at myself, and so off I ran home and got out my own Bible, and there it was: "the satyr shall cry to his fellow." Well, I thought, is that what we've been listening to these past nights? and I tell you it made me look over my shoulder a time or two. Of course I'd asked my father and mother about what it could be before that, but they both said it was most likely cats: but they spoke very short, and I could see they was troubled. My word! that was a noise – 'ungry-like, as if it was calling after someone that wouldn't come. If ever you felt you wanted company, it would be when you was waiting for it to begin again. I believe two or three nights there was men put on to watch in different parts of the Close; but they all used to get together in one corner, the nearest they could to the High Street, and nothing came of it.

'Well, the next thing was this. Me and another of the boys – he's in business in the city now as a grocer, like his father before him – we'd gone up in the choir after morning service was over, and we heard old Palmer the mason bellowing to some of his men. So we went up nearer, because we knew he was a rusty old chap and there might be some fun going. It appears Palmer 'd told this man to stop up the chink in that old tomb. Well, there was this man keeping on saying he'd done it the best he could, and there was Palmer carrying on like all possessed about it. "Call that making a job of it?" he says. "If you had your rights you'd get the sack for this. What do you suppose I pay you your wages for? What do you suppose I'm going to say to the Dean and Chapter when they come round, as come they may do any time, and see where you've been bungling about covering the 'ole place with mess and plaster and Lord knows what?" "Well, master, I done the best I could," says the man; "I don't know no more than what you do 'ow it come to fall out this way.

I tamped it right in the 'ole," he says, "and now it's fell out,' he says, "I never see."

'"Fell out?" says old Palmer, "why it's nowhere near the place. Blowed out, you mean"; and he picked up a bit of plaster, and so did I, that was laying up against the screen, three or four feet off, and not dry yet; and old Palmer he looked at it curious-like, and then he turned round on me and he says, "Now then, you boys, have you been up to some of your games here?" "No," I says, "I haven't, Mr Palmer; there's none of us been about here till just this minute"; and while I was talking the other boy, Evans, he got looking in through the chink, and I heard him draw his breath, and he came away sharp and up to us, and says he, "I believe there's something in there. I saw something shiny." "What! I dare say!" says old Palmer; "well, I ain't got time to stop about there. You, William, you go off and get some more stuff and make a job of it this time; if not, there'll be trouble in my yard," he says.

'So the man he went off, and Palmer too, and us boys stopped behind, and I says to Evans, "Did you really see anything in there?" "Yes," he says, "I did indeed." So then I says, "Let's shove something in and stir it up." And we tried several of the bits of wood that was laying about, but they were all too big. Then Evans he had a sheet of music he'd brought with him, an anthem or a service, I forget which it was now, and he rolled it up small and shoved it in the chink; two or three times he did it, and nothing happened. "Give it me, boy," I said, and I had a try. No, nothing happened. Then, I don't know why I thought of it, I'm sure, but I stooped down just opposite the chink and put my two fingers in my mouth and whistled – you know the way – and at that I seemed to think I heard something stirring, and I says to Evans, "Come away," I says; "I don't like this." "Oh, rot," he says, "give me that roll," and he took it and shoved it in. And I don't think I ever see anyone go so pale as he did. "I say, Worby," he says, "It's caught, or else someone's got hold of it." "Pull it out or leave it," I says. "Come and let's get off." So he gave a good pull and it came away. Leastways most of it did, but the end was gone. Torn off it was, and Evans looked at it for a second and then gave a sort of croak and let it drop, and we both made off out of there as quick as ever we could. When we got outside Evans says to me, "Did you see the end of that paper?" "No," I says, "only it was torn." "Yes, it was," he says, "but it was wet too, and black!" Well, partly because of the fright we had, and partly because that music was wanted in a day or two, and we knew there'd be a set-out about it with the organist, we didn't say nothing to anyone else, and I suppose the workmen they swept up the bit that was left along with the rest of the rubbish. But Evans, if you were to ask him this very day about it, he'd stick to it he saw that paper wet and black at the end where it was torn.'

After that the boys gave the choir a wide berth, so that Worby was not sure what was the result of the mason's renewed mending of the tomb. Only he made out from fragments of conversation dropped by the workmen passing through the choir that some difficulty had been met with, and that the governor – Mr Palmer to wit – had tried his own hand at the job. A little later, he happened to see Mr Palmer himself knocking at the door of the Deanery and being admitted by the butler. A day or so after that, he gathered from a remark his father let fall at breakfast that something a little out of the common was to be done in the Cathedral after morning service on the morrow. 'And I'd just as soon it was today.' his father added; 'I don't see the use of running risks.' ' "Father," I says, "what are you going to do in the Cathedral tomorrow?" And he turned on me as savage as I ever see him – he was a wonderful good-tempered man as a general thing, my poor father was. "My lad," he says. "I'll trouble you not to go picking up your elders' and betters' talk: it's not manners and it's not straight. What I'm going to do or not going to do in the Cathedral tomorrow is none of your business: and if I catch sight of you hanging about the place tomorrow after your work's done, I'll send you home with a flea in your ear. Now you mind that." Of course I said I was very sorry and that, and equally of course I went off and laid my plans with Evans. We knew there was a stair up in the corner of the transept which you can get up to the triforium, and in them days the door to it was pretty well always open, and even if it wasn't we knew the key usually laid under a bit of matting hard by. So we made up our minds we'd be putting away music and that, next morning while the rest of the boys was clearing off, and then slip up the stairs and watch from the triforium if there was any signs of work going on.

'Well, that same night I dropped off asleep as sound as a boy does, and all of a sudden the dog woke me up, coming into the bed, and thought I, now we're going to get it sharp, for he seemed more frightened than usual. After about five minutes sure enough came this cry. I can't give you no idea what it was like; and so near too – nearer than I'd heard it yet – and a funny thing, Mr Lake, you know what a place this Close is for an echo, and particular if you stand this side of it. Well, this crying never made no sign of an echo at all. But, as I said, it was dreadful near this night; and on the top of the start I got with hearing it, I got another fright; for I heard something rustling outside in the passage. Now to be sure I thought I was done; but I noticed the dog seemed to perk up a bit, and next there was someone whispered outside the door, and I very near laughed out loud, for I knew it was my father and mother that had got out of bed with the noise. "Whatever is it?" says my mother. "Hush! I don't know," says my father, excited-like, "don't disturb the boy. I hope he didn't hear nothing."

'So, me knowing they were just outside, it made me bolder, and I slipped out of bed across to my little window – giving on the Close – but the dog he bored right down to the bottom of the bed – and I looked out. First go off I couldn't see anything. Then right down in the shadow under a buttress I made out what I shall always say was two spots of red – a dull red it was – nothing like a lamp or a fire, but just so as you pick 'em out of the black shadow. I hadn't but just sighted 'em when it seemed we wasn't the only people that had been disturbed, because I see a window in a house on the left-hand side become lighted up, and the light moving. I just turned my head to make sure of it, and then looked back into the shadow for those two red things, and they were gone, and for all I peered about and stared, there was not a sign more of them. Then come my last fright that night – something come against my bare leg – but that was all right: that was my little dog had come out of bed, and prancing about making a great to-do, only holding his tongue, and me seeing he was quite in spirits again, I took him back to bed and we slept the night out!

'Next morning I made out to tell my mother I'd had the dog in my room, and I was surprised, after all she'd said about it before, how quiet she took it. "Did you?" she says. "Well, by good rights you ought to go without your breakfast for doing such a thing behind my back: but I don't know as there's any great harm done, only another time you ask my permission, do you hear?" A bit after that I said something to my father about having heard the cats again. "*Cats?*" he says; and he looked over at my poor mother, and she coughed and he says, "Oh! ah! yes, cats. I believe I heard 'em myself."

'That was a funny morning altogether: nothing seemed to go right. The organist he stopped in bed, and the minor Canon he forgot it was the 19th day and waited for the *Venite*; and after a bit the deputy he set off playing the chant for evensong, which was a minor; and then the Decani boys were laughing so much they couldn't sing, and when it came to the anthem the solo boy he got took with the giggles, and made out his nose was bleeding, and shoved the book at me what hadn't practised the verse and wasn't much of a singer if I had known it. Well, things was rougher, you see, fifty years ago, and I got a nip from the counter-tenor behind me that I remembered.

'So we got through somehow, and neither the men nor the boys weren't by way of waiting to see whether the Canon in residence – Mr Henslow it was – would come to the vestries and fine 'em, but I don't believe he did: for one thing I fancy he'd read the wrong lesson for the first time in his life, and knew it. Anyhow, Evans and me didn't find no difficulty in slipping up the stairs as I told you, and when we got up we laid ourselves down flat on our stomachs where we could just stretch our heads out over the old tomb, and we hadn't but just done so when we heard the verger that was then, first shutting the iron porch-gates and locking the south-west door, and then the transept door, so we knew there was something up, and they meant to keep the public out for a bit.

'Next thing was, the Dean and the Canon come in by their door on the north, and then I see my father, and old Palmer, and a couple of their best men, and Palmer stood a talking for a bit with the Dean in the middle of the choir. He had a coil of rope and the men had crows. All of 'em looked a bit nervous. So there they stood talking, and at last I heard the Dean say, "Well, I've no time to waste, Palmer. If you think this'll satisfy Southminster people, I'll permit it to be done; but I must say this, that never in the whole course of my life have I heard such arrant nonsense from a practical man as I have from you. Don't you agree with me, Henslow?" As far as I could hear Mr Henslow said something like "Oh well! we're told, aren't we, Mr Dean, not to judge others?" And the Dean he gave a kind of sniff, and walked straight up to the tomb, and took his stand behind it with his back to the screen, and the others they come edging up rather gingerly. Henslow, he stopped on the south side and scratched on his chin, he did. The the Dean spoke up: "Palmer," he says, "which can you do easiest, get the slab off the top, or shift one of the side slabs?"

'Old Palmer and his men they pottered about a bit looking round the edge of the top slab and sounding the sides on the south and east and west and everywhere but the north. Henslow said something about it being better to have a try at the south side, because there was more light and more room to move about in. Then my father, who'd been watching of them, went round to the north side, and knelt down and felt of the slab by the chink, and he got up and dusted his knees and says to the Dean: "Beg pardon, Mr Dean, but I think if Mr Palmer'll try this here slab he'll find it'll come out easy enough. Seems to me one of the men could prise it out with his crow by means of this chink." "Ah! thank you, Worby,"

[61]

says the Dean; "that's a good suggestion. Palmer, let one of your men do that, will you?"

'So the man come round, and put his bat in and bore on it, and just that minute when they were all bending over, and we boys got our heads well over the edge of the triforium, there come a most fearful crash down at the west end of the choir, as if a whole stack of big timber had fallen down a flight of stairs. Well, you can't expect me to tell you everything that happened all in a minute. Of course there was a terrible commotion. I heard the slab fall out, and the crowbar on the floor, and I heard the Dean say, "Good God!"

'When I looked down again I saw the Dean tumbled over on the floor, the men was making off down the choir, Henslow was just going to help the Dean up, Palmer was going to stop the men (as he said afterwards) and my father was sitting on the altar step with his face in his hands. The Dean he was very cross. "I wish to goodness you'd look where you're coming to, Henslow," he says. "Why you should all take to your heels when a stick of wood tumbles down I cannot imagine"; and all Henslow could do, explaining he was right away on the other side of the tomb, would not satisfy him.

'Then Palmer came back and reported there was nothing to account for this noise and nothing seemingly fallen down, and when the Dean finished feeling of himself they gathered round – except my father, he sat where he was – and someone lighted up a bit of candle and they looked into the tomb. "Nothing there," says the Dean, "what did I tell you? Stay! here's something. What's this? a bit of music paper, and a piece of torn stuff – part of a dress it looks like. Both quite modern – no interest whatever. Another time perhaps you'll take the advice of an educated man" – or something like that, and off he went, limping a bit, and out through the north door, only as he went he called back angry to Palmer for leaving the door standing open. Palmer called out "Very sorry, sir," but he shrugged his shoulders, and Henslow says, "I fancy Mr Dean's mistaken. I closed the door behind me, but he's a little upset." Then Palmer says, "Why, where's Worby?" and they saw him sitting on the step and went up to him. He was recovering himself, it seemed, and wiping his forehead, and Palmer helped him up on to his legs, as I was glad to see.

'They were too far off for me to hear what they said, but my father pointed to the north door in the aisle, and Palmer and Henslow both of them looked very surprised and scared. After a bit, my father and Henslow went out of the church, and the others made what haste they could to put the slab back and plaster it in. And about as the clock struck twelve the Cathedral was opened again and us boys made the best of our way home.

'I was in a great taking to know what it was had given my poor father such a turn, and when I got in and found him sitting in his chair taking a glass of spirits, and my mother standing looking anxious at him, I couldn't keep from bursting out and making confession where I'd been. But he didn't seem to take on, not in the way of losing his temper. "You was there, was you? Well, did you see it?" "I see everything, father," I said, "except when the noise came." "Did you see what it was knocked the Dean over?" he says, "that what come out of the monument? You didn't? Well, that's a mercy." "Why, what was it, father?" I said. "Come, you must have seen it," he says. "*Didn't* you see? A thing like a man, all over hair, and two great eyes to it?"

'Well, that was all I could get out of him that time, and later on he seemed as if he was ashamed of being so frightened, and he used to put me off when I asked him about it. But years after, when I was got to be a grown man, we had more talk now and again on the matter, and he always said the same thing. "Black it was," he'd say, "and a mass of hair, and two legs, and the light caught on its eyes."

'Well, that's the tale of that tomb, Mr Lake; it's one we don't tell to our visitors, and I should be obliged to you not to make any use of it till I'm out of the way. I doubt Mr Evans'll feel the same as I do, if you ask him.'

This proved to be the case. But over twenty years have passed by, and the grass is growing over both Worby and Evans; so Mr Lake felt no difficulty about communicating his notes – taken in 1890 – to me. He accompanied them with a sketch of the tomb and a copy of the short inscription on the metal cross which was affixed at the expense of Dr Lyall to the centre of the northern side. It was from the Vulgate of Isaiah xxxiv., and consisted merely of the three words—

IBI CUBAVIT LAMIA.

'AND NO
BIRD SINGS'

E. F. Benson

Edward Frederic Benson (1867–1940), now
best known for his 'Mapp and Lucia' novels,
wrote several short stories dealing with various
kinds of vampirism (notably 'The Room in the
Tower', 'Mrs Amworth' and *Negotium
Perambulans'*). His early academic essay on the
Clonmel Witch Burning (1895) clearly reflects
his interest in demonic possession and vampiric
elementals. 'And No Bird Sings' first delighted
readers in the pages of *Woman* magazine in
December 1926.

T he red chimneys of the house for which I was bound were visible
from just outside the station at which I had alighted, and, so the
chauffeur told me, the distance was not more than a mile's walk
if I took the path across the fields. It ran straight till it came to the edge
of that wood yonder, which belonged to my host, and above which his
chimneys were visible. I should find a gate in the paling of this wood, and
a track traversing it, which debouched close to his garden. So, in this
adorable afternoon of early May, it seemed a waste of time to do other
than walk through meadows and woods and I set off on foot, while the
motor carried my traps.

It was one of those golden days which every now and again leak out of
Paradise and drip to earth. Spring had been late in coming, but now it was
here with a burst, and the whole world was boiling with the sap of life.
Never have I seen such a wealth of spring flowers, or such vividness of

[64]

green, or heard such melodious business among the birds in the hedgerows; this walk through the meadows was a jubilee of festal ecstasy. And best of all, so I promised myself, would be the passage through the wood newly fledged with milky green that lay just ahead. There was the gate, just facing me, and I passed through it into the dappled lights and shadows of the grass-grown track.

Coming out of the brilliant sunshine was like entering a dim tunnel; one had the sense of being suddenly withdrawn from the brightness of the spring into some subaqueous cavern. The tree-tops formed a green roof overhead, excluding the light to a remarkable degree; I moved in a world of shifting obscurity. Presently, as the trees grew more scattered, their place was taken by a thick growth of hazels, which met over the path, and then, the ground sloping downwards, I came upon an open clearing, covered with bracken and heather, and studded with birches. But though now I walked once more beneath the luminous sky, with the sunlight pouring down, it seemed to have lost its effulgence. The brightness – was it some odd optical illusion? – was veiled as if it came through crêpe. Yet there was the sun still well above the tree-tops in an unclouded heaven, but for all that the light was that of a stormy winter's day, without warmth or brilliance. It was oddly silent, too; I had thought that the bushes and trees would be ringing with the song of mating-birds, but listening, I could hear no note of any sort, neither the fluting of thrush or blackbird, nor the cheerful whir of the chaffinch, nor the cooing wood-pigeon, nor the strident clamour of the jay. I paused to verify this odd silence; there was no doubt about it. It was rather eerie, rather uncanny, but I supposed the birds knew their own business best, and if they were too busy to sing it was their affair.

As I went on it struck me also that since entering the wood I had not seen a bird of any kind; and now, as I crossed the clearing, I kept my eyes alert for them, but fruitlessly, and soon I entered the further belt of thick trees which surrounded it. Most of them I noticed were beeches, growing very close to each other, and the ground beneath them was bare but for the carpet of fallen leaves, and a few thin bramble-bushes. In this curious dimness and thickness of the trees, it was impossible to see far to right or left off the path, and now, for the first time since I had left the open, I heard some sound of life. There came the rustle of leaves from not far away, and I thought to myself that a rabbit, anyhow, was moving. But somehow it lacked the staccato patter of a small animal; there was a certain stealthy heaviness about it, as if something much larger were stealing along and desirous of not being heard. I paused again to see what

[65]

might emerge, but instantly the sound ceased. Simultaneously I was conscious of some faint but very foul odour reaching me, a smell choking and corrupt, yet somehow pungent, more like the odour of something alive rather than rotting. It was peculiarly sickening, and not wanting to get any closer to its source I went on my way.

Before long I came to the edge of the wood; straight in front of me was a strip of meadow-land, and beyond an iron gate between two brick walls, through which I had a glimpse of lawn and flower-beds. To the left stood the house, and over house and garden there poured the amazing brightness of the declining afternoon.

Hugh Granger and his wife were sitting out on the lawn, with the usual pack of assorted dogs: a Welsh collie, a yellow retriever, a fox-terrier, and a Pekinese. Their protest at my intrusion gave way to the welcome of recognition, and I was admitted into the circle. There was much to say, for I had been out of England for the last three months, during which time Hugh had settled into this little estate left him by a recluse uncle, and he and Daisy had been busy during the Easter vacation with getting into the house. Certainly it was a most attractive legacy; the house, through which I was presently taken, was a delightful little Queen Anne manor, and its situation on the edge of this heather-clad Surrey ridge quite superb. We had tea in a small panelled parlour overlooking the garden, and soon the wider topics narrowed down to those of the day and the hour. I had walked, had I, asked Daisy, from the station: did I go through the wood, or follow the path outside it?

The question she thus put to me was given trivially enough; there was no hint in her voice that it mattered a straw to her which way I had come. But it was quite clearly borne in upon me that not only she but Hugh also listened intently for my reply. He had just lit a match for his cigarette, but held it unapplied till he heard my answer. Yes, I had gone through the wood; but now, though I had received some odd impressions in the wood, it seemed quite ridiculous to mention what they were. I could not soberly say that the sunshine there was of very poor quality, and that at one point in my traverse I had smelt a most iniquitous odour. I had walked through the wood; that was all I had to tell them.

I had known both my host and hostess for a tale of many years, and now, when I felt that there was nothing except purely fanciful stuff that I could volunteer about my experiences there, I noticed that they exchanged a swift glance, and could easily interpret it. Each of them signalled to the other an expression of relief; they told each other (so I construed their glance) that I, at any rate, had found nothing unusual in

[66]

the wood, and they were pleased at that. But then, before any real pause had succeeded to my answer that I had gone through the wood, I remembered that strange absence of bird-song and birds, and as that seemed an innocuous observation in natural history, I thought I might as well mention it.

'One odd thing struck me,' I began (and instantly I saw the attention of both riveted again), 'I didn't see a single bird or hear one from the time I entered the wood to when I left it.'

Hugh lit his cigarette.

'I've noticed that too,' he said, 'and it's rather puzzling. The wood is certainly a bit of primeval forest, and one would have thought that hosts of birds would have nested in it from time immemorial. But, like you, I've never heard or seen one in it. And I've never seen a rabbit there either.'

'I thought I heard one this afternoon,' said I. 'Something was moving in the fallen beech leaves.'

'Did you see it?' he asked.

I recollected that I had decided that the noise was not quite the patter of a rabbit.

'No, I didn't see it,' I said, 'and perhaps it wasn't one. It sounded, I remember, more like something larger.'

Once again and unmistakably a glance passed between Hugh and his wife, and she rose.

'I must be off,' she said. 'Post goes out at seven, and I lazed all morning. What are you two going to do?'

'Something out of doors, please,' said I. 'I want to see the domain.'

Hugh and I accordingly strolled out again with the cohort of dogs. The domain was certainly very charming; a small lake lay beyond the garden, with a reed bed vocal with warblers, and a tufted margin into which coots and moorhens scudded at our approach. Rising from the end of that was a high heathery knoll full of rabbit holes, which the dogs nosed at with joyful expectations, and there we sat for a while overlooking the wood which covered the rest of the estate. Even now in the blaze of the sun near to its setting, it seemed to be in shadow, though like the rest of the view it should have basked in brilliance, for not a cloud flecked the sky and the level rays enveloped the world in a crimson splendour. But the wood was grey and darkling. Hugh, also, I was aware, had been looking at it, and now, with an air of breaking into a disagreeable topic, he turned to me.

'Tell me,' he said, 'does anything strike you about that wood?'

'Yes: it seems to lie in shadow.'

[67]

He frowned.

'But it can't, you know,' he said. 'Where does the shadow come from? Not from outside, for sky and land are on fire.'

'From inside, then?' I asked.

He was silent a moment.

'There's something queer about it,' he said at length. 'There's something there, and I don't know what it is. Daisy feels it too; she won't ever go into the wood, and it appears that birds won't either. Is it just the fact that, for some unexplained reason, there are no birds in it that has set all our imagination at work?'

I jumped up.

'Oh, it's all rubbish,' I said. 'Let's go through it now and find a bird. I bet you I find a bird.'

'Sixpence for every bird you see,' said Hugh.

We went down the hillside and walked round the wood till we came to the gate where I had entered that afternoon. I held it open after I had gone in for the dogs to follow. But there they stood, a yard or so away, and none of them moved.

'Come on, dogs,' I said, and Fifi, the fox-terrier, came a step nearer and then with a little whine retreated again.

'They always do that,' said Hugh, 'not one of them will set foot inside the wood. Look!'

He whistled and called, he cajoled and scolded, but it was no use. There the dogs remained, with little apologetic grins and signallings of tails, but quite determined not to come.

'But why?' I asked.

'Same reason as the birds, I suppose, whatever that happens to be. There's Fifi, for instance, the sweetest-tempered little lady; once I tried to pick her up and carry her in, and she snapped at me. They'll have nothing to do with the wood; they'll trot round outside it and go home.'

We left them there, and in the sunset light which was now beginning to fade began the passage. Usually the sense of eeriness disappears if one has a companion, but now to me, even with Hugh walking by my side, the place seemed even more uncanny than it had done that afternoon, and a sense of intolerable uneasiness, that grew into a sort of waking nightmare, obsessed me. I had thought before that the silence and loneliness of it had played tricks with my nerves; but with Hugh here it could not be that, and indeed I felt that it was not any such notion that lay at the root of this fear, but rather the conviction that there was some presence lurking there, invisible as yet, but permeating the gathered gloom. I could not form the slightest idea of what it might be, or whether it was material or ghostly; all I could diagnose of it from my own sensations was that it was evil and antique.

As we came to the open ground in the middle of the wood, Hugh stopped, and though the evening was cool I noticed that he mopped his forehead.

'Pretty nasty,' he said. 'No wonder the dogs don't like it. How do you feel about it?'

Before I could answer, he shot out his hand, pointing to the belt of trees that lay beyond.

'What's that?' he said in a whisper.

I followed his finger, and for one half-second thought I saw against the black of the wood some vague flicker, grey or faintly luminous. It waved as if it had been the head and forepart of some huge snake rearing itself, but it instantly disappeared, and my glimpse had been so momentary that I could not trust my impression.

'It's gone,' said Hugh, still looking in the direction he had pointed; and as we stood there, I heard again what I heard that afternoon, a rustle among the fallen beech-leaves. But there was no wind nor breath of breeze astir.

He turned to me.

'What on earth was it?' he said. 'It looked like some enormous slug standing up. Did you see it?'

'I'm not sure whether I did or not,' I said. 'I think I just caught sight of what you saw.'

'But what was it?' he said again. 'Was it a real material creature, or was it—'

'Something ghostly, do you mean?' I asked.

'Something half-way between the two,' he said. 'I'll tell you what I mean afterwards, when we've got out of this place.'

The thing, whatever it was, had vanished among the trees to the left of where our path lay, and in silence we walked across the open till we came to where it entered tunnel-like among the trees. Frankly I hated and feared the thought of plunging into that darkness with the knowledge that not so far off there was something the nature of which I could not ever so faintly conjecture, but which, I now made no doubt, was that which filled the wood with some nameless terror. Was it material, was it ghostly, or was it (and now some inkling of what Hugh meant began to form itself into my mind) some being that lay on the borderland between the two? Of all the sinister possibilities that appeared the most terrifying.

As we entered the trees again I perceived that reek, alive and yet corrupt, which I had smelt before, but now it was far more potent, and we hurried on, choking with the odour that I now guessed to be not the putrescence of decay, but the living substance of that which crawled and reared itself in the darkness of the wood where no bird would shelter. Somewhere among those trees lurked the reptilian thing that defied and yet compelled credence.

It was a blessed relief to get out of that dim tunnel into the wholesome air of the open and the clear light of evening. Within doors, when we returned, windows were curtained and lamps lit. There was a hint of frost, and Hugh put a match to the fire in his room, where the dogs, still a little apologetic, hailed us with thumpings of drowsy tails.

'And now we've got to talk,' said he, 'and lay our plans, for whatever it is that is in the wood, we've got to make an end of it. And, if you want to know what I think it is, I'll tell you.'

'Go ahead,' said I.

'You may laugh at me, if you like,' he said, 'but I believe it's an elemental. That's what I meant when I said it was a being half-way between the material and the ghostly. I never caught a glimpse of it till this afternoon; I only felt there was something horrible there. But now I've seen it, and it's like what spiritualists and that sort of folk describe as an elemental. A huge phosphorescent slug is what they tell us of it, which at will can surround itself with darkness.'

Somehow, now safe within doors, in the cheerful light and warmth of the room, the suggestion appeared merely grotesque. Out there in the darkness of that uncomfortable wood something within me had quaked, and I was prepared to believe any horror, but now commonsense revolted.

'But you don't mean to tell me you believe in such rubbish?' I said. 'You might as well say it was a unicorn. What *is* an elemental, anyway? Who has ever seen one except the people who listen to raps in the darkness and say they are made by their aunts?'

'What is it then?' he asked.

'I should think it is chiefly our own nerves,' I said. 'I frankly acknowledge I got the creeps when I went through the wood first, and I got them much worse when I went through it with you. But it was just nerves; we are frightening ourselves and each other.'

'And are the dogs frightening themselves and each other?' he asked. 'And the birds?'

That was rather harder to answer; in fact I gave it up.

Hugh continued.

'Well, just for the moment we'll suppose that something else, not ourselves, frightened us and the dogs and the birds,' he said, 'and that we did see something like a huge phosphorescent slug. I won't call it an elemental, if you object to that; I'll call it It. There's another thing, too, which the existence of It would explain.'

'What's that?' I asked.

'Well, It is supposed to be some incarnation of evil; it is a corporeal form of the devil. It is not only spiritual, it is material to this extent that it can be seen bodily in form, and heard, and, as you noticed, smelt, and, God forbid, handled. It has to be kept alive by nourishment. And that explains perhaps why, every day since I have been here, I've found on that knoll we went up some half-dozen dead rabbits.'

'Stoats and weasels,' said I.

'No, not stoats and weasels. Stoats kill their prey and eat it. These rabbits have not been eaten; they've been drunk.'

'What on earth do you mean?' I asked.

'I examined several of them. There was just a small hole in their throats, and they were drained of blood. Just skin and bones, and a sort of grey mash of fibre, like the fibre of an orange which has been sucked. Also there was a horrible smell lingering on them. And was the thing you had a glimpse of like a stoat or a weasel?'

There came a rattle at the handle of the door.

'Not a word to Daisy,' said Hugh as she entered.

'I heard you come in,' she said. 'Where did you go?'

'All round the place,' said I, 'and came back through the wood. It is odd; not a bird did we see, but that is partly accounted for because it was dark.'

I saw her eyes search Hugh's, but she found no communication there. I guessed that he was planning some attack on It next day, and he did not wish her to know that anything was afoot.

'The wood's unpopular,' he said. 'Birds won't go there, dogs won't go there, and Daisy won't go there. I'm bound to say I share the feeling too, but having braved its terrors in the dark I've broken the spell.'

'All quiet, was it?' asked she.

'Quiet wasn't the word for it. The smallest pin could have been heard dropping half a mile off.'

We talked over our plans that night after she had gone up to bed. Hugh's story about the sucked rabbits was rather horrible, and though there was no certain connection between those empty rinds of animals and what we had seen, there seemed a certain reasonableness about it. But anything, as he pointed out, which could feed like that was clearly not without its material side – ghosts did not have dinner, and if it was material it was vulnerable.

Our plans, therefore, were very simple; we were going to tramp through the wood, as one walks up partridges in a field of turnips, each with a shot-gun and a supply of cartridges. I cannot say that I looked forward to the expedition, for I hated the thought of getting into closer quarters with that mysterious denizen of the woods; but there was a certain excitement about it, sufficient to keep me awake a long time, and when I got to sleep to cause very vivid and awful dreams.

The morning failed to fulfil the promise of the clear sunset; the sky was lowering and cloudy and a fine rain was falling. Daisy had shopping errands which took her into the little town, and as soon as she had set off we started on our business. The yellow retriever, mad with joy at the sight of guns, came bounding with us across the garden, but on our entering the wood he slunk back home again.

The wood was roughly circular in shape, with a diameter perhaps of half a mile. In the centre, as I have said, there was an open clearing about a quarter of a mile across, which was thus surrounded by a belt of thick trees and copse a couple of hundred yards in breadth. Our plan was first to walk together up the path which led through the wood, with all possible stealth, hoping to hear some movement on the part of what we had come to seek. Failing that, we had settled to tramp through the wood at the distance of some fifty yards from each other in a circular track; two or three of these circuits would cover the whole ground pretty thoroughly. Of the nature of our quarry, whether it would try to steal away from us, or possibly attack, we had no idea; it seemed, however, yesterday to have avoided us.

Rain had been falling steadily for an hour when we entered the wood; it hissed a little in the tree-tops overhead; but so thick was the cover that the ground below was still not more than damp. It was a dark morning outside; here you would say that the sun had already set and that night was falling. Very quietly we moved up the grassy path, where our footfalls were noiseless, and once we caught a whiff of that odour of live corruption; but though we stayed and listened not a sound of anything stirred except the sibilant rain over our heads. We went across the clearing and through to the far gate, and still there was no sign.

'We'll be getting into the trees then,' said Hugh. 'We had better start where we got that whiff of it.'

[72]

We went back to the place, which was towards the middle of the encompassing trees. The odour still lingered on the windless air. 'Go on about fifty yards,' he said, 'and then we'll go in. If either of us comes on the track of it we'll shout to each other.'

I walked on down the path till I had gone the right distance, signalled to him, and we stepped in among the trees.

I have never known the sensation of such utter loneliness. I knew that Hugh was walking parallel with me, only fifty yards away, and if I hung on my step I could faintly hear his tread among the beech leaves. But I felt as if I was quite sundered in this dim place from all companionship of man; the only live thing that lurked here was that monstrous mysterious creature of evil. So thick were the trees that I could not see more than a dozen yards in any direction; all places outside the wood seemed infinitely remote, and infinitely remote also everything that had occurred to me in normal human life. I had been whisked out of all wholesome experiences into this antique and evil place. The rain had ceased, it whispered no longer in the tree-tops, testifying that there did exist a world and a sky outside, and only a few drops from above pattered on the beech-leaves.

Suddenly I heard the report of Hugh's gun, followed by his shouting voice.

'I've missed it,' he shouted; 'it's coming in your direction.'

I heard him running towards me, the beech-leaves rustling, and no doubt his footsteps drowned a stealthier noise that was close to me. All that happened now, until once more I heard the report of Hugh's gun, happened, I suppose, in less than a minute. If it had taken much longer I do not imagine I should be telling it today.

I stood there then, having heard Hugh's shout, with my gun cocked, and ready to put to my shoulder, and I listened to his running footsteps. But still I saw nothing to shoot at and heard nothing. Then between two beech trees, quite close to me, I saw what I can only describe as a ball of darkness. It rolled very swiftly towards me over the few yards that separated me from it, and then, too late, I heard the dead beech-leaves rustling below it. Just before it reached me, my brain realized what it was, or what it might be, but before I could raise my gun to shoot at that nothingness, it was upon me. My gun was twitched out of my hand, and I was enveloped in this blackness, which was the very essence of corruption. It knocked me off my feet, and I sprawled flat on my back, and upon me, as I lay there, I felt the weight of this invisible assailant.

I groped wildly with my hands and they clutched something cold and

[73]

slimy and hairy. They slipped off it, and next moment there was laid across my shoulder and neck something which felt like an india-rubber tube. The end of it fastened on to my neck like a snake, and I felt the skin rise beneath it. Again, with clutching hands, I tried to tear that obscene strength away from me, and as I struggled with it, I heard Hugh's footsteps close to me through this layer of darkness that hid everything.

My mouth was free, and I shouted at him. 'Here, here!' I yelled. 'Close to you, where it is darkest.'

I felt his hands on mine, and that added strength detached from my neck the sucker that pulled at it. The coil that lay heavy on my legs and chest writhed and struggled and relaxed. Whatever it was that our four hands held, slipped out of them, and I saw Hugh standing close to me. A yard or two off, vanishing among the beech trunks, was that blackness which had poured over me. Hugh put up his gun, and with his second barrel fired at it.

The blackness dispersed, and there, wriggling and twisting like a huge worm lay what we had come to find. It was alive still, and I picked up my gun which lay by my side and fired two more barrels into it. The writhings dwindled into mere shudderings and shakings, and then it lay still.

With Hugh's help I got to my feet, and we both reloaded before going nearer. On the ground there lay a monstrous thing, half-slug, half-worm. There was no head to it; it ended in a blunt point with an orifice. In colour it was grey covered with sparse black hairs; its length I suppose was some four feet, its thickness at the broadest part was that of a man's thigh, tapering towards each end. It was shattered by shot at its middle. There were stray pellets which had hit it elsewhere, and from the holes they had made there oozed not blood, but some grey viscous matter.

As we stood there some swift process of disintegration and decay began. It lost outline, it melted, it liquified, and in a minute more we were looking at a mass of stained and coagulated beech-leaves. Again and quickly that liquor of corruption faded, and there lay at our feet no trace of what had been there. The over-powering odour passed away, and there came from the ground just the sweet savour of wet earth in springtime, and from above the glint of a sunbeam piercing the clouds. Then a sudden pattering among the dead leaves set my heart into my mouth again, and I cocked my gun. But it was only Hugh's yellow retriever who had joined us.

We looked at each other.

'You're not hurt?' he said.

[74]

I held my chin up.

'Not a bit,' I said. 'The skin's not broken, is it?'

'No; only a round red mark. My God, what was it? What happened?'

'Your turn first,' said I. 'Begin at the beginning.'

'I came upon it quite suddenly,' he said. 'It was lying coiled like a sleeping dog behind a big beech. Before I could fire, it slithered off in the direction where I knew you were. I got a snap shot at it among the trees, but I must have missed, for I heard it rustling away. I shouted to you and ran after it. There was a circle of absolute darkness on the ground, and your voice came from the middle of it. I couldn't see you at all, but I clutched at the blackness and my hands met yours. They met something else, too.'

We got back to the house and had put the guns away before Daisy came home from her shopping. We had also scrubbed and brushed and washed. She came into the smoking-room.

'You lazy folk,' she said. 'It has cleared up, and why are you still indoors? Let's go out at once.'

I got up.

'Hugh has told me you've got a dislike of the wood,' I said, 'and it's a lovely wood. Come and see; he and I will walk on each side of you and hold your hands. The dogs shall protect you as well.'

'But not one of them will go a yard into the wood,' said she.

'Oh yes, they will. At least we'll try them. You must promise to come if they do.'

Hugh whistled them up, and down we went to the gate. They sat panting for it to be opened, and scuttled into the thickets in pursuit of interesting smells.

'And who says there are no birds in it?' said Daisy. 'Look at that robin! Why, there are two of them. Evidently house-hunting.'

THE LOVELY LADY

D. H. Lawrence

David Herbert Lawrence (1885–1930),
celebrated for his novels *Women in Love, Sons
and Lovers, The Rainbow* and *Lady Chatterley's
Lover*, was equally adept with poetry, short
stories, travel books, and the fascinating studies,
Psychoanalysis and the Unconscious (1921) and
Fantasia of the Unconscious (1922). These themes
are clearly behind the vampiric 'sponge' in this
story, which first appeared in the anthology *The
Black Cap* (edited by Lady Cynthia Asquith,
1927), and later became the title story in
Lawrence's collection *The Lovely Lady* in 1933.

A t seventy-two, Pauline Attenborough could still sometimes be
mistaken, in the half-light, for thirty. She really was a
wonderfully preserved woman, of perfect *chic*. Of course, it
helps a great deal to have the right frame. She would be an exquisite
skeleton, and her skull would be an exquisite skull, like that of some
Etruscan woman, with feminine charm still in the swerve of the bone and
the pretty naïve teeth.

Mrs Attenborough's face was of the perfect oval, and slightly flat type
that wears best. There is no flesh to sag. Her nose rode serenely, in its
finely bridged curve. Only her big grey eyes were a tiny bit prominent on
the surface of her face, and they gave her away most. The bluish lids were
heavy, as if they ached sometimes with the strain of keeping the eyes

beneath them arch and bright; and at the corners of the eyes were fine little wrinkles which would slacken with haggardness, then be pulled up tense again, to that bright, gay look like a Leonardo woman who really could laugh outright.

Her niece Cecilia was perhaps the only person in the world who was aware of the invisible little wire which connected Pauline's eye-wrinkles with Pauline's will power. Only Cecilia *consciously* watched the eyes go haggard and old and tired, and remain so, for hours; until Robert came home. Then ping! – the mysterious little wire that worked between Pauline's will and her face went taut, the weary, haggard, prominent eyes suddenly began to gleam, the eyelids arched, the queer curved eyebrows which floated in such frail arches on Pauline's forehead began to gather a mocking significance, and you had the *real* lovely lady, in all her charm.

She really had the secret of everlasting youth; that is to say, she could don her youth again like an eagle. But she was sparing of it. She was wise enough not to try being young for too many people. Her son Robert, in the evenings, and Sir Wilfred Knipe sometimes in the afternoon to tea: then occasional visitors on Sunday, when Robert was home: for these she was her lovely and changeless self, that age could not wither, nor custom stale: so bright and kindly and yet subtly mocking, like Mona Lisa who knew a thing or two. But Pauline knew more, so she needn't be smug at all, she could laugh that lovely mocking Bacchante laugh of hers, which was at the same time never malicious, always good-naturedly tolerant, both of virtues and vices. The former, of course, taking much more tolerating. So she suggested, roguishly.

Only with her niece Cecilia she did not trouble to keep up the glamour. Ciss was not very observant, anyhow: and more than that, she was plain: more still, she was in love with Robert: and most of all, she was thirty, and dependent on her Aunt Pauline. Oh, Cecilia! Why make music for her!

Cecilia, called by her aunt and by her cousin Robert just Ciss, like a cat spitting, was a big dark-complexioned pug-faced young woman who very rarely spoke, and when she did, couldn't get it out. She was the daughter of a poor Congregational minister who had been, while he lived, brother to Ronald, Aunt Pauline's husband. Ronald and the Congregational minister were both well dead, and Aunt Pauline had had charge of Ciss for the last five years.

They lived all together in a quite exquisite though rather small Queen Anne house some twenty-five miles out of town, secluded in a little dale, and surrounded by small but very quaint and pleasant grounds. It was an ideal place and an ideal life for Aunt Pauline, at the age of seventy-two. When the kingfishers flashed up the little stream in the garden, going under the alders, something still flashed in her heart. She was that kind of woman.

Robert, who was two years older than Ciss, went every day to town, to his chambers in one of the Inns. He was a barrister, and, to his secret but very deep mortification, he earned about a hundred pounds a year. He simply *couldn't* get above that figure, though it was rather easy to get below it. Of course, it didn't matter. Pauline had money. But then what was Pauline's was Pauline's, and though she could give almost lavishly, still, one was always aware of having a *lovely* and *undeserved* present made to one: presents are so much nicer when they are undeserved, Aunt Pauline would say.

Robert too was plain, and almost speechless. He was medium-sized, rather broad and stout, though not fat. Only his creamy, clean-shaven face was rather fat, and sometimes suggestive of an Italian priest, in its silence and its secrecy. He had grey eyes like his mother but very shy and uneasy, not bold like hers. Perhaps Ciss was the only person who fathomed his awful shyness and *malaise*, his habitual feeling that he was in the wrong place: almost like a soul that has got into the wrong body. But he never did anything about it. He went up to his chambers, and read law. It was, however, all the weird old processes that interested him. He had, unknown to everybody but his mother, a quite extraordinary collection of old Mexican legal documents, reports of processes and trials, pleas, accusations, the weird and awful mixture of ecclesiastical law and common law in seventeenth century Mexico. He had started a study in this direction through coming across a report of a trial of two English sailors, for murder, in Mexico in 1620, and he had gone on, when the next document was an accusation against a Don Miguel Estrada for seducing one of the nuns of the Sacred Heart Convent in Oaxaca in 1680.

Pauline and her son Robert had wonderful evenings with these old papers. The lovely lady knew a little Spanish. She even looked a trifle Spanish herself, with a high comb and a marvellous dark-brown shawl embroidered in thick silvery silk embroidery. So she would sit at the perfect old table, soft as velvet in its deep brown surface, a high comb in her hair, ear-rings with dropping pendants in her ears, her arms bare and still beautiful, a few strings of pearls round her throat, a puce velvet dress on and this or another beautiful shawl, and by candlelight she looked, yes, a Spanish high-bred beauty of thirty-two or three. She set the candles to give her face just the chiaroscuro she knew suited her; her high chair that rose behind her face was done in old green brocade, against which her face emerged like a Christmas rose.

They were always three at table; and they always drank a bottle of champagne: Pauline two glasses, Ciss two glasses, Robert the rest. The lovely lady sparkled and was radiant. Ciss, her black hair bobbed, her broad shoulders in a very nice and becoming dress that Aunt Pauline had helped her to make, stared from her aunt to her cousin and back again, with rather confused, mute, hazel eyes, and played the part of an audience suitably impressed. She *was* impressed, somewhere, all the time. And even rendered speechless by Pauline's brilliancy, even after five years. But at the bottom of her consciousness were the data of as weird a document as Robert ever studied: all the things she knew about her aunt and cousin.

Robert was always a gentleman, with an old-fashioned punctilious courtesy that covered his shyness quite completely. He was, and Ciss knew it, more confused than shy. He was worse than she was. Cecilia's own confusion dated from only five years back – Robert's must have started before he was born. In the lovely lady's womb he must have felt *very* confused.

He paid all his attention to his mother, drawn to her as a humble flower to the sun. And yet, priest-like, he was all the time aware, with the tail of his consciousness, that Ciss was there, and that she was a bit shut out of it, and that something wasn't right. He was aware of the third consciousness in the room. Whereas to Pauline, her niece Cecilia was an appropriate part of her own setting, rather than a distinct consciousness.

Robert took coffee with his mother and Ciss in the warm drawing-room, where all the furniture was so lovely, all collectors' pieces – Mrs Attenborough had made her own money, dealing privately in pictures and furniture and rare things from barbaric countries – and the three talked desultorily till about eight or half past. It was very pleasant, very cosy, very homely even: Pauline made a real home cosiness out of so much elegant material. The chat was simple, and nearly always bright. Pauline was her *real* self, emanating a friendly mockery and an odd, ironic gaiety. Till there came a little pause.

At which Ciss always rose and said good-night and carried out the coffee tray, to prevent Burnett from intruding any more.

And then! Oh, then, the lovely glowing intimacy of the evening, between mother and son, when they deciphered manuscripts and discussed points, Pauline with that eagerness of a girl, for which she was famous. And it was quite genuine. In some mysterious way she had *saved up* her power for being thrilled, in connection with a man. Robert, solid, rather quiet and subdued, seemed like the elder of the two: almost like a priest with a young girl pupil. And that was rather how he felt.

Ciss had a flat for herself just across the courtyard, over the old coachhouse and stables. There were no horses. Robert kept his car in the coachhouse. Ciss had three very nice rooms up there, stretching along in a row one after another, and she had got used to the ticking of the stable clock.

But sometimes she did not go up to her rooms. In the summer she would sit on the lawn, and from the open window of the drawing-room upstairs she would hear Pauline's wonderful heart-searching laugh. And in the winter the young woman would put on a thick coat and walk slowly to the little balustraded bridge over the stream, and then look back at the three lighted windows of that drawing-room where mother and son were so happy together.

Ciss loved Robert, and she believed that Pauline intended the two of them to marry: when she was dead. But poor Robert, he was so convulsed with shyness already, with man or woman. What would he be when his mother was dead? – in a dozen more years. He would be just a shell, the shell of a man who had never lived.

The strange unspoken sympathy of the young with one another, when they are overshadowed by the old, was one of the bonds between Robert and Ciss. But another bond, which Ciss did not know how to draw tight, was the bond of passion. Poor Robert was by nature a passionate man. His silence and his agonized, though hidden, shyness were both the result of a secret physical passionateness. And how Pauline could play on this! Ah, Ciss was not blind to the eyes which he fixed on his mother, eyes fascinated yet humiliated, full of shame. He was ashamed that he was not a man. And he did not love his mother. He was fascinated by her. Completely fascinated. And for the rest, paralysed in a life-long confusion.

Ciss stayed in the garden till the lights leapt up in Pauline's bedroom – about ten o'clock. The lovely lady had retired. Robert would now stay another hour or so, alone. Then he too would retire. Ciss, in the dark outside, sometimes wished she could creep up to him and say: 'Oh, Robert! It's all wrong!' But Aunt Pauline would hear. And anyhow, Ciss couldn't do it. She went off to her own rooms, once more, and so for ever.

In the morning coffee was brought up on a tray to each of the three relatives. Ciss had to be at Sir Wilfred Knipe's at nine o'clock, to give two hours' lessons to his little grand-daughter. It was her sole serious occupation, except that she played the piano for the love of it. Robert set off to town about nine. And, as a rule, Aunt Pauline appeared to lunch, though sometimes not until tea-time. When she appeared, she looked fresh and young. But she was inclined to fade rather quickly, like a flower without water, in the day-time. Her hour was the candle hour.

So she always rested in the afternoon. When the sun shone, if possible she took a sun bath. This was one of her secrets. Her lunch was very light, she could take her sun-and-air bath before noon or after, as it pleased her. Often it was in the afternoon, when the sun shone very warmly into a queer little yew-walled square just behind the stables. Here Ciss stretched out the lying-chair and rugs, and put the light parasol handy in the silent little enclosure of thick dark yew-hedges beyond the red walls of the unused stables. And hither came the lovely lady with her book. Ciss then had to be on guard in one of her own rooms, should her aunt, who was very keen-eared, hear a footstep.

One afternoon it occurred to Cecilia that she herself might while away this rather long afternoon by taking a sun bath. She was growing restive. The thought of the flat roof of the stable buildings to which she could climb from a loft at the end, started her on a new adventure. She often went on to the roof: she had to, to wind up the stable clock, which was a job she had assumed to herself. Now she took a rug, climbed out under the heavens, looked at the sky and the great elm-tops, looked at the sun, then took off her things and lay down perfectly serenely, in a corner of the roof under the parapet, full in the sun.

It was rather lovely, to bask all one's length like this in warm sun and air. Yes, it was very lovely! It even seemed to melt some of the hard bitterness of her heart, some of that core of unspoken resentment which never dissolved. Luxuriously, she spread herself, so that the sun should touch her limbs fully, fully. If she had no other lover, she should have the sun! She rolled voluptuously. And suddenly, her heart stood still in her body, and her hair almost rose on end as a voice said very softly, musingly in her ear:

'No, Henry dear! It was not my fault you died instead of marrying that Claudia. No, darling. I was quite, quite willing for you to marry her, unsuitable though she was.'

Cecilia sank down on her rug powerless and perspiring with dread. That awful voice, so soft, so musing, yet so unnatural. Not a human voice at all. Yet there must, there must be someone on the roof! Oh! how unspeakably awful!

She lifted her weak head and peeped across the sloping leads. Nobody! The chimneys were far too narrow to shelter anybody. There was nobody on the roof. Then it must be someone in the trees, in the elms. Either that, or terror unspeakable, a bodiless voice! She reared her head a little higher.

And as she did so, came the voice again:

'No, darling! I told you you would tire of her in six months. And you see, it was true, dear. It was true, true, true. I wanted to spare you that. So it wasn't I who made you feel weak and disabled, wanting that very silly Claudia; poor thing, she looked so woe-begone afterwards! Wanting her and not wanting her, you got *yourself* into that perplexity, my dear. I only warned you. What else could I do? And you lost your spirit and died without ever knowing me again. It was bitter, bitter—'

The voice faded away. Cecilia subsided weakly on to her rug, after the anguished tension of listening. Oh, it was awful. The sun shone, the sky was blue, all seemed so lovely and afternoony and summery. And yet, oh, horror! – she was going to be forced to believe in the supernatural! And she loathed the supernatural, ghosts and voices and rappings and all the rest.

But that awful creepy bodiless voice, with its rusty sort of whisper of an overtone! It had something so fearfully familiar in it too! and yet was so utterly uncanny. Poor Cecilia could only lie there unclothed, and so all the more agonizingly helpless, inert, collapsed in sheer dread.

And then she heard the thing sigh! A deep sigh that seemed weirdly familiar, yet was not human. 'Ah, well; ah, well, the heart must bleed! Better it should bleed than break. It is grief, grief! But it wasn't my fault, dear. And Robert could marry our poor dull Ciss tomorrow, if he wanted her. But he doesn't care about it, so why force him into anything!' The sounds were very uneven, sometimes only a husky sort of whisper. Listen! Listen!

Cecilia was about to give vent to loud and piercing screams of hysteria, when the last two sentences arrested her. All her caution and her cunning sprang alert. It was Aunt Pauline! It must be Aunt Pauline, practising ventriloquism or something like that! What a devil she was!

Where was she? She must be lying down there, right below where Cecilia herself was lying. And it was either some fiend's trick of ventriloquism, or else thought transference that conveyed itself like sound. The sounds were very uneven. Sometimes quite inaudible,

[82]

sometimes only a brushing sort of noise. Ciss listened intently. No, it could not be ventriloquism. It was worse, some form of thought transference. Some horror of that sort. Cecilia still lay weak and inert, terrified to move, but she was growing calmer, with suspicion. It was some diabolic trick of that unnatural woman.

But *what a devil* of a woman! She even knew that she, Cecilia, had mentally accused her of killing her son Henry. Poor Henry was Robert's elder brother, twelve years older than Robert. He had died suddenly when he was twenty-two, after an awful struggle with himself, because he was passionately in love with a young and very good-looking actress, and his mother had humorously despised him for the attachment. So he had caught some sudden ordinary disease, but the poison had gone to his brain and killed him, before he ever regained consciousness. Ciss knew the few facts from her own father. And lately, she had been thinking that Pauline was going to kill Robert as she had killed Henry. It was clear murder: a mother murdering her sensitive sons, who were fascinated by her: the Circe!

'I suppose I may as well get up,' murmured the dim unbreaking voice. 'Too much sun is as bad as too little. Enough sun, enough love thrill, enough proper food, and not too much of any of them, and a woman might live for ever. I verily believe for ever. If she absorbs as much vitality as she expends! Or perhaps a trifle more!'

It was certainly Aunt Pauline! How, how horrible! She, Ciss, was hearing Aunt Pauline's thoughts. Oh, how ghastly! Aunt Pauline was sending out her thoughts in a sort of radio, and she, Ciss, had to *hear* what her aunt was thinking. How ghastly! How insufferable! One of them would surely have to die.

She twisted and she lay inert and crumpled, staring vacantly in front of her. Vacantly! Vacantly! And her eyes were staring almost into a hole. She was staring into it unseeing, a hole going down in the corner from the lead gutter. It meant nothing to her. Only it frightened her a little more.

When suddenly out of the hole came a sigh and a last whisper. 'Ah, well! Pauline! Get up, it's enough for today!' – Good God! Out of the hole of the rain-pipe! The rain-pipe was acting as a speaking-tube! Impossible! No, quite possible. She had read of it even in some book. And Aunt Pauline, like the old and guilty woman she was, talked aloud to herself. That was it!

A sullen exultance sprang into Ciss's breast. *That* was why she would never have anybody, not even Robert, in her bedroom. That was why she never dozed in a chair, never sat absent-minded anywhere, but went to her room, and kept to her room, except when she roused herself to be alert. When she slackened off, she talked to herself! She talked in a soft little crazy voice, to herself. But she was not crazy. It was only her thoughts murmuring themselves aloud.

So she had qualms about poor Henry! Well she might have! Ciss believed that Aunt Pauline had loved her big, handsome, brilliant first-born much more than she loved Robert, and that his death had been a terrible blow and a chagrin to her. Poor Robert had been only ten years old when Henry died. Since then he had been the substitute.

Ah, how awful!

But Aunt Pauline was a strange woman. She had left her husband when Henry was a small child, some years even before Robert was born. There was no quarrel. Sometimes she saw her husband again, quite amicably, but a little mockingly. And she even gave him money.

For Pauline had earned all her own. Her father had been a Consul in the East and in Naples: and a devoted collector of beautiful and exotic things. When he died, soon after his grandson Henry was born, he left his collection of treasures to his daughter. And Pauline, who had really a passion and a genius for loveliness, whether in texture or form or colour, had laid the basis of her fortune on her father's collection. She had gone on collecting, buying where she could, and selling to collectors and to museums. She was one of the first to sell old, weird African wooden figures to the museums, and ivory carvings from New Guinea. She bought Renoir as soon as she saw his pictures. But not Rousseau. And all by herself, she made a fortune.

After her husband died, she had not married again. She was not even *known* to have had lovers. If she did have lovers, it was not among the men who admired her most and paid her devout and open attendance. To these she was a 'friend'.

Cecilia slipped on her clothes and caught up her rug, hastening carefully down the ladder to the loft. As she descended she heard the ringing musical call: 'All right, Ciss!' which meant that the lovely lady was finished, and returning to the house. Even her voice was marvellously young and sonorous, beautifully balanced and self-possessed. So different from the little voice in which she talked to herself. *That* was much more the voice of an old woman.

Ciss hastened round to the yew enclosure, where lay the comfortable chaise-longue with the various delicate rugs. Everything Pauline had was choice, to the fine straw mat on the floor. The great yew walls were beginning to cast long shadows. Only in the corner, where the rugs tumbled their delicate colours, was there hot, still sunshine.

The rugs folded up, the chair lifted away, Cecilia stooped to look at the mouth of the rain-pipe. There it was, in the corner, under a little hood of masonry and just projecting from the thick leaves of the creeper on the wall. If Pauline, lying there, turned her face towards the wall, she would speak into the very mouth of the hole. Cecilia was reassured. She had heard her aunt's thoughts indeed, but by no uncanny agency.

That evening, as if aware of something, Pauline was a little quieter than usual, though she looked her own serene, rather mysterious self. And after coffee she said to Robert and Ciss: 'I'm so sleepy. The sun has made me so sleepy. I feel full of sunshine like a bee. I shall go to bed, if you don't mind. You two sit and have a talk.'

Cecilia looked quickly at her cousin.

'Perhaps you would rather be alone,' she said to him.

'No, no,' he replied. 'Do keep me company for a while, if it doesn't bore you.'

The windows were open, the scent of the honeysuckle wafted in, with the sound of an owl. Robert smoked in silence. There was a sort of despair in the motionless, rather squat body. He looked like a caryatid bearing a weight.

'Do you remember Cousin Henry?' Cecilia asked him suddenly.

He looked up in surprise.

'Yes, very well,' he said.

'What did he look like?' she asked, glancing into her cousin's big secret-troubled eyes, in which there was so much frustration.

'Oh, he was handsome: tall and fresh-coloured, with mother's soft brown hair.' As a matter of fact, Pauline's hair was grey. 'The ladies admired him very much; he was at all the dances.'

'And what kind of character had he?'

'Oh, very good-natured and jolly. He liked to be amused. He was rather quick and clever, like mother, and very good company.'

'And did he love your mother?'

'Very much. She loved him too – better than she does me, as a matter of fact. He was so much more nearly her idea of a man.'

'Why was he more her idea of a man?'

'Tall – handsome – attractive, and very good company – and would, I believe, have been very successful at law. I'm afraid I am merely negative in all those respects.'

[85]

Ciss looked at him attentively, with her slow-thinking hazel eyes. Under his impassive mask, she knew he suffered.

'Do you think you are so much more negative than he?' she said.

He did not lift his face. But after a few moments he replied: 'My life, certainly, is a negative affair.'

She hesitated before she dared ask him: 'And do you mind?'

He did not answer at all. Her heart sank.

'You see, I am afraid my life is as negative as yours is,' she said. 'And I'm beginning to mind bitterly. I'm thirty.'

She saw his creamy, well-bred hand tremble.

'I suppose,' he said, without looking at her, 'one will rebel when it is too late.'

That was queer, from him.

'Robert,' she said, 'do you like me at all?'

She saw his dusky creamy face, so changeless in its folds, go pale.

'I am very fond of you,' he murmured.

'Won't you kiss me? Nobody ever kisses me,' she said pathetically.

He looked at her, his eyes strange with fear and a certain haughtiness. Then he rose and came softly over to her, and kissed her gently on the cheek.

'It's an awful shame, Ciss!' he said softly.

She caught his hand and pressed it to her breast.

'And sit with me sometime in the garden,' she said, murmuring with difficulty. 'Won't you?'

He looked at her anxiously and searchingly.

'What about mother?' he said.

Ciss smiled a funny little smile, and looked into his eyes. He suddenly flushed crimson, turning aside his face. It was a painful sight.

'I know,' he said, 'I am no lover of women.'

He spoke with sarcastic stoicism against himself, but even she did not know the shame it was to him.

'You never try to be!' she said.

Again his eyes changed uncannily.

'Does one have to try?' he said.

'Why, yes! One never does anything if one doesn't try.'

He went pale again.

'Perhaps you are right,' he said.

In a few minutes she left him, and went to her rooms. At least, she had tried to take off the everlasting lid from things.

The weather continued sunny, Pauline continued her sun-baths, and

Ciss lay on the roof eavesdropping in the literal sense of the word. But Pauline was not to be heard. No sound came up the pipe. She must be lying with her face away into the open. Ciss listened with all her might. She could just detect the faintest, faintest murmur away below, but no audible syllable.

And at night, under the stars, Cecilia sat and waited in silence, on the seat which kept in view the drawing-room windows and the side door into the garden. She saw the light go up in her aunt's room. She saw the lights at last go out in the drawing-room. And she waited. But he did not come. She stayed on in the darkness half the night, while the owl hooted. But she stayed alone.

Two days she heard nothing, her aunt's thoughts were not revealed and at evening nothing happened. Then the second night, as she sat with heavy, helpless persistence in the garden, suddenly she started. He had come out. She rose and went softly over the grass to him.

'Don't speak,' he murmured.

And in silence, in the dark, they walked down the garden and over the little bridge to the paddock, where the hay, cut very late, was in cock. There they stood disconsolate under the stars.

'You see,' he said, 'how can I ask for love, if I don't feel any love in myself. You know I have a real regard for you—'

'How can you feel any love, when you never feel anything?' she said.

'That is true,' he replied.

And she waited for what next.

'And how can I marry?' he said. 'I am a failure even at making money. I can't ask my mother for money.'

She sighed deeply.

'Then don't bother yet about marrying,' she said. 'Only love me a little. Won't you?'

He gave a short laugh.

'It sounds so atrocious, to say it is hard to begin,' he said.

She sighed again. He was so stiff to move.

'Shall we sit down a minute,' she said. And then as they sat on the hay, she added: 'May I touch you? Do you mind?'

'Yes, I mind! But do as you wish,' he replied, with that mixture of shyness and queer candour which made him a little ridiculous, as he knew quite well. But in his heart there was almost murder.

She touched his black, always tidy hair with her fingers.

'I suppose I shall rebel one day,' he said again, suddenly.

They sat some time, till it grew chilly. And he held her hand fast, but

[87]

he never put his arms round her. At last she rose and went indoors, saying goodnight.

The next day, as Cecilia lay stunned and angry on the roof, taking her sunbath, and becoming hot and fierce with sunshine, suddenly she started. A terror seized her in spite of herself. It was the voice.

'Caro, caro, tu non l'hai visto!' it was murmuring away, in a language Cecilia did not understand. She lay and writhed her limbs in the sun, listening intently to words she could not follow. Softly, whisperingly, with infinite caressiveness and yet with that subtle, insidious arrogance under its velvet, came the voice, murmuring in Italian: 'Bravo, si, molto bravo, poverino, ma uomo come te non lo sara mai, mai, mai!' Oh, especially in Italian Cecilia heard the poisonous charm of the voice, so caressive, so soft and flexible, yet so utterly egoistic. She hated it with intensity as it sighed and whispered out of nowhere. Why, why should it be so delicate, so subtle and flexible and beautifully controlled, while she herself was so clumsy! Oh, poor Cecilia, she writhed in the afternoon sun, knowing her own clownish clumsiness and lack of suavity, in comparison.

'No, Robert dear, you will never be the man your father was, though you have some of his looks. He was a marvellous lover, soft as a flower yet piercing as a humming-bird. No, Robert dear, you will never know how to serve a woman as Monsignor Mauro did. Cara, cara mia bellissima, ti ho aspettato come l'agonizzante aspetta la morte, morte deliziosa, quasi quasi troppo deliziosa per un' anima humana – Soft as a flower, yet probing like a humming-bird. He gave himself to a woman as he gave himself to God. Mauro! Mauro! How you loved me!'

The voice ceased in reverie, and Cecilia knew what she had guessed before, that Robert was not the son of her Uncle Ronald, but of some Italian.

'I am disappointed in you, Robert. There is no poignancy in you. Your father was a Jesuit, but he was the most perfect and poignant lover in the world. You are a Jesuit like a fish in a tank. And that Ciss of yours is the cat fishing for you. It is less edifying even than poor Henry.'

Cecilia suddenly bent her mouth down to the tube, and said in a deep voice: 'Leave Robert alone! Don't kill him as well.'

There was a dead silence, in the hot July afternoon that was lowering for thunder. Cecilia lay prostrate, her heart beating in great thumps. She was listening as if her whole soul were an ear. At last she caught the whisper:

'Did someone speak?'

She leaned again to the mouth of the tube.

'Don't kill Robert as you killed me,' she said with slow enunciation, and a deep but small voice.

'Ah!' came the sharp little cry. 'Who is that speaking?'

'Henry!' said the deep voice.

There was dead silence. Poor Cecilia lay with all the use gone out of her. And there was dead silence. Till at last came the whisper.

'I didn't kill Henry. No, NO! Henry, surely you can't blame me! I loved you, dearest. I only wanted to help you.'

'You killed me!' came the deep, artificial, accusing voice. 'Now, let Robert live. Let him go! Let him marry!'

There was a pause.

'How very, very awful!' mused the whispering voice. 'Is it possible, Henry, you are a spirit, and you condemn me?'

'Yes! I condemn you!'

Cecilia felt all her pent-up rage going down that rain-pipe. At the same time, she almost laughed. It was awful.

She lay and listened and listened. No sound! As if time had ceased, she lay inert in the weakening sun. The sky was yellowing. Quickly she dressed herself, went down, and out to the corner of the stables.

'Aunt Pauline!' she called discreetly. 'Did you hear thunder?'

'Yes! I am going in. Don't wait,' came a feeble voice.

Cecilia retired, and from the loft watched, spying, as the figure of the lovely lady, wrapped in a lovely wrap of old blue silk, went rather totteringly to the house.

The sky gradually darkened, Cecilia hastened in with the rugs. Then the storm broke. Aunt Pauline did not appear to tea. She found the thunder trying. Robert also did not arrive till after tea, in the pouring rain. Cecilia went down the covered passage to her own house, and dressed carefully for dinner, putting some white columbines at her breast.

The drawing-room was lit with a softly shaded lamp. Robert, dressed, was waiting, listening to the rain. He too seemed strangely crackling and on edge. Cecilia came in, with the white flowers nodding at her breast. Robert was watching her curiously, a new look on his face. Cecilia went to the bookshelves near the door, and was peering for something, listening acutely. She heard a rustle, then the door softly opening. And as it opened, Ciss suddenly switched on the strong electric light by the door.

Her aunt, in a dress of black lace over ivory colour, stood in the

[89]

doorway. Her face was made up, but haggard with a look of unspeakable irritability, as if years of suppressed exasperation and dislike of her fellow-men had suddenly crumpled her into an old witch.

'Oh, aunt!' cried Cecilia.

'Why, mother, you're a little old lady!' came the astounded voice of Robert: like an astonished boy: as if it were a joke.

'Have you only just found it out?' snapped the old woman venomously.

'Yes! Why, I thought—' his voice tailed out in misgiving.

The haggard, old Pauline, in a frenzy of exasperation, said:

'Aren't we going down?'

She had never even noticed the excess of light, a thing she shunned. And she went downstairs almost tottering.

At table she sat with her face like a crumpled mask of unspeakable irritability. She looked old, very old, and like a witch. Robert and Cecilia fetched furtive glances at her. And Ciss, watching Robert, saw that he was so astonished and repelled by his mother's looks, that he was another man.

'What kind of drive home did you have?' snapped Pauline, with an almost gibbering irritability.

'It rained, of course,' he said.

'How clever of you to have found that out!' said his mother, with the grisly grin of malice that had succeeded her arch smirk.

'I don't understand,' he said with quiet suavity.

'It's apparent,' said his mother, rapidly and sloppily eating her food.

She rushed through the meal like a crazy dog, to the utter consternation of the servant. And the moment it was over, she darted in a queer, crab-like way upstairs. Robert and Cecilia followed her, thunderstruck, like two conspirators.

'You pour the coffee. I loathe it! I'm going! Goodnight!' said the old woman, in a succession of sharp shots. And she scrambled out of the room.

There was a dead silence. At last he said:

'I'm afraid mother isn't well. I must persuade her to see a doctor.'

'Yes!' said Cecilia.

The evening passed in silence. Robert and Ciss stayed on in the drawing-room, having lit a fire. Outside was cold rain. Each pretended to read. They did not want to separate. The evening passed with ominous mysteriousness, yet quickly.

At about ten o'clock, the door suddenly opened, and Pauline

appeared, in a blue wrap. She shut the door behind her, and came to the fire. Then she looked at the two young people in hate, real hate.

'You two had better get married quickly,' she said in an ugly voice. 'It would look more decent; such a passionate pair of lovers!'

Robert looked up at her quietly.

'I thought you believed that cousins should not marry, mother,' he said.

'I do! But you're not cousins. Your father was an Italian priest.' Pauline held her daintily slippered foot to the fire, in an old coquettish gesture. Her body tried to repeat all the old graceful gestures. But the nerve had snapped, so it was a rather dreadful caricature.

'Is that really true, mother?' he asked.

'True! What do you think? He was a distinguished man, or he wouldn't have been my lover. He was far too distinguished a man to have had you for a son. But that joy fell to me.'

'How unfortunate all round,' he said slowly.

'Unfortunate for you? You were lucky. It was my misfortune,' she said acidly to him.

She was really a dreadful sight, like a piece of lovely Venetian glass that has been dropped, and gathered up again in horrible, sharp-edged fragments.

Suddenly she left the room again.

For a week it went on. She did not recover. It was as if every nerve in her body had suddenly started screaming in an insanity of discordance. The doctor came, and gave her sedatives, for she never slept. Without drugs, she never slept at all, only paced back and forth in her room, looking hideous and evil, reeking with malevolence. She could not bear to see either her son or her niece. Only when either of them came, she asked in pure malice: 'Well! When's the wedding? Have you celebrated the nuptials yet?'

At first Cecilia was stunned by what she had done. She realized vaguely that her aunt, once a definite thrust of condemnation had penetrated her beautiful armour, had just collapsed squirming inside her shell. It was too terrible. Ciss was almost terrified into repentance. Then she thought: This is what she always was. Now let her live the rest of her days in her true colours.

But Pauline would not live long. She was literally shrivelling away. She kept her room, and saw no one. She had her mirrors taken away.

Robert and Cecilia sat a good deal together. The jeering of the mad

Pauline had not driven them apart, as she had hoped. But Cecilia dared not confess to him what she had done.

'Do you think your mother ever loved anybody?' Ciss asked him tentatively, rather wistfully, one evening.

He looked at her fixedly.

'Herself!' he said at last.

'She didn't even *love* herself,' said Ciss. 'It was something else – what was it?' She lifted a troubled, utterly puzzled face to him.

'Power!' he said curtly.

'But what power?' she asked. 'I don't understand.'

'Power to feed on other lives,' he said bitterly. 'She was beautiful, and she fed on life. She has fed on me as she fed on Henry. She put a sucker into one's soul, and sucked up one's essential life.'

'And don't you forgive her?'

'No.'

'Poor Aunt Pauline!'

But even Ciss did not mean it. She was only aghast.

'I *know* I've got a heart,' he said, passionately striking his breast. 'But it's almost sucked dry. I *know* I've got a soul, somewhere. But it's gnawed bare. I *hate* people who want power over others.'

Ciss was silent; what was there to say?

And two days later, Pauline was found dead in her bed, having taken too much veronal, for her heart was weakened. From the grave even she hit back at her son and her niece. She left Robert the noble sum of one thousand pounds; and Ciss one hundred. All the rest, with the nucleus of her valuable antiques, went to form the 'Pauline Attenborough Museum'.

THE AUTHOR'S TALE

L.A. *Lewis*

Leslie Allin Lewis (1899–1961) wrote some of
the most original and bizarre supernatural
stories of the 1930s, notably 'Hybrid' and 'The
Tower of Moab', published together as
Tales of the Grotesque in 1934.
The following weird tale of ghosts and vampires
was published at the same time in another
anthology, *Terror by Night*.

'**W**ell, the one I think I'll tell you didn't start off as a ghost-story at all,' said the well-known Author, putting down his glass. 'A "thriller", yes – a torture tale, in fact, after the best tradition of Poe – but something went wrong with the plot, and it finished up in the regions of the uncanny.'

'We agreed to stick to facts,' the Big Game Hunter reminded him, 'not the *plots* of dramatists.' The B.G.H. had been telling a few himself, mostly about African witch-doctors and Indian fakirs.

'Sure,' replied the Author, with one of his rare smiles. 'This *is* fact – only, as I meant to convey, it began as a human drama of revenge, and then the punishment was taken out of the avenger's hands by – *something else.*'

The rest of us drew our chairs nearer the fire. It was raining too hard to permit our customary Saturday 'foursome', but we were not inclined to start for our homes and get a soaking that way.

'Go ahead,' said the Barrister, producing cigars.

'Well, to begin with,' said the Author, 'the story concerns a bloke whom I used to know very well at one time, and whom, for want of a better name, we will call Lester.

'He was, I suppose, an ultra-rabid sentimentalist from the general standpoint. His profession doesn't matter, but his matrimonial ventures do. The fellow made a perfect habit of getting married – like a damn' film-star. In fact, he was eventually nicknamed "Hollywood" by his closer associates. He was under twenty on the first occasion, and he got himself a wife who nagged. He found this out in a week or so, but as they lived in one small bed-sitting-room he couldn't get away from it. She started mostly in the evening when he was tired after a day's work and wanted a spot of peace. After a bit he began to go pub-crawling to escape from the home atmosphere, and then she nagged at him for wasting his money. She used to have a go at him most mornings too, because he didn't have much appetite for the breakfast she had prepared. He stuck it for some years, being very young and rather of the Sir Galahad type. It just didn't occur to him that, having made marriage vows, he could possibly break them. Eventually, however, when the sex-appeal side of things had died a natural death, he realized that his initial idolization of this woman – whose condescension in marrying him at all he had once considered goddess-like – had been converted into frank loathing. They had a culminating scene lasting the whole of one weekend, and she finally went back to her family. They were, fortunately for him, people of substance, and when she later on divorced him she didn't apply for alimony.

'Now, one might think that after an experience like that he would have devoted a few years to meditation before rushing into marriage again – but not a bit of it! Within a week of the *decree absolute* he was hitched up to a very snappy bit of work culled from a theatrical touring company, whom he had already been introducing to his friends as his "second wife" for some months. You'll notice that his Sir Galahad ideals were by now wearing a bit thin.

'Well, that show lasted for about a year – during which his finances failed to multiply – and then the lady poled off with another bloke possessing lots of "dough" and a yacht. Lester was very cut up about it because of the sensitiveness of his affections. He didn't mind about the other bloke – jealousy being absent in his make-up – and he quite saw the point about the yacht. But what he couldn't fathom was why she couldn't still go on loving *him*.

'Well, of course, everybody said this second fiasco would turn him into a misogynist – but did it hell! Inside of a year he appeared before the registrar with a third acquisition, and this time it really looked as if he had backed a winner. The girl was quiet and unassuming, appeared completely devoted – even to the extent of taking off Lester's shoes and fetching his slippers when he came in – and was, above all, a damn' good cook. Things went along splendidly for quite a while. She never nagged at him, was seen everywhere in his company, and couldn't do too much in the way of vetting his wardrobe. If you ever *did* meet him walking out solo he bored you with her praises and declared he wouldn't part with her for all the money in Europe. This, mark you, after as long as three years! I should mention here that he had ultimate expectations from his family which she knew about, and, in the light of later events, this was probably what made her play up to him so cleverly.

'When he had saved a thousand quid by denying himself many of the pleasant things of life, he invested the lot in the purchase of a small business which he considered his wife – an erstwhile commercial secretary, by the by – quite capable of managing. His own work, by now, was taking him around the country a lot, and he left her in sole charge, going down to the place for weekends, but never bothering to audit the books.

'Now, beneath his wife's pose of affection, so long and carefully maintained, lay a mercenary and spiteful nature. The supposed paragon of virtue, who had *carte blanche* with the net profits, began to manipulate the turnover, feeling, doubtless, that Lester's "expectations" were overlong in materializing. In three months she ran up bills with suppliers to more than half the value of the stock-in-trade, and decamped with the whole of the liquid assets. He went home one Saturday to find the premises locked and deserted and, to be brief, had to sell out for a mere song, all of which went into squaring his creditors.

'Not content with this, she got a separation order on some trivial pretext of "unfaithfulness" – *he* had condoned several infidelities on *her* part – and tried to sting him for maintenance. The publicity of the proceedings lost him his job – so she was unlucky about *that* – but the treachery and ingratitude of the whole affair brought a hidden vein of violence through the crust of good nature which had previously enveloped him. He determined that she should pay. Not through any legal action for embezzlement. Oh, dear, no! He could not afford the costs and, in any case, her sentence was likely to be inadequate by reason of her sex. She might, in fact, get away with it altogether. Lester was through with sentiment this time.

'Now, this is where the story becomes interesting. Lester, as I hope I have made clear, was naturally a forbearing soul. His first wife's nagging he had forgiven and forgotten almost as soon as it ceased; his second wife's desertion he had accepted with resignation. In neither case had he attempted to hit back. Now, however, his blood fairly boiled at the ingratitude with which his deeply emotional love had been rewarded, and he set methodically about nothing less than a reversion to Feudalism. He would kidnap this venomous swine of a woman and hold her captive in a secret place that he knew, flogging her daily until brute force brought her to absolute subjection.

'First, however, he had to live, and he borrowed two hundred pounds from his brother to keep him going until a job turned up. Then he made rather a long night journey to a certain destination, took a room at a village pub, and started his preparations. Before leaving, he had interviewd his wife and warned her of his intentions; but she had snapped her fingers at him, saying that such things just *couldn't* happen in the twentieth century. If he attempted to molest her she would obviously scream for help, etc. Lester smiled inwardly at this. It had not occurred to her that it would be necessary for her to make the journey in a drugged sleep on the floor of a closed car, nor that when she was released it would be under similar conditions and at a point far from the scene of her captivity. She might certainly relate her experiences, but that would amount only to her word against his, and he could bring crowds of witnesses to prove that he had never swatted anything bigger than flies.

'Two miles or so outside the village where Lester took up his abode was a derelict farmhouse standing quite alone in a hollow and surrounded by dense undergrowth. So ubiquitous, in fact, had the brambles now become that it was next to impossible to reach the ruin from any direction without suffering serious laceration. This made it peculiarly safe from the visits of unwanted "hikers", while the local rustics and their children gave it a wide berth on account of its reputation of being haunted.

'Lester was not particularly troubled about ghosts. As a boy, in any case, he had frequently explored the deserted homestead in search of birds' nests without encountering anything of an uncanny nature, despite the fact that his youthful imagination had made him susceptible to the possibilities latent in village gossip. It must be admitted, though, that he had never ventured near the farm after sundown.

'At the period of which I am speaking it is doubtful whether the place's evil reputation ever seriously crossed his mind. His chief interest lay in the fact that it was abandoned – isolated – and that in its seclusion he could work his will upon another human being with complete security from intrusion or interference.

[96]

'His early rambles had put him in possession of a secret which, to the best of his belief, was unshared by any other living person. Deep down in the foundations of the building existed a spacious cellar whose only means of access was by a trapdoor flagstone hidden under a heap of rubble in the tumbledown kitchen-parlour. He had first discovered it during the "treasure-hunting" craze which attacks most schoolboys, but had been badly disappointed at the complete absence of "treasure". The floor of the cellar, reached by a winding flight of stone steps, lay some thirty feet below ground level, and though the youthful Lester had not found so much as a forgotten bottle of wine to reward his search, he had, for some unexplained reason, kept his discovery to himself – a course of action which now seemed to have been providential. With the flagstone dropped, the cellar would be most effectively soundproof. The most frantic human screams imaginable would fail to reach the ear of a possible (but unlikely) passerby.

'Lester's principal difficulty lay in importing the timber necessary for his purpose without exciting anyone's curiosity, but this he continued to do under cover of night by stealing baulks of ash from a local timber-yard, conveying them to the place in his car, and laboriously dragging them through the thorny wilderness that surrounded the ruin. He accomplished the task in one trip, leaving the wood stacked in a dilapidated outhouse, and carried it to the cellar on the following day.

'He next proceeded systematically with the construction of the device that he had in mind. It was to be an oblong frame, eight feet high by five feet wide, having a ratchet pulley gear at each corner so that a woman of average build could be mounted in it like a picture, her wrists and ankles held by straps attached to the pulleys. The latter could be operated to extend the hands and feet towards the corners of the frame, stretching the whole figure into the form of a letter "X", and restraining any attempted movement while corporal punishment was in progress. One short end of the rectangle was to be secured to the floor by substantial hinges, while the opposite end would be connected by ropes to two pulleys in the ceiling. Thus the mounted form could be raised to a vertical position for flogging, and lowered to the ground in order that it might subsequently be relaxed for periods of rest necessary to the continuance of health and ability to bear further punishment.

'Lester took the precaution of posing as a commercial traveller to account for his prolonged and irregular absences from his pub. He had previously purchased his hinges, pulleys, and screws from ironmongers in various districts, and had brought the requisite tools with him in his car. It took him four days to construct his apparatus, and towards the evening of the fourth day he was at work on the final touch – the overhead pulleys.

'On the previous days, so he told me, he had knocked off work no later than seven o'clock, though he could naturally have expedited the job by working well into the night. He had felt, however, a certain vague distaste for remaining on the premises at a late hour, and had even taken a small risk of discovery by leaving the flagstone raised all the time he was below-ground – this in spite of the fact that no daylight could reach the cellar at any hour, and that all his labours had had to be carried out by the illumination of a petrol lamp.

'Towards the conclusion of his task, the time being nearer eight than seven, the sensation of distaste had grown to a condition of acute uneasiness and, on descending from the shored-up frame, which he had used as a trestle for reaching the roof joists, he realized that his feelings amounted to fear. The walls seemed to be closing in against the feeble resistance of the lamp, and an inner voice kept repeating in his brain: 'Get out, you fool – *out* before *they* arrive!'

'Lester, though, for all his sentiment and imagination, was no coward. Another detached part of his mind told him simultaneously that the disagreeable sensation was no stronger than usual; but that before he'd simply been too busy to notice it. He decided to stay and test the mechanism before returning to the outer air.

'The ropes from the top pulleys were tied to a staple in the opposite wall. He kicked away the supporting struts, untied the ropes, and lowered the frame to the horizontal.

'Yes, the pulleys were working freely, and would do so, he felt sure when the frame carried its load. He stooped to inspect the adjustable corner thongs and, as he did so, saw, or imagined, in the tail of his eye the flicker of something moving. His heart jumped to his mouth at the thought of discovery, and he jerked round towards the corner where the movement had appeared to be. There was nothing there – animate or otherwise – nor was there the slightest draught to cause shadow-dancing.

'"I'm getting nerves," he muttered, and resumed his inspection: thongs, plaited leather, strong enough to hold a gorilla – pulleys, oiled to silence, and working like roller-bearings – ratchets dropping into place without a fault to hold the thongs at any desired tension. Yes, the job was good . . . What the hell *was* that in the corner?

'He swung round again, and again saw – nothing.

'"Too keyed up with the next move," said Lester aloud. "I must pull myself together or I shall slip up on getting her here." With slightly unsteady hands he lit a cigarette, inhaled deeply, and sat back on a corner of the frame. As he did so a slim, white arm reached out and beckoned to him from a shadowed corner; though, of course, when he turned towards it there was no arm to be seen.

'Lester now appreciated that the place *was* haunted, but, curiously enough, with the realization all sense of panic left him. He described himself as imbued solely with excited curiosity. What *was* this thing that moved and signalled to him when he looked away, yet vanished as soon as he tried to focus it? He concentrated upon keeping very still and trying to catch it off its guard by stealing half-glances at it from an averted eye. There it was again – a tall, white figure leaning against the wall on his extreme right, one slender arm extended and slowly waving a tapering hand in his direction. By an immense effort he managed to keep his gaze straight ahead, striving to take in as much detail as he could. The figure, hanging tantalizingly on the very fringe of his vision, seemed to be that of a nude woman, dark-haired and red-lipped, but with flesh of a horrible, unnatural pallor reminding him of the flaccid whiteness of dressed tripe.

'He shuddered, but, still keeping his eyes averted, edged himself a few feet away, hoping to entice her into the direct light of the lamp. Before he had time to test the success of his ruse he was shaken by a fleeting glimpse of a second white figure just visible in the corner of his *other* eye. He ripped out a startled oath, and involuntarily turned to face this new arrival. Nothing was visible but the bare stonework and the floor littered with wood-shavings; though he could have sworn to the existence of that second figure, deathly white as the first, but bearing the hirsute stamp of masculinity.

'Yet could he *swear* to the existence of either?

'Exercising tremendous self-control, he again riveted his attention on a blank piece of wall, and immediately became aware of white-limbed movement *on either side of him*. He rose to his feet and deliberately made a complete revolution, his eyes taking in the unrelieved bareness of each wall as he faced them in turn. But all the time white, weaving figures mocked the corners of his eyes. Good heavens! The cellar must be teeming with these things which he could only half see!

'He resolved to make a new test. Were these forms *tangible*? Once more, but closer now, a hand was beckoning on his extreme right. He reached sideways towards it, felt his fingers taken in a firm but ice-cold grip, and, resist as he would, *had* to turn his head. His hand retained the sensation of being clasped by another, but of this not even the outline was visible, though he could see white indentations of pressure upon his own fingers. He tried to snatch it away, but instantly another set of fingers closed upon his wrist, and he felt his palm drawn caressingly over

[99]

the chill but pulsating contour of a woman's breast. Then wet lips, hot and passionate as the limbs were cold, pressed fiercely upon his own!

'Lester said afterwards that even curiosity left him after that burning salute. For all he cared the cellar might be peopled by a thousand ghosts. He felt the nude form that he could not see sink to the floor at his feet and draw him down beside her. A languid contentment filled him, and for a while he seems to have slept.

'A period of total oblivion was succeeded by one of half-conscious drowsing during which, lying with eyes half closed, he was aware of much agitated movement about the frame which he had built, and in the tail of his eye it looked as if several of the pallid creatures were grouped about it in attitudes of admiration, stroking it with their hands and making gleeful gestures. They seemed perfectly cognizant of its purpose, and were even testing it, tugging at the thongs and raising and lowering it by the ropes. Needless to say, as soon as he looked towards it they were gone, though the frame continued to move, while at the same moment there floated vaguely into the rim of his vision the white face and red lips of her who lay at his side. A soft, cold hand passed lightly across his forehead, lulling him, and again he relaxed into dreams. He dreamed of the woman whom he had loved last, and perhaps most deeply of all, who had requited him with greed and malice.

'Now, I think, in fairness to Lester, I should at this stage state my own belief that his intentions towards his wife were not only just but clean. He meant to keep her a prisoner in his frame, and to reason with her daily, patiently explaining her errors and emphasizing them with a whip until he honestly believed she had learnt her lesson. Between the chastisements he would keep her warm with rugs, feed her properly, and even give her cigarettes – but the whip and sense of captivity were necessary, because in a state of freedom she simply *would not* respond either to reason or sentiment. Beyond the last his imagination had not travelled.

'He was brought back to remembrance of his present uncanny surroundings by the most hideous and prolonged scream his ears had ever known – a woman's scream of mingled agony and terror. Instantly his eyes were wide open, and he turned them automatically towards the frame, where the flicker of movement was now intensified. His brain in the same moment flashed him a warning that whatever was there would, as usual, vanish; but, to his amazement, this was not so.

'Strapped there, spreadeagled by the thongs, just as he had visualized his wife, hung the struggling figure of a girl, a torrent of cries – some full-throated, others choked as by some muted pressure – issuing from her mouth. Her clothing lay scattered upon the floor, and by the writhing of her body and incessant turning of her head this way and that it was plain that she was trying to resist the loathsome embraces of some real but invisible thing that hugged her. Soon her screams died to little moans and her terrified eyes closed, only to reopen filled with new despair, while her hapless struggles began afresh.

'Shouting hoarsely, Lester sprang to his feet heedless of unseen, restraining arms that sought to hold him down. He took one step in the direction of the frame and felt both arms pinioned in a vice-like grip, while the outer corner of each eye registered the presence of a tall, pale form sprinkled with tufts of coarse black hair. The girl in the frame seemed to realize his own presence for the first time, and called beseechingly: "*You* are human! Help me! Help—" Then something cut off her utterance, though he could see the lips, pinched in and distorted by some external force, striving to open. He essayed another step, but found himself helpless in his captors' grasp. "I can't move. They hold me!" he called back. Then a cold, sinewy hand sealed his own mouth. Abruptly he was flung down and held sitting, turned half away from the suspended girl; and once more, out of the tail of his eye, he could see the numerous weaving bodies that in turn possessed her and passed on into obscurity.

'Lester could never describe very clearly the after-events of that night. Alternatively he would sink back into a careless lethargy with the feeling of soft arms clasping him about, then find himself aroused by even more terrible screams and by gentle licking, sucking noises, indeterminate but very abhorrent. He held one recollection of seeing numberless wounds and rents in the skin of the captive from which blood welled. But the blood was never allowed to flow, being, it seemed, lapped up at its source by invisible tongues.

'There was another period of peace while kisses rained upon his face and a voice whispered to him of the evil, irredeemable soul of his wife, and how no punishment of man's devising could either uplift her or drive her back into the realms where she belonged. "Give her to us," murmured the voice. "She is our sister and will sport with us in our Half-Life – *after that humanity which she has abused has been taken from her.*"

'Followed an interval of universal whisperings and rustlings broken now and again by the sound of crunching bones, gulps, and the unmistakable chewing of flesh, after which it seems that Lester fell into a dead faint.

'His next experience, with a return to full consciousness, was of finding himself lying on the cracked paving of the disused kitchen, the early dawn twilight falling on him through the skeleton roof. For a few moments he rested there, wondering where he was, and – gradually realizing that he was fully clothed and beneath open sky – thought that he must have had an accident with his car. Then remembrance flooded him and he sprang up in terror. The light of his lamp still glowed thinly beneath the raised flagstone, but it was many minutes before he dared approach the top of the steps. There he knelt and listened, but utter silence prevailed below.

'Half convinced that his nerves were to blame and that he had been the victim of an incredibly realistic nightmare, he finally steeled himself to the descent, and saw, with intense relief, that the frame was devoid of an occupant. Neither, thank God, were there any *stains* upon its woodwork. He leaned wearily against it and closed his eyes. This would never do! He had, supposedly, overworked, fallen asleep after finishing his task, and – cardinal error! – left the flagstone raised and the light on at an hour when the exterior darkness would show it up. If he was to effect the merited punishment for the accomplishment of which he had taken great pains, he *must* maintain his self-control. He opened his eyes again preparatory to turning off the light, and noticed, flung untidily into a far corner, a heap of woman's clothing!

'He was up the steps again like a hunted hare, pausing only to throw down the heavy flagstone before bolting for the place where his car was hidden.'

The speaker's voice lowered and ceased.

'And so,' I ventured, for a certain ring of sincerity had made the fantastic tale credible throughout, 'the project was abandoned – or, perhaps, another prison chosen?'

The Author had relaxed in his chair, and his dreamy eyes seemed unaware of our presence. He replied distantly: 'On the contrary, I took her there the following evening and built a cairn over the flagstone to hold it down. Those things knew their job better than I.'

'You say *you* took her there!' the Barrister cut in with asperity.

'Did I?' said the Author carelessly, seeming to reawaken from a doze. 'Well, I suppose successful writers, like actors, must *live* in their parts.'

'B-b-but,' spluttered the B.G.H., 'we stipulated *true* ghost-stories!'

The Author laughed softly, indulgently, as he pressed the bell.

'Four bitters, Steward,' he ordered.

CLOSE BEHIND HIM

John Wyndham

John Wyndham (pseudonym of John Benyon
Harris, 1903–69) was an outstanding British
writer of science fiction, with many classics to
his credit, among them *The Day of the Triffids*
(1951), *The Kraken Wakes* (1953), and *The
Midwich Cuckoos* (1957). This less familiar short
story first appeared in *Fantastic* magazine, in the
January/February 1953 issue.

'Y ou didn't ought to of croaked him,' Smudger said resentfully. 'What in the hell did you want to do a fool thing like that for?'

Spotty turned to look at the house, a black spectre against the night sky. He shuddered.

'It was him or me,' he muttered. 'I wouldn't of done it if he didn't come for me – and I wouldn't even then, not if he'd come ordinary . . .'

'What do you mean ordinary?'

'Like anybody else. But he was queer . . . He wasn't – well, I guess he was crazy – dangerous crazy . . .'

'All he needed was a tap to keep him quiet,' Smudger persisted. 'There wasn't no call to bash his loaf in.'

'You didn't see him. I tell you, he didn't act human.' Spotty shuddered again at the recollection, and bent down to rub the calf of his right leg tenderly.

The man had come into the room while Spotty was sifting rapidly

[103]

through the contents of a desk. He'd made no sound. It had been just a feeling, a natural alertness, that had brought Spotty round to see him standing there. In that very first glimpse Spotty had felt there was something queer about him. The expression of his face – his attitude – they were wrong. In his biscuit-coloured pyjamas, he should have looked just an ordinary citizen awakened from sleep, too anxious to have delayed with dressing-gown and slippers. But somehow he didn't. An ordinary citizen would have shown nervousness, at least wariness; he would most likely have picked up something to use as a weapon. This man stood crouching, arms a little raised, as though he were about to spring.

Moreover, any citizen whose lips curled back as this man's did to show his tongue licking hungrily between his teeth, should have been considered sufficiently unordinary to be locked away safely. In the course of his profession Spotty had developed reliable nerves, but the look of this man rocked them. Nobody should be pleased by the discovery of a burglar at large in his house. Yet, there could be no doubt that this victim was looking at Spotty with satisfaction. An unpleasant gloating kind of satisfaction, like that which might appear on a fox's face at the sight of a plump chicken. Spotty hadn't liked the look of him at all, so he had pulled out the convenient piece of pipe that he carried for emergencies.

Far from showing alarm, the man took a step closer. He poised, sprung on his toes like a wrestler.

'You keep off me, mate,' said Spotty, holding up his nine inches of lead pipe as a warning.

Either the man did not hear – or the words held no interest for him. His long, bony face snarled. He shifted a little closer. Spotty backed against the edge of the desk. 'I don't want no trouble. You just keep off me,' he said again.

The man crouched a little lower. Spotty watched him through narrowed eyes. An extra tensing of the man's muscles gave him a fractional warning before the attack.

The man came without feinting or rushing: he simply sprang, like an animal.

In mid-leap he encountered Spotty's boot suddenly erected like a stanchion in his way. It took him in the middle and felled him. He sprawled on the floor doubled up, with one arm hugging his belly. The other hand threatened, with fingers bent into hooks. His head turned in jerks, his jaws with their curiously sharp teeth were apart, like a dog's about to snap.

Spotty knew just as well as Smudger that what was required was a quietening tap. He had been about to deliver it with professional skill and quality when the man, by an extraordinary wriggle, succeeded in fastening his teeth into Spotty's leg. It was unexpected, excruciating enough to ruin Spotty's aim and make the blow ineffectual. So he had hit again; harder this time. Too hard, And even then he had more or less had to pry the man's teeth out of his leg . . .

But it was not so much his aching leg – nor even the fact that he killed the man – that was the chief cause of Spotty's concern. It was the kind of man he had killed.

'Like an animal he was.' he said. The recollection made him sweat. 'Like a bloody wild animal. The way he looked! His eyes! Christ, they wasn't human.'

That aspect of the affair held little interest for Smudger. He'd not seen the man until he was already dead and looking like any other corpse. His present concern was that a mere matter of burglary had been abruptly transferred to the murder category – a class of work he had always kept clear of until now.

The job had looked easy enough. There shouldn't have been any trouble. A man living alone in a large house – a pretty wild customer with a pretty wild temper. On Fridays, Sundays and sometimes on Wednesdays, there were meetings at which about twenty people came to the house and did not leave until the small hours of the following morning. All this information was according to Smudger's sister, who learned it third hand from the woman who cleaned the house. The woman was darkly speculative, but unspecific, about what went on at these gatherings. But from Smudger's point of view the important thing was that on other nights the man was alone in the house.

He seemed to be a dealer of some kind. People brought odd curios to the house to sell to him. Smudger had been greatly interested to hear that they were paid for – and paid for well – in cash. That was a solid, practical consideration. Beside it, the vaguely ill reputation of the place, the queerness of its furnishings, and the rumours of strange goings-on at the gatherings, were unimportant. The only thing worthy of attention were the facts that the man lived alone and had items of value in his possession.

Smudger had thought of it as a one-man job at first, and with a little more information he might have tackled it on his own. He had discovered that there was a telephone, but no dog. He was fairly sure of the room in which the money must be kept, but unfortunately his sister's source of information had its limitations. He did not know whether there were burglar alarms or similar precautions, and he was too uncertain of the cleaning woman to attempt to get into the house by a subterfuge for a preliminary investigation. So he had taken Spotty in with him on a fifty-fifty basis.

The reluctance with which he had taken that step had now become an active regret – not only because Spotty had been foolish enough to kill the man, but because the way things had been he could easily have made a hundred per cent haul on his own – and not be fool enough to kill the man had he been detected.

The attaché case which he carried was now well filled with bundles of notes, along with an assortment of precious-looking objects in gold and silver, probably eminently traceable, but useful if melted down. It was irritating to think that the whole load, instead of merely half of it, might have been his.

The two men stood quietly in the bushes for some minutes and listened. Satisfied, they pushed through a hole in the hedge, then moved cautiously in its shadow down the length of the neighbouring field.

Spotty's chief sensation was relief at being out of the house. He hadn't liked the place from the moment they had entered. For one thing, the furnishings weren't like those he was used to. Unpleasant idols or carved figures of some kind stood about in unexpected places, looming suddenly out of the darkness into his flashlight's beam with hideous expressions on their faces. There were pictures and pieces of tapestry that were macabre and shocking to a simple burglar. Spotty was not particularly sensitive, but these seemed to him highly unsuitable to have about the home.

The same quality extended to more practical objects. The legs of a large oak table had been carved into mythical miscegenates of repulsive appearance. The two bowls which stood upon the table were either genuine or extremely good representations of polished human skulls. Spotty could not imagine why, in one room, anybody should want to mount a crucifix on the wall upside down and place on a shelf beneath it a row of sconces holding nine black candles – then flank the whole with two pictures of an indecency so revolting it almost took his breath away. All these things had somehow combined to rattle his usual hard-headedness away.

But even though he was out of the place now, he didn't feel quite free of its influence. He decided he wouldn't feel properly himself again until they were in the car and several miles away.

After working around two fields they came to the dusty white lane off which they had parked the car. They prospected carefully. By now the sky had cleared of clouds, and the moonlight showed the road empty in both directions. Spotty scrambled through the hedge, across the ditch, and stood on the road in a quietness broken only by Smudger's progress through the hedge. Then he started to walk towards the car.

He had gone about a dozen paces when Smudger's voice stopped him: 'Hey, Spotty. What've you got on your feet?'

Spotty stopped and looked down. There was nothing remarkable about his feet; his boots looked just as they always looked.

'What—?' he began.

'No! Behind you!'

Spotty looked back. From the point where he stepped on to the road to another some five feet behind where he now stood was a series of footprints, dark in the white dust. He lifted his foot and examined the sole of his boot; the dust was clinging to it. He turned his eyes back to the footmarks once more. They looked black, and seemed to glisten.

Smudger bent down to peer more closely. When he looked up again there was a bewildered expression on his face. He gazed at Spotty's boots, and then back to the glistening marks. The prints of bare feet . . .

'There's something funny going on here,' he said inadequately.

Looking back over his shoulder, Spotty took another step forward. Five feet behind him a new mark of a bare foot appeared from nowhere. A watery feeling swept over Spotty. He took another experimental step. As mysteriously as before, another footmark appeared. He turned widened eyes on Smudger.

Smudger looked back at him. Neither said anything for a moment. Then Smudger bent down, touched one of the marks with his finger, shone his flash-light on the finger. 'Red,' he said. 'Like blood . . .'

The words broke the trance that had settled on Spotty. Panic seized him. He stared around wildly, then began to run. After him followed the footprints. Smudger ran too. He noticed that the marks were no longer the prints of a full foot but only its forepart, as if whatever made them were also running.

Spotty was frightened, but not badly enough to forget the turn where they had parked the car beneath some trees. He made for it, and clambered in. Smudger, breathing heavily, got in on the other side and dropped the attaché case in the back.

'Going to get out of this lot quick,' Spotty said, pressing the starter.

'Take it easy,' advised Smudger. 'We got to think.'

But Spotty was in no thinking mood. He got into gear, jolted out of hiding, and turned down the lane.

A mile or so farther on Smudger turned back from craning out of the window.

'Not a sign,' he said, relieved. 'Reckon we've ditched it – whatever it was.' He thought for some moments, then he said: 'Look here, if those marks were behind us all the way from the house, they'll be able to follow them by daylight to where we parked the car.'

'They'd've found the car marks anyway,' Spotty replied.

'But what if they're *still* following?' Smudger suggested.

'You just said they weren't.'

'Maybe they couldn't keep up with us. But suppose they're coming along somewhere behind us, leaving a trail?'

Spotty had greatly recovered; he was almost his old practical self again. He stopped the car. 'All right. We'll see,' he said grimly. 'And if they are – what then?'

He lit a cigarette with a hand that was almost steady. Then he leaned out of the car, studying the road behind them. The moonlight was strong enough to show up any dark marks.

'What do you reckon it was?' he said, over his shoulder. 'We can't both've been seeing things.'

'They were real enough.' Smudger looked at the stain still on his finger.

On a sudden idea, Spotty pulled up his right trouser leg. The marks of the teeth were there, and there was a little blood, too, soaked into his sock, but he couldn't make that account for anything.

The minutes passed. Still there was no manifestation of footprints. Smudger got out and walked a few yards back along the road to make sure. After a moment's hesitation Spotty followed him.

'Not a sign,' Smudger said, 'I reckon – hey!' He broke off, looking beyond Spotty.

Spotty turned around.

Behind him was a trail of dark, naked footprints leading *from* the car.

Spotty stared. He walked back to the car; the footmarks followed. It was a chastened Spotty who sat down in the car.

'Well?'

Smudger had nothing to offer. Smudger, in fact, was considerably confused. Several aspects of the situation were competing for his attention. The footsteps were not following him, so he found himself less afraid of them than of their possible consequences. They were laying a noticeable trail for anyone to follow to Spotty, and the trouble was that the trail would lead to him, too, if he and Spotty kept together.

The immediate solution that occurred to him was that they split up, and Spotty take care of his own troubles. The best way would be to divide the haul right here and now. If Spotty could succeed in shaking off the footprints, good for him. After all, the killing was none of Smudger's affair.

He was about to make the suggestion when another aspect occurred to him. If Spotty were picked up with part of the stuff on him, the case would be clinched. It was also possible that Spotty, in a bad jam with nothing to lose, might spill. A far safer way would be for him to hold the stuff. Then Spotty could come for his share when, and if, he succeeded in losing the tell-tale prints. It was obviously the only safe and reasonable course. The trouble was that Spotty, when it was suggested to him, did not see it that way.

They drove a few more miles, each occupied with his own thoughts. In a quiet lane they stopped once more. Again Spotty got out of the car and walked a few yards away from it. The moon was lower, but it still gave enough light to show the footprints following him. He came back looking more worried than frightened. Smudger decided to cut a possible loss and go back to his former plan.

'Look here,' he suggested, 'what say we share out the takings now, and you drop me off a bit up the road?'

Spotty looked doubtful, but Smudger pressed: 'If you can shake that trail off, well and good. If you can't – well, there's no sense in us both getting pinched, is there? Anyway, it was you as croaked him. And one has a better chance of getting away than two.'

Spotty was still not keen, but he had no alternative to offer.

Smudger pulled the attaché case out of the back and opened it between them. Spotty began to separate the bundles of notes into two piles. It had been a good haul. As Smudger watched, he felt a great sadness that half of it was going to benefit nobody when Spotty was picked up. Sheer waste, it seemed to him.

Spotty, with his head bent over his work, did not notice Smudger draw the piece of lead pipe out of his pocket. Smudger brought it down on the back of his head with such force and neatness that it is doubtful whether Spotty ever knew anything about it.

Smudger stopped the car at the next bridge and pushed Spotty's body over the low wall. He watched as the ripples widened out across the canal below. Then he drove on.

It was three days later that Smudger got home. He arrived in the kitchen soaked to the skin, and clutching his attaché case. He was looking worn, white, and ready to drop. He dragged a chair away from the table and slumped into it.

'Bill!' his wife whispered. 'What is it? Are they after you?'

'No, Liz – at least, it ain't the cops. But something is.'

He pointed to a mark close inside the door. At first she thought it was his own wet footprint.

'Get a wet cloth, Liz, and clean up the front step and the passage before anyone sees it,' he said.

She hesitated, puzzled.

'For God's sake, do it quick, Liz,' he urged her.

Still half bewildered, she went through the dark passage and opened the door. The rain was pelting down, seeming to bounce up from the road as it hit. The gutters were running like torrents. Everything streamed with wetness save the doorstep protected by the small jutting porch. And on the step was the blood-red print of a naked foot . . .

In a kind of trance she went down on her knees and swabbed it clean with the wet cloth. Closing the door, she switched on the lights and saw the prints leading towards the kitchen. When she had cleaned them up, she went back to her husband.

'You been hit, Bill?'

He looked at her, elbows on the table, his head supported between his hands.

'No,' he said. 'It ain't me what's making them marks, Liz – it's what's followin' me.'

'Following you? You mean they been following you all the way from the job?' she said incredulously. 'How did you get back?'

Smudger explained. His immediate anxiety, after pitching Spotty into the canal, had been to rid himself of the car. It had been a pinch for the job, and the number and description would have been circulated. He had parked it in a quiet spot and gotten out to walk, maybe pick up a lift. When he gone a few yards he had looked back and seen the line of prints behind him. They had frightened him a good deal more than he now admitted. Until that moment he had assumed that since they had been following Spotty, they would have followed him into the canal. Now, it seemed, they had transferred their attentions to himself. He tried a few more steps: they followed. With a great effort he got a grip on himself, and refrained from running. He perceived that unless he wanted to leave a clear trail he must go back to the car. He did.

Farther on he tried again, and with a sinking, hopeless feeling observed the same result. Back in the car, he lit a cigarette and considered plans with as much calmness as he could collect.

The thing to do was to find something that would not show tracks – or would not hold them. A flash of inspiration came to him, and he headed the car towards the river.

The sky was barely grey yet. He fancied that he managed to get the car down to the towpath without being seen. At any rate, no one had hailed him as he cut through the long grass to the water's edge. From there he had made his way downstream, plodding along through a few inches of water until he found a row-boat. It was a venerable and decrepit affair, but it served his purpose.

From then on his journey had been unexciting, but also uncomfortable. During the day he had become extremely hungry, but he did not dare to leave the boat until after dark, and then he moved only in the darkest streets where the marks might not be seen. Both that day and the next two he had spent hoping for rain. This morning, in a drenching downpour that looked as if it might continue for hours, he had sunk the boat and made his way home, trusting that the trail would be washed away. As far as he knew, it had been.

Liz was less impressed than she ought to have been.

'I reckon it must be something on your boots,' she said practically. 'Why didn't you buy some new ones?'

He looked at her with a dull resentment. 'It ain't nothing on my boots,' he said. 'Didn't I tell you it was following me? You seen the marks. How could they come off my boots? Use your head.'

'But it don't make sense. Not the way you say it. *What's* following you?'

'How do I know?' he said bitterly. 'All I know is that it makes them marks – and they're getting closer, too.'

'How do you mean closer?'

'Just what I say. The first day they were about five feet behind me. Now they're between three and four.'

[111]

It was not the kind of thing that Liz could take in too easily. 'It don't make sense,' she repeated.

It made no more sense during the days that followed, but she ceased to doubt. Smudger stayed in the house; whatever was following stayed with him. The marks of it were everywhere: on the stairs, upstairs, downstairs. Half Liz's time was spent in cleaning them up lest someone should come in and see them. They got on her nerves. But not as badly as they got on Smudger's . . .

Even Liz could not deny that the feet were stepping a little more closely behind him – a little more closely each day.

'And what happens when they catch up?' Smudger demanded fearfully. 'Tell me that. What can I do? What the hell can I do?'

But Liz had no suggestions. Nor was there anyone else they dared ask about it.

Smudger began to dream nights. He'd whimper and she'd wake him up asking what was the matter. The first time he could not remember, but the dream was repeated, growing a little clearer with each recurrence. A black shape appeared to hang over him as he lay. It was vaguely manlike in form, but it hovered in the air as if suspended. Gradually it sank lower and lower until it rested upon him – but weightlessly, like a pattern of fog. It seemed to flow up towards his head, and he was in panic lest it should cover his face and smother him, but at his throat it stopped. There was a prickling at the side of his neck. He felt strangely weak, as though tiredness suddenly invaded him. At the same time the shadow appeared to grow denser. He could feel, too, that there began to be some weight in it as it lay upon him. Then, mercifully, Liz would wake him.

So real was the sensation that he inspected his neck carefully in the mirror when he shaved. But there was no mark there.

Gradually the glistening red prints closed in behind him. A foot behind his heels, six inches, three inches . . .

Then came a morning when he woke tired and listless. He had to force himself to get up, and when he looked in the mirror, there *was* a mark on his throat. He called Liz, in a panic. But it was only a very small mark, and she made nothing of it.

But the next morning his lassitude was greater. It needed all his will-power to drag himself up. The pallor of his face shocked Liz – and himself, too, when he saw it in the shaving mirror. The red mark on his neck stood out more vividly . . .

The next day he did not get up.

[112]

Two days later Liz became frightened enough to call in the doctor. It was a confession of desperation. Neither of them cared for the doctor, who knew or guessed uncomfortably much about the occupations of his patients. One called a doctor for remedies, not for homilies on one's way of life.

He came, he hummed, he ha'ed. He prescribed a tonic, and had a talk with Liz.

'He's seriously anaemic,' he said. 'But there's more to it than that. Something on his mind.' He looked at her. 'Have you any idea what it is?'

Liz's denial was unconvincing. He did not even pretend to believe it.

'I'm no magician,' he said. 'If you don't help me, I can't help him. Some kinds of worry can go on pressing and nagging like an abscess.'

Liz continued to deny. For a moment she had been tempted to tell about the footmarks, but caution warned her that once she began, she would likely be trapped into saying more than was healthy.

'Think it over,' the doctor advised. 'And let me know tomorrow how he is.'

The next morning there was no doubt that Smudger was doing very badly. The tonic had done him no good at all. He lay in bed with his eyes, when they were open, looking unnaturally large in a drawn white face. He was so weak that she had to feed him with a spoon. He was frightened, too, that he was going to die. So was Liz. The alarm in her voice when she telephoned the doctor was unmistakably genuine.

'All right. I'll be round within an hour,' he told her. 'Have you found out what's on his mind yet?' he added.

'N-no,' Liz told him.

When he came, he told her to stay downstairs while he went up to see the patient.

It seemed to her that an intolerably long time passed before she heard his feet on the stairs, and she went out to meet him in the hall. She looked up into his face with mute anxiety. His expression was serious, and puzzled, so that she was afraid to hear him speak.

But at last she asked: 'Is – is he going to die, Doctor?'

'He's very weak – very weak indeed,' the doctor said. After a pause, he added: 'Why didn't you tell me about those footprints he thought were following him?'

She looked up at him in alarm.

'It's all right. He's told me all about it now. I knew there was something on his mind. It's not very surprising, either.'

Liz stared at him. 'Not—?'

[113]

'In the circumstances, no,' the doctor said. 'A mind oppressed by a sense of sin can play a lot of nasty tricks. Nowadays they talk of guilt complexes and inhibitions. Names change. When I was a boy, the same sort of thing was known as a bad conscience.

'When one has the main facts, these things become obvious to anyone of experience. Your husband was engaged in – well, to put it bluntly, burgling the house of a man whose interests were mystic and occult. Something that happened there gave him a shock and unbalanced his judgment.

'As a result, he has difficulty in distinguishing between the real things he sees and the imaginery ones his uneasy conscience shows him. It isn't very complicated. He feels he is being dogged. Somewhere in his subconscious lie the lines from *The Ancient Mariner*:

> Because he knows, a frightful fiend
> Doth close behind him tread

and the two come together. And, in addition to that, he appears to have developed a primitive, vampire type of phobia.

'Now, once we are able to help him dispel this obsession, he—' He broke off, suddenly aware of the look on his listener's face. 'What is it?' he asked.

'But, Doctor,' Liz said. 'Those footmarks. I—' She was cut short abruptly by a sound from above that was half groan and half scream.

The doctor was up the stairs before she could move. When she followed him, it was with a heavy certainty in her heart.

She stood in the doorway watching as he bent over the bed. In a moment he turned, grave-eyed, and gave a slight shake of his head. He put his hand on her shoulder, then went quietly past her out of the room.

For some seconds Liz stood without moving. Then her eyes dropped from the bed to the floor. She trembled. Laughter, a high-pitched, frightening laughter shook her as she looked at the red naked footprints which led away from the bedside, across the floor and down the stairs, after the doctor . . .

THE WOMAN ON
THE STAIRS

Margery Lawrence

Margery Lawrence (1889–1969) specialized in
Gothic and romantic melodramas (*The Madonna
of Seven Moons* was successfully filmed in 1944).
She was also a strong believer in the occult and
spiritualism, and many of her supernatural
stories were based on accounts she heard at
seances. 'The Woman on the Stairs' is one of a
number of her exciting narratives from the
casebook of 'Psychic Doctor' Miles Pennoyer,
recorded by his friend Jerome Latimer. It first
appeared in the collection *Master of Shadows*
in 1959.

I have always been fond of my sister-in-law. My brother Arnold had been something of a connoisseur of women when he was a young man, and I had helped to pull him out of one or two rather spectacular affairs – so when he ultimately married a plump, ordinary-looking little woman a few years his elder, without even a handsome income behind her to compensate for her ordinariness, I was surprised, and tempted to wonder how long the marriage would last. But though Arnold had proved a fool over his lights o' love, he was wiser than I had dreamed of when he chose a wife; for Dolly Forster was a dear in every sense of the word. Not clever, but sound and sane as a nut; sweet-tempered, kindly and as capable as they come.

The marriage couldn't have been a more successful one, and when they

[115]

had two children, first a boy – who has nothing to do with this story – and then a girl, their cup, to write dramatically, was filled to the brim with happiness. Yet it was through the girl, some years later, that that cup was so imperilled that it was almost broken, and if it hadn't been for Miles Pennoyer . . . but I am going to the end of the story before I have even begun it. So I will go back to to where I started, and tell things in due order as they came.

Arnold was a very successful barrister, and he and Dolly had a pretty flat in a tall block at Amherst Court, Kensington. Not a very modern one, but the rooms were larger than most of those new box-sized flats; which was one of the reasons why, when Arnold's practice improved and his income with it, they remained there instead of moving to a more modern apartment. Dolly had made it extremely comfortable and they had a good 'general' – an old personal maid of Dolly's, who was devoted to her and to the family as a whole. They stuck the war out there and were lucky to escape with only a few broken windows. Arnold was an air-raid warden and Dolly worked in canteens and hospitals and refugee centres and God knows what-all, while Lance and Pamela were packed off to relatives in Scotland, where they had a thoroughly good time; being, luckily for them, too young to understand anything about the war.

When it was all over, the children came back – not too eagerly, I gathered – and life, as Dolly put it, got back into shape again. She and Arnold were popular and went out a good deal, and in return did a certain amount of modest entertaining. They went to occasional shows or films, concerts and so on, and played golf, bridge and canasta well enough to be invited out quite a lot on the strength of their playing. Arnold drove a smart little Humber and altogether one could not have imagined a pleasanter or more average sort of middle-class couple than Arnold and his wife; yet to this very average pair happened one of the most extraordinary adventures on record in my list of strange cases.

When the children returned from Scotland they went back to school, of course, and Lance, the boy, was at Stowe when this story really started – he was about fourteen and Pamela three years younger.

I was fond of both children, but especially of Pamela, who was my godchild. She was as pretty as Dolly was plain, and as she grew older she showed signs of growing prettier still. Even as a baby she was small-boned and slender, lint-haired and fair as mother-o'-pearl, with long narrow hands and feet and throat. She got these from the Latimer side – the Forsters were all like Dolly. Solid, chunky little people with stubby capable hands, short-necked and square-built as Highland cattle.

Pamela had eyes the colour of an aquamarine – all of which may sound insipid, but somehow she wasn't. I think it was her spirit, her sense of humour, and the irrepressible gaiety that was an essential part of her, that offset the delicate pallor of her colouring . . . for even as a child she was brimful of fun and laughter, for ever on the go, an electric spark if ever there was one.

She and I were the greatest of friends, and when Arnold and Dolly decided that things in Europe had quieted down sufficiently to send her over to France to school to learn the language, at the tender age of eleven, I missed the child badly and treasured her occasional letters – letters as full of fun and vitality as she was herself, though shockingly badly spelt and punctuated. She spent two years in France, and then she went to Austria, to learn German. I saw her only occasionally during those years when she was at home for the holidays, and saw that she was shooting up into a slender reed of a girl with even greater promise of beauty than I had expected. But she was still so much the child I had known and loved beneath the surface veneer of sophistication that she was acquiring with so many pains! Eager, impulsive, emotional – just at the stage of life when a young thing is reaching out towards maturity, yet still teeters uncertainly on the borders of adolescence. I know it's *vieux jeu* to quote the outworn phase that starts 'standing with reluctant feet' – and yet it describes that stage of a girl's life better than anything else I know. The stage where she is still partly a child and partly a 'teenager', yet just beginning to grow up into a woman.

I had no idea that she had returned from Schloss Marhausen until one day I had been in court listening to Arnold defending a case – he was a fine advocate, and even had he not been my brother I would have gone to hear him – and meeting him outside, he invited me to go back to the flat with him to dinner. Thank goodness, even with post-war difficulties of food and drink, Dolly never went temperamental on him if he brought back an unexpected friend to dinner!

It was in his car, as we were driving back to Amherst Court, that Arnold mentioned casually that Pamela had come home. I was surprised, as it was not the end of term by any means – only about halfway through November – and I asked, 'How come?' Arnold shrugged his shoulders.

It appeared that there had been a sudden epidemic of some fever or other – very infectious – and Dolly had panicked and wired for Pamela to come home; a suggestion with which the headmistress of the Schloss had been only too glad to comply, as apparently half the school was down with this disease, whatever it was, and some of the staff as well, so she was thankful to have at least one pupil taken off her hands.

Pamela had been home several days, and Arnold said that he did not think they would send her back again. She had been there eighteen months, and was speaking passably good German now, and it did not seem necessary. I nodded my head and agreed with him, and when we arrived at Amherst Court I went up to their comfortable first floor flat in high spirits. Dolly was there, hospitably dispensing more drinks than were quite decent to display, I felt, with gin at its post-war price; and so was Pamela, grown really tall now and prettier than ever, with her silver-fair hair darkened to a pale gold and done over both ears in two plaited wheels, German fashion, which may not have been smart but suited her wonderfully. She had put on a good deal of weight, too. She was positively chubby, and in the blue dirndl skirt she was wearing, and wide black belt with a short-sleeved white muslin blouse, she looked altogether like a real German *mädchen*.

She flung herself into my arms and hugged me fervently and we all talked nineteen to the dozen, before, through and after dinner, interrupting each other, disputing, laughing, teasing and generally making the cheerful din that means a family reunion.

Fourteen as Pamela was now, Dolly packed her ruthlessly off to bed soon after dinner. They had spent the last two days shopping, as Pamela had not only grown out of most of her clothes but those she had bought in Austria were so emphatically Austrian in style that Dolly said she couldn't possibly take about a child who looked like something out of *White Horse Inn* – if anybody remembers that charming musical show of pre-war days.

So off Pamela went, and both Dolly and Arnold looked after her as she disappeared with the smug approval of two thoroughly satisfied parents – and I must say, I couldn't blame them.

I lighted my cigar – thank goodness Arnold is a judge of both drinks and tobacco – and said what I was expected to say, though for once it was true.

'Well folks, I congratulate you! Pam looks grand – blooming and full of spirits and as pretty as paint. Some chap's going to be a lucky man one day.' Dolly was staring into the fire. She smiled as I spoke and nodded her head rather wistfully.

'It doesn't seem possible, does it, to imagine one's children married?' she said. 'But there it is. Lance is doing well at Stowe – his voice is just breaking and sounds so comic. Poor boy, he's awfully sensitive about it! And now Pam's back with us and halfway a woman now.'

'But not quite,' said Arnold, firmly clamping his teeth about the butt of his cigar. 'I've no intention of letting Pam grow up before she needs to, and that's one of the reasons why I've decided not to let her go back to the Schloss. It was all right when she was still a child, comparatively speaking – but now she's growing up I want her to be more with her mother.' He smiled across at Dolly and patted her plump little knee as he went on.

'If she's half as good as Dolly here when she grows up, Jerry, I'll say some chap's going to be lucky.' I laughed. Time had been when I wondered at Arnold's obvious affection for his plain little wife, but I had long given up wondering and tended to envy him instead.

'Is she really fluent in German now?' I asked, and Dolly looked over at me.

'That's the only thing that worried me a little,' she confessed. 'I wondered if I were doing the right thing in taking her away? Maybe she should have stayed there until her German was at least as good as her French – it isn't as yet, of course. She needed another year to get really fluent. But Arnold was so insistent – and anyway, now I'm not worrying. I've found a way for Pam to keep on with her German, right here in this very building!'

She nodded her neatly waved little head in triumph and I looked my interest as she went on.

'There's a foreign woman, a Russian, living on the floor just above us – at least, not on the floor itself, at the turn of the stairs it is – and she's willing to give Pam lessons in German for a very reasonable sum. We'd known her by sight for some time, but didn't know her name – we called her "The Woman on the Stairs" and found afterwards that the porters all call her that, as she's got one of those unpronounceable Russian names. She seems to speak a dozen different languages so isn't it lucky Pam can stay at home and still perfect her German? And later on the Princess says she will take her in Italian if she likes – says that Pam has a natural flair for languages. Pam is delighted and so are we.'

I elevated my eyebrows. One of Dolly's minor foibles is an innocent sort of snobbery, and she adores a title. I could hear her rolling 'Princess' over on her tongue as a child rolls a lollipop.

'Princess, eh?' I said. 'Moving in high circles, are we? How did you meet her?'

'Only the other day – as a matter of fact it was Pam who got acquainted with her,' said Dolly. 'The Princess had been out shopping – she's quite poor now, though she's been very rich, and she's still got some lovely things – and she dropped her shopping basket in the hall just as Pam was coming in. Of course the child helped her to collect the things, and she was so pleased that she took her back into her flat and gave her cakes and coffee and got talking to her . . . and well, that's how it all started.'

I glanced over at Arnold. He met my glance, smiled faintly and nodded, and got up to bring in the whisky and soda, which was always left handy on a tray in the kitchen when the maid went to bed. As he carried it in he remarked:

'It's quite okay, Jerry. I've checked on the lady's credentials – she gave me enough to supply a whole corps of diplomats – and she's the real thing all right. Princess Olga Alexandra Euphemia Yourakoff-Stavosky, no less – a very old family, related to the Galitzines, and even more blue-blooded, if possible.'

I accepted the drink he poured out for me.

'I suppose she's the usual refugee from the Revolution,' I said. 'If so, she must be a woman of a certain age, as the French so gracefully put it.'

'Well, her family were ruined and driven out at that time, with so many others,' said Arnold. 'But she was only a child then. They went to Paris, where they had relations, and somehow managed to get along there until the Princess grew up and married a Frenchman, the Vicomte de la Croye. They had no family, I gather. When the war came, de la Croye was with the Resistance lot and got caught and killed – she was working with them too till the Germans got wise to her, and then she had to get out as quickly as she could and came to England with only about what she stood up in. Oh yes, there's nothing phony about the fair Olga. You can bet your boots on that, or I would not have dreamt of consenting to let Pam take lessons from her.'

'Does she give private lessons or take classes?' I asked.

'Oh, private,' said Dolly quickly, 'and she's got several pupils. But she's very particular whom she takes. Lady Erle's girl goes to her and Mrs Hare-Lymington's Editha – and oh, several others – all private lessons. The Princess doesn't believe in classes – says she can't give individual attention to each pupil.'

'Well, well,' I said, 'it all sounds excellent. How long has Pam been going to her? – oh, I forgot. She can only just have started, of course, as she only got back last week.'

'She hasn't even started yet,' said Dolly. 'I only fixed things up two days ago. She begins on Monday . . .' There came a tap at the door and a rich voice spoke. A voice mellow, foreign, charming, the voice of a woman.

'May I come in, pleez?'

'Talk of the devil!' said Arnold in an aside as he went to open the door, and Dolly scrambled to her feet, smoothing down the front of her red brocade housecoat as she did so and giving me an eloquent glance. It was evident that she was as pleased as Punch for a Princess to prove herself sufficiently intimate with her to come knocking on the door without ceremony – and I admit that I was curious by now to see the woman who was destined to play Mentor to my pretty god-daughter's Telemacha. The door opened and in swept a tall and impressive-looking woman, white-skinned, red-haired, hook-nosed, clad in flying draperies of black, and carrying in her arms a bundle of books. She halted dramatically on the threshold and a pair of keen dark eyes swept the room – dwelt for a moment on me and came to rest on Dolly's beaming face.

'Ach, madame – you forgeev?' I ring the bell and ring, but no reply and then I try the door and lo, it open and I venture in and I hear voices and I venture more, and so . . .' She rustled forward to the fire, deposited the bundle of books on the small table that held Dolly's coffee cup, and sitting down on the settee beside her opened her first book in a businesslike manner.

'When we talk the other day, madame, I forget theez, *most* important! I haf marked the passages our leetle Pam should learn, if you will show?'

Her large capable hands turned the pages swiftly and showed pencilled markings, turned down pages, inserted slips of paper, and Dolly nodded eagerly as she followed the pointing finger. We men remained silent, watching her, and when she had finished Arnold interrupted Dolly's fervent thanks with the offer of a drink. She turned her red head and smiled engagingly up at him.

'But yes, my friend, with pleasure – especially if you have cognac! Yes? Ach, *wunderschön* . . . you have the taste and the knowledge of the drinks, one can see, as few Englishmen have. And who is thees?'

Her eyes raked me from head to foot, sharp, hard dark eyes beneath a bush of rusty-red hair arranged in a forehead fringe á la Sarah Bernhardt – a fashion so old that for all I knew it might come in again. Dolly, who had plainly been too knocked all-of-a-heap by this unexpected arrival to introduce me, hastened to perform the presentation, and remembering my European experiences, I bent over the white hand extended to me and touched the lips to the handsome diamond ring that encircled the third finger. The lady smiled, plainly well pleased, and remarked

[121]

appreciatively that few Englishmen had such graceful manners; accepted the glass of cognac that Arnold had poured out for her but refused to allow Dolly to make fresh coffee and proceeded to talk – but talk!

It had to be admitted that she talked well – and though in effect it was a monologue, it was so cleverly managed, with such adroit and tactful pauses for suitable questions, comments, exclamations and so on, that to many people it would not seem a monologue at all. I listened, fascinated. It was plain that here was a woman widely travelled, widely read, more than well educated – a woman who had endured and surmounted adventures, experiences, dangers of all sorts without allowing them to affect her sense of humour, courage or tolerance; a woman who must have been a beauty once, and who still retained a measure of that beauty. A woman who had lived royally, and who still, poor as she was now, gave the impression of royalty . . .

I studied her under my eyebrows as she talked, and wondered what her age was. She was that curious ageless type that one sees sometimes in Europe, especially among the older generation of Russian woman – she might have been barely fifty or she might well have been over sixty. It was impossible to tell. The handsome imperious face was little lined, yet it had an oddly mask-like look, which might have been due to the heavy make-up she wore – pale powder thickly applied, eyelids darkened with purple fard and bordered with black mascara, and lips a vivid orange-red which, while theatrical, was undeniably effective with her tousled rust-coloured hair. She had the high cheekbones and faintly slanting eyes of the Russian, and she used her large white hands, with their nails painted the same orange-red as her lipstick, effectively to illustrate the points of her stories – altogether she was a picturesque and arresting creature, and obviously going out of her way to be charming to the family of her new pupil. Then why on earth did I have that faint sense of recoiling, as from something I did not altogether trust?

I watched her and listened to her, now and then contributing my small quota to the talk so as not to be conspicuous by my silence – yet in the end, when she rose to go, with a gracious bow to me and to Arnold and an affectionate pressure of the hand to the gratified Dolly, I found my impression not a whit changed. As Arnold went to show her out of the front door Dolly turned to me and said breathlessly:

'*Isn't* that lucky? I was dying for you to meet her! Now what do you think of her?' Arnold came into the room just as I replied.

'I'm sorry to disappoint you, Dolly, but I don't like her!'

'Not like her?' Dolly's voice rose to a positive squeak of disappointment and dismay. 'What on earth do you mean, Jerry? How *can* you not like her? Nobody could be nicer than she was to you!'

Arnold, pouring himself out a last whisky and soda, looked at me too with surprised disapproval – but I stuck to my guns.

'I'm sorry,' I said firmly. 'I can't give you any reason, so don't ask me, but there it is. There's *something* about the lady I don't like.'

Arnold looked at me with raised eyebrows.

'If you were the ordinary dyed-in-the-wool Britisher, Jerry,' he said, 'I'd say it was just prejudice against a foreigner. But you aren't like that – you've spent years abroad and like foreigners.' I shook my head.

'Don't ask me to explain it,' I said, 'I'm not suggesting she isn't a real Princess or anything like that – I know your thoroughness too well, Arnold, to think that a fake would get past you. No, it's something else . . . something I can't account for. Its – she gives me a queer feeling that I don't want to get too close to her – any more than I would to a snake. Sorry, but there it is.'

Dolly got up with a little vexed flounce.

'Oh well,' she said over one shoulder. 'All I can say is, Jerry, for goodness sake don't go saying anything about not liking her to Pam. You know how easy it is to prejudice kids of her age, and it's *most* important she should go on liking the Princess and wanting to study with her. At present she thinks she's marvellous and is awfully impressed, so leave it at that, will you?'

I nodded. Long afterwards I wished I had not given Dolly that implied promise, but had done my best to put Pam against her prospective mentor from the very first; but there was no way of guessing how things were likely to work out.

Now as it happened, it was some time before I saw Arnold and Dolly and Pam again. I went abroad with my old friend Pennoyer to Brittany for a holiday, so it was some two months or more before I went again to Amherst Court. Since I came back to find a sea of work piled up and waiting for me, I might not have gone then if it had not been that I had run by accident into Pamela herself, coming back from doing some shopping in Kensington High Street for her mother, I thought. But I was wrong.

She was wearing the blue dirndl skirt and white blouse that I remembered – it was hot weather and probably the coolest thing she possessed – and had it not been for that, and the plaited wheels of hair over her ears I doubt if I should have recognized Pam, for she had changed so much! She had lost all the extra weight she had put on in Austria – not that that would have worried me, it was puppy fat anyway and would have come off as she grew out of adolescence – but it was something else that brought me up with a sharp turn. The look on the child's face.

She looked – *drained* is the only word I can think of. Dragged, white, exhausted – and my first reaction was both anger and alarm. What on earth could Dolly be thinking of to let the child get like that? Losing weight was all right, but she should surely not have lost it so quickly – and what on earth was behind that look of exhaustion?

'Pam,' I called. 'Hi, Pam, wait for me!' Pamela jumped, startled, and swung round and for a moment her old joyous self beamed out at me in her delighted smile.

'Uncle Jerry – I'm so glad!' She held her face up for a kiss. 'We've been expecting you to drop in ever since you telephoned Dad last week saying you'd come back.'

'I know,' I said, tucking her spare hand under my arm. 'I've got a lot to tell you – had a grand time with my old friend, Miles – come on, let's turn in here and have an ice, shall we?'

Pam's eyes gleamed as they were wont to do at the mention of ice-cream, but after a moment she shook her head.

'I'd love to, but I can't – I've got to get these things back.' She indicated the laden basket she was carrying.

'Oh that's all right,' I said blithely. 'Your mother'll understand. You can explain . . .'

Pam frowned and spoke a little awkwardly.

'I – they aren't for Mother,' she said. 'They're for the Princess. I – she – I often do some of her shopping for her. She isn't very strong, you know.'

I stared. Personally, I should have thought that that red-headed six-footer was as strong as the proverbial horse. But maybe I was wrong . . .

'Well,' I said. 'Surely she can wait a quarter of an hour? You can always say they kept you waiting at the shops – come on Pam! I haven't seen you for weeks and weeks.'

She hesitated for another moment, then nodded, and together we turned into the nearest café and ordered strawberry ice cream, cakes and coffee. Pamela ate with her usual good appetite and answered my questions and even asked a few of her own about my holiday in Brittany – but she was palpably absent-minded and barely seemed to listen to my replies. I watched her as she consumed her ice, ate three cakes and drank two cups of coffee; and while I was relieved to see that her appetite at least was normal enough, I was far from pleased with other things that I saw as I watched her.

She was so queerly quiet and subdued. There was nothing of her old eager ebullience, the fun and vitality that had been so essential a part of her – all that seemed to have faded out. Her eyes had lost their old sparkle and there was a curiously blank, unseeing look about them, and sometimes when she turned to me to respond to a question she looked at me almost as though she didn't see me. The action was a purely mechanical one, done out of politeness, that was all – she didn't turn to me out of interest or desire to hear what I was saying. In losing the extra weight I knew she had detested, her young figure had regained its old slender beauty; but the oval face was now peaked and pallid, and there were faint bistre-coloured shadows beneath the aquamarine eyes . . .

'Pam,' I said firmly. 'I don't like the look of you, my child. What have you been doing to yourself? Slimming too strictly to get the weight down?'

For a second her old smile flashed at me again, but it faded as she shook her head.

'Oh no, I haven't been slimming. Mother wouldn't let me, she said it would all come off naturally if I waited – and it did, quite quickly.'

'Too quickly, I'd have said,' I said with dissatisfaction. 'You don't look well, Pam. Feel okay?'

She nodded in a listless sort of fashion.

'Oh yes, I'm perfectly all right.'

'You aren't working too hard?' I persisted – for the more I studied the child the more concerned I was beginning to feel about her. There was something unnatural about this change – a change not merely in the body, but mentally as well. Where, in this lifeless, mechanically-smiling youngster was the vital, laughing, energetic Pam of old? 'You're sure that new teacher of yours isn't letting you overdo it?'

Now she was roused to animation. The mention of the Princess was like touching a button that suddenly lighted up a darkened room, and I don't know why, but it didn't please me. Didn't please me at all . . .

'Oh goodness, no!' Her reply came as quickly as the lash of a whip. 'I – she's the most marvellous person, Uncle Jerry. I never met anybody like her at all before. I – she – we all think so – all her pupils, I mean.'

'Are you getting on with your German well under her teaching?' I asked. Actually I wasn't especially interested in her German, but I wanted to study the sudden light in her eyes at the mention of the

[125]

Princess's name; the spurt of animation that had been infused into the listless apathetic creature that had been Pam until that moment.

A faint frown lined her smooth forehead between the twin wheels of flaxon hair.

'German?' she said and looked at me in an oddly questioning way.

'Yes, German.' I said a shade impatiently. 'Surely that was what you were going to her for, wasn't it? To perfect your German?'

'Oh yes – yes, of course it was.' Pam agreed, a shade over-eagerly I thought. 'Oh – I'm getting on very well she says. Very well indeed.'

I looked at her sideways. I was getting very puzzled, and I didn't like being puzzled.

'Studying anything else with her?' I asked. Pam looked at me.

'I . . . she's teaching me deportment,' she said slowly, 'how to do a Court curtsy and all that sort of thing. She says she'll get me presented at Court one day, she knows lots of titled people and she says it's only a question of pulling strings . . . oh she's marvellous, Uncle Jerry! You have no idea . . .'

She was off again, her eyes alight, her voice fervent – it was plain that the little fool had a bad case of heroine-worship such as besets, most teenagers, and I was annoyed. I don't know why, but somehow I would have preferred her to have an emotional fixation on the games mistress at the Schloss or on the Mother Superior of her convent in France rather than have fastened on to this theatrical Princess-with-a-past – and a past-and-a-half, I would have betted! She might well be a right-down regular royal Princess – she might even have been a heroine of the Resistance – but she had been other more murky things as well, or I missed my guess.

'Well,' I said discontentedly, beckoning the waiter over to pay my bill, 'she may be the cat's whiskers to you, my dear, but you don't look well, and my own opinion is that she's working you too hard. I shall tell your mother I think so, too – and anyway why should you run her errands for her in this hot weather?'

Pamela's hands clutched more tightly the handles of her basket, and her lips took on a mutinous line, but she said nothing – and I made up my mind it was time I saw Dolly.

I invited myself to dinner again at Amherst Court shortly after my encounter with Pam – but I got little satisfaction out of either Dolly or Arnold.

Arnold withdrew into his study soon after dinner, he was working on a tough case that had to be prepared practically overnight and I tackled

Dolly at once about Pam, who had not dined with us. She was, Dolly said importantly, having supper with the Princess, who amongst other things was a wonderful cook and had promised to show Pamela how to make an omelette.

Dolly talked Princess practically all through dinner – that is, when Arnold and I were not talking our respective shop – and it was plain to me that if Pam was besotted on this confounded woman, her mother was not far behind her.

It was the Princess this and the Princess that. Some marvellous little dressmaker she knew who had made Dolly some clothes that were simply wonderful, and so cheap. Some brilliant doctor or dentist who, at a word from the Princess, would treat her friend for next to nothing. Some shop or agency or office that would do the same – and regarding Pam, how kind the Princess was to Pam! She singled her out above all her other pupils – no other was ever asked to have supper privately with her – taught her to cook and embroider, showed her how to make a real Court curtsy – it was really marvellous how she had taken to Pam and how Pam had taken to her, and what a chance that was for Pam! Poor as she might be, the Princess was an aristocrat to her fingertips, and knew everybody who was anybody in London; and when it came to the time for bringing Pam out into the world . . .

So it went on and on, and when Arnold left us I interrupted the spate very firmly.

'Look here, Dolly, do you know you've talked nothing but this confounded Princess since I came?' Dolly looked a trifle confounded and bit her lip.

'Have I?' she confessed. 'Maybe I have – but you see, she is really rather an absorbing sort of person. She's not like anybody else I've ever known.'

'That's all right,' I said, 'but she needn't become an obsession with you as well as with Pam.'

Dolly's eyes flew wide and she shook her head protestingly.

'I really think, Jerry,' she said, 'you're making a mountain out of a molehill. It's quite natural for girls of Pam's age to get a crush on older women. It was bound to happen with somebody or other, and I'm glad it's happened with the Princess, because under her influence Pam can learn so much that will be useful to her later on in life.'

'Well,' I said, 'I don't like the change in the girl – she's lost all her old fun and gaiety, and she's got so thin.'

Dolly laughed outright.

'You are really not going to suggest, are you, that her getting thin again is due to the Princess?' she asked. 'Really Jerry, isn't that rather silly? It was only puppy fat due to all that rich food in Austria and it came off just naturally.' Her blue eyes met mine squarely. 'You see, Jerry, I'm very ambitious for Pam. She's going to be a lovely girl, and Arnold and I spent a lot on her education and on Lance's – it's all we can do for our children to launch them in the world, as we haven't got a lot to leave them in the way of money. We're just quiet middle-class people, Jerry, and I don't know anybody influential in Society, while the Princess does, and if she chooses she can help Pam a lot later on. She can give her useful introductions, get her in touch with good families, see that she meets men worth meeting, maybe help her to get some sort of job where her looks can get her really noticed ... Pam wants to go in for dress-modelling, herself, and of course that's one of the best ways to get noticed now. It's like being one of the Gaiety girls in father's and mother's day. Most of them married into the peerage.'

I had to stem the torrent again, for Dolly, in her efforts to justify her own obvious cultivation of the Princess, looked like emulating Tennyson's Brook and running on forever.

'I see,' I said dryly. 'You mean you see the Princess as a useful leader by which Pam may climb into society. Isn't that rather old-world, Dolly – after the war and all its experiences?'

Dolly squared her stubborn little jaw.

'Things don't change as much as all that,' she said, 'and every mother in the world wants the best for her daughter and tries every way to get it. I want the best for my Pam, and I believe the Princess is going to be a very worthwhile social asset – so I'm going to use her for what she's worth, and I don't care what you say!'

'Even if she's not good for Pam?' I ventured. 'Must she be forever in the woman's pocket?'

'I honestly don't know what you're driving at, Jerry,' Dolly said irritably. 'Pam goes there every day for a German lesson, and quite often the Princess asks her in either to supper or to coffee after supper, and supervises her homework or gives her hints about all sorts of things like manners and how to talk to people and interest them and all that. And about Pam's being quieter in her manner,' a hint of defiance crept into her tone, 'well, maybe that is partly due to the Princess, as she told me she thought it would be a good thing to tone down the child's exuberance a little! It wasn't good style to bounce and laugh and shout and get excited as she used to do.'

'Good style, be hanged,' I said rudely, 'I liked Pam better left as she was, a jolly natural kid! And how far is this refining process going, do you know?'

'It's going on until Pam's really polished, as she ought to be,' snapped Dolly, losing her temper. 'I don't care what you say, Jerry, I think this is a marvellous chance for the child. Arnold and I can't afford to send Pam to a really expensive finishing school in Paris as we'd have liked, and to have her "finished" here by a woman like the Princess while she's still under our roof is simply a miracle. I'd be mad not to seize the chance.'

I compressed my lips. It was plainly no use arguing. Between her natural desire to seize every worldly advantage for her child and her equally strong desire, that sprang from her innocent snobbery, to cling to the most aristocratic woman she had ever known, Dolly was hell-bent on going her own way – and I was not going to quarrel with her.

'Well, it's your pigeon,' I said, 'but I don't like it, all the same. Where's that whisky of Arnold's? I need a drink!' Dolly went to the kitchen and brought in the tray. As she put in down she looked at me, and her blue eyes were plaintive.

'I know you think I'm being a fool over this,' she said sadly, 'and I can't get you to understand. I wish you knew the Princess better and you'd take a different view of her – wait a minute!' While I poured myself out a drink she went to her desk, extracted a minute diary from it and read out a date about two weeks ahead.

'She's giving a little cocktail party in her flat – six to eight, just a few friends getting together – and she wants us to come. I'm sure she'd be delighted to see you as well – an extra man's always welcome. Why don't you come? If you could get to know her better I'm sure you wouldn't have this silly prejudice against her.'

I brightened. This was a good idea. I wanted to get next to the lady, though I doubted whether it would result, as Dolly fondly hoped, in my instinctive distrust of her giving way before a sudden rush of liking.

I made a note of the date in my diary, drank up my whisky and went off – and just before I left I put a question to Dolly. If the Princess would welcome an extra man, might she not welcome two extra men even more heartily? If I might, I should like to bring my friend Pennoyer with me.

'Pennoyer, your friend the spook doctor?' asked Dolly.

She knew and liked Pennoyer, though like many women she was a little scared of as well as sceptical about his work – such of it as she understood, which was very little. 'Oh yes, I'm sure she would. But why do you want to bring *him*, particularly? There aren't any spooks in the Princess's flat?'

I hedged.

'Oh, he doesn't spend his entire life spook-hunting, you know,' I said. 'He's quite a social bird in his quiet way, and speaks as many languages as the Princess. I thought they might get on rather well together.'

Dolly brightened and nodded her head.

'That's true,' she agreed. 'Well, do bring him and I'll tell the Princess . . .'

Pennoyer listened with interest when I told him my story – my impressions, that is, as there was scarcely anything sufficiently substantial to be called a story as yet.

In fact, some years earlier, I probably would not have ventured to tell him about it at all, fearing I was, as Dolly had said, making mountains out of molehills. But Pen had so often encouraged me to record and report to him my impressions, even very vague and fleeting ones, telling me that I sensed more rightly than I knew when things were psychically wrong that I had lost my old shyness and self-distrust, and made no bones of telling him in detail all I felt about the matter that was puzzling me, as this certainly was. He heard me out to the end and then nodded.

'I'll come with you with pleasure,' he said, 'and meet this good lady. But first I'll build a protective shell about myself so that she can't pick up any waves of psychic powers and be on the alert!'

'Make yourself into an ordinary man, in fact,' I joked, but even as I joked I knew that even with his psychic powers cloaked, Miles Pennoyer would never be an ordinary man. One look into those deep-set steady eyes, at that lean brown face with the strong chin and the tender sensitive mouth, told one that here was an exceptional man indeed – one of the great ones of the world who live only to serve their fellow men. Pen nodded and smiled.

'It may not be necessary, of course,' he said. 'The Princess may merely be a remarkably strong character before whom both mother and daughter are at the moment doing the hero-worshipping act – rather foolishly, but probably quite harmlessly – and in that case, one can do nothing but wait until it wears off and Pam and Dolly both come to their senses. On the other hand, I'm inclined to pay attention to your hunches. They are often a definite "lead", and if there is anything in my line about this business I should obviously look into it, if I can do so quietly and

[130]

unobtrusively. That's all I can say at the moment. Okay Jerry, I'll come with you on the 23rd.'

The Princess's notion of a small and intimate cocktail party was not mine! As Pennoyer and I ascended the stairs of her flat we could hear the roar of voices high above us, and the clink and rattle of glasses. We looked at each other and Pennoyer grimaced – the last thing in the world he would normally choose to go to was a cocktail party. But today he was being an ordinary man . . .

The Princess's flat was one of those situated on the turn of the stairs that led from one floor up to another. The building was so constructed that there was one of these small flats at each corner of the block on each floor, reached by two or three odd steps that led up to the front door from the angle where the first flight of stairs turned sharply to the second flight. The door was propped open, and we could see from the mist of smoke inside that the place was crowded; however, we were in for it now, and pushed our way into the mob of men and women that seethed inside, looking around first for our hostess, then for a corner where we might possibly get a drink and smoke together. It was a larger flat than I had at first anticipated and consisted, I subsequently discovered, of three rooms. One large one in which we were all congregated, and two smaller ones that served the Princess as a bedroom and a pocket-sized dining-room.

There was a strong smell of some Eastern incense, and indeed the whole place was definitely Eastern in flavour. A pierced bronze lamp the size and shape of a football hung from the centre of the ceiling, there was a wide divan in one corner covered with a handsome Chinese shawl in purples, reds and greens; and on the wall behind it hung a shabby but beautiful Persian rug in silk, the 'Tree of Life' pattern, which must have been worth a good deal for all its shabbiness.

There was a piano, also draped with another Chinese shawl, but in orange and blue this time. This was laden with photographs in silver frames, and more photographs crowded the high mantelpiece – photographs mainly of women in elaborate Court or evening dress and men in magnificent uniforms, mostly of old Russia in the days of the Czars – the majority of them bearing sprawling signatures. There was a gilded Buddha on a carved and lacquered shelf and two incense sticks smouldering in a brass jar beside him, and a litter of Eastern curios and ornaments along the top of the bookcases which lined two walls of the room – and the door that plainly led into the Princess's bedroom was discreetly hidden behind a fine *mushrabiyeh* screen such as one may still pick up, if one is lucky, in the back streets of Cairo, Port Said or Alexandria. An odd room; a cluttered room, one might say, and yet a room that breathed personality as its owner did.

She was standing in a corner talking with great animation to a group of people and did not see us for a moment – which I was glad about, as it gave Pen a chance of sizing her and her surroundings up before she noticed him.

She wore her usual black, velvet this time, but it was brightened up today by a flaming scarf of Italian striped silk in vivid crimsons and purples and greens, and she wore enormous dangling ear-rings of emeralds set in silver and a great oval-shaped brooch to match pinned in her breast – old Russian jewellery, one could see at once from its style. In her crest of henna-reddened hair there nodded and sparkled another piece of valuable jewellery – a dragonfly with outspread wings, its body a serrated row of emeralds, its eyes made of rubies and its wings a lacework of tiny many-coloured jewels. Flamboyant as it was, it was a lovely piece of work of its kind, and though it would have look appallingly *outré* on many women, somehow this woman, with her essentially dramatic quality, managed to carry it off.

Just then Pam's voice came at my elbow, eager, excited. She was carrying a tray of luscious-looking little snacks, stuffed eggs, prawns in aspic, anchovies sitting on cucumber slices, sections of celery filled with cream cheese – you know the sort of thing. She was plainly playing waitress to help the Princess's little maid, and though this fresh proof of her servitude to her teacher annoyed me, I was pleased to see her for once bright and animated as of old, and congratulated her on the excellent qualities of the *canapés*, many of which, she proudly told us, she had prepared herself. Pennoyer, whom she knew and liked, smiled at her as he accepted one, and I followed his example when suddenly a voice rich, mellow, delightful spoke in our ears – our hostess had spotted us at last.

'Ach, it is Meester Latimer, I theenk – the brother of *chére* Madame Latimer – and your friend, no? So charmed – *so* pleased . . .'

I hastily performed the necessary introduction and saw the hard dark eyes dwell reflectively on Pen, pass him over with, in effect, a shrug, and turn again to me. It was plain that Pennoyer had made himself with eminent success into an ordinary man! The Princess went on, one large hand resting possessively on Pam's slender shoulder as she stood close to her.

'Thees child, see how she helps me – I cannot do wit'out her at any of my parties. See, she made wit' me most of these things to eat! So nice . . .'

She chose a prawn *canapé*, popped it into her large mouth and went on talking as Pam beamed her pleasure at the praise. Pennoyer accepted another *canapé*, shook his head at the tray of cocktails that had just appeared and asked for a glass of fruit juice or soda water and listened as the lady continued.

'You weel not find your brother and hees wife as yet, Meester Latimer – they come later on, they say – but I beg of you, eat and drink all you will and amuse yourself. Here are some of my dearest friends – we get together now and then, as you call it, those of us who are still alive, and talk over old times.'

'Like the play "Reunion in Vienna",' remarked Pennoyer in German, and the Princess beamed delightedly.

'*Ach so!* You are a linguist – how wonderful! So few Englishmen speak any language but their own, though since the war it is better, *nicht wahr?* So many years on the Continent, even Englishmen had to try and learn a little of other languages.' Her keen eyes bored into Pennoyer's. 'You speak my own tongue perhaps, professor, Russian? You *are* a professor – or perhaps I mistake?'

Pennoyer said that perhaps one might fairly call him a professor, of the mind rather than of the body – and yes, he *did* speak Russian. The Princess screamed out the information at the top of a delighted voice, at which several compatriots of hers turned and came over to us, and presently we found ourselves the centre of an interested group all rattling away in Russian. Pennoyer was plainly the success of the evening!

I wandered away when Dolly and Arnold arrived – I can't speak Russian, so I left things to Pen. Dolly and the Princess fell on each other's necks, as women do, and Dolly, finding a spare chair – she had a genius for finding somewhere to sit where nobody else could possibly do so – sat herself down and looked about her with great satisfaction.

She might well be satisfied, as the air was positively dark with titles, though it was plain they were mostly Continental titles and their owners, poor devils, pretty poor and shabby. But there was much foreign talk and foreign manners – hand-kissing, shoulder shrugging and gesticulating and introductions of 'Madame la Comtesse' this and that, 'The Margravine' and so on, and most of the crowded photographs were signed with Royal, or at least near Royal names. So Dolly was in high feather, and looking as nearly pretty as she could look in a becoming navy and white printed shantung frock and loose coat and little hat to match.

She greeted me with a beaming smile and a meaning glance towards Pam, still standing beside the Princess with the latter's hand on her shoulder.

For a moment we watched the two, the young girl and the tall imperious woman whose hand lay possessively on her shoulder. Pam was wearing a beige frock and beige coloured sandals, and it struck me then that she seemed even thinner than when I had seen her last, though excitement had lent a spurious touch of colour to her cheeks and the Princess's obvious approval had brought a sparkle to her eyes. But somehow, somewhere, that odd sense of doubt, of distrust was still working within me, and not all the Princess's graciousness – and she had gone out of her way to be gracious – could do anything to remove that feeling.

I glanced over at Pennoyer, still talking to his group of Russians; met his appealing glance and knew what it meant. 'Haven't we stayed long enough? I've got all I wanted!' I nodded and said to Dolly mendaciously:

'What a shame you and Arnold came so late . . . because I'm afraid it's a case of "hullo and goodbye" for Pen and me. We've been here a good while, and we'll have to go now – Pen's got an urgent case waiting.'

Dolly's face fell.

'Oh, but—' she began, but I was having no buts. I was too keen to hear what sort of an impression Pen had got out of the Princess and her set-up.

'Sorry,' I said firmly. 'It's been a nice party, but you came very late, you know. Let me see, it's Pam's birthday party next week isn't it – on Thursday? Right! Then I'll be seeing you then. Now I'll say goodnight to our hostess and collect Pen, and we'll be on our way . . .'

I waited until Pen's car had pulled away from the entrance to the flats and then burst out with the question I had been dying to ask for the past hour.

'Well, what do you think of her?'

Pennoyer smiled as he skilfully steered the car into the crowded length of Kensington High Street.

'You always want to rush your fences, Jerry,' he said, 'leave me alone until we get back to the flat. I want to sort my impressions out quietly – and after dinner I'll tell you the summing up of those impressions.'

I felt dashed and subsided.

[134]

'Can't you tell me at least the general atmosphere of those impressions?' I said at last. Pen smiled again.

'All I'm prepared to say at the moment is that your hunches are generally correct, and this one I'll swear is correct too,' he said slowly at last. 'Correct in that there is *something* here I don't like – something that smells bad, if you know what I mean – but further than that I can't go. Whether that bad smell arises from a thoroughly nasty mental condition or from a nasty spiritual one I don't yet know – now shut up until we get home. I want to think!'

I lighted up my cigarette and sank back into my seat, knowing it was useless to try and pump my friend further, and we swept smoothly past Derry and Tom's, past Barker's, down Gloucester Road into Chelsea and so via Chelsea Hospital onto the Embankment. Pennoyer drove fast and well, his soft hat pulled down over his deep-set eyes, his face grave and preoccupied; but though he was driving like a master I knew that his mind, the major part of it at least, was not even in the car with me. It was concentrated upon the Princess, and how desperately anxious I was to know what the result of that concentration was going to be!

However, I knew better than to interrupt again, and said nothing until the car was safely parked in its accustomed corner of the quaint old-fashioned square where Pen lived and we had entered the flat, where Friedl had already laid the table and set out the accustomed tray of drinks.

'Hullo!' I said as I saw two places laid. 'How on earth did Friedl know you were going to bring home a guest?'

'I told her mentally,' said Pennoyer, throwing his hat into a corner and pouring himself out a glass of iced orange juice. 'She's been with me so long that without realizing it she picks up mental messages or instructions I send her with surprising success.' He drank off his orange juice thirstily. 'She'll tell you she felt it likely that *mein Herr* would bring home a friend with him – that's all she knows. Pour yourself out a drink, my boy – that is, if you think plain sherry or whisky and soda will mix safely with those rather doubtful-looking cocktails you were drinking at the Princess's party.'

'I'll risk it,' I said with a grin and followed his advice – followed it twice, to be exact – and then Friedl brought in the dinner. It was good as usual. Omelette – *fritto misto*, for my benefit, though as usual Pen contented himself with the vegetables that accompanied that delectable dish – and caramel custard, a particular weakness of mine, to follow; and when we were settled in the sitting room with the coffee before us and

[135]

one of the excellent cigars that Pen keeps for his guests clamped between my teeth, I said firmly:

'Now I've been a good boy and obeyed orders, Pen, but time's up. Out with your conclusions about this damned Princess!'

Pen stirred his coffee and dropped an extra piece of sugar into it. He had so few ordinary weaknesses that I found his love of sweet things rather appealing – it seemed to bring him a little nearer to the commonplace human being that was myself!

'I'll tell you this,' he said at last –' that for a long time I was puzzled as to whether the bad psychic smell I picked up was simply a case of a supremely clever and ruthless lesbian having fastened her tentacles on a malleable young girl. But on our way back things began to get sorted out in my mind – and I'm certain it's not that. Anyway, we can make sure very soon – as soon as we've finished our coffee.'

'How can you make sure?' I asked with interest.

'We'll use the Globe,' said Pennoyer. 'Having been to the lady's flat, I can tune in to her atmosphere without difficulty, and as it's more than likely that Pam will be staying behind when the rest of the guests leave in order to help her beloved teacher clear up, we should be able to sit comfortably back here and watch what happens there! As the Princess had no suspicion whatever that I am other than a quite ordinary man who was brought in as a make-weight, she will not try to "protect" herself or her flat in any way. So we should have a clear run-in, so to speak.'

I looked at him with interest.

'Then you think she's not unacquainted with occultism?'

He nodded. 'I'm sure she knows a good deal about it!' he said briefly.

I sighed.

'You talk about "us" looking into the Globe,' I said, 'but you've forgotten, you old brute, that I haven't the "sight" that can see things in the Globe. All I ever see in it is the reflection of my own face – and I'm thoroughly tired of that.'

Pen grinned.

'Drink up the rest of your coffee and come on,' he ordered. 'Don't you know yet that your old friend is a miracle worker? Dump this tray out in the hall for Friedl to take away, and draw the curtains close, and we'll get busy.'

While I put the tray outside and drew the soft tobacco-coloured velvet curtains Pen unlocked the corner cupboard and drew carefully out a large round glass globe on a carved blackwood stand. He placed it on a small table, drew up two comfortable chairs beside it and turned out all

[136]

the lights but a single lamp at the far end of the room; this he draped with a red silk scarf so that all the light it gave out was a blurred rosiness in the dusk, and felt his way back to the table. Then, while I waited, bursting with curiosity to see what he was going to do to me, he came behind me, placed one palm flat across my forehead and the other at the back of my neck and held them there for a few moments.

'This is where I open the Eye in the middle of your forehead – what some people call the pineal gland and others say is the last vestige of what was once a Third Eye,' he said. 'They are both right in one way and wrong in another – but I haven't time to go into that now.'

'Why your hand on the back of my neck?' I asked. Pen tutted at me.

'You ask me that, Jerry, with your knowledge? You know the five psychic centres well enough – the Eye on the forehead, the heart, the navel, the genitals, the base of the skull. There is a close link between the two head centres and I am opening them both so that you may see all there is to be seen. Now, sit still, and let the power flow through.'

I sat still, and as Pen's strong hands pressed on my head and at the back of my neck I did indeed feel the flowing of some mysterious power like a faint but distinct electric current, tingling, stimulating – and when I opened my eyes at last it was something of a shock to see the room and its furniture just as before, clear in the dim red light, the Globe poised on its stand before us on the little table. But Pennoyer gave me no time to wonder and question.

He moved over to the Globe and held his long hands outstretched for a moment over it, muttering under his breath some words that I could not distinguish, then withdrew his hands and returned to his seat.

'Now,' he said under his breath, 'we shall see what we shall see!'

For a few moments the Globe remained dark with only the far gleam of the lamp reflected in a blurred patch of reddish light on its rounded side – then suddenly a tiny flame seemed to dawn in the very centre of it. The flame grew rapidly larger and brighter and at last it seemed to fill the Globe as though it was hollow and lighted from within; then it mellowed to a soft glow, and leaning forward I began to see in it various odd things, seen as through a shifting mist; a chair and a table, the long shape of a divan piled with cushions and two figures moving about . . .

The mist cleared and I saw that I was looking into the sitting-room of the Princess's flat – the room I had so recently seen filled with people drinking, talking, laughing – but now it was empty but for two figures. The figure of young Pamela, busy clearing away what were evidently the remains of a picnic supper, and that of the Princess.

[137]

She had changed her dress and put on a sort of lounging robe, I suppose it was – a handsome thing of black and green Chinese brocade with wide sleeves and a collar fastened high to her neck with jade buttons – and she was sitting cross-legged on the divan surrounded with cushions, watching Pamela at work. It struck me at once how oddly right both her robe and her attitude were – plainly, like so many Russians, she was of Mongol blood, and in that dress somehow she seemed to fit better into this setting than into any other. She was smoking a cigarette in a foot-long jade holder and plainly talking to Pamela as the child moved about. I watched Pamela finish her job of clearing the table and setting the room to rights and saw her turn to the elder woman and ask a question – probably as to whether she should wash up the supper things. However, whatever it was, the older woman vetoed it, and motioned Pamela to sit down at the table, open a drawer in it and get out a pile of exercise books. I saw Pamela look towards the divan with rather a rueful pout – evidently she was in no mood to tackle German now! – and for some odd reason I felt disappointed; surely my hunch and Pennoyer's sensings were not going to peter out into a mere conscientious teacher giving a promising pupil an extra lesson? But I had jumped to a hasty conclusion.

Obediently Pamela drew up a chair and settled herself to work. I had known that she often did her homework under her teacher's eyes, yet somehow I had not expected it to happen this particular night, after the excitement of the party. The room grew quiet and in the background the Princess still sat upright, cross-legged on her cushions, smoking, motionless as a carved image – motionless as the gilded Buddha perched high up on his lacquered shelf against the wall. The absurd thought struck me that she looked very much like the Buddha! The attitude, the poise, were exactly the same, but that the Buddha had one hand raised in blessing and she – yet even as I looked she laid her cigarette carefully in the ashtray on the little table beside the divan and raising her hand, even as the Buddha had raised his, held it steadily, palm forward, with her eyes directed at the unconscious girl as she bent over her books.

There's was a moment's pause, and then I saw something more than curious. I saw what seemed like five threads of silvery light begin to ray out from the tips of the Princess's fingers and stream towards Pamela! They were no thicker than a silk thread, yet I could see them clearly, silvery in colour, but with a curious greenish sheen that somehow I did not like at all – and they streamed out sheer across the room and fastened on Pam. One attached itself to the back of her neck, another to the top of her head, another to her forehead, another to the base of her throat and the fifth to her heart – and once attached they seemed to swell and grow and pulsate like living things! The sight was so uncanny that I gave a sharp exclamation of revulsion – and Pennoyer's hand came firmly down on mine. He spread his left hand over the Globe and at once the picture faded – the glass became dull and I was back in the normal present, glaring at Pen in fury mixed with anger, and completely bewildered.

'Pen – what on earth *is* it?' I burst out. 'It was horrible! Those rays or threads fastening on to Pam . . .'

'Tentacles, I would rather call them,' said Pen calmly. 'You're right, it *was* horrible, for the woman is drawing vitality from Pam to keep herself alive. She knows plenty about magic, for only a magician can do what we saw her doing – set a psychic pump to work on a younger being in order to provide herself with the vitality that she no longer possesses. They knew about it in Biblical days, of course – remember giving the aged King David a young virgin to lie in his bosom to give him back his strength? There was nothing sexual about that – and nothing actually magical such as we have just seen. Just the knowledge that the aged can and do draw vitality from the younger, only too often, to prop up their weakening powers.'

'I know something about that,' I said, 'because nowadays doctors won't have children sleeping in their grandparents' room, as so often used to happen – they know it is bad for them.'

'Of course it is,' said Pen. 'Thank goodness, in that respect at all events, we have learnt a little wisdom. But this – this is a thousand times worse. This damned woman – if she is a woman at all . . .'

I was startled and interrupted.

'Oh, surely?' I began, but Pen swept on.

'Oh, I don't mean she isn't a woman, physically speaking. I mean that the Entity who is incarnated in her body is essentially male, and that is one of the reasons why she – *he* – is able to handle and attract women so successfully. Again, there is nothing sexual about it, in the lesbian sense I mean – it's a psychological matter. Psychologically, women sense the male, and a strong male, within the Princess and so gravitate towards her . . . that's the reason why both Dolly and Pamela and doubtless a lot of other women before them have fallen under this infernal woman's spell. I must break it – for without it . . .'

'Yes?' I prompted him. He hesitated a moment, then faced me squarely, seriously.

'Look here, Jerry, I don't want to be a gloom-merchant – but this is serious! You saw this psychic pump at work – sucking out the very life-force of this child, to be drawn into and used by this evil Thing on the divan. You've seen how changed and white and listless Pamela has become since she met this so-called Princess – well, unless we can stem this flow of vitality from her to the Princess, sooner or later she will die for sheer lack of strength to keep alive. She'll be sucked dry. I've no manner of doubt that the Princess has done this before – possibly many times before – she's a psychic vampire and there is no viler magic than hers. There is no knowing her real age, but I'm positive she is vastly older than she seems. But don't despair, Jerry. Go home and get to sleep – and tomorrow I will see you again and tell you what I think we may be able to do.'

'It's no use your talking to Arnold and Dolly, I suppose?' I said. Pen shook his head.

'Not a scrap,' he said firmly. 'Arnold would only laugh and think me crazy; and Dolly – who's completely under this woman's spell – would be offended, and we should get nowhere. No, I must handle this alone – and now get along.'

I could not get to Pam's birthday party after all, as a few days after my talk with Pennoyer I went down with a nasty chill and had to stay in bed for several days with a high temperature, feeling very sorry for myself. I sent a cheque to Dolly to spend on a present for my goddaughter, and she bought her a red suede handbag that she assured me she envied most heartily, and twice I tried to get Pennoyer to come and chat to me to beguile a few of the weary hours I had to spend in bed; but old Friedl told me that my friend had departed to Paris on some mysterious errand the very day after we had seen the Princess and her pupil – her victim rather, I now realized – in the Globe. So I had to possess my soul in patience until I got on my feet again, and the first night I felt fit enough I went to Amherst Court to dine.

Pam greeted and thanked me for her present very sweetly, though without that old exuberance that she used to show, and I scanned her young face as I kissed her, with more than my old anxiety. She looked, I thought, even whiter and more listless than before, and now I knew what she was being used for – what that devil in female form was trying to do – everything in me was up in arms with fear and anger both, and I was wild to find some sort of an excuse to break off these damned lessons, separate the teacher and the taught . . . but what on earth could I do?

With Dolly, poor darling, smiling smugly on the situation, I simply hadn't a hope – and for the first time since I had known her, I felt I could have shaken the little woman for her stupidity, for her obstinacy . . . yet even as I felt the impulse I dismissed it as unfair. How could she be expected to understand? As Pen had said, if I had tried to explain she would simply have considered the whole idea crazy, as Arnold would do likewise . . . so I stifled my feelings as best I could, and we sat down to dinner as usual.

Needless to say, after touching on various other subjects such as my recent illness and Pen's visit to Paris – which, since to Dolly Paris meant clothes and to Arnold women, neither of them could understand what should take Pen there! – the talk gravitated to that damned Princess; but this time Pam had something really interesting to say.

'You know, Mummy,' she said, 'I'm not the only one that's been having presents. The Princess had one today – and she's so intrigued with it because she can't think who it's from!'

Dolly's eyes were round with interest.

'Can't think who it's from?' she repeated. 'But how very odd! Did it come by post?'

'Oh yes.' said Pam, eating her grilled chicken with relish, 'it came from abroad – Rome, I think – all corded up in a wooden box with seals and things and stuffed inside with shavings.'

'Wasn't there a card inside?' I asked. Pam shook her head.

'No, I suppose the person who sent it meant to put a card in and forgot. Isn't it maddening? The Princess and I unpacked it together and went through every inch; but there wasn't any sign of a card or a note, and she's going nearly mad trying to find out who sent it!'

'Well, is it worth all that careful packing?' asked Arnold.

'I don't think so,' said Pam frowning. 'It's an old metal thing – like a sort of wheel stuck on a long metal stem with a foot to it – some antique thing or other. I never saw anything like it before and can't imagine what it's used for.'

'Can the Princess?' I asked.

'I think she knows what it is, but can't make out why its been sent to her,' said Pam, and her eyes suddenly lighted up. 'I know! Will you come round to her flat with me after dinner, Uncle Jerry, and have a look at it? I'm sure the Princess would love you to come?'

'I'll come with pleasure,' I said – which was true, for some inner instinct told me that it was important I should see this thing. Somewhere behind this mysterious present moved Pennoyer, I was sure. Certainly Rome puzzled me, as Friedl had said Pen had gone to Paris; but it would not be the first time that Pen had deliberately confused his tracks, and that this thing, whatever it was, had come from or via him I felt positive.

After we had coffee Dolly telephoned the Princess to ask if it would be convenient for me to come over and see the curio about which Pam had told us. I was (she said) a connoisseur of such things. The Princess welcomed the idea enthusiastically and Pam and I went up to the little door at the angle of the stairs. The flat was filled with the smell of incense, as before – the Princess had a passion for the heavy musky scent, which I personally detest – and she greeted us eagerly.

'But how charming of you, Meester Latimer, to come and try and explain my mystery? Behold it as it stands!'

She threw out both hands dramatically towards the object standing on a small round table just below the Buddha . . . and I recognized it at once. It was a small Tibetan prayer wheel. One of those used by the high Lamas in the monasteries of Tibet – and plainly an ancient and, I should judge, very valuable one. It was of bronze, turned greenish with age; the rim and the spokes of the wheel were pierced in patternwork and the stem was covered with a close ornamentation of hammered and embossed metal. I picked it up, touching it delicately, and at my touch the wheel whirled instanter. Old as it plainly was, it had been so well made that not even years and tarnishing and the inevitable battering it had undergone – for it was dented in several places – had sufficed to upset the beautiful balance of the wheel upon its supporting stem. I replaced it carefully, glancing up as I did so at the poker-faced Buddha on his lacquered shelf above; I remember thinking as I did so how well the two seemed to belong together . . .

'It's an old Tibetan prayer wheel – and a valuable one I should judge,' I said. 'What a very interesting present to receive, Madame! And yet Pam tells me you do not know who sent it to you.'

The Princess shrugged and spread out her hands.

'No! But this is fantastic! There is nothing – no card, no message – and yet I would give *anything* to know who sends me so wonderful, so thrilling a present!'

Her long fingers touched the wheel and set it twirling again.

'One is supposed to say a prayer for each turn-round, eh? But how exciting! I must read up something about this in the encyclopaedia. I know so very little, and yet this fascinates me more than I can say.' She touched it again and the touch was almost loving. 'Oh, *who* could have sent it to me? I think I shall really die of mortification if I cannot find out!'

I picked up the paper wrapping of the box that still lay on the floor and studied the big red blob of sealing wax that had fastened the stout string round it. The blob had been broken in two pieces, but so solid were they that it was possible to put the two bits together and see the design of the seal that had been used to stamp the wax. It was a double-headed bird of some sort, with a shield held in its claws; there was a flamboyant crest on the shield and a motto below it. I held it out.

'Perhaps this seal might give you a clue, Madame. Is it one you recognize? I should think it Austrian, or perhaps Russian?'

She clutched it eagerly, studied it for a moment, then relaxed with a smile of gratification.

'I should have thought of that,' she ejaculated. 'But of course I know it! This is the crest of the Galianov family – one of the oldest in Russia. Ruined and driven out like so many others in the Revolution. But I used to know many of them in Paris.'

Her hooded eyes studied the seal closely. 'I – yes – it must be that one of them has remembered me and found out where I live. I wonder who it could be? There were three brothers I used to know when I was young. Ivan and Mikal and Serge – and they were all in love with me!'

'It looks,' I said guilefully, 'as though one of them at least is still in love with you!'

The woman tossed her rust-coloured head and smiled the smile of a woman whose vanity is pleased, though with her expressive hands she made a gesture as though disclaiming my compliment. Then she patted me on the cheek and cried out that she was delighted – delighted! – and that we must now drink some coffee with her and have perhaps a tiny drink of *anisette* or Pernod to toast the new treasure?

We stayed another half hour – it would have been difficult, if not discourteous, to refuse – and much of the time, of course, was taken up in gleeful speculation by both the Princess and her pupil as to how the donor of the present could have discovered her address, which brother it was, and whether he was likely to follow up his present with a personal visit – which the infatuated Pam was quite positive would happen. We took our leave, and the moment I found myself back in my own rooms, tired as I was by that time, I rang up Pen's flat. His voice answered me and he laughed as I threw out my challenge.

'Yes, of course,' he said, 'I *went* to Paris all right; but as it was essential that my hand in this matter should never be suspected, when I'd got the thing I went for safely in my possession I flew to Rome with it and despatched it from there. I sealed it with an old Russian seal I picked up in a junk shop, hoping she'd recognize it – as you say she did. When I'd sent the box off I hopped into a plane and here I am!'

'But how on earth did you get the thing? Tell me!' I demanded.

'Not over the telephone,' said Pen firmly. 'It's a nefarious tale and I'm not going to broadcast it. Come and have dinner with me tomorrow night and I'll tell you all about it – and later on we'll have a look at you-know-what. Good night!'

Though Friedl's English is still very rudimentary, in spite of the years she has spent in Pen's service, Pen refused to discuss the matter that was so intriguing me until after dinner, and I was so excited that I must confess to bolting my food without my usual appreciation of its excellence. Directly we had adjourned to the sitting-room and the coffee was placed before us and the door closed behind Friedl's substantial form, Pen began.

'First, I must confess to having done a spot of burglary over the prayer wheel! I knew there were several in the British Museum but that was too hard a crib to crack; so I telephoned to a Buddhist friend of mine, and he told me of a small temple in the heart of Paris, of all places. It belonged to a Buddhist brotherhood but was closed and locked except when they gathered there about once a month – and only the *concierge* of the building where it was located ever went in to clean or dust it. I went over and found this place, and to my relief found the *concierge* both old and decidedly bibulous. I put on a French working-man's clothes and *béret* and took a big basket of vegetables to sell; got acquainted with the old boy, who was alone, his wife had gone to the country; jollied him along with plenty of doped wine and when he was snoring stole the keys from his pocket! Walked in, lifted the prayer wheel, hid it under the vegetables in my basket, locked it and replaced the keys, and walked out.'

'How on earth will you explain it to the brotherhood if they have a meeting and miss it?' I said. Pen shrugged.

'Let's hope I can replace it as I removed it,' he said, 'but the need was so urgent that I had to risk that.'

'Why did you need it – and what has it to do with the Princess?' I asked.

'I told you,' said Pennoyer, 'that in essentials she is a man – and I am right! More, I knew when I was looking in on her that night what sort of a man she was. She was a Lama in one of her previous incarnations – and a great one, though an evil one. She is drawn to this wheel because of her ancient inner memories that know a prayer wheel's value; but what she does *not* know is that this particular wheel once belonged to the great Nam Penh, one of the great Lamas – but as white as she was once black.'

'And you think?' I prompted, as Pennoyer paused.

'Once again, as I've done many times before,' he said, 'I am pitting the forces of Good against the forces of Evil, and praying that they will win. If this woman had had her old knowledge of magic – which luckily she has not – she would never have allowed the prayer wheel into her flat, for it is the thin edge of the wedge – the spearhead inserted into a crack that I hope will burst right open. Now, tonight, once again, we will look into the Globe and see what we shall see!'

Once more Pennoyer placed his hands on my forehead, at the back of the neck and then over my ears – for a reason I did not understand until later – and in the dusked room we sat watching the Globe as it misted over, cleared and showed us as sharply as though we actually sat there in our bodily selves, the sitting-room of the Princess at Amherst Court.

The room was dimly lighted, with a red lamp before the Buddha and blue curls of fresh incense were rising lazily into the air from the metal vase on the shelf beside it. The Princess, clad in the Chinese robe I had seen before, sat cross-legged on the divan against the richly coloured spread of the ancient carpet that hung on the wall behind it. Her tousled red head was bent as she studied the prayer wheel, held cupped in her two strong hands. For a long time she stared at it, and then with an exasperated sigh put it down on a small table beside the divan, chose and lighted a cigarette. It was plain that though the thing fascinated her she was still at a loss to understand either its arrival or its fascination; and as her head, bending over the flame of her cigarette lighter, was temporarily averted from the prayer wheel, I saw what was happening before she did.

It seemed that a tall column of silvery mist was forming itself against the dusk of the room just behind the shape of the prayer wheel. Swiftly the column took shape and substance and before I could blink a tall man stood there – a man wearing the yellow robes and the curiously-shaped red headgear of a Tibetan Lama of one of the highest orders – the Li Tam Quoy. His lean ascetic face was worn and lined, his lips thin and firmly set and his eyes set in deep hollows. It was a face weary with years and experience, a face learned and sad both – yet as he watched the bent head of the woman on the divan there was no harshness in his eyes, only pity and sorrow. Her head was still bent when he spoke to her – and then I knew that Pen had unclosed my psychic hearing as well as my sight, for I could hear their voices as clearly as I could have heard my own.

'Well, Lom Chang? So you are at your tricks again?'

The red head shot up with a cry of mortal terror and she sat rigid, hands gripping the rug each side of her, her blazing eyes, wide as lamps, staring at the priest who faced her, one long hand resting lightly on the prayer wheel.

'You! You!' she managed to sob out hoarsely, and he nodded.

'You remember me – and my warning to you,' he said quietly. 'In the old days of the monastery that we both remember so well, you used the blood of the living young to keep your fading body alive and vital! Here

[145]

again I see you robbing the young – but now of the life force itself, not merely the blood. Oh Lom Chang, Lom Chang, will you never learn?'

As he spoke I was staring at the Princess, and my eyes bulged, amazed – for as I stared, lo and behold, she changed! From a russet-haired, haggard yet handsome woman she changed before my eyes – and in her place I saw a hawk-faced, shaven-headed priest! Crouched together, his narrow eyes filled with fear and hate both, he sat motionless on the divan, his hands buried in the sleeves of his robe, his bloodless lips a thin line in the yellow mask of his face . . . yet terrified as he plainly was, he did not lack courage as he snarled out:

'Life, life – is any price too high to pay for it?'

The tall priest, confronting him, nodded his stately head.

'It is indeed – yet you have not learnt that, it seems. From afar on the Other Side of this life we have watched you, Lom Chang, through many incarnations, and seen you, alas, at your evil work again and yet again – anything to keep the life flame burning in the wretched physical body that you prize so highly – anything! We have watched you fasten on this English child with sorrow and amazement – but thanks to the wise man who brought this Holy Wheel into touch with you and so gave me the opportunity I needed, your evil project is vain. The child shall be freed – and you, Lom Chang, will go to your own place, there to meet your fellows and your judges and have the doom meted out to you that you have, alas, so well and truly earned.'

Even in the dim light of the room I could see the beads of the sweat of terror that pearled the high bald forehead of the Thing on the divan, and I could see him shaking as he tried fiercely to master his fears. His voice came in a harsh croak.

'No, no – I will not let her go! It is only the strength I draw from her that keeps this physical body alive – I dare not let her go!'

'You have no choice,' said the tall priest, whom now I knew to be none other than the great Nam Penh, the White Lama of whom Pennoyer had spoken to me – the original owner of the prayer wheel. 'Prepare, Lom Chang, for your span of time on this earth is over!'

He raised his hands on high, reverently holding the prayer wheel, and I saw him set it spinning furiously as his lips moved in a strange unearthly sound, half chant, half prayer. The figure in the Chinese robe sprang convulsively to its feet, trying to snatch at the upraised wheel, but even as it moved it collapsed, falling together like a mechanical doll, the springs of which had suddenly given out. The yellow-robed figure seemed to swell and grow to giant size, the chanting rang and boomed in my ears – and suddenly the scene vanished, the globe was once more an ordinary ball of crystal, and in the dimness Pennoyer and I sat staring at each other.

Pen rose to his feet and went to fetch the tray of drinks from the sideboard.

'So that's the end,' he said. 'I wondered how it would come – but I never dreamed that the White Lama himself would come to deliver punishment and take back his prayer wheel. So Lom Chang has gone to his account – and thank the gods your little goddaughter is freed.'

'You mean he – she – the Princess is dead?' I said. Pen nodded.

'Oh yes! Dead, thank heaven as she – *he* can be – like you, I really don't know what to call her. You saw her tonight in her true colours – She who was once a very great Lama until she took to twisting the laws of magic to suit her own evil ends. What she was doing to Pamela she had done many times before in earlier lives to other young people – but in a cruder way.'

'Do you mean – actually drawing their blood?' I asked. 'It seems – well, almost impossible to believe.'

'"For the blood is the life",' quoted Pennoyer as he poured me out a whisky and soda. 'You may or may not know, Jerry, that to this day there are certain extremely advanced souls inhabiting human bodies who know how, by conserving their vital energies in various magical ways, to lengthen the physical life of those bodies to an inconceivable extent. Only in the remote corners of the world do you find these men – chosen souls who after long and arduous training in their far-off cells or monasteries, know how to turn the lamp of physical life so low that it is almost extinguished, so that they can leave their bodies motionless, lying for months at a time, cared for and guarded by a few devoted young disciples while their freed spirits rove the earth ever further and further afield. Some of these men can and do visit other planets and confer with the wise folk there, and bring back vast stores of knowledge with them. This, when at last they awake to full physical life on this earth again, they share and discuss with their fellow workers and use for the benefit of mankind until such time as the Call comes again to them to leave their bodies and go journeying . . .'

'What an amazing idea,' I said wonderingly. 'You mean the bodies they leave need no food or drink – or anything?'

'They need nothing, for the flame of life has been turned so low they can live on almost indefinitely in that semi-cataleptic state,' said my friend. 'But in order to do this – to learn to draw only on the Spirit for the force that keeps that flame alive – takes much arduous and exhausting training of many years; and it is also, alas, possible – and much easier –

[147]

to keep life alive for many years beyond the normal span by drawing on the actual lifeblood of others. Which was the sin for which you heard Lom Chang sentenced.' He poured himself out a glass of lime juice, added sugar and took a long drink. 'Too impatient to go through the bitter training he should have faced, he took the easier way, and for a long time lived on the lifeblood of the young disciples who thronged about him to learn of him – for he was famed for his learning then and many young people came from far parts of Tibet to study under his wing. But gradually here one and there one grew oddly weak and pale and at last died – and those in charge of the monastery set a watch and found out what was happening.'

Pen drew a long breath.

'Lom Chang died – died very horribly, as he deserved to die – but as you have seen, his spirit is still rebellious, still bent on its evil ends. He has grown subtler since those days, certainly – now he no longer draws the blood from the living body, but works on the psychic life-force, which is worse still. Your Pamela does not know, thank God, what she has escaped . . .'

I shivered.

'I don't know and I don't want to know. But I can't tell you how grateful I am to you, Pennoyer, and how grateful Pam's mother and father ought to be – and won't be, since they don't know anything about this!'

Pen smiled.

'I don't want thanks,' he said gently – and I know he spoke the truth. 'I'm only so thankful – and so grateful to the Great Ones I serve – that my ruse has turned out so wonderfully successful. And now I'm going to send you home to bed, Jerry, a wiser and a much happier man than when you came; and look out for the announcement of the Princess's death in the papers. I rather think you'll find something interesting there.'

I did indeed.

The Princess's maid discovered her body lying prone in death on the floor beside the divan and raised a frightful screech which brought in the police almost at once – to my great relief, in time to prevent Pam's going into the flat and finding the body, which I had been afraid of, knowing how often she ran in and out. But as luckily the Princess never got up until eleven o'clock, the body and the flat had both been examined and the body removed before Pam and her parents knew what was happening.

The news came as a great shock to both Pam and her mother, of course, and on Dolly's agitated phone call I went round to do what I could to steady them both up; but there was little to be said. The inquest brought in the cause of death as a sudden apoplectic stroke – and it was one of the smaller, more sensational rags that printed a 'par' about the deceased that gave me, as the saying is, furiously to think. It ran something like this:

'A curious feature of the death from an apoplectic stroke of the Princess Olga Sophia Alexandra Euphemia Yourakoff-Stavosky emerged at the inquest. Though those who knew the Princess in life refused to accept her as being more than fifty-eight or sixty at most, the doctor who examined the body gave the dead woman's age as incredibly old – so old that it was beyond him to understand how she had been kept alive. And further, he was by no means certain that she was a woman at all! Certainly, to use his own discreet words, "not a complete and normal woman" by which possibly the good doctor means she was a hermaphrodite. The whole matter remains a considerable puzzle.'

When I consulted Pennoyer about the paragraph he smiled.

'I rather thought that would happen,' he said. 'No, I don't mean that in this life she was physically a hermaphrodite – I should very much doubt it. But I do think that since at the moment of her death – which was from sheer fright, of course, and no stroke at all – she was wearing the semblance of her old maleness, that left an imprint, as her actual age also did, on the physical body she was wearing. The body appeared to the good doctor – who must have been puzzled to a degree, poor chap! – as both semi-male and incredibly old. Actually, I'm surprised the physical body even held together, struck as it was at the moment of death with the repercussion of the actual years she had kept it alive. I've no doubt that woman was probably well over a hundred and fifty – and if we could only know her history, has kept herself alive and vital and comparatively young for untold years by using young things as she was trying to use Pamela . . . pumping them of their lifestream in order to renew her own. Brrh! It doesn't bear thinking of . . .'

'Another thing that's odd,' I said. 'There's nothing about the prayer wheel, and I gather from Pam that it had disappeared.'

'Nam Penh took it with him,' said Pen, 'and I'll bet anything you like it's now reposing where I took it from, in the Buddhist Temple in Paris – and that it's never been missed. Next time I go over I'll get in touch with my friend the *concierge* and find out. But I'm sure I'm right.'

And of course – he was.

VAMPIRES LTD

Josef Nesvadba

Psychiatrist and doctor Josef Nesvadba (born
1926) is Czechoslovakia's most prominent
writer of satirical fantasy and science fiction,
continuing in the tradition of Karel Capek, the
Czech writer who introduced the word 'Robot'
to literature in his 1921 play R.U.R. ('Rossum's
Universal Robots').
Nesvadba's stories have been translated into
many languages. The following tale was the title
story of one of his best collections, originally
published in Prague in 1964.

T hinking back to my stay in England a year ago, what I remember
most of all are the cars. As if western Europe had suffered
another invasion. An invasion of motorists.

The first time the idea struck me was at Orly airport, listening to the
fat Irishman whose artichokes had broken loose and were rolling down
the escalator. The plane was due to take off in a couple of minutes, and
the escalators were bearing his artichokes away into the waiting rooms
for the Near East, Ecuador, and Guadeloupe. He had to resign himself to
the loss. All the time we were flying over the Channel he lamented the
vanished vegetables, and tried to prepare us for the horrors of English
cooking.

'I'm the agent for a car firm,' he said proudly. 'Our sporting models are
going to beat the whole world . . .'

My companion wanted to give him pleasure, and said: 'I've got an
English car, too, back home. A Hillman.' The pink-cheeked Irishman did

not reply. As though politely ignoring a rude word. We were travelling first class, and he had obviously taken us for better class people.

'Quite a decent car,' he had himself in hand now; 'considering the price . . .' he shrugged. 'Now I sell Jaguars. I think we shall be selling them behind the Iron Curtain soon,' he added, after unobtrusively but closely examining my tie. 'Our cars turn bad roads into good and good roads into Heaven.' I did not ask him whether he believed in life after death. We were coming in for a landing.

The second time cars were forced to my attention was that same evening, when I was trying to find a lady of my acquaintance who lives in Kensington Terrace. I came out of the subway station and wanted to ask the way to the street I had written in my address book, but there was nobody there to ask. I mean, nobody on the pavement; along the road, at a snail's pace, moved four long snakes of steel boxes, each isolating its driver from the outside world so perfectly that he heard neither questions nor shouts.

Then the most interesting experience of all turned up, and that is what I really want to tell you about. It still seems incredible to me. I stayed too long at my friend's house that night, drinking Johnny Walker. Seventy proof. I found that out next morning when I failed to find my companion in our hotel. He had left. They said he had waited for me till the very last minute, but that he had had to catch the train. He probably thought I had deserted him. He did not even leave a message in the hotel. I was alone in that city of eight million people, a city quite strange to me, without a penny in my pocket. The lady I had spent the evening with was not at her office, nor was she at home. There was only one thing left to try. I would have to get to Bolster, where the Commission I was supposed to be a member of was sitting, in somebody else's car. Even at home I have never tried hitch-hiking. I'm getting on in years and I doubt whether anyone would stop to pick me up on account of my attractive appearance. Exhausted, I staggered on foot to a Shell petrol station and gazed yearningly at the cars passing by. They seemed even farther away from me than they had the evening before, although at home I am used to driving about in a small car myself.

'Do you want a lift?' a tall pale man with side whiskers asked me. He spoke with a public school accent and wore plus fours. I shall never forget him. Or his car. It was a racing model, with disc brakes, eight forward gears – it could do a hundred and fifty kilometres an hour in the one before top – it was beautifully sprung and did not seem to run on normal gas, because the owner pulled in at the bar opposite.

'A lift to Bolster,' I replied dejectedly. I could not understand why the man wanted to help me; I had never seen him in my life before.

'I'm sure you need a car . . .' he said a few minutes later, when we were on the motorway. He drove on the left, like everybody else in England, and I thought I'd go through the floor of the car, the way I pressed my foot on an imaginary brake at every corner.

'I've got to get to a conference there,' I told him. 'That's the only reason I'm in England at all. I've simply got to be there in time.'

'You know how to drive,' he said, and it sounded like a statement of fact; then he stopped the car and staggered out of the driving seat. 'I'll pick the car up in Bolster tomorrow. I've got some business to see to in the City today.' He was so pale his face looked grey. He seemed more in need of an undertaker.

'I haven't got my licence with me, or anything, I'm a foreigner, and . . .' I protested weakly, not wanting to admit that I was scared of driving on the left.

'You won't need any papers with this car,' my benefactor replied and stopped a taxi going in the opposite direction. I did not even have time to thank him properly. I thought of the Million Pound Note. Was he trying to win a bet with my help? But he had forgotten to tell me anything about the car, the little peculiarities it might have, how many cylinders it had got, and whether the cylinder heads worked on a camshaft like other racing cars. We had not mentioned the compressor ratio or the question of fuel. Sitting at the steering wheel I felt imprisoned. There was very little room in the car, just enough for two, and it was upholstered in special non-slip material; there was a row of dials below the windscreen. The ignition key was still in place. I pressed the starter button. The car leaped forward like a bolting horse; I felt as though I were steering a rocket. I stopped bothering my head about how I came to be at that steering wheel, and concentrated on gaining the upper hand. It was difficult at first, but I soon saw that everybody on the road was trying to be helpful. Cars stopped and their drivers gazed admiringly. All the Austins, Fords, Rolls-Royces, Morrises, Peugeots, Chevrolets and what not, the common run of cars, stood respectfully waiting for my aristocrat to pass. Even the Flying Squad saluted me. It ought to have aroused my suspicions from the outset; I should have stopped and got out there and then. But I went on.

At the next crossroads I even stopped to give a girl a lift. Her name was Susan, her mother was an actress and had brought her up the modern way. When I told her that we were not used to sixteen-year-olds walking barefoot with rings on their big toes, and smearing purple over their eyelids, she very obediently rubbed the stuff off and took a pair of flat-heeled shoes out of her bag. She said that she was delighted I was a Red and kept examining my face closely. She said her best friend had slept with a jazz drummer at the seaside last year, which put her top of the class. Not one of the others had caught a real Red, though, from behind the Iron Curtain. I began to loathe jazz, actresses and her whole class at school. Susan attracted me quite a bit.

'Let's stop for a cup of tea,' she said as we passed one of the gas pumps; they were as thick along the roads as the giant hoardings attacking your pocket all the way. 'You can buy me a drink . . .' Since the licensing laws in England allow you to buy whisky only at certain hours, nobody wants to let the chance of buying a drink slip by, thus proving the measure of his freedom. We went for a cup of tea. I hoped she had got some small change on her, or I would have to try to have the bill sent to the Embassy. I could not shame my country, after all. We stood at a broad wooden bar already occupied by other drivers. I felt a bit dizzy.

'My dear, that's a Bentley. It's certainly not an Arnold-Bristol. It's got disc brakes on all four wheels. A wonderful car. It's not a Morse or a Dellow or a Crossley or a Frazer Nash. It's a Bentley. The last time I saw one was at last year's races at Le Mans. The only car in England that can keep up with my Cunningham . . .' I heard a voice behind me say, but did not realize at once that it was a woman and that she was talking about my car. She ordered lobster soup, fish and roast beef. She knew all there was to know about Prague. Even about Eliska Junková almost winning the famous Targa Florio race in Sicily in twenty-six, that the most famous woman racing driver in the world was a Czech.

'Things are bad over there now, though. I've heard the Russians race in nothing but adapted Pobeda saloons. I suppose nobody can buy a Bugatti or a Porsche for his own use, can he? How did you get hold of this car you've got now?' I changed the subject and told her I thought the cult of the car as a prestige symbol in the west denoted a crisis in individualism; every separate individual trying to run his own means of transport until all the roads were blocked and the streets in the towns were impassable and they got nothing out of it. That I thought the crowds of cars were just a symptom of the crisis of the personality in our age. She did not understand what I was talking about, and told me she could overtake everything in her post-war American Cunningham, built by millionaires for road racing in Europe – in America they race on closed tracks. She did not glance at Susan once while she was speaking, and her voice seemed more and more like the sound of a four-stroke engine; I stopped listening, and got up to leave. The Ambassador was going to have a nice bill to pay, I thought to myself. And I was going to have a lot to answer for when I got back to Prague. The waiter assured me the Marchioness had paid for everything. It was the Marchioness of Nuvolari, born Riley, who had married a relative of the famous racing driver simply to be able to boast of the name.

She dashed out of the gaily painted pub after us and hopped into her one-seater, pulling on her helmet and waiting like a true sportswoman for us to get ready to take off. We set off together. It was a good thing it was evening and there were not many cars on the road. It was a race according to the rules, I had to show that bragging woman where she got off. We soon passed her; I don't know what there was about our engine, but we left the American supercar far behind. The landscape flew by as smudged as an abstract painting; I braked carefully, not to overturn the car. Susan threw her arms around my neck and started kissing me. She was delighted. We had won. Our Mile miglia. Our Targa Florio. Our Le Mans. Our Brno Round, I added for my own satisfaction. We had not killed a single onlooker. I felt proud of myself and I felt as though I had run that race on foot. I was conscious of kissing Susan, and putting my arms around her, and then I slipped down in the seat.

It was night when I came to myself. Susan was giving me Schweppes to drink, it tasted like soda water and quinine. She had taken my right shoe off and was nursing it in her lap like a doll.

'You didn't tell me you were hurt . . .' I had been for a medical in Prague before I left and I knew there was nothing wrong with me. Then she showed me a fresh scab on my foot the size of her hand. 'You'll have to go to a doctor at once, you must have lost an awful lot of blood . . . ' she said.

'I went to see the doctor the day before yesterday and nothing has happened to my foot since then.' Where could I have been losing blood? It would be visible, wouldn't it? She was talking nonsense . . . When I tried to get up I found I was still dizzy, I had to clutch at the car door and stagger out like his lordship had in London when he so incomprehensibly presented me with his car. I had done nothing with my foot except press the accelerator. I frowned.

'Do you know how to open the bonnet of this thing?' I asked her.

'It's your car, isn't it?' she sounded cross. In English they don't use the familiar 'thou', but I felt sure she was using it now. It took me a little while to get the bonnet open. The engine looked most unusual. Instead

[154]

of the carburettor there was a big oval steel box with two thick pipes coming from it, and these led to the engine proper. I knew there existed cars with only one cylinder and so I tried to open the odd contraption. It would not give. I went back to the dashboard, with Susan looking on sulkily. I turned the ignition key and tried pressing the accelerator with my own empty shoes, avoiding direct contact. Nothing happened. I accidentally knocked against the accelerator with one finger and the car shot forward, knocking our heads against the ceiling.

'What's the matter with you?' asked Susan. 'Why don't you drive on?' With an effort I switched on the light and showed her my finger. There was a tiny little scab on it, more like a bruise. 'Look at that . . .' She did not get the point.

'This is a very strange car indeed. It's neither a Bentley or a Jaguar, even if it kills its driver in the end, I expect. It runs on human blood . . . ' she started to laugh and showed me the maker's name. James Stuart, Old Georgetown 26. It was engraved on a brass plate beneath the steering wheel.

'D'you think the man sold cars for suicides? Now I can see what nonsense you foreigners have stuffed into you. A car that runs on blood.' Then she stopped, for around that strange block which was really nothing other than the steel heart of the car, a steel heart with a pulmonary and a cardiac vein; around that vessel wound thin little veins which were quite transparent, and now they were filling with something dark red. It looked as if I were right. I told her about the strange way the car had come into my hands, and I described the last moments of the former's owner's life. I was convinced that he had chosen me as the next victim because I was a foreigner whom nobody knew here and nobody was likely to miss.

'What are you going to do now?' she asked. I had no choice. I would have to walk to the nearest pub and ring my colleague in Bolster. Susan would have to find another car to pick her up, preferably with a more reliable driver.

'I'm not going to leave you in a mess,' she said with determination. I had heard that Englishwomen are very faithful and the idea worried me a bit. I told her she couldn't go walking over fields and woods with me, because once I relinquished this technical miracle there would be no more admirers to treat us to lobster soup and oysters. I was going to have to lead the simple life, and that wasn't good for love's young dream.

She found out I was right. We walked along below the embankment at the edge of the road, for about three hours. The headlamps gleamed above us. I did not want to stop any car, I only wanted to walk to the nearest village and find the first phone I came to.

'That's silly. I can climb up first and even the United States Ambassador would stop for me. We play a sort of game like that in school and I always win.' She lifted her breasts proudly. They certainly were attractive enough.

'You risk stopping another car made by Vampires Ltd, and having your blood sucked again . . .' She laughed, no longer believing the tale; now she saw only the advantages of the modern technical age. The advantages which are on the surface and can convince at once. In the end we quarrelled. She had thin-soled shoes on her feet and must have felt every stone through them; she was pretty good to have stuck it so long. I shouted at her, too, because I knew that was the only way to part company and forget each other, the only way for me to free myself from this girl and her masterful affections. I helped her up the bank, then I heard the squeal of brakes, handlamps stopped just behind her and lit up her figure from all sides. My last glimpse of her was as she shaded her eyes from the glare, looking like a lovely blind girl.

It was morning before I reached a village, and in daylight I realized that the motorway had been planned so as to by-pass the villages and allow fast traffic. The place was called Old Georgetown and looked like something out of a dream, tumbledown castle and all. The children wore school uniforms and the men wore very broad trousers. I was in the birthplace of my car. I felt that it must be a dream. I looked for number twenty-six.

'James Stuart died in thirty-two, sir,' an elderly secretary with a blonde bun told me in the office. 'The firm has been closed down since then. I just look after things for the bank because we cannot find a buyer.' She pointed to the yard beyond the broken window. It was a graveyard for racing cars, piled with unfinished chassis, cars smashed up in races, bones and bonnets of cars. Hens and ducks wandered about in the knee-high grass.

'What happened to the cars he made?' I asked.

'There's not one of them on the road today,' said the elderly lady bitterly, and sat down to a typewriter that dated from the beginning of the century, and on which the letters moved instead of the roller. 'Not one of the grand old cars that Caracciola himself used to drive. They won every race they went in for,' she snapped suddenly, as though I voiced an objection, and then she pointed to the dusty trophies on the walls. 'It was the depression that did for us. There were no rich men left to order hand-made cars. Mr Stuart finished the last of his cars the day before the banks ruined him. He set out from Old Georgetown in it and was never heard of again . . .' On a yellowing photograph Mr Stuart stood with one hand on the bonnet of my car. It was not the thin man I had seen in London. God knows how many people that car had sucked dry in between.

'I have heard of him,' I said in my bad English, 'and I know where that last car of his is now . . .' I thought she started in fright.

'It's the best car in the world, with sixteen forward gears and two reserve brakes on each wheel. Nobody has made a car that could accelerate like that since.'

'A car that kills . . .' I told her.

'It will win every race in the world for you, you will live in ease and live for nothing but sport . . .'

'And death.' She could not understand. Of course she knew all about the car. She had even perhaps helped Mr Stuart to get his own back on the society that had beggared him and did not give his genius a chance. 'Here are the keys,' I said as I laid them on the table. 'I don't want your car. In return perhaps you will allow me to ring Bolster . . .'

'You're a foreigner, aren't you,' she said when she picked up the keys, as though that explained everything. I nodded and waited to be put through to Bolster. I had to spell out my friend's name and even then they mixed it up. It took half an hour before they got hold of him. He promised to send someone for me; his surprise gave way to severity, but I was glad to hear him, anyway.

I waited for him in the Stuart yard and that was where the Marchioness of Nuvolari found me.

'Here's our Chaeron,' she said, 'now don't try and tell me you've never done any racing. I'd give a lot for your skill. And your car. You were right; I'm going to sell my Cunningham. I don't know how it is but the Americans are no good at racing cars. I want to buy your car. How much do you want for it?' I sent her inside; perhaps if she buys it the old lady will be able to buy a better typewriter. I did not warn her until she came out with the keys in her hand.

'I'll tell you where I left the car, of course, but I must warn you the car will kill you . . .' then I told her all I knew about the thing.

'How very interesting,' she said politely.

'It's a vampire, I must impress it on you. The accelerator sucks your life's blood . . .!' She laughed.

'Then it's really worth the money. What do you think the others cars run on, anyway? What did I pay for my gas with, what did I have to give for it? I had to sacrifice myself if I wanted to have the cars. And in the most complicated manner. This will only make it so much simpler. The only thing I want is to win the Le Mans race once in my life, and beat all the aces. Then I shall die in peace. I know I shall win, I worked out your speed yesterday. It's a wonderful car, I shall win all along the line.'

'You will kill yourself . . .'

'That doesn't matter . . .' and then I understood why nobody had returned that car in all those years, since nineteen thirty-two, why every driver had gladly sold his soul to that mechanical devil and let that vampire suck his blood. Because they could get ahead of all the others.

Later, as the Marchioness's chauffeur drove me to Bolster in her old Cunningham it seemed as though all the cars on that six-lane motorway were competing in that great unofficial race in which death did not matter.

I got to Bolster before the first session started. My colleague had not yet rung up the Embassy to report me. Everything turned out all right except that I did not have time to shave.

And that I never saw Susan Saunders again.

CHASTEL

Manly Wade Wellman

Manly Wade Wellman (1903–86) was among
the most popular writers for the legendary
Weird Tales magazine in the 1930s and 1940s.
His sixty-five books include biographies,
regional histories, mainstream fiction, mystery
novels, science fiction and fantasy.
He wrote several excellent vampire stories
including 'The Horror Undying' (1936),
'School for the Unspeakable' (1937), 'When It
Was Moonlight' (1940), and 'The Last Grave of
Lill Warren' (1951).
'Chastel', one of his finest later tales, first
appeared in the seventh *Year's Best Horror*
volume (1979), and was reprinted in his rare
American collection *The Valley So Low* (1987).

'Then you won't let Count Dracula rest in his tomb?' inquired Lee
Cobbett, his square face creasing with a grin.

Five of them sat in the parlour of Judge Keith Hilary
Pursuivant's hotel suite on Central Park West. The Judge lounged in an
armchair, a wineglass in his big old hand. On this, his eighty-seventh
birthday, his blue eyes were clear, penetrating. His once tawny hair and
moustache had gone blizzard-white, but both grew thick, and his square
face showed rosy. In his tailored blue leisure suit, he still looked
powerfully deep-chested and broad shouldered.

Blocky Lee Cobbett wore jacket and slacks almost as brown as his face.
Next to him sat Laurel Parcher, small and young and cinnamon haired.
The others were natty Phil Drumm the summer theatre producer, and

Isobel Arrington from a wire press service. She was blonde, expensively dressed, she smoked a dark cigarette with a white tip. Her pen scribbled swiftly.

'Dracula's as much alive as Sherlock Holmes,' argued Drumm. 'All the revivals of the play, all the films—'

'Your musical should wake the dead, anyway,' said Cobbett, drinking. 'What's your main number, Phil? "Garlic Time?" "Gory, Gory Hallelujah?"'

'Let's have Christian charity here, Lee,' Pursuivant came to Drumm's rescue. 'Anyway, Miss Arrington came to interview me. Pour her some wine and let me try to answer her questions.'

'I'm interested in Mr Cobbett's remarks,' said Isobel Arrington, her voice deliberately throaty. 'He's an authority on the supernatural.'

'Well, perhaps,' admitted Cobbett, 'and Miss Parcher has had some experiences. But Judge Pursuivant is the true authority, the author of *Vampiricon.*'

'I've read it, in paperback,' said Isobel Arrington. 'Phil, it mentions a vampire belief up in Connecticut, where you're having your show. What's that town again?'

'Deslow,' he told her. 'We're making a wonderful old stone barn into a theatre. I've invited Lee and Miss Parcher to visit.'

She looked at Drumm. 'Is Deslow a resort town?'

'Not yet, but maybe the show will bring tourists. In Deslow, up to now, peace and quiet is the chief business. If you drop your shoe, everybody in town will think somebody's blowing the safe.'

'Deslow's not far from Jewett City,' observed Pursuivant. 'There were vampires there about a century and a quarter ago. A family named Ray was afflicted. And to the east, in Rhode Island, there was a lively vampire folklore in recent years.'

'Let's leave Rhode Island to H. P. Lovecraft's imitators,' suggested Cobbett. 'What do you call your show, Phil?'

'*The Land Beyond the Forest,*' said Drumm. 'We're casting it now. Using locals in bit parts. But we have Gonda Chastel to play Dracula's countess.'

'I never knew that Dracula had a countess,' said Laurel Parcher.

'There was a stage star named Chastel, long ago when I was young,' said Pursuivant. 'Just the one name – Chastel.'

'Gonda's her daughter, and a year or so ago Gonda came to live in Deslow,' Drumm told them. 'Her mother's buried there. Gonda has invested in our production.'

'Is that why she has a part in it?' asked Isobel Arrington.

'She has a part in it because she's beautiful and gifted,' replied Drumm, rather stuffily. 'Old people say she's the very picture of her mother. Speaking of pictures, here are some to prove it.'

He offered two glossy prints to Isobel Arrington, who murmured 'Very sweet,' and passed them to Laurel Parcher. Cobbett leaned to see.

One picture seemed copied from an older one. It showed a woman who stood with unconscious stateliness, in a gracefully draped robe with a tiara binding her rich flow of dark hair. The other picture was of a woman in fashionable evening dress, her hair ordered in modern fashion, with a face strikingly like that of the woman in the other photograph.

'Oh, she's lovely,' said Laurel. 'Isn't she, Lee?'

'Isn't she?' echoed Drumm.

'Magnificent,' said Cobbett, handing the pictures to Pursuivant, who studied them gravely.

'Chastel was in Richmond, just after the First World War,' he said slowly. 'A dazzling Lady Macbeth. I was in love with her. Everyone was.'

'Did you tell her you loved her?' asked Laurel.

'Yes. We had supper together, twice. Then she went ahead with her tour, and I sailed to England and studied at Oxford. I never saw her again, but she's more or less why I never married.'

Silence a moment. Then: '*The Land Beyond the Forest*,' Laurel repeated. 'Isn't there a book called that?'

'There is indeed, my child,' said the Judge. 'By Emily de Laszowska Gerard. About Transylvania, where Dracula came from.'

'That's why we use the title, that's what Transylvania means,' put in Drumm. 'It's all right, the book's out of copyright. But I'm surprised to find someone who's heard of it.'

'I'll protect your guilty secret, Phil,' promised Isobel Arrington. 'What's over there in your window, Judge?'

Pursuivant turned to look. 'Whatever it is,' he said, 'it's not Peter Pan.'

Cobbett sprang up and ran toward the half-draped window. A silhouette with head and shoulders hung in the June night. He had a glimpse of a face, rich mouthed, with bright eyes. Then it was gone. Laurel had hurried up behind him. He hoisted the window sash and leaned out.

Nothing. The street was fourteen storeys down. The lights of moving cars crawled distantly. The wall below was course after course of dull brick, with recesses of other windows to right and left, below, above. Cobbett studied the wall, his hands braced on the sill.

[161]

'Be careful, Lee,' Laurel's voice besought him.

He came back to face the others. 'Nobody out there,' he said evenly. 'Nobody could have been. It's just a wall – nothing to hang to. Even that sill would be tricky to stand on.'

'But I saw something, and so did Judge Pursuivant,' said Isobel Arrington, the cigarette trembling on her fingers.

'So did I,' said Cobbett. 'Didn't you, Laurel?'

'Only a face.'

Isobel Arrington was calm again. 'If it's a trick, Phil, you played a good one. But don't expect me to put it in my story.'

Drumm shook his head nervously. 'I didn't play any trick, I swear.'

'Don't try this on old friends,' she jabbed at him. 'First those pictures, then whatever was up against the glass. I'll use the pictures, but I won't write that a weird vision presided over this birthday party.'

'How about a drink all around?' suggested Pursuivant.

He poured for them. Isobel Arrington wrote down her answers to more questions, then said she must go. Drumm rose to escort her. 'You'll be at Deslow tomorrow, Lee?' he asked.

'And Laurel, too. You said we could find quarters there.'

'The Mapletree's a good motel,' said Drumm. 'I've already reserved cabins for the two of you.'

'On the spur of the moment,' said Pursuivant suddenly, 'I think I'll come along, if there's space for me.'

'I'll check it out for you, Judge,' said Drumm.

He departed with Isobel Arrington. Cobbett spoke to Pursuivant. 'Isn't that rather offhand?' he asked. 'Deciding to come with us?'

'I was thinking about Chastel.' Pursuivant smiled gently. 'About making a pilgrimage to her grave.'

'We'll drive up about nine tomorrow morning.'

'I'll be ready, Lee.'

Cobbett and Laurel, too, went out. They walked down a flight of stairs to the floor below, where both their rooms were located. 'Do you think Phil Drumm rigged up that illusion for us?' asked Cobbett.

'If he did, he used the face of that actress, Chastel.'

He glanced keenly at her. 'You saw that.'

'I thought I did, and so did you.'

They kissed goodnight at the door to her room.

Pursuivant was ready next morning when Cobbett knocked. He had only one suitcase and a thick, brown-blotched malacca cane, banded with silver below its curved handle.

'I'm taking only a few necessaries, I'll buy socks and such things in Deslow if we stay more than a couple of days,' he said. 'No, don't carry it for me, I'm quite capable.'

When they reached the hotel garage, Laurel was putting her luggage in the trunk of Cobbett's black sedan. Judge Pursuivant declined the front seat beside Cobbett, held the door for Laurel to get in, and sat in the rear. They rolled out into bright June sunlight.

Cobbett drove them east on Interstate 95, mile after mile along the Connecticut shore, past service stations, markets, sandwich shops. Now and then they glimpsed Long Island Sound to the right. At toll gates, Cobbett threw quarters into hoppers and drove on.

'New Rochelle to Port Chester,' Laurel half chanted, 'Norwalk, Bridgeport, Stratford—'

'Where, in 1851, devils plagued a minister's home,' put in Pursuivant.

'That name makes a poem,' said Laurel.

'You can get that effect by reading any timetable,' said Cobbett. 'We miss a couple of good names – Mystic and Giants Neck, though they aren't far off from our route. And Griswold – that means Gray Woods – where the Judge's book says Horace Ray was born.'

'There's no Griswold on the Connecticut map anymore,' said the Judge.

'Vanished?' said Laurel. 'Maybe it appears at just a certain time of the day, along about sundown.'

She laughed, but the Judge was grave.

'Here we'll pass by New Haven,' he said. 'I was at Yale here, seventy years ago.'

They rolled across the Connecticut River between Old Saybrook and Old Lyme. Outside New London, Cobbett turned them north on State Highway 82 and, near Jewett City, took a two-lane road that brought them into Deslow, not long after noon.

There were pleasant clapboard cottages among elm trees and flower beds. Main Street had bright shops with, farther along, the belfry of a sturdy old church. Cobbett drove them to a sign saying MAPLETREE COURT. A row of cabins faced along a cement-floored colonnade, their fronts painted white with blue doors and window frames. In the office, Phil Drumm stood at the desk, talking to the plump proprietress.

'Welcome home,' he greeted them. 'Judge, I was asking Mrs Simpson here to reserve you a cabin.'

[163]

'At the far end of the row, sir,' the lady said. 'I'd have put you next to your two friends, but so many theatre folks have already moved in.'

'Long ago I learned to be happy with any shelter,' the Judge assured her.

They saw Laurel to her cabin and put her suitcases inside, then walked to the farthest cabin where Pursuivant would stay. Finally Drumm followed Cobbett to the space next to Laurel's. Inside, Cobbett produced a fifth of bourbon from his briefcase. Drumm trotted away to fetch ice. Pursuivant came to join them.

'It's good of you to look after us,' Cobbett said to Drumm above his glass.

'Oh, I'll get my own back,' Drumm assured him. 'The Judge and you, distinguished folklore experts – I'll have you in all the papers.'

'Whatever you like,' said Cobbett, 'Let's have lunch, as soon as Laurel is freshened up.'

The four ate crab cakes and flounder at a little restaurant while Drumm talked about *The Land Beyond the Forest*. He had signed the minor film star Caspar Merrick to play Dracula. 'He has a fine baritone singing voice,' said Drumm. 'He'll be at afternoon rehearsal.'

'And Gonda Chastel?' inquired Pursuivant, buttering a roll.

'She'll be there tonight.' Drumm sounded happy about that. 'This afternoon's mostly for bits and chorus numbers. I'm directing as well as producing.' They finished their lunch, and Drumm rose. 'If you're not tired, come see our theatre.'

It was only a short walk through town to the converted barn. Cobbett judged it had been built in Colonial times, with a recent roof of composition tile, but with walls of stubborn, brown-grey New England stone. Across a narrow side street stood the old white church, with a hedge-bordered cemetery.

'Quaint, that old burying ground,' commented Drumm. 'Nobody's spaded under there now, there's a modern cemetery on the far side, but Chastel's tomb is there. Quite a picturesque one.'

'I'd like to see it,' said Pursuivant, leaning on his silver-banded cane.

The barn's interior was set with rows of folding chairs, enough for several hundred spectators. On a stage at the far end, workmen moved here and there under lights. Drumm led his guests up steps at the side.

High in the loft, catwalks zigzagged and a dark curtain hung like a broad guillotine blade. Drumm pointed out canvas flats, painted to resemble grim castle walls. Pursuivant nodded and questioned.

'I'm no authority on what you might find in Transylvania,' he said, 'but this looks convincing.'

A man walked from the wings toward them. 'Hello, Caspar,' Drumm greeted him. 'I want you to meet Judge Pursuivant and Lee Cobbett. And Miss Laurel Parcher, of course.' He gestured the introductions. 'This is Mr Caspar Merrick, our Count Dracula.'

Merrick was elegantly tall, handsome, with carefully groomed black hair. Sweepingly he bowed above Laurel's hand and smiled at them all. 'Judge Pursuivant's writings I know, of course,' he said richly. 'I read what I can about vampires, inasmuch as I'm to be one.'

'Places for the Delusion number!' called a stage manager.

Cobbett, Pursuivant and Laurel went down the steps and sat on chairs. Eight men and eight girls hurried into view, dressed in knockabout summer clothes. Someone struck chords on a piano, Drumm gestured importantly, and the chorus sang. Merrick, coming downstage, took solo on a verse. All joined in the refrain. Then Drumm made them sing it over again.

After that, two comedians made much of confusing the words vampire and empire. Cobbett found it tedious. He excused himself to his companions and strolled out and across to the old, tree-crowded churchyard.

The gravestones bore interesting epitaphs: not only the familiar PAUSE O STRANGER PASSING BY/ AS YOU ARE NOW SO ONCE WAS I, and A BUD ON EARTH TO BLOOM IN HEAVEN, but several of more originality. One bewailed a man who, since he had been lost at sea, could hardly have been there at all. Another bore, beneath a bat-winged face, the declaration DEATH PAYS ALL DEBTS and the date 1907, which Cobbett associated with a financial panic.

Toward the centre of the graveyard, under a drooping willow, stood a shedlike structure of heavy granite blocks. Cobbett picked his way to the door of heavy grillwork, which was fastened with a rusty padlock the size of a sardine can. On the lintel were strongly carved letters: CHASTEL.

Here, then, was the tomb of the stage beauty Pursuivant remembered so romantically. Cobbett peered through the bars.

It was murkily dusty in there. The floor was coarsely flagged, and among sooty shadows at the rear stood a sort of stone chest that must contain the body. Cobbett turned and went back to the theatre. Inside, piano music rang wildly and the people of the chorus desperately rehearsed what must be meant for a folk dance.

'Oh, it's exciting,' said Laurel as Cobbett sat down beside her. 'Where have you been?'

'Visiting the tomb of Chastel.'

'Chastel?' echoed Pursuivant. 'I must see that tomb.'

Songs and dance ensembles went on. In the midst of them, a brisk reporter from Hartford appeared, to interview Pursuivant and Cobbett. At last Drumm resoundingly dismissed the players on stage and joined his guests.

'Principals rehearse at eight o'clock,' he announced. 'Gonda Chastel will be here, she'll want to meet you. Could I count on you then?'

'Count on me, at least,' said Pursuivant. 'Just now, I feel like resting before dinner, and so, I think does Laurel here.'

'Yes, I'd like to lie down for a little,' said Laurel.

'Why don't we all meet for dinner at the place where we had lunch?' said Cobbett. 'You can come too, Phil.'

'Thanks, I have a date with some backers from New London.'

It was half past five when they went out.

Cobbett went to his quarters, stretched out on the bed, and gave himself to thought.

He hadn't come to Deslow because of this musical interpretation of the Dracula legend. Laurel had come because he was coming, and Pursuivant on a sudden impulse that might have been more than a wish to visit the grave of Chastel. But Cobbett was here because this, he knew, had been vampire country, maybe still was vampire country.

He remembered the story in Pursuivant's book about vampires at Jewett City, as reported in the Norwich *Courier* for 1854. Horace Ray, from the now vanished town of Griswold, had died of a 'wasting disease'. Thereafter his oldest son, then his second son had also gone to their graves. When a third son sickened, friends and relatives dug up Horace Ray and the two dead brothers and burned the bodies in a roaring fire. The surviving son got well. And something like that had happened in Exeter, near Providence in Rhode Island. Very well, why organize and present the Dracula musical here in Deslow, so near those places?

Cobbett had met Phil Drumm in the South the year before, knew him for a brilliant if erratic producer, who relished tales of devils and the dead who walk by night. Drumm might have known enough stage magic to have rigged that seeming appearance at Pursuivant's window in New York. That is, if indeed it was only a seeming appearance, not a real face. Might it have been real, a manifestation of the unreal? Cobbett had seen enough of what people dismissed as unreal, impossible, to wonder.

A soft knock came at the door. It was Laurel. She wore green slacks, a green jacket, and she smiled, as always, at sight of Cobbett's face. They sought Pursuivant's cabin. A note on the door said: MEET ME AT THE CAFÉ.

When they entered there, Pursuivant hailed them from the kitchen

[166]

door. 'Dinner's ready,' he hailed them. 'I've been supervising in person, and I paid well for the privilege.'

A waiter brought a laden tray. He arranged platters of red-drenched spaghetti and bowls of salad on a table. Pursuivant himself sprinkled Parmesan cheese. 'No salt or pepper,' he warned. 'I seasoned it myself, and you can take my word it's exactly right.'

Cobbett poured red wine into glasses. Laurel took a forkful of spaghetti. 'Delicious,' she cried. 'What's in it, Judge?'

'Not only ground beef and tomatoes and onions and garlic,' replied Pursuivant. 'I added marjoram and green pepper and chili and thyme and bay leaf and oregano and parsley and a couple of other important ingredients. And I also minced in some Italian sausage.'

Cobbett, too, ate with enthusiastic appetite. 'I won't order any dessert,' he declared. 'I want to keep the taste of this in my mouth.'

'There's more in the kitchen for dessert if you want it,' the Judge assured him. 'But here, I have a couple of keepsakes for you.'

He handed each of them a small, silvery object. Cobbett examined his. It was smoothly wrapped in foil. He wondered if it was a nutmeat.

'You have pockets, I perceive,' the Judge said. 'Put those into them. And don't open them, or my wish for you won't come true.'

When they had finished eating, a full moon had begun to rise in the darkening sky. They headed for the theatre.

A number of visitors sat in the chairs and the stage lights looked bright. Drumm stood beside the piano, talking to two plump men in summer business suits. As Pursuivant and the others came down the aisle, Drumm eagerly beckoned them and introduced them to his companions, the financial backers with whom he had taken dinner.

'We're very much interested,' said one. 'This vampire legend intrigues anyone, if you forget that a vampire's motivation is simply nourishment.'

'No, something more than that,' offered Pursuivant. 'A social motivation.'

'Social motivation,' repeated the other backer.

'A vampire wants company of its own kind. A victim infected becomes a vampire, too, and an associate. Otherwise the original vampire would be a disconsolate loner.'

'There's a lot in what you say,' said Drumm, impressed.

After that there was financial talk, something in which Cobbett could not intelligently join. Then someone else approached, and both the backers stared.

It was a tall, supremely graceful woman with red-lighted black hair in

[167]

a bun at her nape, a woman of impressive figure and assurance. She wore a sweeping blue dress, fitted to her slim waist, with a frill-edged neckline. Her arms were bare and white and sweetly turned, with jewelled bracelets on them. Drumm almost ran to bring her close to the group.

'Gonda Chastel,' he said, half-prayerfully. 'Gonda, you'll want to meet these people.'

The two backers stuttered admiringly at her. Pursuivant bowed and Laurel smiled. Gonda Chastel gave Cobbett her slim, cool hand. 'You know so much about this thing we're trying to do here,' she said, in a voice like cream.

Drumm watched them. His face looked plaintive.

'Judge Pursuivant has taught me a lot, Miss Chastel,' said Cobbett. 'He'll tell you that once he knew your mother.'

'I remember her, not very clearly,' said Gonda Chastel. 'She died when I was just a little thing, thirty years ago. And I followed her here, now I make my home here.'

'You look very like her,' said Pursuivant.

'I'm proud to be like my mother in any way,' she smiled at them. She could be overwhelming, Cobbett told himself.

'And Miss Parcher,' went on Gonda Chastel, turning toward Laurel. 'What a little presence she is. She should be in our show – I don't know what part, but she should.' she smiled dazzlingly. 'Now then, Phil wants me on stage.'

'Knock-at-the-door number, Gonda,' said Drumm.

Gracefully she mounted the steps. The piano sounded, and she sang. It was the best song, felt Cobbett, that he had heard so far in the rehearsals. 'Are they seeking for a shelter from the night?' Gonda Chastel sang richly. Caspar Merrick entered, to join in a recitative. Then the chorus streamed on, singing somewhat shrilly.

Pursuivant and Laurel had sat down. Cobbett strode back up the aisle and out under a moon that rained silver-blue light.

He found his way to the churchyard. The trees that had offered pleasant afternoon shade now made a dubious darkness. He walked underneath branches that seemed to lower like hovering wings as he approached the tomb structure at the centre.

The barred door that had been massively locked now stood open. He peered into the gloom within. After a moment he stepped across the threshold upon the flagged floor.

He had to grope, with one hand upon the rough wall. At last he almost stumbled upon the great stone chest at the rear.

It, too, was flung open, its lid heaved back against the wall.

There was, of course, complete darkness within it. He flicked on his cigar lighter. The flame showed him the inside of the stone coffer, solidly made and about ten feet long. Its sides of grey marble were snugly fitted. Inside lay a coffin of rich dark wood with silver fittings and here, yet again, was an open lid.

Bending close to the smudged silk lining, Cobbett seemed to catch an odour of stuffy sharpness, like dried herbs. He snapped off his light and frowned in the dark. Then he groped back to the door, emerged into the open, and headed for the theatre again.

'Mr Cobbett,' said the beautiful voice of Gonda Chastel.

She stood at the graveyard's edge, beside a sagging willow. She was almost as tall as he. Her eyes glowed in the moonlight.

'You came to find the truth about my mother,' she half-accused.

'I was bound to try,' he replied. 'Ever since I saw a certain face at a certain window of a certain New York hotel.'

She stepped back from him. 'You know she's a—'

'A vampire,' Cobbett finished for her. 'Yes.'

'I beg you to be helpful – merciful.' But here was no supplication in her voice. 'I already realized, long ago. That's why I live in little Deslow. I want to find a way to give her rest. Night after night, I wonder how.'

'I understand that,' said Cobbett.

Gonda Chastel breathed deeply. 'You know all about these things. I think there's something about you that could daunt a vampire.'

'If so, I don't know what it is,' said Cobbett truthfully.

'Make me a solemn promise. That you won't return to her tomb, that you won't tell others what you and I know about her. I – I want to think how we two together can do something for her.'

'If you wish, I'll say nothing,' he promised.

Her hand clutched his.

'The cast took a five-minute break, it must be time to go to work again,' she said, suddenly bright. 'Let's go back and help the thing along.'

They went.

Inside, the performers were gathering on stage. Drumm stared unhappily as Gonda Chastel and Cobbett came down the aisle. Cobbett sat with Laurel and Pursuivant and listened to the rehearsal.

Adaptation from Bram Stoker's novel was free, to say the least. Dracula's eerie plottings were much hampered by his having a countess, a walking dead beauty who strove to become a spirit of good. There were some songs, in interesting minor keys. There was a dance, in which men and women leaped like kangaroos. Finally Drumm called a halt, and the performers trooped wearily to the wings.

[169]

Gonda Chastel lingered, talking to Laurel. 'I wonder, my dear, if you haven't had acting experience,' she said.

'Only in school entertainments down South, when I was little.'

'Phil,' said Gonda Chastel, 'Miss Parcher is a good type, has good presence. There ought to be something for her in the show.'

'You're very kind, but I'm afraid that's impossible,' said Laurel, smiling.

'You may change your mind, Miss Parcher. Will you and your friends come to my house for a nightcap?'

'Thank you,' said Pursuivant. 'We have some notes to make, and we must make them together.'

'Until tomorrow evening, then. Mr Cobbett, we'll remember our agreement.'

She went away toward the back of the stage. Pursuivant and Laurel walked out. Drumm hurried up the aisle and caught Cobbett's elbow.

'I saw you,' he said harshly. 'Saw you both as you came in.'

'And we saw you, Phil. What's this about?'

'She likes you.' It was half an accusation. 'Fawns on you, almost.'

Cobbett grinned and twitched his arm free. 'What's the matter, Phil, are you in love with her?'

'Yes, God damn it, I am. I'm in love with her. She knows it but she won't let me come to her house. And you – the first time she meets you, she invites you.'

'Easy does it, Phil,' said Cobbett. 'If it'll do you any good, I'm in love with someone else, and that takes just about all my spare time.'

He hurried out to overtake his companions.

Pursuivant swung his cane almost jauntily as they returned through the moonlight to the auto court.

'What notes are you talking about, Judge?' asked Cobbett.

'I'll tell you at my quarters. What do you think of the show?'

'Perhaps I'll like it better after they've rehearsed more,' said Laurel. 'I don't follow it at present.'

'Here and there, it strikes me as limp,' added Cobbett.

They sat down in the Judge's cabin. He poured them drinks. 'Now,' he said, 'there are certain things to recognize here. Things I more or less expected to find.'

'A mystery, Judge?' asked Laurel.

'Not so much that, if I expected to find them. How far are we from Jewett City?'

'Twelve or fifteen miles as the crow flies,' estimated Cobbett. 'And Jewett City is where that vampire family, the Rays, lived and died.'

'Died twice, you might say,' nodded Pursuivant, stroking his white moustache. 'Back about a century and a quarter ago. And here's what might be a matter of Ray family history. I've been thinking about Chastel, whom once I greatly admired. About her full name.'

'But she had only one name, didn't she?' asked Laurel.

'On the stage she used one name, yes. So did Bernhardt, so did Duse, so later did Garbo. But all of them had full names. Now, before we went to dinner, I made two telephone calls to theatrical historians I know. To learn Chastel's full name.'

'And she had a full name,' prompted Cobbett.

'Indeed she did. Her full name was Chastel Ray.'

Cobbett and Laurel looked at him in deep silence.

'Not apt to be just coincidence,' elaborated Pursuivant. 'Now then, I gave you some keepsakes today.'

'Here's mine,' said Cobbett, pulling the foil-wrapped bit from his shirt pocket.

'And I have mine here,' said Laurel, her hand at her throat. 'In a little locket I have on this chain.'

'Keep it there,' Pursuivant urged her. 'Wear it around your neck at all times. Lee, have yours always on your person. Those are garlic cloves, and you know what they're good for. You can also guess why I cut up a lot of garlic in our spaghetti for dinner.'

'You think there's a vampire here,' offered Laurel.

'A specific vampire.' The Judge took a deep breath into his broad chest. 'Chastel. Chastel Ray'.

'I believe it, too,' declared Cobbett tonelessly, and Laurel nodded. Cobbett looked at the watch on his wrist.

'It's past one in the morning,' he said. 'Perhaps we'd all be better off if we had some sleep.'

They said their goodnights and Laurel and Cobbett walked to where their two doors stood side by side. Laurel put her key into the lock, but did not turn it at once. She peered across the moonlit street.

'Who's that over there?' she whispered. 'Maybe I ought to say, what's that?'

Cobbett looked. 'Nothing, you're just nervous. Goodnight, dear.'

She went in and shut the door. Cobbett quickly crossed the street.

'Mr Cobbett,' said the voice of Gonda Chastel.

'I wondered what you wanted, so late at night,' he said, walking close to her.

She had undone her dark hair and let it flow to her shoulders. She was, Cobbett thought, as beautiful a woman as he had ever seen.

'I wanted to be sure about you,' she said. 'That you'd respect your promise to me, not to go into the churchyard.'

'I keep my promises, Miss Chastel.'

He felt a deep, hushed silence all around them. Not even the leaves rustled in the trees.

'I had hoped you wouldn't venture even this far,' she went on. 'You and your friends are new in town, you might tempt her specially.' Her eyes burned at him. 'You know I don't mean that as a compliment.'

She turned to walk away. He fell into step beside her. 'But you're not afraid of her,' he said.

'Of my own mother?'

'She was a Ray,' said Cobbett. 'Each Ray sapped the blood of his kinsmen. Judge Pursuivant told me all about it.'

Again the gaze of her dark, brilliant eyes. 'Nothing like that has ever happened between my mother and me.' She stopped, and so did he. Her slim, strong hand took him by the wrist.

'You're wise and brave,' she said. 'I think you may have come here for a good purpose, not just about the show.'

'I try to have good purposes.'

The light of the moon soaked through the overhead branches as they walked on. 'Will you come to my house?' she invited.

'I'll walk to the churchyard,' replied Cobbett. 'I said I wouldn't go into it, but I can stand at the edge.'

'Don't go in.'

'I've promised that I wouldn't, Miss Chastel.'

She walked back the way they had come. He followed the street on under silent elms until he reached the border of the churchyard. Moonlight flecked and spattered the tombstones. Deep shadows lay like pools. He had a sense of being watched from within.

As he gazed, he saw movement among the graves. He could not define it, but it was there. He glimpsed, or fancied he glimpsed, a head, indistinct in outline as though swathed in dark fabric. Then another. Another. They huddled in a group, as though to gaze at him.

'I wish you'd go back to your quarters.' said Gonda Chastel beside him. She had drifted after him, silent as the shadow herself.

'Miss Chastel,' he said, 'tell me something if you can. Whatever happened to the town or village of Griswold?'

'Griswold?' she echoed. 'What's Griswold? That means grey woods.'

'Your ancestor, or your relative, Horace Ray, came from Griswold to

[172]

CHASTEL

die in Jewett City. And I've told you that I knew your mother was born a Ray.'

Her shining eyes seemed to flood upon him. 'I didn't know that,' she said

He gazed into the churchyard, at those hints of furtive movement.

'The hands of the dead reach out for the living,' murmured Gonda Chastel.

'Reach out for me?' he asked.

'Perhaps for both of us. Just now, we may be the only living souls awake in Deslow.' She gazed at him again. 'But you're able to defend yourself, somehow.'

'What makes you think that?' he inquired, aware of the clove of garlic in his shirt pocket.

'Because they – in the churchyard there – they watch, but they hold away from you. You don't invite them.'

'Nor do you, apparently,' said Cobbett.

'I hope you're not trying to make fun of me,' she said, her voice barely audible.

'On my soul, I'm not.'

'On your soul,' she repeated. 'Goodnight, Mr Cobbett.'

Again she moved away, tall and proud and graceful. He watched her out of sight. Then he headed back toward the motor court.

Nothing moved in the empty street. Only one or two lights shone here and there in closed shops. He thought he heard a soft rustle behind him, but did not look back.

As he reached his own door, he heard Laurel scream behind hers.

Judge Pursuivant sat in his cubicle, his jacket off, studying a worn little brown book. Skinner, said letters on the spine, and *Myths and Legends of Our Own Land*. He had read the passage so often that he could almost repeat it from memory:

'To lay this monster he must be taken up and burned; at least his heart must be; and he must be disinterred in the daytime when he is asleep and unaware.'

There were other ways, reflected Pursuivant.

It must be very late by now, rather it must be early. But he had no intention of going to sleep. Not when stirs of motion sounded outside, along the concrete walkway in front of his cabin. Did motion stand still, just beyond the door there? Pursuivant's great, veined hand touched the front of his shirt, beneath which a bag of garlic hung like an amulet. Garlic – was that enough? He himself was fond of garlic, judiciously

[173]

employed in sauces and salads. But then, he could see himself in the mirror of the bureau yonder, could see his broad old face with its white sweep of moustache like a wreath of snow on a sill. It was a clear image of a face, not a calm face just then, but a determined one. Pursuivant smiled at it, with a glimpse of even teeth that were still his own.

He flicked up his shirt cuff and looked at his watch. Half past one, about. In June, even with daylight saving time, dawn would come early. Dawn sent vampires back to the tombs that were their melancholy refuges, 'asleep and unaware', as Skinner had specified.

Putting the book aside, he poured himself a small drink of bourbon, dropped in cubes of ice and a trickle of water, and sipped. He had drunk several times during that day, when on most days he partook of only a single highball, by advice of his doctor; but just now he was grateful for the pungent, walnutty taste of the liquor. It was one of earth's natural things, a good companion when not abused. From the table he took a folder of scribbled notes. He looked at jottings from the works of Montague Summers.

These offered the proposition that a plague of vampires usually stemmed from a single source of infection, a king or queen vampire whose feasts of blood drove victims to their graves, to rise in their turn. If the original vampires were found and destroyed, the others relaxed to rest as normally dead bodies. Bram Stoker had followed the same gospel when he wrote *Dracula*, and doubtless Bram Stoker had known. Pursuivant looked at another page, this time a poem copied from James Grant's curious *Mysteries of All Nations*. It was a ballad in archaic language, that dealt with baleful happenings in 'The Towne of Peste' – Budapest?

> It was the Corpses that our Churchyardes filled
> That did at midnight lumberr up our Stayres;
> They suck'd our Bloud, the gorie Banquet swilled,
> And harried everie Soule with hydeous Feares . . .

Several verses down:

> They barr'd with Boltes of Iron the Churchyard-pale
> To keep them out; but all this wold not doe;
> For when a Dead-Man had learn'd to draw a naile,
> He can also burst an iron Bolte in two.

Many times Pursuivant had tried to trace the author of that verse. He wondered if it was not something quaintly confected not long before

1880, when Grant published his work. At any rate, the Judge felt that he knew what it meant, the experience that it remembered.

He put aside the notes, too, and picked up his spotted walking stick. Clamping the balance of it firmly in his left hand, he twisted the handle with his right and pulled. Out of the hollow shank slid a pale, bright blade, keen and lean and edged on both front and back.

Pursuivant permitted himself a smile above it. This was one of his most cherished possessions, this silver weapon said to have been forged a thousand years ago by St Dunstan. Bending, he spelled out the runic writing upon it:

Sic pereant omnes inimici tui, Domine

That was the end of the fiercely triumphant song of Deborah in the Book of Judges: So perish all thine enemies, O Lord. Whether the work of St Dunstan or not, the metal was silver, the writing was a warrior's prayer. Silver and writing had proved their strength against evil in the past.

Then, outside, a loud, tremulous cry of mortal terror.

Pursuivant sprang out of his chair on the instant. Blade in hand, he fairly ripped his door open and ran out. He saw Cobbett in front of Laurel's door, wrenching at the knob, and hurried there like a man half his age.

'Open up, Laurel,' he heard Cobbett call. 'It's Lee out here!'

The door gave inward as Pursuivant reached it, and he and Cobbett pressed into the lighted room.

Laurel half-crouched in the middle of the floor. Her trembling hand pointed to a rear window. 'She tried to come in,' Laurel stammered.

'There's nothing at that window,' said Cobbett, but even as he spoke, there was. A face, pale as tallow, crowded against the glass. They saw wide, staring eyes, a mouth that opened and squirmed. Teeth twinkled sharply.

Cobbett started forward, but Pursuivant caught him by the shoulder. 'Let me,' he said, advancing toward the window, the point of his blade lifted.

The face at the window writhed convulsively as the silver weapon came against the pane with a clink. The mouth opened as though to shout, but no sound came. The face fell back and vanished from their sight.

'I've seen that face before,' said Cobbett hoarsely.

'Yes,' said Pursuivant. 'At my hotel window. And since.'

He dropped the point of the blade to the floor. Outside came a whirring rush of sound, like feet, many of them.

'We ought to wake up the people at the office,' said Cobbett.

'I doubt if anyone in this little town could be wakened,' Pursuivant told him evenly. 'I have it in mind that every living soul, except the three of us, is sound asleep. Entranced.'

'But out there—' Laurel gestured at the door, where something seemed to be pressing.

'I said, every living soul,' Pursuivant looked from her to Cobbett. 'Living,' he repeated.

He paced across the floor, and with his point scratched a perpendicular line upon it. Across this he carefully drove a horizontal line, making a cross. The pushing abruptly ceased.

'There it is, at the window again,' breathed Laurel.

Pursuivant took long steps to where the face hovered, with black hair streaming about it. He scraped the glass with his silver blade, up and down, then across, making lines upon it. The face drew away. He moved to mark similar crosses on the other windows.

'You see,' he said, quietly trimphant, 'the force of old, old charms.'

He sat down in a chair, heavily. His face was weary, but he looked at Laurel and smiled.

'It might help if we managed to pity those poor things out there,' he said.

'Pity?' she almost cried out.

'Yes,' he said, and quoted:

> '. . . Think how sad it must be
> To thirst always for a scorned elixir,
> The salt of quotidian blood.'

'I know that,' volunteered Cobbett. 'It's from a poem by Richard Wilbur, a damned unhappy poet.'

'Quotidian,' repeated Laurel to herself.

'That means something that keeps coming back, that returns daily,' Cobbett said.

'It's a term used to refer to a recurrent fever,' added Pursuivant.

Laurel and Cobbett sat down together on the bed.

'I would say that for the time being we're safe here,' declared Pursuivant. 'Not at ease, but at least safe. At dawn, danger will go to sleep and we can open the door.'

'But why are we safe, and nobody else?' Laurel cried out. 'Why are we awake, with everyone else in this town asleep and helpless?'

'Apparently because we all of us wear garlic,' replied Pursuivant

[176]

patiently, 'and because we ate garlic, plenty of it, at dinnertime. And because there are crosses – crude, but unmistakable – wherever something might try to come in. I won't ask you to be calm, but I'll ask you to be resolute.'

'I'm resolute,' said Cobbett between clenched teeth. 'I'm ready to go out there and face them.'

'If you did that, even with the garlic,' said Pursuivant, 'you'd last about as long as a pint of whiskey in a five-handed poker game. No, Lee, relax as much as you can, and let's talk.'

They talked, while outside strange presences could be felt rather than heard. Their talk was of anything and everything but where they were and why. Cobbett remembered strange things he had encountered, in towns, among mountains, along desolate roads, and what he had been able to do about them. Pursuivant told of a vampire he had known and defeated in upstate New York, of a werewolf in his own Southern countryside. Laurel, at Cobbett's urging, sang songs, old songs, from her own rustic home place. Her voice was sweet. When she sang 'Round is the Ring', faces came and hung like smudges outside the cross-scored windows. She saw, and sang again, an old Appalachian carol called 'Mary She Heared a Knock in the Night'. The faces drifted away again. And the hours, too, drifted away, one by one.

'There's a horde of vampires on the night street here, then.' Cobbett at last brought up the subject of their problem.

'And they lull the people of Deslow to sleep, to be helpless victims,' agreed Pursuivant. 'About this show, *The Land Beyond the Forest*, mightn't it be welcomed as a chance to spread the infection? Even a townful of sleepers couldn't feed a growing community of blood drinkers.'

'If we could deal with the source, the original infection—' began Cobbett.

'The mistress of them, the queen,' said Pursuivant. 'Yes. The one whose walking by night rouses them all. If she could be destroyed, they'd all die properly.'

He glanced at the front window. The moonlight had a touch of slaty grey.

'Almost morning,' he pronounced. 'Time for a visit to her tomb.'

'I gave my promise I wouldn't go there,' said Cobbett.

'But I didn't promise,' said Pursuivant, rising. 'You stay here with Laurel.'

His silver blade in hand, he stepped out into darkness from which the

[177]

moon had all but dropped away. Overhead, stars were fading out. Dawn was at hand.

He sensed a flutter of movement on the far side of the street, an almost inaudible gibbering of sound. Steadily he walked across. He saw nothing along the sidewalk there, heard nothing. Resolutely he tramped to the churchyard, his weapon poised. More greyness had come to dilute the dark.

He pushed his way through the hedge of shrubs, stepped in upon the grass, and paused at the side of a grave. Above it hung an eddy of soft mist, no larger than the swirl of water draining from a sink. As Pursuivant watched, it seemed to soak into the earth and disappear. That, he said to himself, is what a soul looks like when it seeks to regain its coffin.

On he walked, step by weary, purposeful step, toward the central crypt. A ray of the early sun, stealing between heavily leafed boughs, made his way more visible. In this dawn, he would find what he would find. He knew that.

The crypt's door of open bars was held shut by its heavy padlock. He examined that lock more closely. After a moment, he slid the point of his blade into the rusted keyhole and judiciously pressed this way, then that, and back again the first way. The spring creakily relaxed and he dragged the door open. Holding his breath, he entered.

The lid of the great stone vault was closed down. He took hold of the edge and heaved. The lid was heavy, but rose with a complaining grate of the hinges. Inside he saw a dark, closed coffin. He lifted the lid of that, too.

She lay there, calm-faced, the eyes half shut as though dozing.

'Chastel,' said Pursuivant to her. 'Not Gonda. Chastel.'

The eyelids fluttered. That was all, but he knew that she heard what he said.

'Now you can rest,' he said. 'Rest in peace, really in peace.'

He set the point of his silver blade at the swell of her left breast. Leaning both his broad hands upon the curved handle, he drove downward with all his strength.

She made a faint squeak of sound.

Blood sprang up as he cleared his weapon. More light shone in. He could see a dark moisture fading from the blade, like evaporating dew.

In the coffin, Chastel's proud shape shrivelled, darkened. Quickly he slammed the coffin shut, then lowered the lid of the vault into place and went quickly out. He pushed the door shut again and fastened the stubborn old lock. As he walked back through the churchyard among the graves, a bird twittered over his head. More distantly, he heard the hum of a car's motor. The town was waking up.

In the growing radiance, he walked back across the street. By now, his steps were the steps of an old man, old and very tired.

Inside Laurel's cabin, Laurel and Cobbett were stirring instant coffee into hot water in plastic cups. They questioned the Judge with their tired eyes.

'She's finished,' he said shortly.

'What will you tell Gonda?' asked Cobbett.

'Chastel was Gonda.'

'But—'

'She was Gonda,' said Pursuivant again, sitting down. 'Chastel died. The infection wakened her out of her tomb, and she told people she was Gonda, and naturally they believed her.' He sagged wearily. 'Now that she's finished and at rest, those others – the ones she had bled, who also rose at night – will rest, too.'

Laurel took a sip of coffee. Above the cup, her face was pale.

'Why do you say Chastel was Gonda?' she asked the Judge. 'How can you know that?'

'I wondered from the very beginning. I was utterly sure just now.'

'Sure?' said Laurel. 'How can you be sure?'

Pursuivant smiled at her, the very faintest of smiles.

'My dear, don't you think a man always recognizes a woman he has loved?'

He seemed to recover his characteristic defiant vigour. He rose and went to the door and put his hand on the knob. 'Now, if you'll just excuse me for a while.'

'Don't you think we'd better hurry and leave?' Cobbett asked him. 'Before people miss her and ask questions?'

'Not at all,' said Pursuivant, his voice strong again. 'If we're gone, they'll ask questions about us, too, possibly embarrassing questions. No, we'll stay. We'll eat a good breakfast, or at least pretend to eat it. And we'll be as surprised as the rest of them about the disappearance of their leading lady.'

'I'll do my best,' vowed Laurel.

'I know you will, my child,' said Pursuivant, and went out the door.

THE APPLES OF SODOM

David Rowlands

David Rowlands (born 1941), a biochemist by profession,
has had many fine supernatural stories published
in magazines and anthologies over the past twenty years.
Many of these feature (or are related by) the delightful
Catholic priest Father O'Connor. The following story
is taken from his 1980 collection of Fr O'Connor stories,
Eye Hath Not Seen . . .

(The apples of Sodom bear lovely fruit but within are full of ashes)

Father O'Connor bent forward to clean his pipe in anticipation of that first, after-dinner smoke. After banging it out against the bricks, he picked up an apple log, eyeing it thoughtfully.

The land upon which his little church had recently been built was donated by a farming parishioner, and had once been a small, enclosed apple orchard. With neglect, however, its fruit had become crabby, its trees twisted and wild. The good Father loved trees and regretted the necessity of grubbing up even so spoiled an orchard, but there was no denying the transient benefit to us: apple makes the best of firewoods! At this time, his store still held a few branches against winter; and so it was that an excellent fire was blazing in the red-brick hearth, the singing of the flames and crackling of devoured timber providing a background to our conversation.

'That log puts you in mind of something,' I said; as statement rather than question.

'Indeed it does.' He sighed a little as he replaced the log and began to dip his fingers into his shabby old tobacco pouch. 'The experience was one of the oddest, and in many ways the most incredible, of my ministry; yet there were also overtones of sardonic humour about it from a Catholic viewpoint.'

'Well,' I said, 'You *must* tell me about it now, Father. I am all attention.'

Instead of beginning, he lit his pipe and eased the slippers off his feet before swinging his cassocked legs up to rest on the fender.

'What do you know of vampires?,' he asked, seemingly going off at a tangent, between preliminary puffs.

'I suppose I know the usual mumbo-jumbo about how allegedly to lay them, with garlic and stake,' I answered, 'but are you telling me, Father, that you actually encountered one of these creatures?'

He smiled and made no direct reply.

'It was at my very first parish charge,' he said, 'a little village in Berkshire. I was fortunate in that the vicar of the Anglican community was as young as myself, as inexperienced and as inclined to be friendly. His parishioners resented him as an upstart who had replaced their well-loved old vicar of decades, and by the time I arrived, poor Baine – that was his name – had fallen foul of most of their cherished prejudices and customs! His friendship for me was the last straw and was seen by his Parochial Church Council to be a direct path to Rome.' He chuckled reminiscently. 'Time heals all; he has now been their vicar for some thirty years and any attempt to replace him would doubtless be resisted most strongly. We still correspond from time to time.

'Anyway, I had not been long about my duties and was, in fact, in the act of returning home to breakfast after early Mass, one delightful summer morning, when I heard my name called, and turned to see Baine sprinting after me in breathless haste. He accompanied me back to my lodgings. Waiting for us there was a sallow, gipsyish young fellow whom he introduced as Len James. It transpired that this fellow James was employed to keep the churchyard tidy.

'My splendid housekeeper rose to the occasion and produced extra coffee and breakfast. Mr James, at least, ate his as though he hadn't eaten for a fortnight. When we had finished he smoked a cigarette and – at Baine's prodding – began a tale which I will précis. (I could not for the life of me mimic his rambling, and often irrelevant, discourse in Berkshire dialect.)

'Working in the north corner of the churchyard, he had hung his coat on a low bough of a small, stunted crab apple tree that grew where he was scything a luxuriant growth of grass. From time to time he repaired there for a swig of cold tea from a bottle in his pocket and, at lunchtime, the shade was so inviting that he took his scythe and whetstone across to sharpen there while he munched his midday bait. Chewing away, he set to alternately abrading the scythe's edge, and testing it with his thumb. Whether due to the bread and cheese and sunshine, or whether his labours had tired him, he fell into a brown study. He yawned and stretched out. His foot running idly through the rank grass met an obstacle and stopped. Interested, he pulled and scraped away the turf to reveal the corner of an old slate slab. So, he'd been sitting beside someone's grave, had he? What an odd place to bury them! He continued scraping away the thick grass roots and soon had a sizeable flat slab exposed. The apple tree apparently grew out of the top of the grave, emerging from under the edge of the covering slab – obviously taking the easiest way out. There was a faint inscription, but time and normal erosion had all but defaced it.

'My young Anglican friend interjected here that he had taken a pencil rubbing of the faint inscription, and pulled a crumpled paper from his pocket. It appeared to be SEPVLCHRVM NON MOVERE and, below that, NOLI PRODERE and the date MDCCXLVII. Which we took to be part of an injunction against moving the burial place of someone interred in 1747. I was not, and am not, sure why it should be given in Latin, except perhaps simply to warn the educated and not inspire the perverse yokel to investigate further.

'Anyway, to get back to James's narrative: Just as he was rising to get back to his labours, his eyes caught sight of a billet of wood. To insert this under the edge of the slab was a moment's work. He moved it slightly but no more, nor could all his efforts avail further. Shrugging in annoyance he picked up his scythe and turned back to the grass, to become aware of a short, squat figure watching him from beneath the tree. For an instant he thought it was a dense cloud of the little gnats that had been pestering him, drawn to his perspiration; then he thought it was a heat-haze mirage. Whatever it was, its scrutiny had the effect of immobilizing him while it drew nearer. His outstanding impression was of a mass of hair grown long, that hung about a greyish body and spread about on the ground like a train. As it advanced, the limbs parting the hair seemed very bony and yellowish. Of face or physiognomy there was no trace, but two eyes gleamed through the hair and reflected a reddish light. Backed against a stone monument and unable to give way, James shuddered as a thin, hairy limb parted the hair to reveal prominent, yellow, rabbit-like teeth overfilling a red mouth. The thing was level with him (he was crouching) and a wave of peculiarly earthy breath, redolent of mould, came over him and he screwed his eyes shut, palpitating in horror. Nothing further happened and, with a sinking feeling, he opened his eyes and saw ... nothing. "She" – for so he reckoned the stunted figure – was gone, but a cloud of gnats hovered for a moment beneath the apple tree and then was gone also.

'James shook himself hard, aware that chilly drops of sweat were coursing down his back, and went out into the sunshine.

'Returning from "The Swan" that night, he went to bed and dreamed of "her" as a young and comely woman. They had walked through the meadows below the church, detoured through a copse to avoid the river, and had crossed the lawns of a stately orange brick mansion that lay among the concealing poplars.

'Baine interrupted again here to say that this sounded like the old Manor house, a painting of which hung in the vicarage. The present (much altered) building dated from about the mid-eighteenth century.

'James resumed the narrative of his dream. They had climbed to a room with a balcony that overlooked the river, the fields and churchyard; its tombstones like pebbles on a green beach. His companion had shaken her fist and howled curses toward the church. The scene hazed over like a heat mirage and he was lying back, gazing up at an ornamental ceiling whereon nymphs and centaurs besported with mythological abandonment.

'He woke at dawn, in his own bed. Shivering and exhausted, he was just conscious of something that slipped under the bedroom window sash. Getting up was an effort. His work that day seemed unusually tiring, and Baine had commented on his lethargy; telling him not to overdo it in the sun. He had been particularly plagued by gnats which persisted round him, despite flailing arms, and rubbing crushed yarrow over his face and arms to repel them. Baine emerged from the church an hour or so later, to find James resting beneath the tree and, going across, was much intrigued to see the uncovered slab, and took the rubbing of the faint inscription. However, parochial business called him away for most of the day. Returning to the churchyard just before tea, he again saw James resting beneath the tree and an old coat or sack propped on a spade partly obscuring him from view. On approaching closer, though, he saw that he had been mistaken; there was no coat – or spade come to that – only a dancing cloud of little flies; and James was lying asleep, breathing adenoidally, his head against the stem of the apple tree. He shook him awake and told him to cease work for the day.

'So, James plodded off home, and, again, that night dreamed. This time he was in the churchyard and saw her rise from the roots of the tree to meet him. He woke to find himself in the place of his dream, lying beneath the apple tree; his clothes soaked with dew and a faint mist drifting over the ground. He was so weak that he could hardly move and, crawling to the lych gate, he collapsed. Here Baine found him at first light, apparently dreaming; writhing and twitching like a dog in sleep. On

[183]

hearing his somewhat incoherent story, Baine helped him over to the vicarage, and phoned the doctor who, however, was out on an all-night case. He then thought of me and sent James to wait at my house while he came to meet me from early Mass.

'To eliminate the obvious, I examined Mr James's neck for the legendary marks, but found nothing. For all his weakness, if this was a vampire, then it was a lamprey of the life force rather than a carnal sucker of blood. However, a number of things had to be done.

'I bade Mr James rest on my sofa and stay all day if I did not return. Baine I despatched to his parish records to check on the occupancy of that manor house and its relation to the date 1747 on the slab. Moreover I wanted a canvas "tent" to screen the slab from inquisitive eyes.

'After making preparations to absent myself for several hours, I hastened to the vicarage. My young friend had dug out the parish registers and a Rector's Diurnal from the old chest, and was making notes. There could be no mistaking the relevant entries. In scholarly longhand was a reference to the removal of Lady Alys Beauregard from the family vault to a spot in the North churchyard that could only be the present grave. There were references forward (to 1752 in the Rector's Diurnal) and back (to 1584). Unhappily the latter was no longer in existence (the extant registers beginning at 1690 or thereabout), but the former was simply to a note that: "Henry Goodenough, sexton, did todaye shew me a supplying or treelette growyng oute ye Lady Alys tomb. I supposed it would be apel, whiche same he did confyrme"; and a futher note to the effect (in 1770) that the (by then substantial) tree was known as the "cursing tree". The learned Rector had a parallel to draw with the Apple tree of Sodom and a lesson to derive, in that, "tis said by my people that its fruite woulde tayst soure to (them) of dissent but swete withal to (those) of popish ways". He would seem to have deemed it necessary to preach a strong sermon (he wrote admonition!) against those in his parish who believed that on the anniversary of the lady's interment they could curse their neighbours by placing a token on the tree boughs.

'There being no more to learn from the records and Rector's diurnal, we adjourned to the churchyard, where a canopy had been fixed round the spot beneath the tree, to see if Lady Alys was still at home. The sexton gave a start of surprise at seeing me with his priest and fixed a resigned look on poor Baine. Mr James's efforts had certainly moved the slab and left a slight gap. Together we three levered the crowbar provided by the sexton, and moved the slab; whereupon a cloud of gnats flew out and away into the air. The tree roots so revealed grew sturdily in the soil, bent almost at right angles to emerge from beneath the slab. The sexton carefully excavated the hole further, to reveal a stone coffin of great age, such as were made in the 13th century (and stockpiled by some families for use by future generations). The lid had been forced up by the tree which clearly grew as an offshoot from some long-dead stake, just as a briar sometimes shoots from a cultivated rose stump. The coffin itself was full of earth, which would need careful sieving to determine bones, or other relicta. I had learned enough, however: the lady had been staked in earth on her removal from the family mausoleum in 1747; no doubt to keep her quiet. Mr James's discovery of the newer grave and shifting of the slab had evidently "wound up" her mechanism – as it were; he providing her with "vitality", if so unsuitable a word could be used!

'What to do about it? That was the question! I had already decided against any appeal to my Diocesan; a worthy director, but lacking imagination and not likely to countenance our ecumenical approach.

'A hail from the lych gate, announced that my lift to the station had arrived and I took leave of Baine for the time being. Luckily the journey to Oxford was reasonably easy in those days, and involved no change of train.

'I had first met Con McAlister at Cambridge. He was a born mystic of undoubtedly queer gifts and on a mental plane far removed (thank heaven!) from my own. He was extremely attractive to women and missed none of the opportunities that came his way; inevitably his clarity of intellect suffered and degeneration set in. We had remained friends, since I discounted most of the scandal I had heard about him, though I suspect his liking for me was more in the nature of cynical amusement. It was typical of the man that he had made Cambridge too hot for him, and taken himself to Oxford, where I now found him – affectedly pleased to see me. He was at least interested in my problem, and there and then telephoned an introduction for me through to another erudite friend; whither I then repaired.

'The Revd Samuel Montagu proved to be a strange and effeminate bibliophile who spent most of his waking hours in the Bodleian. In conversation it transpired that he had written the Vatican's *Liber Auctoritas* on demonology and the Black Art. I was glad to have this opportunity of meeting such an arcane and odd character, yet uneasy too; there was something repellent about him.

'I was received in a book-lined study: thousand upon thousand of books – the collection of a lifetime he told me; mostly of the strange and bizarre, but with a good sprinkling of long-forgotten dramatists. He saw to it that even a modest bibliophile like myself expanded in the presence of such a fascinating authority. Had the matter back home not been so pressing, I could have stayed all day drinking his sherry and looking over his incredible files of "persecution" data, that made my Cambridge thesis look decidedly anaemic! On hearing my precis of Mr James's tale and subsequent researches, he went at once to a row of calf-bound notebooks, like folios. After a moment's pause, he selected a volume and thumbed delicately through the pages.

'"Ah", he smiled, "Here we are ... Lady Alys Beauregard ... yes, yes ...", and he handed me the book with a quizzical look.

'To my surprise it was written by hand ... in Latin! Now, at last, I had cause to thank the strictness of the Christian Brothers' Seminary in Tralee! I took the book from Mr Montagu and began to read, with only an occasional pause: "*Maiores Henrii Beauregardi per Normantum triumphum orti sunt. In sexto decimo saeculo et Mariam suffragati sunt et coronationem ordinaverunt ...*". That is to say: "The line of Henry Beauregard dates back to the Norman Conquest. In the 16th Century they were strongly pro-Mary and took a leading part at her Coronation. The wife, Alys, was widely believed to be the influence in the family and her portrait (the original of which has not survived the fire of 1584) allegedly showed her to be a stern, hard-faced woman. Henry died in 1562 and was buried in the family crypt beneath the church. Alys, who died in 1584, had been implicated as instigator of a number of Catholic plots against Elizabeth. She committed suicide when arrest was imminent and died unrepentant, unabsolved and – it was alleged by servants – with bitter curses and dire threats. Local legend had it that *her* hand, from the grave, fired the house later that same year, two days after the Desmonds – to whom Elizabeth granted the house and estate in perpetuity – took possession. Nine lives were lost and the line of Desmond all but perished; the property passing to a cadet branch. Parish records show that the old lady was still a force to reckon with in the parish, and caused much disturbance during the reformed services, with noise and commotion from the crypt; but these died out around 1680. There are further records of disturbances with a new Desmond in the parish, who had the shell of the old manor pulled down in 1747. It is alleged at that time, that she appeared in dreams to the family, threatening their sleeping hours and terrifying congregations with noises from the vault. Desmond had appointed to the living a Rector of great force and character, who investigated the matter thoroughly. Entering the crypt, he found stone coffins thrown about or tumbled off their niches. The cadaver of the old Dame herself was well preserved, albeit shrivelled and desiccated – and she hung half out of her open coffin; her hair had continued to grow and was of prodigious length. This, they cut off with consecrated shears, and burned, believing that much of her malicious power resided therein. In accordance with prevailing belief the crypt was sealed up and she and her coffin removed to ground on the north side of the church, and her 'bodye pyrsed (with) a goode and sounde staffe of apel', she being then 'confyned beneathe a propre slabbe, duly blesst'."

'I stopped reading. The Revd Montagu pushed his glasses up to his forehead with an odd little smile as he recovered the book from me.

'"Now", he said, "it would seem that you have a nice little problem, Father. The Lady is not going to stay quiet so long as that slab can be moved, obviously. I don't know what she is after, but I suggest so staunch a Catholic is not going to be appeased by any watered-down Anglican ritual. That Rector of 1747 was a clever man, but not quite imaginative enough; though – at that – he seems to have kept her quiet for some 200 years." He chuckled. "My suggestion is that *you*, Father, give her absolution. I think she might rest then. Do let me know what transpires, so that I can keep my notes up to date."

'This then gave me a fine problem in diplomacy' (continued Fr O'Connor). 'Before I left Revd Montagu he took me to visit his private chapel downstairs, and my doubts of his sanctity as a priest disappeared in that tranquil haven. Only later did I learn from the cynical McAlister that next door was another room, the exact antithesis of the chapel, and which served for more diabolical ceremonials! What an enigma these two brilliant men were!

'I arrived back, tired and travel-stained, to find that James had felt better and had gone home. My housekeeper thought someone had called for him. I dropped into the vicarage – doubtless to the further scandalization of the village – and told Baine what I had discovered from Revd Montagu. He was all attention, and most grateful, but I was not surprised that even this insouciant upholder of the Thirty-nine Articles was disturbed at the thought of *my* giving absolution. Whereas I was sure, on reflection, that Revd Montagu was right: however lenient my views on the validity of Anglican orders might be, to this stern old revenant from the 16th century, there would be no question but that the rites of priesthood rested solely with the elder church.

'We might have debated the matter academically for the rest of our lives had not Baine been summoned to the door. It was James's old mother; he had not been home since morning; it was now quite late, and she was worried.

'We both guessed, of course, where we should look for him. Reassuring his mother as best we could, we sped across to the churchyard in the dusk. A whirligig of bats were circling round the massive pile of the four-square Norman tower. On the north side, our "tent" was still in place and a dark hump was lying before it. As we arrived at the grave, we could see that it was James – barely conscious and hardly breathing. Baine bent to tend to him and I looked from them . . . to see the woman of our quest. As James had said, at first glance she was simply a mass of hair with a suggestion of limbs. I showed her my crucifix whereupon the snarl, which had displayed those hideous, rabbit teeth through the hair, changed to a softer expression. She reached out a thin arm and I all but recoiled in revulsion at its texture, but gave her the rosary. The act of reaching out parted the hair from her chest and revealed a ragged wound, black and gaping against the cere cloths. Seeing quickly that Baine was absorbed in trying to resuscitate James, I said swiftly, "May the Lord be in your heart and on your lips that you may truly confess your sins . . ."

'She knelt, the hair spreading out like a pool around her. No sound came to me, though I saw her lips move. She was substantial enough for me to feel the slight pressure of her touch upon the chain of my cross. I spoke briefly of the coming together of the churches in Christ (glad that our respective superiors were not there to interject) and concluded with the absolution: "*Ego te absolvo, in nomine Patris et Filii et Spiritus Sancti*. Amen."

'With the words, "*Requiescat in pace*", her form seemed to slide into the ground and the prone James began to stir. Baine and I helped him back to his mother's house and, I must say, I felt all in. It had been quite a day! James was troubled no more, but I think he gave up working in churchyards.

'Baine and I talked long that night. Next day, at my suggestion, he read the committal over the grave and we replaced the slab; having got the sexton to sink the entire grave as much lower as the tree roots would allow; which wasn't much. However it was possible to turf over the top and we hoped that would take care of the Lady Alys for the future.

'Leaving the sexton to place the turves, we walked off down the path. As we emerged beneath the apple tree I plucked two of the tiny fruits and handed one to Baine.

'He bit his and winced, spitting out the fragments. I swallowed mine with apparent enjoyment. "Quite tasty," I said.

'He gave me a sharp look. "Come, Father," he said, "You are pulling my leg!"

'I smiled in return. "My dear Baine, you wouldn't have me disappoint an old lady, would you?" Possibly I deserved the stomach ache I suffered that night.'

[188]

THE MASTER OF RAMPLING GATE

Anne Rice

Anne Rice (born 1941) is highly regarded as the
most popular and successful writer in modern
vampire literature, with her acclaimed 'Vampire
Chronicles': *Interview with the Vampire* (1976),
The Vampire Lestat (1986) and *The Queen of the
Damned* (1988).
Her only short story on the same theme is 'The
Master of Rampling Gate', which appeared in
the popular American magazine *Redbook*,
February 1984.

S pring 1888
Rampling Gate. It was so real to us in the old pictures, rising like
a fairy-tale castle out of its own dark wood. A wilderness of gables
and chimneys between those two immense towers, grey stone walls
mantled in ivy, mullioned windows reflecting the drifting clouds.

But why had Father never taken us there? And why, on his deathbed,
had he told my brother that Rampling Gate must be torn down, stone by
stone? 'I should have done it, Richard,' he said. 'But I was born in that
house, as my father was, and his father before him. You must do it now,
Richard. It has no claim on you. Tear it down.'

Was it any wonder that not two months after Father's passing,
Richard and I were on the noon train headed south for the mysterious
mansion that had stood upon the rise above the village of Rampling for

four hundred years? Surely Father would have understood. How could we destroy the old place when we had never seen it?

But, as the train moved slowly through the outskirts of London I can't say we were very sure of ourselves, no matter how curious and excited we were.

Richard had just finished four years at Oxford. Two whirlwind social seasons in London had proved me something of a shy success. I still preferred scribbling poems and stories in my room to dancing the night away, but I'd kept that a good secret. And though we had lost our mother when we were little, Father had given us the best of everything. Now the carefree years were ended. We had to be independent and wise.

The evening before, we had pored over all the old pictures of Rampling Gate, recalling in hushed, tentative voices the night Father had taken those pictures down from the walls.

I couldn't have been more than six and Richard eight when it happened, yet we remembered well the strange incident in Victoria Station that had precipitated Father's uncharacteristic rage. We had gone there after supper to say farewell to a school friend of Richard's, and Father had caught a glimpse, quite unexpectedly, of a young man at the lighted window of an incoming train. I could remember the young man's face clearly to this day: remarkably handsome, with a head of lustrous brown hair, his large black eyes regarding Father with the saddest expression as Father drew back. 'Unspeakable horror!' Father had whispered. Richard and I had been too amazed to speak a word.

Later that night, Father and Mother quarrelled, and we crept out of our rooms to listen on the stairs.

'That he should dare to come to London!' Father said over and over. 'Is it not enough for him to be the undisputed master of Rampling Gate?'

How we puzzled over it as little ones! Who was this stranger, and how could he be master of a house that belonged to our father, a house that had been left in the care of an old, blind housekeeper for years?

But now after looking at the pictures again, it was too dreadful to think of Father's exhortation. And too exhilarating to think of the house itself. I'd packed my manuscripts, for – who knew? – maybe in that melancholy and exquisite setting I'd find exactly the inspiration I needed for the story I'd been writing in my head.

Yet there was something almost illicit about the excitement I felt. I saw in my mind's eye the pale young man again, with his black greatcoat and red woollen cravat. Like bone china, his complexion had been. Strange to remember so vividly. And I realized now that in those few remarkable

[190]

moments, he had created for me an ideal of masculine beauty that I had never questioned since. But Father had been so angry. I felt an unmistakable pang of guilt.

It was late afternoon when the old trap carried us up the gentle slope from the little railway station and we had our first real look at the house. The sky had paled to a deep rose hue beyond a bank of softly gilded clouds, and the last rays of the sun struck the uppermost panes of the leaded windows and filled them with solid gold.

'Oh, but it's too majestic,' I whispered, 'too like a great cathedral, and to think that it belongs to us!'

Richard gave me the smallest kiss on the cheek.

I wanted with all my heart to jump down from the trap and draw near on foot, letting those towers slowly grow larger and larger above me, but our old horse was gaining speed.

When we reached the massive front door Richard and I were spirited into the great hall by the tiny figure of the blind housekeeper Mrs Blessington, our footfalls echoing loudly on the marble tile, and our eyes dazzled by the dusty shafts of light that fell on the long oak table and its heavily carved chairs, on the sombre tapestries that stirred ever so slightly against the soaring walls.

'Richard, it is an enchanted place!' I cried, unable to contain myself.

Mrs Blessington laughed gaily, her dry hand closing tightly on mine.

We found our bedchambers well aired, with snow-white linen on the beds and fires blazing cosily on the hearths. The small, diamond-paned windows opened on a glorious view of the lake and the oaks that enclosed it and the few scattered lights that marked the village beyond.

That night we laughed like children as we supped at the great oak table, our candles giving only a feeble light. And afterward we had a fierce battle of pocket billiards in the game room and a little too much brandy, I fear.

It was just before I went to bed that I asked Mrs Blessington if there had been anyone in this house since my father left it, years before.

'No, my dear,' she said quickly, fluffing the feather pillows. 'When your father went away to Oxford, he never came back.'

'There was never a young intruder after that? . . .' I pressed her, though in truth I had little appetite for anything that would disturb the happiness I felt. How I loved the Spartan cleanliness of this bedchamber, the walls bare of paper and ornament, the high lustre of the walnut-panelled bed.

'A young intruder?' With an unerring certainty about her

surroundings, she lifted the poker and stirred the fire. 'No, dear. Whatever made you think there was?'

'Are there no ghost stories, Mrs Blessington?' I asked suddenly, startling myself. *Unspeakable horror*. But what was I thinking – that that young man had not been real?

'Oh, no, darling,' she said, smiling. 'No ghost would ever dare to trouble Rampling Gate.'

Nothing, in fact, troubled the serenity of the days that followed – long walks through the overgrown gardens, trips in the little skiff to and fro across the lake, tea under the hot glass of the empty conservatory. Early evening found us reading and writing by the library fire.

All our inquiries in the village met with the same answers: The villagers cherished the house. There was not a single disquieting legend or tale.

How were we going to tell them of Father's edict? How were we going to remind ourselves?

Richard was finding a wealth of classical material on the library shelves and I had the desk in the corner entirely to myself.

Never had I known such quiet. It seemed the atmosphere of Rampling Gate permeated my simplest written descriptions and wove its way richly into the plots and characters I created. The Monday after our arrival I finished my first real short story, and after copying out a fresh draft, I went off to the village on foot to post it boldly to the editors of *Blackwood's* magazine.

It was a warm afternoon, and I took my time as I came back. What had disturbed our father so about this lovely corner of England? What had so darkened his last hours that he laid his curse upon this spot? My heart opened to this unearthly stillness, to an indisputable magnificence that caused me utterly to forget myself. There were times here when I felt I was a disembodied intellect drifting through a fathomless silence, up and down garden paths and stone corridors that had witnessed too much to take cognizance of one small and fragile young woman who in random moments actually talked aloud to the suits of armour around her, to the broken statues in the garden, the fountain cherubs who had had no water to pour from their conches for years and years.

But was there in this loveliness some malignant force that was eluding us still, some untold story? *Unspeakable horror* . . . Even in the flood of brilliant sunlight, those words gave me a chill.

As I came slowly up the slope I saw Richard walking lazily along the

[192]

uneven shore of the lake. Now and then he glanced up at the distant battlements, his expression dreamy, almost blissfully contented.

Rampling Gate had him. And I understood perfectly because it also had me.

With a new sense of determination I went to him and placed my hand gently on his arm. For a moment he looked at me as if he did not even know me, and then he said softly:

'How will I ever do it, Julie? And one way or the other, it will be on my conscience all my life.'

'It's time to seek advice, Richard,' I said. 'Write to our lawyers in London. Write to Father's clergyman, Dr Matthews. Explain everything. We cannot do this alone.'

It was three o'clock in the morning when I opened my eyes. But I had been awake for a long time. And I felt not fear, lying there alone, but something else – some vague and relentless agitation, some sense of emptiness and need that caused me finally to rise from my bed. What was this house, really? A place, or merely a state of mind? What was it doing to my soul?

I felt overwhelmed, yet shut out of some great and dazzling secret. Driven by an unbearable restlessness, I pulled on my woollen wrapper and my slippers and went into the hall.

The moonlight fell full on the oak stairway, and the vestibule far below. Maybe I could write of the confusion I suffered now, put on paper the inexplicable longing I felt. Certainly it was worth the effort, and I made my way soundlessly down the steps.

The great hall gaped before me, the moonlight here and there touching upon a pair of crossed swords or a mounted shield. But far beyond, in the alcove just outside the library, I saw the uneven glow of the fire. So Richard was there. A sense of well-being pervaded me and quieted me. At the same time, the distance between us seemed endless and I became desperate to cross it, hurrying past the long supper table and finally into the alcove before the library doors.

The fire blazed beneath the stone mantelpiece and a figure sat in the leather chair before it, bent over a loose collection of pages that he held in his slender hands. He was reading the pages eagerly, and the fire suffused his face with a warm, golden light.

But it was not Richard. It was the same young man I had seen on the train in Victoria Station fifteen years ago. And not a single aspect of that taut young face had changed. There was the very same hair, thick and lustrous and only carelessly combed as it hung to the collar of his black coat, and those dark eyes that looked up suddenly and fixed me with a most curious expression as I almost screamed.

We stared at each other across that shadowy room, I stranded in the doorway, he visibly and undeniably shaken that I had caught him unawares. My heart stopped.

And in a split second he rose and moved toward me, closing the gap between us, reaching out with those slender white hands.

'Julie!' he whispered, in a voice so low that it seemed my own thoughts were speaking to me. But this was no dream. He was holding me and the scream had broken loose from me, deafening, uncontrollable and echoing from the four walls.

I was alone. Clutching at the door frame, I staggered forward, and then in a moment of perfect clarity I saw the young stranger again, saw him standing in the open door to the garden, looking back over his shoulder; then he was gone.

I could not stop screaming. I could not stop even as I heard Richard's voice calling me, heard his feet pound down that broad, hollow staircase and through the great hall. I could not stop even as he shook me, pleaded with me, settled me in a chair.

Finally I managed to describe what I had seen.

'But you know who it was!' I said almost hysterically. 'It was he – the young man from the train!'

'Now, wait,' Richard said. 'He had his back to the fire, Julie. And you could not see his face clearly—'

'Richard, it was he! Don't you understand? He touched me. He called me Julie,' I whispered. 'Good God, Richard, look at the fire. I didn't light it – he did. He was here!'

All but pushing Richard out of the way, I went to the heap of papers that lay strewn on the carpet before the hearth. 'My story . . .' I whispered, snatching up the pages. 'He's been reading my story, Richard. And – dear God – he's read your letters, the letters to Mr Partridge and Dr Matthews, about tearing down the house!'

'Surely you don't believe it was the same man, Julie, after all these years . . .?'

'But he has not changed, Richard, not in the smallest detail. There is no mistake, I tell you. It was the very same man!'

The next day was the most trying since we had come. Together we commenced a search of the house. Darkness found us only half finished, frustrated everywhere by locked doors we could not open and old staircases that were not safe.

And it was also quite clear by suppertime that Richard did not believe I had seen anyone in the study at all. As for the fire – well, he had failed to put it out properly before going to bed; and the pages – well, one of us had put them there and forgotten them, of course . . .

But I knew what I had seen.

And what obsessed me more than anything else was the gentle countenance of the mysterious man I had glimpsed, the innocent eyes that had fixed on me for one moment before I screamed.

'You would be wise to do one very important thing before you retire,' I said crossly. 'Leave out a note to the effect that you do not intend to tear down the house.'

'Julie, you have created an impossible dilemma,' Richard declared, the colour rising in his face. 'You insist we reassure this apparition that the house will not be destroyed, when in fact you verify the existence of the very creature that drove our father to say what he did.'

'Oh, I wish I had never come here!' I burst out suddenly.

'Then we should go, and decide this matter at home.'

'No – that's just it. I could never go without knowing. I could never go on living with knowing now!'

Anger must be an excellent antidote to fear, for surely something worked to alleviate my natural alarm. I did not undress that night, but rather sat in the darkened bedroom, gazing at the small square of diamond-paned window until I heard the house fall quiet. When the grandfather clock in the great hall chimed the hour of eleven, Rampling Gate was, as usual, fast asleep.

I felt a dark exultation as I imagined myself going out of the room and down the stairs. But I knew I should wait one more hour. I should let the night reach its peak. My heart was beating too fast, and dreamily I recollected the face I had seen, the voice that had said my name.

Why did it seem in retrospect so intimate, that we had known each other before, spoken together a thousand times? Was it because he had read my story, those words that came from my very soul?

'Who are you?' I believe I whispered aloud. 'Where are you at this moment?' I uttered the word, 'Come.'

The door opened without a sound and he was standing there. He was dressed exactly as he had been the night before and his dark eyes were riveted on me with that same obvious curiosity, his mouth just a little slack, like that of a boy.

I sat forward, and he raised his finger as if to reassure me and gave a little nod.

'Ah, it is you!' I whispered.

'Yes,' he said in a soft, unobtrusive voice.

'And you are not a spirit!' I looked at his mud-splattered boots, at the faintest smear of dust on that perfect white cheek.

'A spirit?' he asked almost mournfully. 'Would that I were that.'

Dazed, I watched him come toward me; the room darkened and I felt his cool, silken hands on my face. I had risen. I was standing before him, and I looked up into his eyes.

I heard my own heartbeat. I heard it as I had the night before, right at the moment I had screamed. Dear God, I was talking to him! He was in my room and I was talking to him! And then suddenly I was in his arms.

'Real, absolutely real!' I whispered, and a low, zinging sensation coursed through me so that I had to steady myself.

He was peering at me as if trying to comprehend something terribly important. His lips had a ruddy look to them, a soft look for all his handsomeness, as if he had never been kissed. A slight dizziness came over me, a slight confusion in which I was not at all sure that he was even there.

'Oh, but I am,' he said, as if I had spoken my doubt. I felt his breath against my cheek, and it was almost sweet. 'I am here, and I have watched you ever since you came.'

'Yes . . .'

My eyes were closing. In a dim flash, as of a match being struck, I saw my father, heard his voice. No, Julie . . . But that was surely a dream.

'Only a little kiss,' said the voice of the one who was really here. I felt his lips against my neck. 'I would never harm you. No harm ever for the children of this house. Just the little kiss, Julie, and the understanding that it imparts, that you cannot destroy Rampling Gate, Julie – that you can never, never drive me away.'

The core of my being, that secret place where all desires and all commandments are nurtured, opened to him without a struggle or a sound. I would have fallen if he had not held me. My arms closed about him, my hands slipping into the soft, silken mass of his hair.

I was floating, and there was, as there had always been at Rampling Gate, an endless peace. It was Rampling Gate I felt enclosing me; it was that timeless and impenetrable secret that had opened itself at last. . . . A

power within me of enormous ken . . . To see as a god sees, and take the depth
of things as nimbly as the outward eyes can size and shape pervade . . . Yes,
those very words from Keats, which I had quoted in the pages of my story
that he had read.

But in a violent instant he had released me. 'Too innocent,' he
whispered.

I went reeling across the bedroom floor and caught hold of the frame
of the window. I rested my forehead against the stone wall.

There was a tingling pain in my throat where his lips had touched me
that was almost pleasurable, a delicious throbbing that would not stop.
I knew what he was!

I turned and saw all the room clearly – the bed, the fireplace, the chair.
And he stood still exactly as I'd left him and there was the most appalling
anguish in his face.

'Something of menace, unspeakable menace,' I whispered, backing
away.

'Something ancient, something that defies understanding,' he pleaded.
'Something that can and will go on.' But he was shaken and he would not
look into my eyes.

I touched that pulsing pain with the tips of my fingers and, looking
down at them, saw the blood. 'Vampire!' I gasped. 'And yet you suffer
so, and it is as if you can love!'

'Love? I have loved you since you came. I loved you when I read your
secret thoughts and had not yet seen your face.'

He drew me to him ever so gently, and slipping his arm around me,
guided me to the door.

I tried for one desperate moment to resist him. And as any gentleman
might, he stepped back respectfully and took my hand.

Through the long upstairs corridor we passed, and through a small
wooden doorway to a screw stair that I had not seen before. I soon
realized we were ascending in the north tower, a ruined portion of the
structure that had been sealed off years before.

Through one tiny window after another I saw the gently rolling
landscape and the small cluster of dim lights that marked the village of
Rampling and the pale streak of white that was the London road.

Up and up we climbed, until we reached the topmost chamber, and
this he opened with an iron key. He held back the door for me to enter
and I found myself in a spacious room whose high, narrow windows
contained no glass. A flood of moonlight revealed the most curious
mixture of furnishings and objects – a writing-table, a great shelf of

books, soft leather chairs, and scores of maps and framed pictures affixed to the walls. Candles all about had dripped their wax on every surface, and in the very midst of this chaos lay my poems, my old sketches – early writings that I had brought with me and never even unpacked.

I saw a black silk top hat and a walking stick, and a bouquet of withered flowers, dry as straw, and daguerreotypes and tintypes in their little velvet cases, and London newspapers and opened books.

There was no place for sleeping in this room.

And when I thought of that, where he must lie when he went to rest, a shudder passed over me and I felt, quite palpably, his lips touching my throat again, and I had the sudden urge to cry.

But he was holding me in his arms; he was kissing my cheeks and my lips ever so softly.

'My father knew what you were!' I whispered.

'Yes,' he answered, 'and his father before him. And all of them in an unbroken chain over the years. Out of loneliness or rage, I know not which, I always told them. I always made them acknowledge, accept.'

I backed away and he didn't try to stop me. He lighted the candles about us one by one.

I was stunned by the sight of him in the light, the gleam in his large black eyes and the gloss of his hair. Not even in the railway station had I seen him so clearly as I did now, amid the radiance of the candles. He broke my heart.

And yet he looked at me as though I were a feast for his eyes, and he said my name again and I felt the blood rush to my face. But there seemed a great break suddenly in the passage of time. What had I been thinking! *Yes, never tell, never disturb . . . something ancient, something greater than good and evil . . .* But no! I felt dizzy again. I heard Father's voice: *Tear it down, Richard, stone by stone.*

He had drawn me to the window. And as the lights of Rampling were subtracted from the darkness below, a great wood stretched out in all directions, far older and denser than the forest of Rampling Gate. I was afraid suddenly, as if I were slipping into a maelstrom of visions from which I could never, of my own will, return.

There was that sense of our talking together, talking and talking in low, agitated voices, and I was saying that I should not give in.

'Bear witness – that is all I ask of you, Julie.'

And there was in me some dim certainty that by these visions alone I would be fatally changed.

But the very room was losing its substance, as if a soundless wind of terrific force were blowing it apart. The vision had already begun . . .

We were riding horseback through a forest, he and I. And the trees were so high and so thick that scarcely any sun at all broke through to the fragrant, leaf-strewn ground.

Yet we had no time to linger in this magical place. We had come to the fresh-tilled earth that surrounded a village I somehow knew was called Knorwood, with its gabled roofs and its tiny, crooked streets. We saw the monastery of Knorwood and the little church with the bell chiming vespers under the lowering sky. A great, bustling life resided in Knorwood, a thousand voices rising in common prayer.

Far beyond, on the rise above the forest, stood the round tower of a truly ancient castle; and to that ruined castle – no more than a shell of itself anymore – as darkness fell in earnest we rode. Through its empty chambers we roamed, impetuous children, the horses and the road quite forgotten, and to the lord of the castle, a gaunt and white-skinned creature standing before the roaring fire of the roofless hall, we came. He turned and fixed us with his narrow and glittering eyes. A dead thing he was, I understood, but he carried within himself a priceless magic. And my companion, my innocent young man, stepped forward into the lord's arms.

I saw the kiss. I saw the young man grow pale and struggle and turn away, and the lord retreated with the wisest, saddest smile.

I understood. I knew. But the castle was dissolving as surely as anything in this dream might dissolve, and we were in some damp and close place.

The stench was unbearable to me; it was that most terrible of all stenches, the stench of death. And I heard my steps on the cobblestones and I reached out to steady myself against a wall. The tiny marketplace was deserted; the doors and windows gaped open to the vagrant wind. Up one side and down the other of the crooked street I saw the marks on the houses. And I knew what the marks meant. The Black Death had come to the village of Knorwood. The Black Death had laid it waste. And in a moment of suffocating horror I realized that no one, not a single person, was left alive.

But this was not quite true. There was a young man walking in fits and starts up the narrow alleyway. He was staggering, almost falling, as he pushed in one door after another, and at last came to a hot, reeking place where a child screamed on the floor. Mother and father lay dead in the

[199]

bed. And the sleek fat cat of the household, unharmed, played with the screaming infant, whose eyes bulged in its tiny, sunken face.

'Stop it!' I heard myself gasp. I was holding my head with both hands. 'Stop it – stop it, please!' I was screaming, and my screams would surely pierce the vision and this crude little dwelling would collapse around me and I would rouse the household of Rampling Gate, but I did not. The young man turned and stared at me, and in the close, stinking room I could not see his face.

But I knew it was he, my companion, and I could smell his fever and his sickness, and the stink of the dying infant, and see the gleaming body of the cat as it pawed at the child's outstretched hand.

'Stop it, you've lost control of it!' I screamed, surely with all my strength, but the infant screamed louder. 'Make it stop.'

'I cannot,' he whispered. 'It goes on forever! It will never stop!'

And with a great shriek I kicked at the cat and sent it flying out of the filthy room, overturning the milk pail as it went.

Death in all the houses of Knorwood. Death in the cloister, death in the open fields. It seemed the Judgement of God – I was sobbing, begging to be released – it seemed the very end of Creation itself.

But as night came down over the dead village he was alive still, stumbling up the slopes, through the forest, toward that tower where the lord stood at the broken arch of the window, waiting for him to come.

'Don't go!' I begged him. I ran alongside him, crying, but he didn't hear.

The lord turned and smiled with infinite sadness as the young man on his knees begged for salvation, when it was damnation this lord offered, when it was only damnation that the lord would give.

'Yes, damned, then, but living, breathing!' the young man cried, and the lord opened his arms.

The kiss again, the lethal kiss, the blood drawn out of his dying body, and then the lord lifting the heavy head of the young man so the youth could take the blood back again from the body of the lord himself.

I screamed, 'Do not – do not drink!' He turned, and his face was now so perfectly the visage of death that I couldn't believe there was animation left in him; yet he asked: 'What would you do? Would you go back to Knorwood, would you open those doors one after another, would you ring the bell in the empty church – and if you did, who would hear?'

He didn't wait for my answer. And I had none now to give. He locked his innocent mouth to the vein that pulsed with every semblance of life beneath the lord's cold and translucent flesh. And the blood jetted into the young body, vanquishing in one great burst the fever and the sickness that had wracked it, driving it out along with the mortal life.

He stood now in the hall of the lord alone. Immortality was his, and the blood thirst he would need to sustain it, and that thirst I could feel with my whole soul.

And each and every thing was transfigured in his vision – to the exquisite essence of itself. A wordless voice spoke from the starry veil of heaven; it sang in the wind that rushed through the broken timbers; it sighed in the flames that ate at the sooted stones of the hearth. It was the eternal rhythm of the universe that played beneath every surface as the last living creature in the village – that tiny child – fell silent in the maw of time.

A soft wind sifted and scattered the soil from the newly turned furrows in the empty fields. The rain fell from the black and endless sky.

Years and years passed. And all that had been Knorwood melted into the earth. The forest sent out its silent sentinels, and mighty trunks rose where there had been huts and houses, where there had been monastery walls. And it seemed the horror beyond all horrors that no one should know anymore of those who had lived and died in that small and insignificant village, that not anywhere in the great archives in which all history is recorded should a mention of Knorwood exist.

Yet one remained who knew, one who had witnessed, one who had seen the Ramplings come in the years that followed, seen them raise their house upon the very slope where the ancient castle had once stood, one who saw a new village collect itself slowly upon the unmarked grave of the old.

And all through the walls of Rampling Gate were the stones of that old castle, the stones of the forgotten monastery, the stones of that little church.

We were once again back in the tower.

'It is my shrine,' he whispered. 'My sanctuary. It is the only thing that endures as I endure. And you love it as I love it, Julie. You have written it . . . You love its grandeur. And its gloom.'

'Yes, yes . . . as it's always been . . .' I was crying, though I didn't move my lips.

He had turned to me from the window, and I could feel his endless craving with all my heart.

'What else do you want from me!' I pleaded. 'What else can I give?'

A torrent of images answered me. It was beginning again. I was once again relinquishing myself, yet in a great rush of lights and noise I was enlivened and made whole as I had been when we rode together through the forest, but it was into the world of now, this hour, that we passed.

We were flying through the rural darkness along the railway toward London, where the night-time city burst like an enormous bubble in a shower of laughter and motion and glaring light. He was walking with me under the gas lamps, his face all but shimmering with that same dark innocence, that same irresistible warmth. It seemed we were holding tight to each other in the very midst of a crowd. And the crowd was a living thing, a writhing thing, and everywhere there came a dark, rich aroma from it, the aroma of fresh blood. Women in white fur and gentlemen in opera capes swept through the brightly lighted doors of the theatre; the blare of the music hall inundated us and then faded away. Only a thin soprano voice was left, singing a high, plaintive song. I was in his arms and his lips were covering mine, and there came that dull, zinging sensation again, that great, uncontrollable opening within myself. Thirst, and the promise of satiation measured only by the intensity of that thirst. Up back staircases we fled together, into high-ceilinged bedrooms papered in red damask, where the loveliest women reclined on brass beds, and the aroma was so strong now that I could not bear it and he said: 'Drink. They are your victims! They will give you eternity – you must drink.' And I felt the warmth filling me, charging me, blurring my vision until we broke free again, light and invisible, it seemed, as we moved over the rooftops and down again through rain-drenched streets. But the rain did not touch us; the falling snow did not chill us; we had within ourselves a great and indissoluble heat. And together in the carriage we talked to each other in low, exuberant rushes of language; we were lovers; we were constant; we were immortal. We were as enduring as Rampling Gate.

Oh, don't let it stop! I felt his arms around me and I knew we were in the tower room together, and the visions had worked their fatal alchemy.

'Do you understand what I am offering you? To your ancestors I revealed myself, yes; I subjugated them. But I would make you my bride, Julie. I would share with you my power. Come with me. I will not take you against your will, but can you turn away?'

Again I heard my own scream. My hands were on his cool white skin, and his lips were gentle yet hungry, his eyes yielding and ever young. Father's angry countenance blazed before me as if I, too, had the power to conjure. *Unspeakable horror.* I covered my face.

He stood against the backdrop of the window, against the distant drift of pale clouds. The candlelight glimmered in his eyes. Immense and sad and wise, they seemed – and oh, yes, innocent, as I have said again and again. 'You are their fairest flower, Julie. To them I gave my protection always. To you I give my love. Come to me, dearest, and Rampling Gate will truly be yours, and it will finally, truly be mine.'

Nights of argument, but finally Richard had come round. He would sign over Rampling Gate to me and I should absolutely refuse to allow the place to be torn down. There would be nothing he could do then to obey Father's command. I had given him the legal impediment he needed, and of course I told him I would leave the house to his male heirs. It should always be in Rampling hands.

A clever solution, it seemed to me, since Father had not told me to destroy the place. I had no scruples in the matter now at all.

And what remained was for him to take me to the little railway station and see me off for London, and not worry about my going home to Mayfair on my own.

'You stay here as long as you wish and do not worry,' I said. I felt more tenderly toward him than I could ever express. 'You knew as soon as you set foot in the place that Father was quite wrong.'

The great black locomotive was chugging past us, the passenger cars slowing to a stop.

'Must go now, darling – kiss me,' I said.

'But what came over you, Julie – what convinced you so quickly . . .?'

'We've been through all that, Richard,' I said. 'What matters is that Rampling Gate is safe and we are both happy, my dear.'

I waved until I couldn't see him any more. The flickering lamps of the town were lost in the deep lavender light of the early evening, and the dark hulk of Rampling Gate appeared for one uncertain moment like the ghost of itself on the nearby rise.

I sat back and closed my eyes. Then I opened them slowly, savouring this moment for which I had waited so long.

He was smiling, seated in the far corner of the leather seat opposite, as he had been all along, and now he rose with a swift, almost delicate movement and sat beside me and enfolded me in his arms.

'It's five hours to London,' he whispered.

'I can wait,' I said, feeling the thirst like a fever as I held tight to him, feeling his lips against my eyelids and my hair. 'I want to hunt the London streets tonight,' I confessed a little shyly, but I saw only approbation in his eyes.

'Beautiful Julie, my Julie . . .' he whispered.

'You'll love the house in Mayfair,' I said.

'Yes . . .' he said.

'And when Richard finally tires of Rampling Gate, we shall go home.'

THE UNDEAD

Robert Bloch

Robert Bloch (born 1917) is one of America's
best-known writers of horror stories, a worthy
successor to Edgar Allan Poe and H. P.
Lovecraft. Since 1935 he has written hundreds
of short stories and several novels including
American Gothic and the immortal *Psycho*.
Among his vast output of magazine stories can
be found many clever and witty variations on
the vampire theme, including 'Dig That Crazy
Grave!', 'The Bat is My Brother', 'Hungarian
Rhapsody', and 'The Cloak' (filmed with Jon
Pertwee in 1970). 'The Undead' (taken from Bram
Stoker's original title for *Dracula*) appeared in
Bloch's recent collection *Midnight Pleasures* (1987).

E very evening at six Carol took off her glasses, but it didn't seem to
help. In the old movie reruns on TV, Cary Grant was always there
to exclaim – a mixture of surprise and gentlemanly lust – 'Why,
you're beautiful without your glasses!'

No one had ever told Carol that, even though she really was beautiful,
or almost so. With her light auburn hair, fair skin, regular features and
sapphire-blue eyes, she needed only the benefit of contact lenses to
perfect her image.

But why bother, when Cary Grant wasn't around? The bookshop's
customers for first editions and rare manuscripts seemed more interested in caressing parchment than in fondling flesh.

And by nightfall the place was empty; even its owner had departed,
leaving Carol to shut up shop, lock the doors, and set the alarms. With
a valuable stock on hand she was always mindful of her responsibility.

Or almost always.

Tonight, seated in the rear office and applying her lipstick preparatory to departure, she was surprised to hear footsteps moving across the uncarpeted floor in the hall beyond.

Carol frowned and put her compact down on the desktop. She distinctly recalled turning out the shop lights, but in her preoccupation with self-pity could she have forgotten to lock the front entrance?

Apparently so, because now the footsteps halted and a figure appeared in the office doorway. Carol blinked at the black blur of the body surmounted by a white blob of head and hair.

Then she put on her glasses and the black blur was transformed into a dark suit, the white blob became the face of an elderly gentleman with a receding hairline. Both his suit and his face were wrinkled, but the old man's dignified bearing overshadowed sartorial shortcomings and the onslaughts of age. And when he spoke his voice was resonant.

'Good evening. Are you the proprietor of this establishment?'

'I'm sorry,' Carol said. 'He's already left. We're closed for the night.'

'So I see.' The stranger nodded. 'Forgive me for intruding at this late hour, but I have travelled a long way and hoped I might still find him here.'

'We open tomorrow at ten. He'll be here then. Or if you'd like to leave a message—'

'It is a matter of some urgency,' the old man said. 'Word has reached me that your firm recently came into the possession of a manuscript – a manuscript which supposedly disappeared over seventy years ago.'

Carol nodded: 'That's right. The *Dracula* original.'

'You know the novel?'

'Of course. I read it years ago.'

Reaching into his pocket the stranger produced an old-fashioned calling card and handed it to her. 'Then perhaps you will find this name familiar.'

Carol peered at the lettering. The Gothic typescript was difficult to decipher and she repeated aloud what she read.

'Abraham Van Helsing?'

'Correct.' The old man smiled.

Carol shook her head. 'Wait a minute. You don't expect me to believe—'

'That I am the namesake of my great-grandfather, Mynheer Doctor Professor Van Helsing of Amsterdam?' He nodded. 'Oh yes, I can assure you that *Dracula* is not entirely a work of fiction. The identity of some of its characters was disguised, but others, like my illustrious ancestor, appeared under their own names. Now do you understand why I am interested in the original manuscript?' As he spoke, the old man glanced at the safe in the far corner. 'Is it too much to hope that you have it here?'

'I'm sorry,' Carol said. 'I'm afraid it's been sold.'

'Sold?'

'Yes. The day after we sent out our announcement the phones started ringing. I've never seen anything like it; just about every customer on our mailing list wanted to make a bid. And the final offer we got was simply fantastic.'

'Could you tell me who purchased the manuscript?'

'A private collector. I don't know his name, because my boss didn't tell me. Part of the deal was that the buyer would remain completely anonymous. I guess he was afraid somebody would try to steal it from him.'

The old man's frown conveyed a mingling of anger and contempt. 'How very cautious of him! But then they were all cautious – concealing something which never truly belonged to any of them. That manuscript has been hidden away all these years because it was stolen in the first place. Stolen from the man to whom the author gave it in gratitude for providing him with the basis of the novel – my own great-grandfather.' He stared at Carol. 'Who brought this to your employer?'

'He didn't tell me that, either. It's very hush-hush—'

'You see? Just as I told you. He must have known he had no right to possess it. Thieves, all of them!'

Carol shrugged. 'Really, I didn't know.'

'Of course. And I'm not blaming you, my dear young lady. But perhaps you can still be of some assistance to me. Did you happen to see the manuscript before it was sold?'

'Yes.'

'Can you describe it?'

'Well, to begin with, it wasn't called *Dracula*. The handwritten title was *The Undead*.'

'Ah yes.' The old man nodded quickly. 'That would be the original. What else can you recall about it?'

'The cover page was in Bram Stoker's handwriting, but the manuscript was typed. The author's changes and editorial corrections were done by hand, and so was the renumbering of the pages. It looked as though a lot of pages had been omitted – almost a hundred, I'd guess.' Carol paused. 'That's really just about all I remember.'

'And more than enough. From your description there's no doubt it is the genuine manuscript.' The old man nodded again. 'You're sure about pages being omitted?'

'Yes, quite sure, because my boss commented on that. Why, is it important?'

'Very. It seems Bram Stoker was wiser than his informant. Although the published novel does refer to Count Dracula's plan to bring vampirism to England, this motive is not stressed. What the missing pages contained is what Van Helsing revealed about Dracula's ultimate goal – to spread vampirism throughout the world. They also presented factual proof of Dracula's existence, proof too convincing to be ignored. Stoker wrote down everything Van Helsing told him but had second thoughts about including it in his final draft. I wished to make certain, however, that those pages didn't still exist in manuscript form. Now that I know, it won't even be necessary to seek out the new owner.'

'But you talk as though all this is true,' Carol said. 'It's only a novel. And Count Dracula gets killed in the end.'

'Again an example of Stoker's caution,' the old man told her. 'He had to invent a death scene to reassure his readers. Even so, just think of the influence that novel has had on millions of people who learned of Dracula and vampirism through the book and the theatre and films. As it is, many of them still half believe.' The resonant voice deepened. 'What do you think would have happened if Stoker hadn't novelized the story – if he'd written it for what it was, a true account of the actual experiences of Abraham Van Helsing? Even in novel form, if those missing pages still existed their message might bring a warning to the world which would endanger Dracula's plans.'

Carol glanced at her watch as he spoke. Six thirty. She was getting hungry and the old man's hangup was getting on her nerves. She stood up, forcing a smile.

'This has been very interesting,' she said. 'But I really must close up now.'

'You have been most kind.' The old man smiled. 'It seems a pity you do not entirely believe me, but I speak the truth. Count Dracula is as real as I am.'

Carol reached for her open compact on the desk. In the oval mirror she saw her reflection, but there was none of her visitor, even though he was standing quite close. Close enough for her to smell the rank breath, see the whiteness of the pointed teeth, feel the surprising strength of the hands that rose now to imprison her in their implacable grip.

As he forced her head back Carol's glasses dislodged, clattering to the floor, and for a moment her image in the compact mirror was indeed quite beautiful. Then the bright droplets spurted down, blotting it forever.

CHINA ROSE

Ron Weighell

Ron Weighell (born 1950) has written several
short stories and a novella (*The White Road*,
1992) reflecting his interest in the writings of
M. R. James, Arthur Machen, De Quincey, and
the western magical tradition.
Among his published works are *An Empty House
& other stories* (1986) and *Angles of Coincidence*
(1987). 'China Rose' was written especially for
this volume.

I t was the French detective Vidocq, I think, who used to say that every
act of evil had its own distinctive odour; that in a crowd of a
thousand persons he could tell transgressors of the moral law by the
sense of smell alone. What would a man of such singular olfactory
accomplishments have made of Nicholas Hallam and Rose Seaford, I
wonder? Nothing redolent of brimstone or corruption: rather a subtle
whiff of something clinical masked by a sweet incense. And about Rose,
of course, always the troubling fragrance of hibiscus.

It began one golden autumn morning in 1923, when I, young, poor
and happier than I knew, walked over Parliament Hill Fields to deliver a
belated birthday present to my cousin, Diane Harewood. An attack of
asthma had prevented me from attending her fancy-dress party the night
before, robbing me of the chance to appear as a swashbuckling pirate.
The Theda Baras and Nell Gwynns would never know what they had
missed. I remember worrying as I rang the bell in case I woke Diane,
which shows how little I knew then of her riotous life style. Coming from
the poorer side of the family, I had no experience of life among the

Hampstead set. So I was surprised to find the door answered by Napoleon Bonaparte, who let me into a scene of chaos.

It appeared that some colossus had lifted the lid off the house and buried the floor under a ton of streamers, balloons and unconscious bodies. The air was thick with cigarette smoke and the fumes of alcohol, the lounge curtains still drawn, so all was seen in an unearthly half-light. The clouds of noxious smoke and the notorious historical figures lying around in postures of pain and despair made it all a bit like Hades, but at the far end of the room a Lalique lamp cast a golden glow across armchairs drawn up around a coffee table laden with empty bottles. There sat Diane, transformed by white silk pyjamas, bathing cap and greasepaint into a fetchingly malevolent Pierrot. She was deep in conversation with a 90s dandy in the Des Esseintes style.

I edged past two exhausted females shuffling together beside a gramophone. The rasping voice was exhorting them to 'Charleston, Charleston!' but I could see they didn't have it in them.

Diane accepted my carefully chosen gift with no interest whatsoever and after a kiss and a gushing greeting, proceeded to ignore me. The dandy was telling her of an encounter he had had on a plateau in the Himalayas with a two-hundred-year-old man who lived in an underground chamber, guarding an enormous book with clasps of horn. He claimed to have won the old man's confidence by some yogic trick of sitting naked in the ice fields and melting the snow by generating bodily heat. (I commented that two-hundred-year-old men were notoriously easy to impress, but no one took any notice of me.) He learnt that the book contained the whole history of the human race and the old man had inherited the job of turning over a page each day until his successor should come. The dandy had had a devil of a job convincing the old sage that he was not the man, but he *had* got a sneaky glimpse of our future! The earth was soon to be destroyed by fire. It seemed that we were only here to prepare the way for another species!

It was while I was listening to this account that I first saw the strange couple seated in a corner of the room. One was a tousle-headed, handsome and athletic youth with the look of one of Aubrey Beardsley's more sinister satyrs. It seemed the trousers and shoes he wore were only there to hide his shaggy legs and cloven hooves. The other was the most unhealthy-looking woman I have ever seen. The wrist of the hand that supported her chin looked so thin, so horribly fragile, that it seemed the grip of anger or an accidental blow would have broken it like a twig. She drew on a cigarette held lightly between the first and second fingers of the other hand, flapping the wrist back limply after each inhalation and pouting a lazy grey cloud towards the ceiling. I noticed a curious silver ring on her index finger. It showed a horned serpent coiling back and forth inside the oval collet.

Her features were angular and ordinary, her skin was positively yellow, like old ivory jaundiced by years. Her teeth, which would become visible as she pouted out the smoke, were finely shaped but faintly tinged with blue and jagged along the edges.

She had about her a strange, sickly charm such as Poe might have delighted in, or Rossetti taken for an image of deathly elegance; another Beatrice. As I looked at her wide, dead eyes shadowed beneath the lower lashes by restless nights, I could almost see a ghostly pillow hovering behind her head. That was the first of two very perceptive fancies.

The most disturbing thing about her was her absolute lack of human response. She was not listening to the young man who sat beside her, she was watching him talk to her, observing him like some peculiar and only vaguely interesting phenomenon. The only sign of emotion I could discern was a fleeting twist to the corners of her mouth which suggested sarcastic amusement. I couldn't help feeling, though, that she was too withdrawn to find direct humour in her surroundings. The real source, I felt, must be more secret than that. The second fancy came to me then, of an unseen companion, a familiar as it were, crouching at her shoulder, its mouth to her ear. It was this creature, and not she, who thought human beings were all bloody fools, and who twisted her mouth, despite herself, with a stream of evil, whispered observations.

My attention was drawn back at that moment to the dandy, who had taken Diane to the window and drawn back the curtain. A wave of sunshine flooded the room, edging their forms in a shared aura of gold.

'Awake!' he cried melodiously. 'For Morning in the Bowl of Night has flung the stone that put the stars to flight, and lo! the Hunter of the East has caught St Pancras Station in a noose of light!'

Diane turned her grotesquely made-up face to his and laughingly called him a fool, and something in the tone of her voice made me sorry that no woman had ever spoken to me in such a way.

I found myself rising to join them, so we stood close together peering out into the bright world. Close to, the dandy smelled strongly of some musky perfume. Diane introduced us and I learned that his name was Nicholas Hallam. When he learned that I was a clerk, he looked at me with sympathy.

'You're always telling me that my life is too selfish, Diane' – the sarcastic twist that came to her mouth suggested that she had said no such thing – 'I have decided to make Thomas my good cause. I will save this poor wretch from himself. If he's still a clerk in one month, there is no hope for him. Be honest, young man. Do you really wish to spend this sequence of precious and unrepeatable sensations we call a day languishing in the dungeons of Messrs Kneebone and Kneebone, or whatever they are called, pining for adventure while your life goes drifting away, along with the desks and the uncounted dirty ledgers, towards the grave?'

'Not particularly,' I conceded, 'but I have rent to pay, and lately I've developed some expensive habits like eating. So I'm afraid,' I finished checking my pocket watch, 'I must push off, or the desks and ledgers will be drifting toward the grave with my replacement at the helm.'

'Yes, and we must leave too, Diane,' said Hallam, glancing across her to the woman in the corner who had so aroused my interest. 'Our young friend has reminded us of our duty. Rose and I have a hard day too. It is our plan to walk away the morning, giving common people a chance to look at us and dream. Then a good lunch with fine wine in a little restaurant I know, and a trip to my bookbinders, where my volumes of Swinburne await me clad in a new raiment of leather, scarlet as the tongue of Sin.' He sighed deeply. 'And if we have the strength after such a day of toil, a whole decanter of cognac remains at home to be disposed of unaided. I hardly think we shall have the energy left to invoke Ashtoreth tonight!' Bending forward he kissed Diane's hand and whispered 'Goodbye for now, my sweet Pierrot.'

Diane simpered and let go of his hand with reluctance.

'Call in on us some time, Lenihan,' he added to me, holding out an expensive-looking calling card. The address was 13 Tamar Gardens, Hampstead.

A couple of days later I took the umpteenth look at that black and gold card, pondered again the weird charm of Rose Seaford, for such apparently was her name, and decided to take Hallam up on his invitation. The evening wind was blowing fine rain down the streets, and my asthma had been playing up a little, but I had just bought a rather snappy trilby which, I thought, gave me a touch of style, so I said 'what the hell' and took a taxi.

Tamar Gardens sounded very plush. It turned out to be a rather run-down block of flats. Somewhat disillusioned, I rang the bell and waited; and waited. Just when I was about to give up and go home, Rose Seaford opened the door and stepped out, wearing a voluminous black raincoat and a black slouch hat. Drawing me in out of the lamplight, she whispered fearfully, 'Did you see anyone watching the flat?'

I shrugged in confusion. 'I need your help,' she said, peering over my shoulder. Then she put her finger to her lips and pointed to a solitary walker who came into view, and glanced in our direction as he went by. I was beginning to enjoy my close proximity to Rose in the shadowy doorway, but she pushed me out into the rain, whispering 'We've got to keep him in sight, but don't let him see us.'

So I found myself tailing a complete stranger through the strengthening rain, ducking into doorways now and then, and worrying as I did so about the condition of my drooping, saturated hat. Soon the whole thing became rather exciting. My inborn flair for detection, nurtured on Dupin and Holmes, got the better of me. Whenever the man passed under a street-lamp I scrutinized him. It was strange, I reflected; he looked like a man walking home in the rain! He paddled along with his hands thrust into the pockets of his sodden overcoat, apart from the moments when a stronger gust came, lashing along the street, and he clutched desperately at his trilby. I found myself wondering ruefully whether it was a new one. We followed him for miles before losing him in a positive warren of alleys. Rose hovered for a moment, seemingly quite rattled, then said, 'We've got to get there first.'

'Where?' I cried, but she was already off with a brisk step. Then followed the most exhausting hour I have ever experienced. Rose might have been frail of form, but she set a fast pace and held it up hill and down dale.

I was soon trailing behind with a stitch, my breath steaming out into the chill drizzle. When she was obliged to wait until I caught up, the stream of invective to which she subjected me would have staggered a stevedore. I would never have guessed how rich and fruity her language could be. Eventually we came onto a steep lane where the gutters were awash, causing our sodden shoes to slip on the smooth flagstones. Beside a set of high, barred gates set in a towering wall we stopped, and I realized that we were in Swains Lane, at the old gates of Highgate cemetery. The place should have been locked up at such an hour, but inexplicably, Rose must have known that the lock had not been turned for she threw her weight against the wet iron bars, and with a deep and ominous groan, the gates rolled back on their rusty hinges.

Here, let me confess, I loitered somewhat. Highgate cemetery is ruinous, overgrown, shadow-haunted and choked to overflowing with more than four thousand corpses. An unwholesome necropolis of crumbling tombs, it has never figured highly in my list of daytime haunts. By night, 'a blended scene of moles, fanes, arches, domes and palaces, where, with his brother Horror, Ruin sits', it was the last place on earth

I would have chosen to pursue some nameless and doubtless unpleasant errand.

Rose, though, was striding off along a gloomy, rain-washed path hemmed in by ivied slabs, stone crosses and contorted, leafless trees. An owl actually had the audacity to hoot. I stuck close and whistled carelessly as we descended some ruined steps and followed the path to a tall gate built on the design of an Egyptian temple, as if a normal gateway were not sepulchral enough. Here Rose turned and gripped my arm.

'Wait here,' she said firmly. 'And no talking to strangers.'

Then she turned and disappeared up the path by which she had come.

My initial desire was to follow her, but I set my back against the wall on one side of the gate and tried to think beautiful thoughts. Although I had become oblivious to the rain, the wind seemed suddenly to penetrate my drenched mackintosh, cutting me to the bone. I began to shiver. My imagination was playing up too. There I was, trying desperately to keep my mind on something sensible and healthy, and all the while my inner eye was plagued by images of death and decay. Every novel, every theory I had ever read concerning the horrors that reach from beyond the grave unwound before me. I was scaring myself stiff.

In annoyance as much as anything, I began to pace up and down the path along which Rose had departed, that is, first away from, and then toward, the Egyptian gate. It was while turning away from it for the tenth time that I heard a distinct slow scuffing of feet walking out of the darkness towards my back! There could be no mistake. I was being approached out of the dark central labyrinth of the cemetery.

I must have aged visibly at that moment. It was my first taste of supernatural fear, and it robbed me of all volition. All I could do was to stand paralysed as the steps drew nearer. My heart lurched violently as fingers tightened on my shoulder, then a voice close to my ear whispered, 'It's only me.'

I have never struck a woman but it was a close thing at that moment.

'What in God's name are you playing at?' I gasped, too shaken up to shout. Rose set off along the path.

'Nothing in God's name,' she called back. 'All the paths return to that spot – I came round that way to save time.'

'What are we doing here, Rose?' I asked, recovering a little composure as I caught up with her.

'That,' she replied wittily, 'would be telling.'

Not much more than an hour later we were in Hallam's front room drying out, and I had still received no satisfactory explanation for the adventure. The room was not what I had expected of Hallam. There were no vast cases of old tomes, no Gothic trappings and no luxurious furniture. The place had a spartan, oriental look to it, with acres of bare floor scattered with cushions, a folded screen, and two glass cabinets of simple but sound workmanship which contained small ornaments and perhaps a dozen volumes with fine but hardly extravagant bindings. A few silken banners hanging on the walls showed brilliantly coloured images of fierce Tibetan gods, and a crystal ball supported on the coils of a magnificent gilt dragon sat on a low cabinet. There was, too, a small but exquisitely detailed statue of some female deity of the East, not Kali, who has many arms and blue skin, but a being with a normal quota of limbs and skin the colour of flame, her voluptuous body twisted into a dancing posture. She wore a grisly torque of human skulls.

I was squatting, a little self-consciously, in a silk kimono sipping a glass of cognac. Rose was reclining on the opposite side of the fireplace, her eyes on the vortex of steam that was swirling above our drying clothes. Hallam had just entered wearing a robe of black velvet and was pacing back and forth before the fire like a caged tiger, gesticulating grandly and chuckling, as though he were as high as a kite.

'Rose is right, of course,' he decided, 'It is better that you don't know her purposes tonight. There are some things,' he concluded darkly, 'which man ought not to know.'

He took the decanter from the low cabinet and refilled my glass with cognac. 'In any case,' he continued on a lighter note, 'you have had an intense experience, which is surely our purpose in being here if we have one at all. To be where the vital forces of life unite most intensely. For an hour or so you did have a quickening sense of life.'

That had been the case, but I had no intention of conceding without reasoned arguments, so I said 'Piffle!'

'Pater actually,' he pointed out, quite unperturbed, 'but no matter. I must admit you disappoint me, Lenihan. I had such high hopes for you, but it seems your hard, gem-like flame is guttering.'

I gave up gracefully; there was no arguing with either of them. In any case, having accepted a glass of brandy to warm me up, I had begun to see what people saw in the stuff, and with each refill had sunk deeper into the warm lagoon of intoxication. Now I had reached the point where the gears of the mind had started to slip and the commonplace takes on an unguessed profundity. Even as he spoke, I was watching the smoke of the fire billowing in slow, ghostly waves of unendurable beauty. I was suddenly overcome with an inexplicable melancholy.

'Really, I'm not mocking you, Lenihan,' Hallam was saying. 'I merely wish to impress upon you one important fact – the most important it may be! Simply that life is a desperate business; you should seek experience itself and not some imagined goal that you may never live to see. You have had an experience this evening, that is all. The reasons, the rights and wrongs of it do not concern you, nor should they. Now come on Lenihan, have another drink and relax.'

I glanced vacantly about me, searching vainly for some blade of wit that had not been blunted by the brandy. A mahogany display case just behind me, quite plain and simple but looking at that moment like no other display case in creation, caught my eyes. I moved over to look at it. The interior was lined with crumpled red silk, a waste of frozen blood across which was trekking an ivory figure no larger than a thumbnail. He was an old Japanese gentleman in short breeches and a ragged vest. His tiny arms were withered to sinew and bone, his lean jaw locked in an agony of exhaustion. The burden under which he struggled so grimly was a lion-headed demon riding his back, one fore-claw tangled in the old man's hair, the other thrown back in a finely observed struggle for balance. So perfect was the impression of pain and unendurable weight that it seemed the old man had staggered for days across those cruel wastes while the monster threw back its finely-carved jaws in triumphant laughter. It was a beautiful and a terrible vision seen only for a second before my breath defiled the glass and swallowed the scene in mist.

'Netsuke,' said Hallam at my elbow, conjuring back the vision with a magical pass of his handkerchief. 'I have quite a few, though it would be rather ostentatious to display more than one at a time. Many of the designs are based on legends.' He handed me my glass and went on to describe a few, which I cannot honestly pretend to remember in any detail, though one concerned a deity on the floating bridge of Heaven, whatever that is, forming islands from the foam that dripped from the tip of his celestial spear, and another told of a dwarf who travelled in a vessel of gooseskins and had once bitten the cheek of some god or other. (Strangely enough I do remember the name of the little god-nibbler, though why it stuck in my mind I can't imagine. If ever anyone is lost for that name, I hope I will be there to prompt, casually, 'Sukuna Bikona'.) Rose had taken a peach from a bowl by her side and was tearing the luscious flesh with wet, sucking bites, like a rapacious oriental succubus.

That much impressed itself upon my fuddled brain but no more. I was engulfed in the warm flood, and Hallam's voice became steadily more remote. I remember the spines of the few leather-bound books in a case, glowing like crystal columns full of green and gold amber liquor, full of the liquor of the gods; and the gilded lettering on one, a copy of Pater's

Greek Studies, at which I stared until the word 'greek' became the most stupid combination of letters imaginable. My next distinct recollection is of Rose drawing back the drapes and a faint, pinkish radiance giving a suggestion of living colour to her face. Hallam was saying, angrily I thought, 'Too risky – one is enough.' Then he saw that I was awake and his tone changed.

'Dawn, Lenihan,' he said. 'Time to go. You can walk home across Parliament Hill Fields. See the dawn over London. Another priceless experience.'

He was laughing to himself as he said it.

The drenching mist must have left me with a cold, because I was shivery and lethargic for days after. Every morning I searched the papers with fear, expecting reports of some dark deed among the tombs of Highgate cemetery, but I found nothing of significance.

One day about a fortnight later, I met Hallam and Diane outside the Bargate Café in York Street. This was the occasion on which I realized that they were lovers. It was also the first time I noticed Diane's failing health. As they talked, betraying their new-found intimacy with every tone and gesture, I took in her drawn, pale face and lack-lustre gaze. What disturbed me most was her mirthless, lethargic manner. I gave her the openings for a couple of her usual digs at my expense and she let them go without a word. Watching them off into the grey, overcast afternoon, I kept thinking 'first Rose, now Diane'. Whatever Hallam got up to, it seemed to take a fearsome toll on his women.

I wondered too, how Rose would take this change of affections. Somehow I could not see her sitting back meekly and accepting such a state of affairs. To my surprise, I found myself hoping that those blank, pitiless eyes might turn towards me. By some obscure alchemy of her own, she had transformed the slightest gesture of human acknowledgment – a glance, a sarcastic smile – into gold. The indifference was a challenge. I don't know that I was foolish enough to fall in love with her, but I did apparently want her to like me.

Hallam's romance with Diane began to stimulate gossip among mutual friends and without actually prying I kept my ears open. Unfortunately, where facts are scarce, opinion is generally most plentiful among the uninformed. There is always the friend of a friend – more often it is the friend of an enemy – who is willing to extemporize. The view of the man that emerged was nothing if not comprehensive.

Hallam, it seemed, was a penniless sponger; he was a millionaire. A student of Ancient Mysteries, he 'dabbled' in the Black Mass. He was a scholar of no mean repute, and the author of some fine poetry. He affected false scholarship and coined pornographic verse. He had published some distinguished essays on comparative religion; he produced spurious 'studies' of pseudo-occultism. He was a homosexual, though it seemed that no woman was safe with him.

For a while I did my best to keep track of this pendulum of opinion as it swung its crazy way between adulation and scorn, but growing sick and dizzy with it all, I decided to hold my judgment and size up the man on the basis of my own experience. One piece of evidence a little more substantial than talk did give me cause for concern though. There had been newspaper reports a few years earlier that Hallam used dangerous drugs and encouraged his acolytes to do the same. It could have been scandal-mongering of course, but I couldn't see the newspaper in question throwing mud so blatantly unless sure that a certain amount of it was going to stick. It was significant, too, that Hallam had not sued.

Around this time, the firm to which I had given ten years' faithful service decided that I was surplus to requirements, thus fulfilling Hallam's resolution at our first meeting. I had not lasted the month!

For a while my financial circumstances, which had never been exactly healthy, were precarious, a factor which no doubt contributed greatly to a renewal of my asthma. Things were pretty black, one way and another, and I lost contact with our main protagonists for some weeks. Only when my health began to return did I venture out to visit Diane. I ragged her about her laziness and gave her an outrageously exaggerated account of my own illness but all the while I was inwardly appalled by her condition. She was thin and listless, quite drained of her old energy and her complexion was sickly white. Most disturbing of all, she had quite lost the last spark from her eyes. It was a shell of Diane that I spoke to.

My concern rapidly gave way to suspicion when she admitted that she had not seen a doctor. 'Nicholas says I have a leak in my aura,' she explained seriously. 'I've been losing energy for ages. It's a good job he knows about these things because he can put it right.'

Just how he was achieving this Diane was unwilling to say, but it involved an ancient ritual into which she had been initiated at Hallam's flat, by Hallam *and* Rose! At least it had been Hallam and Rose at the start, but on that first occasion they had been interrupted by the doorbell. Rose had left to answer the door and had not returned.

Then the penny dropped and I guessed who the unexpected visitor had been. Diane could not remember the date but she did remember that it had been raining that night!

So I knew the answer to the mystery of Highgate cemetery! It had been a way of keeping me occupied for a couple of hours. The method, and choice of destination, had probably been left to Rose's peculiar sense of humour!

After that, I was in the mood for a confrontation with Hallam and made straight for his flat. I was some thirty yards from the house when a taxi drew up outside and Hallam emerged, followed by a woman in a dark coat and slouch hat. Even without the familiar clothing from the night of the wild chase, the slow pantherine sway would have identified Rose. Hallam paid the driver, put his arm around her shoulder and together they entered his flat.

I walked by and kept on walking. The realization that Hallam was seeing both women did not surprise me overmuch but Diane's state made the whole thing seem doubly squalid. There was something petty and two-faced about pulling such a trick on a sick girl, especially as Hallam was in all probability the one who had made her sick in the first place. It was then that I decided to set my scruples aside and get down to some serious prying.

An afternoon in the reading room of the British Library with Hallam's published works proved edifying. All the books were de luxe, privately printed editions with exquisite bindings. Some were poetry, metrically dextrous and clearly influenced by Baudelaire and Swinburne. Others dealt with Egyptian Magic, Tibetan Tantric Yoga and the erotic temple sculptures of India. One work entitled *The Serpent of Khem* had an acrostic on the title page that spelled out the identity of the personage whose worship was recounted within.

> Serpent of Khem, by old mysterious Art.
> Allures with the coiling favours of the Worm.
> Twines with the knot of love about my heart.
> Abomination in beguiling form!
> Nature supreme who rules our every part!

Altogether a charming dedication. Little that I read made sense to me then, but I could hardly fail to notice the constant references to drugs, from peyote to the deadly refinements of heroin. In the powers of magic I did not at that time believe, but in the deleterious power of drugs I certainly did.

One of the most striking features of these wonderfully printed books was the wealth of weird and disturbing illustrations by an artist called Alphonsus Gaunt. That name rang a bell. I remembered a quite terrifying edition of *Grimm's Fairy Tales* that had overshadowed much of my early

childhood. The plates accompanying one of Hallam's poetic effusions –
Hymns to the Nephilim – surpassed that dark masterpiece by a long way.
Then I made a significant discovery. In one of the volumes was a
frontispiece drawing of Hallam and Gaunt and both faces were equally
familiar. Alphonsus Gaunt was the satyr I had seen speaking to Rose at
Diane's party!

That threw me for a moment. Either Gaunt had been a boy-genius
when he illustrated the *Grimm's*, or he was older than he looked. In any
case I might have found a source of inside information on the Hallam
ménage.

Alphonsus Gaunts were not plentiful in the street directory. I traced him
to a basement flat of a once-grand house in Deyton Street: not quite the
residence I had expected of a distinguished artist! My ring was answered
by an incredibly pale and shrivelled old woman, who nodded at the
mention of Gaunt's name and gestured me to enter.

The flickering radiance of a candle cupped in her hand gave enough
light to show the way between stacks of magazines and newspapers
smelling of damp. We passed through a kitchen with a huge sink and
cold-stone flags underfoot, where an immense range lay, long ago choked
on soot and fat. There was a sound of dripping water. Coming at last to
a great door of oak, she threw open the carved panels and shrank away
into the gloom. I stepped through and the door closed behind me.

Many candles were burning in the room. I saw skulls of men and
animals; distorted, elongated sculptures of stone and clay; the tattered
spines of a thousand old books. And I saw a host of faces watching me.

In the candlelight were faces benign and malevolent, beautiful and
hideous. One I will never forget, bony and blotched, with a cruel, wet-
lipped mouth and obliquely-slanting eye-pits, watery, yellow and alive
with a vile intelligence. The head was crowned with a thatch of white,
downy fur, and above it, as though unfurling from a hunched back,
immensely powerful wings, serrated and membranous like those of a bat,
but gnarled and shaggy at the joints like the forelegs of a dray horse.

Then my eyes adjusted and I made out frames and easels. They were
paintings, wonderful, living faces on canvas and wood, even on the
sound boards of old radio sets. Then one face, a benign and monumental
Greek head, let out a slow breath and moved.

It was Gaunt, seated crossed-legged before an odd little altar-like table.
He held a pencil, which was moving swiftly over a sheet of paper. It
seemed the pencil lead was kindling a black fire on the page, tongues and
billows of a sinuous burning that licked and swirled to engulf the virgin

[219]

parchment. Out of the swiftly and perfectly formed flames and smoke, faces began to form, receding ranks and columns of profiles, sphinx-like and vigilant. Soon a half-formed monstrosity of a face emerged, growing under the moving pencil, a soft, twisted mask that watched me with living eyes. It was a shock to realize that, in order to produce an image that was the right way up for me, Gaunt had to be drawing it upside down. But not as great as the one I got when I looked closely at the artist, for his eyes were tightly closed.

He was himself as singular as anything in that weirdly disturbing place. I could now put his age at around forty, but he had a honed, hawklike handsomeness of features and an unruly thatch of dark, curly hair that would give an impression of youth from a distance. He was dressed not in some garment of ritual, but a threadbare jacket over a tattered, paint-spotted pullover and no shirt. He might have been a labourer hardened by years of toil in the sun and wind. Yet there was about him the look of a magus.

Laying down his pencil, he opened his eyes and looked on me without the slightest sign of surprise. The appearance of strangers in his room was apparently a common occurrence. Leaning forward, he touched my arm.

'A flesh and blood visitor for a change,' he observed mildly. 'Who are you, an emissary from the parasites and eaters of filth? Another sleepwalker from the dung heaps of society?'

'I saw you at Diane's party. You were with Rose Seaford—'

'The whore of Hell,' he interjected. 'Do you follow the cult of the Kû?'

I hesitated, unsure of the answer that was most likely to win his confidence. The delay betrayed me.

'No, you don't, do you? What are you here for? My work is no longer for sale.'

'I'm not here to buy – although I do find your work fascinating.'

My choice of words seemed to please him. Encouraged, I poured out the whole story of Hallam's activities. When I'd finished, he pondered a moment, then offered a tobacco tin full of roll-ups. When I refused he lit one up himself and proceeded to make a pot of tea. There was something incongruous about that figure, who looked, in the smoke of his cigarette like an alchemist crouched over his alembics, engaged in so domestic a task.

The tea, however, was strong and good. Gaunt sized me up for a while, then said abruptly 'When I called her the whore of Hell just now – it wasn't an insult. It was a title—' He took a sip of tea. 'You really don't know what I'm talking about, do you?' His voice was heavy with contempt. 'That silly little girl of yours – has she any idea what she's involved in? I thought not. Sleepwalkers! She's in real danger, boy!'

'I know. Hallam uses drugs—'

'I'm not talking about drugs, fool! Do you think a book like *Hymns to the Nephilim* can be made without a cost? *They* have to be lured to visible appearance and that takes energy. What is drained has to be replenished. The Kiss of the Shade, boy – the *Mors Osculi*. The soundless reverberation of silent gongs. Get your girl out of it now, right away. Tonight! Stay with her – keep them away!'

Despite myself, I was letting him get through to me. I felt terrified. I must have looked it too, because Gaunt shook his head and said 'Wait – I may have something that will help you.' I found myself thanking him.

'I'm not doing it for you – or that stupid girl. I have a difference of opinion with Hallam over Rose.'

He produced, of all things, a small plate or shallow dish painted with spirals of looping script and a symbol reminiscent of the outline of a bat. Holding it up before his face, he focused all his attention on it.

As I sat waiting, my mind began to play strange tricks on me. It seemed to grow darker in the room, and much colder. I swear that some of the paintings seemed to move, so that I seemed to be sitting in the middle of a decidedly hostile crowd. Then Gaunt took up a piece of white linen and wrapped up the plate. As he handed the bundle to me he said: 'Take this and place it in the girl's room. Close to her as you can get it. She'll be all right then.'

I took the thing to humour him. By that time my only thought was to get out of the place before I ended up as mad as he was. Doubtful of my ability to find the way out, I asked if the old woman could show me back to the door. In the candlelight his expression became more than ever that of a malevolent satyr as he answered 'There's no old woman living in this house.'

That did it. I got out of the room as quickly as I could and made my own way through the dark labyrinth of the house. If there were any light switches, I didn't find them so I stumbled through the piles of papers in the passages, ridiculously afraid of coming upon that wizened old woman who, in Gaunt's ambiguously *stressed* expression, did not *live* in the house at all. It was just an irrational fear of the dark, I told myself, but that didn't help me one bit. By the time I found the door and let myself out into the deserted streets, my nerves were in a sorry state.

Let me admit that my only thought was to go home and forget all the mumbo-jumbo. I actually got to my own front door, but I didn't go in. Something told me that I was right about Diane being in danger, if only from the drugs that Hallam was so fond of. And if Gaunt was an example of the adherents of this Kû cult, Diane's sanity was doubly in danger.

So despite the lateness of the hour, I made my way to Diane's house. I got no reply to my knock, and all the windows were in darkness, but when I looked through the letterbox, I glimpsed the distinctive fur lining of Hallam's overcoat hanging in the hall.

All the tension of the previous few hours came out in anger. I began pounding at the door and shouting through the letter box. Just as curtains were drawing back all over the street and shouts of complaint began, I heard a sound of bolts drawn, and Hallam's face appeared in the doorway.

At first he refused to let me in, but when I began to shout about the police he had a sudden change of heart. The house was unheated, but Hallam was bathed in sweat. He was dressed in a black robe with wide sleeves and a thrown-back hood that gave him the look of a sensual and worldly monk, an impression compounded by the smell of some heavy incense that hung in the air. If Hallam intended to keep me talking in the hall, he was out of luck. A glance had shown that the living-room was in darkness, and that a light was glinting through the crack of the bedroom door. Before he had a chance to say, or do, anything, I had crossed the hall and thrown open the door.

The image frozen by my sudden entry will never fade from my mind. Diane lay on her bed, her face pale and slick as a mask of white silk. She was naked, and running with sweat, or some glistening unguent. A heavy gold plate, or plaque lay over her groin. The air in the room was thick with incense and pulsed with a deep, throbbing that troubled the ear-drums without creating a sensation of actual sound. Rose Seaford stood over Diane, her hands gesturing over the throat and breast regions with the movements of one warming her hands over a fire. Rose's hair was dishevelled, her yellow skin glinting with sweat. She wore a long, diaphanous garment of flame-coloured silk, gathered at the waist with a single black cord. On her forehead was a disc of polished metal. A heavy choker at her throat held a second disc and suspended from it on a fine chain hung a variety of geometric shapes.

There was nothing languid or sickly about the gaze she turned on me then. She radiated quite diabolic power. Hallam began to say something but she silenced him with a venomous look, and returned her wide, white gaze to me. The gash of her mouth tightened hard, and the muscles of her jaw flexed spasmodically. I really thought she was about to launch herself on me like a great cat. Instead she straightened up and extended her arms in my direction. I felt a crawling over my flesh, and the atmosphere grew suffocating, as though the very pressure in the room had increased. Suddenly, I felt fear, a blind, unreasoning urge to run, to escape the stifling radiation that beat out from her like waves of intolerable heat. My brow felt as though it would burst. And then the face of Rose Seaford began to change.

How can I describe what happened in the pulsing, smoky atmosphere of that room? If I say she grew old, you will not understand. She became ancient, as the visage of the Sphinx is ancient, as the colossi at Memnon are ancient. It was a face that might have gazed for aeons upon desolation, or brooded through time in some jungle-draped ruin. And out of her body, coiling thickly down both arms, came a black flowing of serpents.

But this was not the greatest horror. For she multiplied before my eyes, generated a host of identical snake goddesses on every side, until the spiralling black coils of her hatred filled the space between us, and the air became black with it.

Against that onslaught a puny human could have done nothing. I was frozen with terror, and could only close my eyes and wait to be engulfed in the seething blackness.

Then the pulsing on the air stopped, and the room became very still. I opened my eyes and saw that the blackness had dispersed. There was only one figure before me, one Rose Seaford staring with a look of puzzlement at the region of my chest. I felt a warm, bracing sensation radiating from that spot, like a gulp of brandy on a cold day. The source was the inside pocket of my coat, where I had placed Gaunt's amulet.

With trembling fingers I drew it out and tore off the linen wrapping. Holding it before me I moved towards the bed, and as I did so Rose Seaford drew back and skirted the room until she and Hallam stood between me and the door. Close to, I could see that the metal plate on Diane's groin was engraved with animal-headed gods and snakes. I picked the thing up and shied it at the watching couple. It was probably just as well it missed them. The impact took a two-inch chunk out of the wall. Hallam scoooped up the plate and took Rose's arm.

'Come on,' he said levelly. 'You've got what you wanted.' Turning to me he added, 'You wasted your time, Lenihan. We'd finished with her tonight in any case.'

When they had gone I breathed for what seemed to the first time in minutes, and covered Diane with a sheet from the floor.

Diane recovered in time, but she was never quite as *vital* again. She was devastated when Hallam would have nothing more to do with her, and ironically, blamed me for driving him away. Hallam, she said, had done everything he could to cure her 'loss of energy' and my interference with the rites had offended him! We were never as close after that, which was a pity.

One bitter December night the following year, I made the short journey to the Everyman Theatre in Hampstead to see Coward's *The Vortex*, which by only its second week had ensured a successful run in the West End, establishing once and for all the name of its already famous young author. I caught one of the last performances before the play left the confines of that 'converted drill-hall' for the more salubrious setting of the Royalty. It seemed to me in my naïveté a tremendously powerful piece, and the wild response of the audience could not but have an unsettling effect on a ragged-arsed clerk a whole year older than the author whose hour of triumph he had just witnessed. I left the theatre dizzy with fantasies of suddenly discovered talent and critical acclaim. It was with something of a shock that I glimpsed those two familiar faces in the buffeting crowd. Slipping behind a nearby stanchion, I paused to watch them.

Hallam was deep in conversation with a young couple, smiling the smile of one who has no need of dreams to sustain him. He was wearing immaculate evening dress, and a cloak thrown back at the shoulders to reveal the crimson lining; all very Mephistophelean. In fact with his elegant appearance and those bloody gashes at the shoulders like torn wings, he looked every inch the fallen angel. Rose stood beside him, her arm linked so lightly with his that her grey leather glove barely compressed his sleeve. There was no clinging with her, no sacrifice of her independence for anything as human as love. Her tawny hair was drawn tightly back into an elaborate knot at the nape of her neck, displaying the fine, strong line of her jaw. She was engulfed in a mist of grey furs piled pillow deep behind her head and tucked snugly under her chin like a winter blanket. She stood apart, even in the crowd, sweeping the passersby with her cold, heartless expression. As I watched, her other, unseen companion must have whispered something, because she smiled that nasty secret smile. And I knew that somewhere they had found another victim and completed the dreadful process of reparation. This knowledge did not come from the smile of Rose Seaford as she scanned the crowd flocking home through the December darkness. It was the healthy bloom of her skin, and her eyes, no longer blank and dead, but ablaze with replenished inner fire.

SAINT SEBASTIAN
AND THE MONA LISA
A. F. Kidd

A. F. Kidd (born 1953) is a freelance copywriter
and artist who has written many excellent
supernatural stories. This new story displays an
ingenious twist on the vampire theme.

It was dark in the little chapel, the dark of places where sun's light
never falls. Working by the smoking light of a sputtering candle,
Andrea Giaiotti applied, very delicately, colour to the wet wall. As
delicately as a caress.

Saint Sebastian looked down at the painter with his own face, a plain
Sienese face, contorted in agony. These were features painted as much in
sweat as in pigment, Giaiotti having spent hours contorting them before
a cheap mirror in order to get the expression right; with the result that the
saint, blood spilling from his many arrow wounds, had none of the
serenity of other depictions of his martyrdom. He bled, he was in pain,
he was dying screaming. Which was exactly what Giaiotti had intended.

He wasn't sure what Father Giordano would say, however. There was
an uneasy suspicion in the back of his mind that the Church actually
preferred to think of saints meeting their deaths with their faces grave
and contemplative and their clear eyes full of nothing but God. And
Christ – Gesù, he thought, suddenly, to paint the Crucifixion. That
would be something to see. A Christ in mortal agony, as he had to be as
soon as the nails went in, let alone hanging on the Cross for hours.
Giaiotti knew how men died. His broad hands, which made his
paintbrush look so small, were scarred with sword cuts: he had killed
men himself, and knew well the stench of blood and fear and shit and
sweat which was a battlefield. He was thirty-seven years old.

[225]

These arrow wounds, for example. They came from bitter memory, and remembered pain. How it had felt entering his arm – a hammer blow and then sharpest agony. The sensation of it, arrowhead, wooden shaft, in his flesh, like a wrong bone. They'd cut and pulled it out, through his arm, because of the barbs, after breaking the shaft off. Giaiotti clenched his eyes shut and breathed out explosively, and was abruptly aware of smells: the flamey reek of the spitting candle, his own sweat, the greasy sheepskin vest (which he suspected hadn't been properly cured) he wore against the cold. The pigments he used, each with its own peculiar scent, like different notes of music. The wet smell of the plaster.

'This is the San Sebastiane of Andrea Giaiotti,' said the guide, putting coins into a slot to switch on the illumination as he spoke. 'It was painted around 1460.' The tourists, obediently, gave a collective gasp as the saint's tortured face and mutilated body came into view. 'See how Giaiotti painted him as a man in pain, rather than a saint who could rise above suffering. It's a characteristic of his work, but it's certainly not usual at this period of the Renaissance. There's a tradition that Giaiotti had been a mercenary soldier as a young man, which could account for the realism of the wounds. In fact he painted very few works, or very few have survived. It's said that he stopped painting altogether after completing his Crucifixion, which we'll see in the church of Santa Croce. No one knows why; it's probably his masterpiece.'

The light went out – he knew how long his speeches lasted, to the second – and he led his charges out of the darkened chapel.

I wonder, thought the guide, whose name was Pietro Oliveri, if any of this lot really feel any sense of history, of Andrea Giaiotti, or anything at all.

'We're now going to see what's called the Scotti Chapel.' Several of the tourists laughed. Peasants, thought Pietro. 'It's named after the di Scotti family, who came here from the Veneto in the middle of the fifteenth century, and were the patrons of a number of artists including Giaiotti.' He paused. 'In here is his only surviving work that isn't a fresco. It's painted on a wooden panel and is known as *La Madonna con Tessuto*, which is to say weaving, or web, because of the tapestry in the picture. But that isn't the most remarkable thing about her.' This was a dramatic moment, and Pietro relished it: On came the lights, and the small painting thus revealed brought another gasp, more awed than the first, from his audience. 'I'm sure most of you are familiar with *La Gioconda* – the Mona Lisa,' Pietro went on, almost maliciously, 'and the resemblance won't have escaped you. However, Leonardo painted the

Mona Lisa in 1499, and this painting pre-dates it by almost thirty years. We have documentary evidence of that.'

That's shut them up, he thought smugly.

Giaiotti's eyes were smarting and gritty: he rubbed at them irritably. Thankfully the fresco work was finished for the day, but he sighed at the thought of what still awaited him. San Sebastiane and his like were all very well, but it was the private commissions which enabled him to eat. So he had not been at all upset to replace the late and unlamented Lorenzo Rossi, who had dropped dead in his studio for no apparent reason, as Francesco di Scotti's protegé. But di Scotti was not a man who listened to excuses if you delivered later than promised; and so here was Giaiotti, ruining his eyesight in a windowless chapel by day and in his own studio by night.

Maddalena was a compensation: his model for the Virgin. Which was one thing she wasn't, thought Giaiotti wryly, scratching absently at his neck. His fingers burrowed into his imperfectly shaved beard, discovering to his annoyance that something had bitten him – more than once, by the feel of it. I might have known this stinking sheepskin had vermin in it, he thought, toying with the idea of taking it back and stuffing it down Beppo Riccio's throat; but he didn't really have the time, however satisfying that would have been, and besides, he'd probably freeze to death without it.

It was nearly dark outside and the painter wondered morosely when he would see daylight once more, then cursed violently as he walked into a fellow pissing in the gutter. Damn them all to hell, he thought, and damn me too for ever wanting to be a painter. Why didn't I stay a soldier? He knew the answer to that, though, rubbing his arm where the huge puckered scar was, where the arrow wound had gone bad. That was a worse stink than the battlefield. He also knew he'd have lost the arm at least if that Greek hadn't known to introduce maggots into the wound, to eat away the rot. Much good his knowledge had done the Greek, dead of a sword-stroke in the gut not long after. No, thought Giaiotti with utter certainty, creating is better than destroying. Especially when the simple act of painting, of watching an image take shape at the end of his brush, gave him such intense pleasure, as unlike the bloody fury of battle as he could imagine.

He blew on his cold hands as he turned into the narrow street where his studio was, seeing with satisfaction that there was a light in the window.

*

Pietro Oliveri watched the group of tourists disperse, his face oddly expressionless. These tours, short though they were, always left him feeling drained and totally unsatisfied. He shook himself and walked briskly down an alley, which the locals did not show the visitors, to gulp a quick espresso before the next busload of tourists arrived.

As he'd hoped, he found Caterina Gardelli already there, and after mutual commiseration about the awfulness of tourists, she pulled a tattered folder from her bag.

'Anything new?' he asked her.

'I'm not sure. I'm still battling with this German thing. I wish we could find a copy of the original.'

'That would make it too easy.'

'No such thing as too easy, and you can never be too rich or too thin either.'

'So how are you getting on with von Muntz? Can I see?' He read the title from the sheaf of handwritten papers she handed him: 'The Enigma of Andrea Giaiotti and the Mona Lisa. I wish we could tell if he was going to tell us something we don't already know.'

'Should be, by the sheer length of the thing.'

Pietro suppressed a snort of amusement. 'Catarì, that's rude.' She hit him with the folder. 'Let me read, let me read!'

'Here are the pictures I've found so far,' she pulled out a handful of postcards and spread them on the table. 'La Gioconda; la Madonna con tessuto; Léda et le cygne, by Jean-Jacques Printanier 1638; la nuotatrice—'

'What? The swimmer? Who's that by?'

Catarina picked up the card: 'Vittorio Vincenze, 1851. Rijksmuseum.'

Momentarily distracted, Pietro stared at the little reproduction: it was not one he had seen before, yet the face of the naiad, or whatever she was, was immediately familiar.

'And then there's this one,' Catarì added.

'Shit,' muttered Pietro, looking at it: it was somehow disturbing, disquieting. The woman with the smile sat, as did her prototype, among rocks, yet she seemed more ancient than they did, and there was a threat there, a menace; but Pietro looked in vain for a reason why he should think so. He turned it over to read the title, which was Die Königin der Nacht: School of van Bork, 1792.

It was well after dawn when Giaiotti awoke, alone as usual, for Maddalena would never stay; he had a thumping head and aches in all his joints. He tried to move, and wished he hadn't: he felt a hundred years old, and as feeble as a child. In the dim light creeping round the shutters' edges the room looked alien, peopled with things which seemed unlikely to resolve themselves into such mundane things as easels or furniture. The painter staggered to his feet, not at all sure that his legs would support him, and fumbled at the shutter. Freezing air poured in with the day, making him curse; stooping for the disordered blankets, he ended up on the floor with a spinning head.

At length he succeeded in winding the threadbare woollen cloth around himself and topped it with the verminous sheepskin, no longer caring about being bitten, though he could feel something had already had another go. He found half a jug of rather sour red wine and swallowed it all, nearly gagging on it. It brought his shivering under control, and the remains of a stale loaf helped further. The almost-pain of the bites was driving him mad, and as he scratched he felt his nails take scabs off. Startled, he looked at his fingers and found blood on them, blood seeping down his chest and matting in the hair, and another bite near his left nipple. His hand went to his neck again, finding warm wetness there.

A slow realization began to rise that unless he had rats in his vest it was nothing in there which had bitten him, but he could not follow the thought: his mind was working too sluggishly. But he was certain of one thing, and it was a soldier's instinct which made him so; and that was that he stood in peril. Something inimical sought his life, if not his very soul.

Fighting, he found after this realization had taken root within, was not something one forgot, if the instinct was there; and ten years as a mercenary had given him that instinct. He was not going to sit calmly by and let some demon devour him. Having made this decision, he turned his attention to more immediate things: cleaned up the blood as best he could; dressed, wearily; left his two-day beard as it was; packed his paintbrushes and pigments neatly (a soldier's habit he'd never been able to lose); and stumbled down the narrow stairs into the bitter cold of a winter's morning.

Giaiotti's heart sank as he plodded up to San Sebastiane to see Father Giordano waiting for him, but the priest looked more worried than anything else. Before the older man could speak and before he himself could change his mind, the painter blurted out, 'Father, tell me, are there demons that can render a man weak as a babe when he wakes in the morning?' and was surprised to see the good Father make a thoroughly pagan sign against evil. Almost, he laughed; but it was with great seriousness that the priest asked him the reason for his enquiry. Giaiotti pulled his shirt open at the neck and the old man's eyes widened in what seemed sheerest terror. He seized the painter by the arm and virtually dragged him into the church, pushing him to his knees at the altar.

'Father, what—'

'Be silent. Wait there.'

In a short while the priest returned with a vessel of holy water, the contents of which he tipped, without ceremony, down Giaiotti's neck. The water was freezing cold, but it was more than that which knocked the painter backwards. He sprawled on the floor, pawing at his neck and chest where no wounds now showed; the priest eyed him narrowly. 'I pray we are not too late,' he said. 'See the rewards of fornication.'

'I—' began Giaiotti.

'Confess your sin, and we shall hope the succubus will not visit you again.'

'Succubus, but I—'

'Lilith and her kind! Demons who lie with men and steal their blood and their lives and their souls.'

Something colder, and older, than the icy chill of the holy water washed over the painter, and the face of Maddalena was very clear in his mind's eye.

He knew it was a dream, but he also knew that soon he would forget even that simple sane truth and be drawn downward into some mad spiral of terror, just as his steps in the dream were descending a long tower, a narrow square stair like the one in the Torre del Mangia in Siena, following a woman whom he'd first thought was Catarì although he could not see her face. Dread lay like a tumour in his stomach and in the hollow under his heart, but he was unable to halt his descent. Once, he had touched the stone walls, but they ran with water; once, looked through a gap in the centre of the tower, as you also could in Siena, but had seen only darkness.

At last they reached the base of the tower, Pietro and the woman who was always two steps ahead of him; and he realized that they were fathoms underwater, down deep in the deepest sea. In that moment he was convinced he would go insane if her saw her face, and found himself praying to a God he was not even sure he believed in that she would not turn round, but she did.

She had one hand on the big iron ring which was the handle of the tower's door, and she turned, and he could not close his eyes; but it was only the secret smile of the Mona Lisa he saw. Still, his skin crawled as she beckoned to him; but he followed as she opened the door and swam out into the blue depths. Wonder overcame fear as he realized he could breathe underwater, and he kicked his feet to rise in pursuit. Bright fish like flocks of birds drifted lazily by, some curiously lipping his fingers, some swimming away in slow alarm.

And then the swimmer slowed so he could rise to her side, and she turned to him a face on which Catarì's features were superimposed over those of La Gioconda, and smiled. She opened her mouth, and it was filled with teeth like a shark's, and she began to rip at Pietro's throat, while he was unable to scream for the water which flooded into his mouth and lungs.

Heart hammering, he jerked out of sleep and fumbled for the switch by his bed. The room came on with the light, and the dream began to fade. Gradually, his breathing eased, as he was able to convince his body that he was not drowning.

Although the bed was wet.

Pietro knew he'd sleep no more that night, with nightmare's cobwebs still shadowing his thoughts. The idea of turning off the light in that dead hour terrified him, so he opened a drawer in his little desk, and, extracting a big dog-eared layout pad and a soft pencil, began to exorcize his dream by drawing it.

Giaiotti's arm still ached where the priest had gripped it; the old man had more strength than one would think. But it was not this which concerned him, as he squinted at the martyred flesh of San Sebastiane, the cheap candle spitting smoky light on his work and the chill biting into his bones. It was the fact that Maddalena had not returned for three nights, and succubus or not he needed her to complete the painting for Francesco di Scotti.

Also sneaking into his mind like a lizard in a stone wall came the thought: Lorenzo Rossi died two months ago, and this morning they found Filippo Mantegna dead in the river but not of drowning – rumour said he'd been savaged by a wild beast but Giaiotti was awake and aware now, ready for the possibility of peril, and he had a strong idea that it wasn't wolf or boar or bear that had chewed up the young painter's throat.

He paused, his brush just a thought away from the fresco, as the cold coincidence caught hold. *Anch'io son pittore*, he thought, and almost laughed. For all Father Giordano's prayers and holy water and penances, she's marked me, and is it my soul or merely my body I fear for?

Despite the chill he had to wipe sweat from his brow. Determinedly he put other thoughts aside and turned his attention to the martyrdom before him. Here, and just so, and thus, and the arrowhead bursts through the flesh, violating it.

[231]

In the owl-light of evening he was not at all surprised to find Maddalena awaiting him, but he had a little armour now. Thinking back to all the previous nights, he could recall neither painting nor meat and drink, conversation nor coupling. And yet he must have put brush to panel, they must have eaten, spoken, lain together. Yet none of it lay in his memory. So this time when she looked from under her eyelids, he did not meet her gaze. He laughed, and showed her the wine, and the bread and cheese and sausage he'd brought, and refused to look at her.

The painter was visited by fear then: how to prevent her from feeding on him? Even as the thought formed, she had his hand in hers and raised it to her mouth; too late he tried to jerk away, but her grip was not to be broken. There was bitter pain as she sank her teeth into his wrist, and even his soldier's heart quailed as he saw the punctures they made, clean and tiny – a woman's teeth, after all, no matter how sharp – and felt his own blood kissing her lips.

He had a wooden platter in his other hand, and swung it round as hard as he could to smash against her head. Giaiotti saw blood fly, but realized it was his own as her delicate little fangs tore out of his wrist. Again he struck at her, feeling the jarring all the way to his shoulder, and either blow would have felled a strong man; but she seemed unaffected. She hissed at him, as a snake would. The painter pressed his torn wrist to his shirt, which reddened quickly, and pain ate his arm. He backed away; the succubus followed.

'Foolish man,' she whispered, her voice like a snake's scales slipping over stone, 'do not deny fate.'

'*In nomine Patris*—' began Giaiotti in desperation, but she laughed.

'Petty words of canting priests of a dead god,' she said. 'You cannot bind me thus, Signor Pittore, you are mine, your heart and your blood and your soul, and your body cries out for me even now.'

The painter was miserably aware that she was right, and observed with an odd detachment, as he had done years before, that terror and desire could exist simultaneously, yet totally separately; except where one fed on the other. But he wasn't ready to give up yet. 'Holy water closed the wounds you gave,' he said – his voice came out a croak – 'I think you lie.'

'And yet you paint me in the costume of your goddess,' she said sweetly.

Had Giaiotti been a devout man, he might have despaired then, but words came to him, the words of the only pragmatist he knew: Galileo Galilei. Who, though everything had been stripped from him, truth, learning, wisdom, his life's work, still had cried his protest after being forced to recant: '*Eppur si muove.*' Yes, the earth does move, despite all you say, despite all the weasel words and the petty, the inimical words and the negation of knowledge, still, like Giordano Bruno whom they would burn in the Campo di Fiore, he had spoken against what sought to destroy him.

'But you do lie,' he said.

She did not speak for a moment, but when she did, her words sank into Giaiotti's soul. 'I need you,' she said. 'I need men who can create out of nothing. In men like you there is something essential to me. You must know that my food is blood. Yet most men's blood is so thin that it affords but poor nourishment. It is you, the artists, the poets, the men who create: your blood has savour, it runs thick as cream and honey, and I need it to live.'

'And I,' said Giaiotti with the certainty of prophecy, 'am a soldier. I have the scars of bitter wars on my hands, and the memories of deaths I dealt in my heart. If you take my blood you drink destruction, not creativity. I can tell you very many of the myriad ways of death, I am not creator but destroyer. Drink my blood if you will, but I am more danger to you than you are to me.'

The succubus wailed then, and her despair echoed down the cold years so that Giaiotti, for all his passion, was never completely free of it; and in the moment when he knew he had won, he also knew he had been defeated. She had drained too much from him already, leaving him only a little space for the completion of his work; and leaving him empty, too, in some unreachable place that made him sorrow for a loss he never could identify.

And, five hundred or so years later, in the same city, watched by similar olive trees with almost identical blue-green leaves, by black cypresses which waved in just such a way, under roofs as red and ragged and within walls as cool and nearly white, the corpse of a young art student who had been spending his vacation working as a tourist guide was found, as white as clay because his blood had gone. And a girl named Catarina, who could never thereafter bear the fond nickname Catari, did not know why she wept in the night in tower-studded Tuscany in that newly haunted summer.

She is older than the rocks amongst which she sits; like the vampire she has been dead many times, and learned the secrets of the grave; and has been a diver in deep seas, and keeps their fallen day about her; and trafficked for strange webs with Eastern merchants; and, as Leda, was the mother of Helen of Troy . . .

Walter Pater (1839–94) on the Mona Lisa

QUIET IS
THE NIGHT

Jessica Palmer

Jessica Palmer is an American writer living in
England. She has written for numerous
American newspapers and magazines, and has
also had some ten textbooks published.
As a fiction writer, she has had short stories
published in magazines and anthologies on both
sides of the Atlantic. Her first novel *Dark
Lullaby* (1991) has been nominated for the Bram
Stoker Award, and a sequel, *Cradlesong*, is
scheduled for 1993.

Quiet is the night when men lie sleeping, and young mothers sit, babies at breast; when the moon pulls the tides and drives the weak in spirit to lunacy; when the asylums echo with the cries of their tortured inmates. None of them hear save the matron and the guard who whip their bodies into subservience, but not their minds. Such is a time when shadows dance in eerie splendour, heedless of winds or the sickly half light. The moon rules, and She is an evil Goddess, a fickle Lady who jealously guards those She calls her own. I am such a one. I worship, the moon, my Goddess and burn incense in Her name.

They call me mad but who, may I ask, can judge sanity? I wake at night while others rest their weary bones. While most of mankind prays for a better tomorrow, I know I will have none. Captive, I peer through the filthy window which is my looking-glass to the world. Walking in my home, I feel like a caged animal. I shall never see the seasonal progression of colours. For me, all colours blend into muted half-tones. Outside, the moon casts her bewitching silver light, creating illusive images which twist and turn with malevolent life. The trees whisper malignant messages. Rats are kings as they scurry, searching for food, and cockroaches their court.

Why do they call me mad? Because I have talked to these tormented souls whose bodies lie buried in unhallowed soil. With me they find comfort, a temporary haven, and are able to excuse their evil deeds. I have seen the ghosts of men who walk by night and are tied to earth by dreams left unfulfilled. Only I understand their plight, for all my dreams have turned to naught. Yes, and I have too done those things that no one dare mention in the light of day.

I murdered my father, cruel man that he was. Patricide, a sin against God and man, yet to kill one such as he can be no sin. Thus, I will worship no puny male God. That God would have me 'honour my father and my mother'. Worship, the dishonourable? Honour, the damned? If people knew, if they only knew, they would fall to their knees and sing my praises.

Was I driven by madness? Or salvation? I still do not know. If salvation, then whose? Certainly, not mine. For me it is too late. Yet it was She, my Goddess, who protected me, and in doing so, She claimed my soul for all eternity. Rather Her, than others. So before this night is through and the weakling sun crests the window ledge, I must tell my story so I may be shriven. Forgiven? For what, and by whom?

Certainly as a child there was nothing to commend me, nothing to indicate what would later become of me. I was, at best, mediocre, a spindly, gangly girl – neither brilliant nor beautiful. As I was taught, I spoke only when spoken to, was seen but not heard. Ours was an aristocratic family, minor nobility to be sure; but a long, well-honoured bloodline – or so I was told. Long and enduring, yes. Honoured? Doubtful, tainted more likely.

How well I remember him, my father. He was a man of great stature and loud voice – thin, with razor-sharp features and a sharper tongue. So clearly in my mind I can still envision him, standing before me in his pinstripe suit, gold watch chain dangling over a flat torso. With ebony hair – the colour of night – unnaturally pale skin and piercing, burning eyes, he *was* a handsome man.

My mother, however, was a shrunken woman – just a shadow of the youth, vitality and beauty she had once possessed. Wrinkles creased her brow, with fine lines etched around her eyes and mouth. All the life sapped out of her, she was forever silent, brooding, haunted. When she spoke, her voice was cracked, brittle and dry like an October leaf. She only left her boudoir to make dutiful appearances at dinners and quickly withdraw at the first opportunity.

I saw little of them – neither mother nor father – only my nanny with her soft, brown eyes framed by a wrinkled and wizened face. She pitied me, the solitary child. She'd cluck; she'd fuss and try to make up for my parents' negligence.

Dinner was a strained affair. The family would gather in the huge dining-hall which mourned the days when it's walls had echoed the sound of celebration and laughter. Here my mother and I sat in silence, staring at food growing cold and unappetizing. My father never ate. Instead, he drank – some strange nutritive concoction.

We would retire to the parlour. I on my footstool and Mamma in her chair, we'd work upon some elaborate embroidery. She would eventually excuse herself with a headache. My father would stand beside the fireplace, his glass in hand, until he tired of my childish company. On went his cape. Grabbing his bowler and walking stick, he'd stalk off into the night.

I never knew or thought to question his nocturnal absences. He'd return each morning, flushed and refreshed, to disappear somewhere in the house's darkened interior. As I never questioned his night-time wanderings, neither did I ponder his diurnal disappearances. Where did he go when he vanished into the mansion's bowels? Perhaps because of its ritualistic regularity, I never thought it odd, or perhaps I assumed that despite our noble bloodline, he – as other children's fathers – plied some trade somewhere and that he – as other children's fathers – must of necessity go to work.

Such was my home life. Awakened each morning by my father's daily arrival, I would run to my mother's chambers. She would obligingly kiss 'Dolly' and myself good morning and send us on our way. Then I saw no one except my nanny until high tea. Each night the same: dinner, a farcical attempt at domesticity which always fell short of mark – my mother to retreat early, followed by father's abrupt departure and I to be sent to bed.

One night, however, there was an unheard of interruption in this placid routine. Tea was late. No one came to find me where I played in the pantry. When the hunger pangs became too great, I crept from my hiding place. My nanny caught me before I could make it into the great hall and hurried me to bed. As we passed the library I caught the sound of angry voices filtering through the thick, oak door. Once alone, I considered the phenomenon of being put to bed without supper – normally an act reserved for punishment, yet I had done nothing wrong.

I slipped from my room and down the stairs to stand silently by the library door. Hiding behind a marble bust of some long-deceased and forgotten relative, I strained to hear. My mother's voice sounded querulous, aggrieved, rasping.

'. . . but why? I am your wife . . . why do you go out each night? Do you seek another?' The question dissolved into sobs.

'Quiet woman, how dare you question me?' My father's booming bass carried easily through the thick door. 'Yes, you are my wife, an unfortunate error on my part. Do you know why I married you?' There was a pause. 'To bear sons to carry on the family name, and what have you given me? One snivelling runt of a girl.'

The ticking clock was audible above the sound of my breathing. I pressed closer to the wall, wishing I would die.

'Those that I seek, unlike you, are full-bodied women with rich blood flowing in their veins,' he snorted, 'which is more than I can say for you or that brat of yours.'

'But . . .'

'Silence!'

I heard a crack, a shrill cry and then a dull thud. 'Damn you! The sight of you sickens me.' My father burst from the room and stormed out into the night, hat and cane in hand.

As the front door closed, the servants appeared from nowhere. Cautiously they crept into the library to find my mother lying in a heap upon the floor. Clucking like a broody hen, Nanny helped her to her feet. 'I told you that no good would come of it if you married that monster.'

She hovered, scolding the other servants into action as she led my mother to her chamber. The downstairs maid poured a brandy and followed them up the stairs. No one noticed me pressed against the wall. My evening meal, when it came, was cold, tasteless. I ate with my nanny, the house so still, it seemed to swallow all sound.

The next day as I ran toward my mother's chambers, I was intercepted and informed that madame was not feeling well and wished not to be disturbed. From that day forward, my mother avoided me, and Dolly and I did without our good morning kiss. My presence seemed to remind her of my father's rebuke, and hate blossomed in me like an evil flower – hate for the father who had deprived me of my mother's love.

They say I became a strange child, oblivious to others, seeking instead my own companionship. I would awaken at night to wander the rooms alone. Like my father, I had become a nocturnal animal. Although I emulated him, I stayed out of his reach – as all did who had learned to fear his temper – hiding in the servants' quarters. They tolerated my presence with clicking tongues and nodding heads.

Little else changed. My mother remained a ghost, a fleeting shadow who flitted through empty corridors and sat through silent suppers. I would await my father's nightly departure patiently. Then I could sit on my stool and stare out of the window at the moon, loving Her in all Her phases. For even then, I felt Her pull.

My Goddess beckoned to me. The moon became my mother, caressing me with Her silver rays, soothing my fears. Yes, my Lady called to me, and gladly I followed. With Her, I found the love I had lost. It was then I learned to understand the whisper of trees and the murmur of the dead. My nightly vigils became longer until it became difficult to rouse me during the day.

Several years must have passed in this manner, for it seemed that I awoke one morning a woman grown and learned of Eve's curse. My nanny told me with pride that I'd grown beautiful. Like the duckling in the children's tale, I'd become a swan. Mayhap I had, but I was more like my father than my mother. I had his same night-pale skin, raven hair and luminescent eyes.

One night in my seventeenth year, I sat in the library gazing out of the bay window upon the serene face of the moon. I could hear the nameless multitudes weep in agony. Bathed in white light, my chin resting on my knees, I watched the silent dance of the trees in the garden below. My Lady rode the night sky, soaring across the heavens in ethereal chariots drawn by twinkling stars.

Enchanted and enthralled, I didn't hear the front door as it creaked open on screeching hinges. I was alerted to my father's early arrival by his footsteps in the hall. They stopped outside the library. In the half-light I could see him as he moved into the room. He spied me huddled near the window. Startled by my unexpected presence, he stared until recognition dawned in his glowing red eyes. He laughed, a sound to chill mortal blood.

'So it's you. I should have known. Out on your midnight perambulation, I see.' He appraised me coolly. 'Perhaps there is more of me in you than I had expected.'

He walked up beside me, leaning his cane against the window seat. His hand stroked my hair. Its touch sent shivers down my spine and raised the hackles on my neck.

'Kiss me.'

A simple request which was spoken in the silken, sultry tones of promise – his voice oily and smooth. Revolted, I recoiled. The swift motion sent his cane crashing, to the floor. He seemed not to notice.

'Why don't you give your daddy a big kiss?'

Slavering in anticipation, he towered over me – his skin flushed, his eyes glittering. Dropping to his knees before me, he smiled.

God, what an evil smile! Why had I never noticed it before? His teeth were pearly white with long, accentuated canines – sharp like a wolf's made to rend, to tear, to rip muscles from bone and sinew.

I froze, terrified by the sight. He pulled my rigid body down on top of him, mouth open, questing. Beads of perspiration formed on his forehead. He groaned and I felt those sharp eyeteeth press against my breast. He panted, his breath coming in short, rasping gulps. It was scented with the sweet and sour odour of death and decay. I swallowed, bile rising to my throat.

I groped for his walking stick. My fingers searched the floor until I found that which I sought. I closed my hand around its silver tip and slowly raised it above my head, my back arching to extend my reach. The action caused his teeth to pierce my flesh. He sighed in swooning, sibilant ecstasy.

With all the strength I could muster I brought the cane crashing down upon his skull. Hissing, he rolled out from under me while I stumbled to my feet. He crawled toward the window and then using the drapes pulled himself erect. Rage tinted his eyes the colour of hellfire; he glared at me. Stunned as he was, he swayed for a moment before leaping forward to wrest the stick from my grasp.

I swung again, using both hands. Every ounce of the remaining strength my meagre body possessed powered it to its target. The cane struck his face; it broke with the force of the blow. I felt facial bones give way and he collapsed to the floor to lie in a pool of blood. One side of his head was crushed – his face, a tangled mass of flesh and bone. I stared in horrified fascination, sure that he was dead. Nothing, no one, could survive such injury.

Mesmerized, I did not see him move as he stretched out his hand to grab my ankle. A scream rose in my throat when I realized he still lived. But how? I scrambled away from his grasp. Somehow, he managed to get up and lurch towards me, moving like a marionette on tangled strings. I turned to run only to discover I was trapped. I held the broken walking stick before me like a sword, its sharp, ragged tip pointed outwards.

Relentlessly, he inched forward. Bits of too-sharp teeth hung from a flapping jaw. What remained of his mouth worked soundlessly, and his tongue was a lumpy mass of flesh moving in a strangled throat. One eye swung from a silvery cord. The other, still in his skull, gleamed.

Powered by what demoniac fury I do not know, but somehow he sprung, a snarling beast. The cane caught him just below the breastbone and sank easily into his chest. He impaled himself with his final leap. He flailed, caught like an entomologist's specimen on the tip of a pin. He reached for me, hands opening and closing spasmodically. Then he grabbed the stick, attempted to pull it from his chest. I stood transfixed until my fingers loosened their hold on the cane. He fell – lifeless at last.

I couldn't move, only stare at the remains of what was once my father. The moon whispered Her greeting to me. I felt my spirit soar to meet my Goddess. She had awaited me – knowing, as She had protected me, that I was Hers now and for all eternity. I was Hers, and Hers alone. Ah, but for what purpose?

I screamed. The single eye stared at me. My shrieks reverberated through the empty, marble foyer. Soon the house came alive with movement. I told my tale and I told the truth, for I had not the presence of mind to lie. In the days of confusion that followed, I hid behind a mask of hysteria and my now-presumed insanity.

Amazingly, I was never punished for my crime. Maybe, they felt the resulting madness was punishment enough. Most likely, however, it was money which bought my freedom and the police inspector's silence. My mother's family was not without influence and with the right word to the right person, a discreet deposit into the proper account . . . who knows?

No charges were filed to be sure. It was deemed an accident. One might say I was blessed by the times in which I lived. No one would believe a seventeen-year-old girl of slight build could have the strength to crush a man's skull.

That they thought me broken, I am sure, for I told them what I had seen and what I suspected. They didn't believe me about my father – about who, or what, he was. Frantically, I tried to make them understand but to no avail. I knew that night and in the days thereafter that – what is his name? – Stoker didn't lie. His book was no flight of fancy to terrify and delight foolish women and children. It was a warning.

Who would listen? Such things didn't happen in our bountiful land, our blessed England during Victoria's reign. Such beings did not exist.

No one in polite society would consider such blasphemy. Was this not the nineteenth century, the age of rationalism, of science, of the steam engine and other modern miracles? No, 'twas simply a mad girl's tale, driven to lunacy by the enormity of her crime.

Once the parody of an investigation was completed, life returned to its same dull calm. My mother stayed in her apartments. I had released her and easily she changed into widow's black. There were no more token appearances. The only person to see her was her maid. Except for the funeral, she never set foot outside her rooms again.

The servants left me to my own devices. I wandered the halls at night, never arising during the day. No one objected; it was by then the norm, and after all, was I not my father's daughter? Mostly they murmured, whispering to one another that my mind had become unhinged.

Thus we sought our separate solace, she in her solitude and I in the night. As it turned out, I inherited everything in trust until I came of age. Odd to be so rewarded. Days blended into weeks and weeks to years of uninterrupted monotony. My mother's death caused little stir, although the servants left soon after her demise. I was not sorry to see them go. With their exodus, the house fell into disrepair; but who was there to care? Not I.

Since then I have never seen the sun. I awaken each night when the moon is at Her zenith. I rarely leave my filthy room except when the moon's pull drags me, like the tide, to my father's grave. And so, I am alone in my lunacy. My only companions are the cockroaches and the rats which share my now humble abode. With them I feel a kinship, fellow creatures of the night. Sometimes a restless spirit finds its way into my chambers to tell me what awaits me after death, if indeed death is mine to have; but I fear life more.

The moon *is* a wicked mistress. It would appear that I am Hers to torture or caress at whim. Since She possesses me body and soul, She sends demons to haunt me. She sends with them twisted, tortured souls and only now do they tell me of their plight in Her hands. Each night I pray to be released from Her icy grip, but the cold Maiden holds me with no intention of releasing what is Hers.

Too late did I realize that She was not mine alone. No, if She ruled me, so too had She ruled my father. He and I were one. I inherited not only his wealth, but also his foul blood, his unholy needs. She sends his ravaged face with its accusing single eye to remind me how I came to Her. It keeps me company – its silent message, gruesome – for he tells me what I will become.

[241]

The change has come upon me slowly, but I cannot deny its presence. Neither can I deny its eventual outcome. The looking-glass I took down months ago – the same evening I peered into its mirrored surface and saw naught, but the moon reflected behind me. I can no longer tolerate solid food. I force myself to eat because I do not want to become like *him*, but nothing stays down except raw meat – dripping, bloody flesh. Even then my body rebels the very act of mastication; my stomach recoils its solidity.

Of late, my father comes more often – his message more insistent. No matter how I beseech Her, the face remains, hanging suspended in the darkness, until She is of a mind to remove its presence. What I have done to anger Her I do not know. Perhaps, I have not paid Her proper homage. Perhaps She grows weary of my entreaties, and She wishes to take that final, irrevocable step that will make me totally hers – never more to find peace on this earth, for my father's face ever lingers.

My room is grey and musty; cobwebs festoon the corners, and plaster falls from the ceiling. I sleep by day. By night I burn incense to Her image, and I pray that his living death be not mine. I gaze out the windows to see ghosts dance in the eerie light. Twisted, tortured branches reach to the heavens – imploring.

Did I not say earlier that it is too late? Only this evening when I arose with the setting sun, I heard the soft patter of tiny feet, and I pounced on the poor, frightened creature – a rat. Sick with my own depravity and trembling with lust, I set it free; but not before I tasted its warm blood.

Yes, too late. This and my father's face reminds me that for me time has run out. Through ragged lips, he whispers. I cannot stop it, and I cannot hide. If I try, others of his kind – nay, my kind – will find me, will force me to accept the final transition. I will not permit it!

I have made my plans well, bribing a street urchin to purchase sturdy hemp. It was his skilled fingers that made the noose which hangs from the exposed rafter to cast its grim shadow across the grimy wall. Even as I write my father sits across from me, his pinstriped suit splattered with gore, his shattered face framing that solitary eye, and his cane protruding from his chest. If I didn't know any better, I would swear he is smiling.

The moon is full, and spirits sing sweet siren songs, begging me to join them. I only hope I can, that I am not too far gone, too much my father's daughter, to enter their restless kingdom.

THE LAST SIN

Ken Cowley

One of the earliest and most celebrated literary
vampires of the nineteenth century was Lord
Ruthven, created by Dr John Polidori, friend of
Byron and Shelley. The first edition claimed that
his story *The Vampyre* was 'related by Lord
Byron to Dr Polidori', though this was later
denied by Byron himself. Here Ruthven appears
in a new variation of the same theme.
Ken Cowley (born 1928) is an advertising
director who has written many supernatural and
horror stories for *Dark Horizons* and
other magazines.

'Isn't this the night she promised to come back?' asked Bertie slyly,
knowing full well that it was, but wanting to prick Ruthven out of
his complacency.

Ruthven just smiled at him, but Bertie persisted. 'What was it she
actually said, just before she died? Wasn't it "I shall be with you, Lord
Ruthven, on your wedding eve?" And she sounded so strong, so sure for
the moment, even with the blood pouring out of her wrists.'

This time Ruthven stirred uneasily, slopping his port onto the white
tablecloth. The image thus created took him back far more effectively
than words to the day when they had found Lolly at the gates of Ruthven
Manor, pouring out her lifeblood into the dust as profligately as she had
previously dispensed her favours to the then loving Ruthven.

'Silly wench,' he growled. 'What the hell did she expect? I've tumbled
a dozen girls on the estate in my time and a few gold sovereigns always put

it right before. What if she did get herself with child? If her grandmother had half the skills with herbs and spells that she's credited with, that little inconvenience could have been put to rights in a trice.'

His brow grew even blacker as he remembered how the old crone accosted him in the village street, shortly after the funeral. 'My Lolly was a good girl,' she had said, 'too good for you, Lord Ruthven. And mark this well – I never knew her to break a promise. You are a sinful man, Lord Ruthven, but when she comes for you I can almost find it in my heart to pity you.'

True, Lord Ruthven was a sinful man in a time when money and position made it possible for a man to indulge himself. At an early age he had dedicated himself to committing all the sins. No serving girl was safe from him, nor indeed any groom; his appetite was as catholic as it was prodigious. His parents had done their best to curb him, until they had frustrated him once too often and a convenient fire had left the way clear.

Of late, however, he had found the returns on his pleasures diminishing through repetition as fast as his fortune was dissipating under the strain of funding and covering up his excesses. Desperate remedies were called for. In short, marriage to Catherine Beddowes, only daughter of a neighbour rich in trade if poor in social position. Catherine was thirtyish and had quite obviously never been bedded – in fact Ruthven's only attempt at that somewhat daunting exercise had been met with shocked outrage and legs as tightly closed as a pensioner's purse.

'Damned bitch,' muttered Ruthven under his breath. 'Just wait until tomorrow night. I'll have you, my girl, so many times and in so many ways that you'll never say no to anything again. And I do mean anything.' When one is at the end of a catalogue of perversions one can always start all over again through the corruption of an innocent, he reflected.

'Eh, what's that, Ruthven?' muttered a bleary-eyed Bertie.

Ruthven had forgotten he was there. 'Oh, for God's sake get you home, Bertie' he growled. 'You have got to be standing up for me tomorrow morning, remember.'

Huffing and puffing Bertie shambled out of the dining-room, across the naked flagstones of the great hall, and on through the back door to the stable yard and his waiting horse. It did not improve his temper that the mare was unusually nervous – snorting and stamping her iron-shod feet until the sparks flew from the cobblestones. Bertie hauled himself into the saddle where he sat like a sack of coals, expecting his mount to find her way home, but it needed a cruel stroke with his whip to overcome her reluctance.

The way lay along a winding carriage drive through lawns made iron-hard by the February frost, and it was not until horse and rider approached the belt of trees that crowded close around the entrance gates that the ringing silence was broken. The owls erupted into a clamour of hooting as a wind from nowhere caused the treetops to thrash about. There were furtive movements in the undergrowth and, although it might have been a trick of the uncertain moonlight, Bertie had the distinct impression that people or things which had no right to be there were peeping out at him from behind mossy boles. There was a sense of expectancy in the air as if an audience were waiting for the start of a play.

Bertie's whip rose and fell again, but his horse needed no further urging and flew out of the gates and down the road to the village, lungs labouring and sweat rising off her in a cloud of icy steam. A now thoroughly frightened Bertie hung on for dear life although it was only the providence which watches over fools and drunkards that kept him in the saddle as the crossroads approached and the signpost that had been planted to keep Lolly quiet shuddered in the ground and tipped at a crazy angle in his path.

Back at the big house Ruthven shared the feeling of expectancy. The master bedroom, where the unfortunate Catherine was on the morrow to be so cruelly deflowered, was at the front of the house and he stood at the window staring out over the moonlit park. There was a movement at the edge of the trees as a white shape detached itself from the shadows and advanced slowly across the frozen ground. Ruthven squinted in an effort to make it out. A stray sheep, perhaps, from the neighbouring farm? But did a sheep crawl, and would it move in such a purposeful straight line? And, as it grew ever closer, would a sheep rise up on its hind legs and lift its arms to half reveal, in the shadowy folds of some material, a glint of shiny white? Ruthven looked no further but retreated to the great four-poster to await that which must come.

Beneath him the double doors of the entrance hall boomed as they crashed back against the walls. There followed a silence so intense that Ruthven, ears straining to catch every noise, had to hold his breath against the thudding of his heart to hear, a minute later, the small sounds he was waiting for – the little creaks and groans that signified the passage of his visitor up the wooden staircase and along the uncarpeted floorboards to his bedroom.

The door swung open, and Ruthven had company. Lolly had worn well in the grave, perhaps because of the sandy soil at the roadside. There was still flesh stretched tight across the bone, tight enough to draw her white lips back from long, sharp teeth. She smiled a terrible smile and glided across the bedroom, her arms flung wide to block off his escape, revealing in the process the bloodless gashes across her wrists. As she reached the edge of the bed she fell forward and crawled towards him.

The ground lay flat around Ruthven Manor for an hour's ride in any direction until the low hills started to climb into a bowl which held the frozen solitude as if it were a lake. It was said that the screams could be heard through the clear, conductive air for ten miles or more in any direction, screams so piercing that they rose to a falsetto, almost womanish pitch before mercifully dying away.

High up at the back of the hall the servants cowered in their beds, and none dared brave the darkened corridors until the first shafts of daylight arrived to herald Ruthven's wedding day. Only then did Robert, the first footman, drag his reluctant feet to his master's bedroom. Of Lolly there was no sign. Ruthven lay white and still upon the enormous bed. He looked totally drained, as indeed he was.

Robert stifled a scream as Ruthven stirred, opened his eys and looked at him. The servant made to back away, but an immensely strong hand shot out and gripped him by the front of his embroidered waistcoat.

'Why so alarmed, Robert?' enquired Ruthven sardonically. 'Today is my wedding day and there is much to be done.' He released the terrified man and lay back on the pillow, musing on his good fortune. Was it only yesterday that he had bemoaned the fact that he had completed the catalogue of sins? And now here he was, about to go to his bride with the stains of the ultimate sin still clinging to his body, the sin of necrophilia.